I0822367

**KEEPER OF SCARLET PETALS**


Aethon Books
www.aethonbooks.com

Print and eBook formatting by Steve Beaulieu.

Published by Aethon Books LLC.

# I

The first and final steps in the path of a Keeper were death. Their order was not one of glory, nor was it one of joy. To be a Keeper was to dedicate one's life, completely and utterly, to protecting another.

They were far more than mere bodyguards. When the time came for thought, they were advisors. When the time came for war, they were soldiers. When the time came for peace, then they were butlers. They were what they needed to be – and more.

Upon the day that Jasmine joined the order of the Keepers, her first death came to pass. Her ties to the outside world were cut, her name stricken from the Whitewater Kingdom's records.

There was nothing left for her outside the tall, obsidian walls of the Sanctum – not until she graduated from the training program and earned the right to serve the King's line.

And that was exactly how she wanted it.

It had been six months since she'd begun her training as a Keeper, and she'd loved nearly every second of it.

Nearly every second.

Jasmine leaned back as a sword whistled through the air before her face, passing so closely to her that she could feel the wind from its passing. She shifted her weight and drove her shoulder into Asher's chest.

He staggered backward with a grunt. Even as he caught his balance and raised his blade to defend himself, Jasmine hooked her leg behind his and yanked his feet out from under him. The man fell, rolling as he hit the ground.

Jasmine lunged, aiming to land a strike on him while he was down. Asher rolled as if he had eyes on the back of his head, his own sword striking out like a snake and knocking Jasmine's to the side.

He grabbed a handful of sand and flung it into her face. Jasmine staggered back, squeezing her eyes shut with a curse. Her hand moved, flicking out in a mixture of instinct and training.

A loud clang rang out as her blade struck Asher's and flung it from his hand. They froze, both breathing heavily. Jasmine took a step back, catching her breath as she wiped the sand from her eyes.

"I win," Jasmine said. "You should rely on real swordsmanship, you know. There isn't always sand to use."

"If there isn't sand, there'll be something else." A smirk flickered across Asher's tanned features, and his golden eyes twinkled in amusement. If he hadn't looked so much like a smug cat, Jasmine might have considered him handsome. "I always find a way to win in the end."

"That's what you've said every time you've lost, but I don't see you winning much anymore. How long has it been? Maybe you should try a little harder."

"Maybe so. Then again, I actually know how to split my time. Fighting isn't the only thing a Keeper should be able to do."

Jasmine grimaced. And, in the instant that she was distracted,

Asher's foot whipped out. He knocked her legs out from under her and she slipped back, falling onto the sand with a pained grunt.

Moving with the grace of a snake, Asher shot forward and slammed Jasmine's hands back to the ground before she could raise them. He sat on her chest and locked eyes with her, his smug grin growing wider.

"The match was over. That was a cheap blow." Jasmine growled.

"No fight is over until someone is dead."

"Just get off me."

Asher snickered and rose to his feet, releasing Jasmine. He held a hand out, but she ignored it and stood up on her own. Asher hadn't been wrong. There was a lot more to being a Keeper than knowing how to kill, but none of it was anywhere near as interesting.

Asher padded over to the side of the small stone room and grabbing his shirt from where it hung on a rack. The toned muscles on his back glimmered with sweat as he pulled his shirt on. Jasmine was tempted to avert her eyes, but she knew better. That would have left an opening, and she didn't put it past him to try to attack again.

"Ninety-six to ninety-seven," Asher said begrudgingly as he turned away from the rack and pushed a strand of long, brown hair out of his eyes. "You're officially better than me. As you pointed out, that wasn't an official match."

The words felt hollow to Jasmine's ears. The only thing she had was fighting. Asher led the class in every other aspect a Keeper was trained on in their first year – diplomacy, etiquette, strategy, and butlery.

He was insufferable.

"If you realize that you've got shortcomings, you should probably spend some time fixing them," Asher advised. "It's not like you couldn't do it if you spent a tenth as much effort as you do on fighting."

"If I wanted advice, I'd speak to Keeper Esther. You can keep yours." Jasmine stalked to the other side of the room, taking a towel from a rack and wiping herself down before pulling a Keeper uniform over her leather-padded undershirt.

*He's not wrong, but that just makes it even more annoying. Keeper Esther is going to have my head if I don't manage to start rounding my skills out. Watcher's Ass, this is frustrating.*

"Internally scolding yourself?" Asher asked. "I'm telling you, it's not just hard. Just pay attention in class."

"Shut up," Jasmine said with a huff. "Stop doing that."

"Doing what? Reading your mind?"

"You can't read my mind. You aren't a Starvein, so you don't have any magic in you. You're just a competent asshole."

"I'd say I'm more than just competent." Asher cleaned his sword off, then slid it into a sheath that hung at his side. He turned back to Jasmine and cocked an eyebrow. "And was I wrong?"

*No.*

"Yes. I was just thinking of more humiliating ways I could beat you in our next sparring match."

"That's the problem. Instead of that, you should be thinking of ways to avoid insulting Keeper Esther during our etiquette training." Asher opened the door in the back wall and stepped out into an open-air pathway. Just below the railing at its edge stretched the top of the Sanctuary's great walls, wide enough to take several wagons across side by side, if one were so inclined. The black stone shimmered in the moonlight, and large guard towers rose up all along it.

Beyond the walls were the sloping grass fields of the mountain that the massive school had been built upon. They were split in twain by a thick, winding river that came from the mountains behind Sanctuary. The river ran straight through the center of Sanctuary and down the side of the mountain.

It led up to a city by the name of Rodrige that was just a little under a week's travel away – one that Jasmine didn't care to remember. Even though it should have been nothing more than a distant memory, the scents from the vendors lining the streets and the loud calls of the morning market were still sharp in her mind.

"You going to just stand there forever?" Asher asked, tilting his head to the side. "This is a bit too much introspection, even for you. Are you that worried about failing Etiquette? I could tutor you – for a price."

"I wouldn't spend more time with you if you even if someone paid me to."

"Could have fooled me. You love our sparring sessions."

"Just because I respect your ability with a sword does not mean I respect *you.*"

"I'm hurt," Asher said, placing a hand on his chest and feigning sadness. "You know, if you keep falling for cheap tricks, are they even cheap anymore?"

"That one won't catch me again."

"That's why I've always got more." Asher raised a hand in farewell and set off, chuckling to himself. "See you tomorrow."

Jasmine did her best not to look too annoyed. She turned and headed down the path in the other direction toward her housing, resisting the urge to look back at Asher as he left. Even though they were both Keepers in training, Asher had gotten lucky with his dormitory assignment. It was at the center of Sanctuary, right next to just about anything one could want.

Jasmine's, on the other hand, was a small building at the edge. It was close to the training fields, and that was about it.

Of course, compared to the Starvein Halls on the other side of the Sanctuary, all the Keeper dormitories were plain and uninspiring. She'd only seen them once before, and only briefly. The Starveins were haughty enough when she occasionally ran into them in the markets, and Jasmine had absolutely no desire to run into any more of the arrogant mages than she needed to.

*Almost makes me wonder why I'm dedicating eight years of my life learning how to protect one of them, but as far as jobs for a gutter rat go, I don't think I could have gotten luckier unless I was a Starvein myself.*

Even if she didn't have the fancy, gold clad halls of a Starvein to keep her company, Jasmine didn't mind. The training areas were the most important parts of Sanctuary – not counting the markets on Tenthday, when merchants came in selling all sorts of confectionery that she happily spent the majority of her allowance on. She didn't care much for the rest of the Sanctuary.

*And screw Etiquette class. I can just make something up. All you have to do is be nice. That's not that hard. Hey, I could practice by being nice after I beat Asher in another sparring match tomorrow morning. I can't let myself get lax. I'm only one win ahead of him.*

A small grin crawled across Jasmine's lips as she walked, already envisioning the coming day.

*Tomorrow's match will be fun.*

That match never came.

# 2

Asher had never been so much as been late before. But, as rays of sunlight peeked through the windows along the wall of the training room, Jasmine started to realize that Asher might not just be late – she was pretty sure he wasn't coming at all.

A frown crossed her face. He was a lot of things, but he'd never been a coward. It didn't make sense for him to skip out on their training. She'd expected him to be even more eager to fight since he'd finally lost the lead he'd had over her.

*Is he planning a sneak attack or something? It wouldn't be the first time, but he's never held off this long before. There's no way he's actually that mad about losing to me, is there? He's Rank 1 in basically everything other than combat.*

She waited for a few more minutes, but nobody joined her. Eventually, the sun rose high enough that she couldn't risk standing around any longer. It wouldn't be long before the morning class started, and Keeper Esther did not appreciate when her students showed up late.

The trip to class was strangely quiet. Without Asher ribbing her the entire way back, it almost felt empty – but there was also a degree of peace that Jasmine would vehemently insist that she enjoyed.

Walking alone through the morning air had a certain charm to it.

Just not as much charm as walking back after a victory while Asher sported a smarting bruise.

Jasmine arrived at the lecture room and stepped inside. There was no door blocking the doorframe – it was just a large archway that went a long way in illuminating the entire large area while the sun was still across from it.

One hundred stone seats were carved into the ground, each with a single, worn thin cushion placed atop them. They were arranged in a semicircle before a large dais. Only eleven of the seats were full, and Keeper Esther stood by the dais, leaning on a bone staff.

Esther was an elderly woman well into her seventies, but even in spite of her graying hair and lame leg, her body was still toned and muscular. She moved with terrifying grace and had sent Jasmine home beaten black and blue after enough sparring matches to instill enough respect to last a lifetime.

Jasmine took her seat, and the blonde girl in the chair beside her sent her a conspiratorial eyebrow wiggle. "You're early today. What happened?"

"Nothing. And, Lydia, before you ask, I mean that in the literal sense."

"Really? You didn't train?" Lydia's green eyes widened in shock and she glanced over her shoulder, as if to see if anybody else had overheard. She looked back to Jasmine and lowered her voice. "Are you sick? Did you injure yourself?"

"No, I'm fine. My partner just skipped out on me."

"You're kidding. Asher bailed?"

"That's what I was thinking," Jasmine said, leaning back and letting out a sigh. "What a waste of time. The smug bastard is probably pouting that I pulled ahead of him.."

"You pulled ahead? Damn, Jas. Good job. Asher deserves to lose at something. He's a prick. I didn't think he'd actually get that annoyed about losing, though. Who would have thought." Lydia scrunched her nose. "Still cute, though."

"You didn't think that when he demolished you in our last set of ranking battles," Jasmine said with a wry grin. "I recall you using a few choice words that even Keeper Esther hadn't heard before."

"Yeah, well, he cheated. He had dried pepper in his pockets. Pepper! Who carries a pocket of pepper around?"

"Not arguing with you there," Jasmine said. She resisted the urge to look over her shoulder and check if Asher had arrived yet. They had a mutual agreement to keep their matches out of the classrooms to avoid disciplinary action, but she wouldn't put any underhanded strategies past him.

Jasmine heard two more sets of footfalls enter the classroom, but she could tell by their gait that neither belonged to Asher. The other students all whispered in hushed tones to each other, but Jasmine paid them little mind.

"We have all arrived," Keeper Esther said, tapping her staff on the ground to draw their attention. "All that will be arriving today, at least. Today's lecture will be different than our norm."

Esther's voice echoed through the room, silencing everyone. All fourteen of them. Fifteen, if Asher had been here. For a room that had once been meant to house classes of one hundred, it often felt oppressively empty.

"What about Asher?" Lydia asked. She'd never been one to wait long for an answer, and today was clearly no exception.

"That is the matter which we will discuss." Esther's voice was more somber than Jasmine was used to, and her words drew the attention of every Keeper-in-training that sat in the room.

"Asher will no longer be with us," Esther said.

Everyone stared at her in shock.

"What?" Jasmine exclaimed. "He dropped out of Sanctuary?"

"He left the Keeper order," Esther said, inclining her head. "Due to personal circumstances. It is not my place to speak any further on this matter, but the decision is final."

"Why would he do something like that?" Jasmine pressed. "Are you sure there wasn't a mix up or something? We were just training yesterday. I don't see why he'd leave."

"It is not the place of a Keeper to wonder. It is our place to act," Esther said, her words carrying an underlying note of steel that would take no response other than acceptance. Jasmine sank back into her chair, repressing the urge to start arguing with the older woman. The last thing she needed was disciplinary action.

*I just don't understand. Why would he just leave for no reason? It doesn't make sense. I'm not going to let that sneaky bastard just slip away like this. I'll find Asher and drag him back until he begs Esther to let him back in.*

"I understand you are surprised," Esther said. There was an uncharacteristic note of sympathy in her voice. "But we must all continue on. Loss is a part of our order that will never leave. Just be thankful that he is not dead."

"That's got to suck," Lydia leaned over and whispered into Jasmine's ear. "Good luck finding someone else that wants to spar every morning. Then again, maybe this is good. We can practice not setting the kitchen on fire."

Jasmine grunted, not even trying to hide the mixture of disappointment, annoyance, and sadness in her chest. It didn't sit right with her at all. Asher hadn't shown any signs of wanting to leave the order. He'd been completely normal the previous day.

*What happened?*

"I wished to gather you all to inform you of the loss to our numbers, but that is not the only announcement I have today," Esther said. They all looked back at her.

"Are we getting a new Keeper to replace Asher?" Brock, a bushy-browed boy with heavy features asked from behind Jasmine. "Fifteen is already the smallest Year One Keeper class in years, isn't it? Now we're down a member."

"You're just hoping someone new joins so you don't have to be last in the rankings anymore," Lydia said.

"Says the girl in tenth place. You're not much better."

"There's more to being a Keeper than swinging a sword," Lydia countered. She glanced at Jasmine out of the corner of her eye and cleared her throat as she looked back to Brock. "Do I really need to remind you what happened the last time you tried baking? I think I've still got the lump of coal you called bread sitting around somewhere."

Brock let out an undignified grumble. He was rescued by Esther, who sent Lydia a sharp glance.

"A Keeper also knows when to hold her words for a better time," Esther said. "And you, Lydia, are as snippy as a field mouse. About as dangerous as one as well."

All of them chuckled. It was a tense, awkward laugh that would have been far lighter the previous day. Keeper Esther paused for a moment, then pursed her lips.

"What's the announcement, then?" Lydia asked.

"There has been a change in plans," Esther said after a few more moments. She let out a small sigh. "Against my *very* firm recommendations, the order has decided that your training must be accelerated in order to accommodate for the significant losses we have experienced in recent years. Even though you are just three months into your first year, all of you will be starting your Year Two practice on top of your current work."

"Don't we actually begin working for a Charge in Year Two?" Brock asked, his eyebrows furrowing. "Are... we ready for that?"

"No," Esther replied. "You are not. Unfortunately, you must be. It will not be permanent. We will simply be adding some extra elements to your preparations. I am confident that, even in spite of this, you will all persevere."

*Great. Just what I needed. More work.*

"Given the weight of this information, I will be dismissing all of you early. Take some time to think. You will not often get this opportunity, so cherish it," Esther suggested. She waved her hand and tapped her staff on the ground. "Go."

"Wow. Today's like a dozen horses of bad news hitting you in a row, isn't it?" Lydia asked Jasmine as the other Keepers-in-training stood all around them. A dull roar of muted conversation washed over Jasmine's ears.

"I'm not sure where you got a dozen. And the only bad news is the last part. What a waste of time."

"You know, all things considered, it might be a good idea for you to spend a little less time fighting and a little more–"

Jasmine silenced Lydia with a glare. A second passed, and Lydia shrugged.

"Hey, just saying. And really? You aren't even slightly mad about Asher?"

"Oh, I'm pissed," Jasmine said, clenching her fists. "But I'll just drag him back to the order. I can't believe he'd just leave us like that."

Lydia snickered and stood up. Jasmine mirrored her, and they started toward the door.

"Do you even know where he lives?" Lydia asked as they reached the archway.

"Not really," Jasmine admitted. "But I'm sure I'll–"

"Jasmine," Esther called.

Jasmine glanced back at her teacher. "Yes, Keeper Esther?"

"Remain in the lecture hall for a little longer. I have something I need to discuss with you."

Lydia and Jasmine exchanged a confused glance.

"What did you do?" Lydia whispered.

"Nothing," Jasmine hissed back. She shook her head and jerked her chin toward the hall. "I'm sure this won't take long, but you can leave if you want to."

"I'll just wait. I'm not going to pass up on something interesting," Lydia replied with a grin. She stepped out of the hall and Jasmine headed back down to rejoin Esther.

The rest of the students left the room, and it wasn't long before Jasmine was alone with the older Keeper. Jasmine adjusted her stance, her brow furrowed.

"Is something wrong?" Jasmine asked.

"No, no. I'm just distracted," Esther said with a shake of her head. "I called you in to discuss a few things in private. You haven't done anything wrong."

"Oh. That's good." Jasmine breathed a small sigh of relief. "What things?"

"I hear that you've been making great improvements in your combat abilities as of late. It's rare I see someone so dedicated."

*Why does it sound like she found out before I told Lydia in class today? Maybe she's actually a Starvein and is just hiding it. That wouldn't surprise me at all.*

"Thank you," Jasmine said carefully, but Esther wasn't done.

"And it's rarer that I see someone so dedicated to just one aspect of their training while completely neglecting every other one," Esther finished.

Jasmine winced.

"I'll get on that, Keeper Esther. I won't lag behind for long."

"I'm sure you won't. Today, I called on you specifically because of your dedication to your combat skills." Esther leaned her staff against the dais and interlaced her fingers, watching Jasmine's expression closely.

*Come on! Just spit it out already. What do you want to say?*

Instead of voicing her thoughts, Jasmine sat silently. Esther gave her a wry smile, but it quickly faded.

"You've been selected, Jasmine."

# 3

"Selected? For what?" Jasmine asked, baffled. "The thing you talked about in class?"

"Something similar, but it is not the exact same circumstance."

Jasmine couldn't contain her distaste this time around. "Oh. Do I have to do this?"

"I'm afraid so."

"Figures. Maybe Lydia was right. What am I supposed to do, then? Protecting a fake target from bandits or the like? That could be interesting."

Esther's brow furrowed. "I'm afraid you may have misconceptions about what I meant, Jasmine. This is not a drill. You will be assigned to a minor noble whose family was killed in an attack, and you will be expected to fulfill every duty that a Keeper should."

Jasmine choked and she stared at Esther, waiting for the older woman to start laughing at the joke. Unfortunately, there wasn't a single hint of humor in Esther's eyes. She was deadly serious.

"Why me?" Jasmine asked. "I'm not exactly..."

"Well rounded?" Esther finished. "No, you are not, much to my disappointment. However, there are no available Year Two Keepers. They are all already assigned to charges. We do not have the bodies to spare – and as we just discussed, you are more than capable in a fight, which is exactly what is needed."

"You make it sound like this is more than just a training exercise."

"I'm afraid it is. The noble you are being assigned to is in genuine need of a Keeper. He has been granted a Keeper until the time at which he is able to defend himself."

"I'm going to be working for a noble? That's impossible. I can't," Jasmine said, shaking her head vehemently. "Keeper Esther, you've seen–"

"Your limitations are well known to me," Esther said curtly. "But this is not up to discussion, Jasmine. I am displeased with this as well, but there are no Keepers that can be spared for a relatively unimportant noble. If it were not for the King's command, no Keeper would be assigned."

"The King himself commanded it?" Jasmine blinked.

"He did. I do not know why. It was a damn foolish command to make. You will have to work twice as hard to keep up with the rest of your class, and you already have much work on your plate."

"If the order comes straight from the King, then I'll do it. I wouldn't even be here if it wasn't for him. He's the one that allowed me into the order."

*And he's the one that got me out of the gutters. I can't fail this. If I get booted out of the Sanctuary and sent back to that Watcher-damned hell-hole, I'll have a dagger in my back before I can blink. I won't go back. I'd rather die on my own terms.*

Jasmine's mouth was dry as a bone. She swallowed heavily, but it did little to cure her parched throat. No matter what she wanted, an order from the King wasn't a request. She didn't have much of a choice in the matter.

*Did Asher somehow hear about this and drop out early? That sneaky piece of – that would be just like him.*

If Esther noticed Jasmine's hands clenching at her sides, she didn't mention anything.

"Good. Do not fall too far behind, Jasmine. This will not exempt you from any of your normal responsibilities or the consequences that will come from failing to complete them."

Jasmine swallowed, then nodded. "I understand. Will the noble be coming to Sanctuary?"

"They are part of the Starvein program and are already present," Esther replied. "Your belongings have already been moved to room K15 in the Starvein Halls."

Jasmine opened her mouth, then closed it with a click.

"I have to move?" Jasmine asked weakly. "I thought–"

"You are performing the full role of a Keeper. The *full* role," Esther said with a shake of her head. "That includes defending your charge from threats at all times of the day."

*Lovely. Lydia was definitely right. Today is awful.*

Jasmine repressed her emotions, keeping them from showing on her face. It felt like a storm had been set off in her stomach. Following the King's orders felt considerably less gratifying when it sounded like it would come at such a high cost.

"I will be here to help where I can," Esther said in a gentle tone. "I am sorry. You should not have been put in this situation."

*That really fixes everything. Thanks. Now that you're sorry, I won't have the rest of my free time stolen by some random noble that the King decided was worth basically sacrificing me to. They weren't important enough to get assigned a proper Keeper, so they just tagged me with it instead. Fantastic.*

"Is that all?" Jasmine asked, struggling to keep her face devoid from emotion. Her stomach felt like it was knotting itself and her ears rang with blood.

"Yes. You may leave."

Jasmine strode out, nearly walking straight into Lydia. She'd completely forgotten that her friend had been waiting for her.

"You were in there a while. Was Keeper Esther congratulating you on being the rank one fighter now that Asher ran like a baby," Lydia started with a grin, but it fell away as soon as she saw Jasmine's face. "Jas? What happened?"

"I got selected to be a Keeper," Jasmine muttered. "In the middle of my first year."

"I thought we were all going to have to do the extra stuff. It's not *that* bad. Sure, we'll have a bit less free time, but things could be worse. We're still students, you know."

Jasmine stared at Lydia. Lydia's face paled.

"You mean you *actually* have to be a Keeper? A real one? Not training?"

"Not training. Some noble's family got killed and the King decided that I'm the one that has to baby him because they don't want to spare a real Keeper. Not important enough for someone that's actually relevant, but still important enough to completely destroy my life," Jasmine said.

"Maybe it won't be so bad?" Lydia offered, but it was clear by the tone of her voice that she knew just how weak the suggestion was. "I mean, we're training to be Keepers anyway, right?"

"Training being the key word," Jasmine muttered. She ran a hand through her black hair, tugging at it in frustration before starting off down the hall at a brisk pace. Lydia jogged to catch up with her.

"You'll probably learn a lot."

"It's more likely that I won't learn anything at all," Jasmine said with a huff. "I'm not ready for this. I've barely got any training. I enjoy learning to be a Keeper, but I still wanted to *live* a little too, you know? These years were going to be the last properly free ones I had."

"Maybe you'll really like the noble."

Jasmine sent a flat stare at Lydia, who cleared her throat.

"Okay, that's probably a reach. It's not permanent though, right? It's just for a while."

"Yeah." Jasmine sighed. "That's the one lucky bit, I guess. I only have to put up with it until the King decides this guy is safe again. If I'm lucky, it'll be over quickly."

*And if I'm not, I'm stuck with him forever.*

Jasmine could tell that the same thought was passing through Lydia's head. Lydia glanced away and cleared her throat.

"I'm sorry. Do you know why they chose you?"

"Yeah. Because I was the best fighter in our year."

Lydia's eyes widened and she missed a step. "Damn, that's unlucky. So Asher would have gotten chosen if this happened a few days ago? That really sucks. I wonder if he somehow heard about this and dropped just in case. I bet a noble would have preferred someone who was pretty good at fighting and great at everything else to – well, you know."

"Thanks. I definitely haven't heard that enough today," Jasmine said dryly. "You might be right, though. I can't believe him."

"When I see him next, I'm going to shove my foot up where the sun doesn't shine," Lydia declared.

Jasmine burst into laughter. Lydia's fiery personality translated poorly into her fighting abilities, so the image of her furiously chasing after Asher was absurd enough that Jasmine couldn't help it.

"Thanks, Lydia," Jasmine said. "I appreciate you trying to make me feel better. I think I'm supposed to go report to my new room."

"Want me to come?"

"Better not. They might get ideas and decide one Keeper trainee isn't enough."

Lydia paled. "Would they really?"

"I was joking."

*Mostly.*

Lydia shuddered. "Don't joke like that. Though, if I did have to properly do the duties of a Keeper this early on, I'd rather partner with you than anyone else."

"Thanks," Jasmine said dryly. "That would work for me as well. I could do the fighting, and you could do everything else."

They reached a fork in the path and came to a stop. Jasmine looked out over the railing. Abandoned buildings covered the ground beneath them, relics of when Sanctuary had once been a massive city. The lower levels had supposedly been the most populous. Now, they had more ghosts than people.

The path to the right – the one that overlooked the city below – led back to her former dormitory room. The one to the left branched off and headed deeper into the upper levels of the city.

"This is me," Jasmine said, nodding to the path. "I guess I'll be seeing you in class. Esther said those will be the only time I actually get a break from my new job."

*Except I won't be because I'm not going to have time to go to class. How am I supposed to say that, though?*

Lydia nodded. She searched for words for a few moments, but found none. Jasmine didn't wait around to make the scene any more uncomfortable. She just raised her hand in farewell and set off down the path, leaving Lydia behind her.

Jasmine remembered little of the walk to the Starvein Halls. It felt like she was in a daze. Everything had moved so quickly that she could barely even register what had happened since waking up that day.

But, when Jasmine arrived at her destination, she had no choice but to take a moment and stare in awe. The Halls were undeniably beautiful. Their towering ceilings rising hundreds of feet in the air. Beautiful gold trimmed the marble and obsidian pillars arranged in neat rows, and ancient murals adorned every inch of the walls. Though much of it had faded in recent years, it was still an imposing sight to behold.

She had only been to the Halls briefly in the past, and it took her almost an hour of largely aimless wandering before she finally located the dormitory wing.

The ceiling in it was a much more reasonable ten feet tall, but it wasn't any less decorated than the rest of the area. Jasmine had to keep herself from gawking as she walked.

It wasn't much of a surprise to her that the Starvein Halls were so much nicer than the Keeper section of Sanctuary. Almost anyone could become a Keeper – or, at least, almost anyone could try.

But a Starvein - Only a noble could be a Starvein. The two words were basically synonymous. Starveins could cast magic, and that made them noble. Or perhaps it was the other way around. Jasmine wasn't sure, but she didn't care all that much about the semantics at the moment.

Jasmine came to a stop before one of the doors about halfway down the hall. The haze that had been enveloping her thoughts finally lifted as found herself standing before a beautiful metal plaque that read S15. It had been pounded into the wall beside an obsidian door with gold trimmings.

Beneath the plaque, on a small bronze plate that was so rusted that Jasmine had to scratch at it to get a better look, K15 had been carved.

Several seconds passed as Jasmine stood in silence, debating what to do. Part of her was tempted to just turn around and wander off as if she'd never seen the door in the first place. But, eventually, she forced her reluctant body to obey her commands and raised her hand, knocking twice.

No more than a few seconds later, the door swung open. Jasmine opened her mouth to introduce herself, then froze. Staring back at her were two golden eyes that she would have recognized anywhere.

"Asher?"

# 4

"Jasmine?" Asher asked, stunned. He looked tired. There were dark bags under his eyes, and he blinked heavily like he were trying to dismiss a hallucination. "What are you doing here?"

"What are *you* doing here?" Jasmine demanded.

"I asked first."

"Are you really going to pretend like you didn't know?" Jasmine crossed her arms in front of her chest and glared at him. "As if you didn't hear that someone was going to get chosen. Lucky me that I ran into you, though. I was going to–"

"I'm not coming back to be a Keeper," Asher said, a harsh note to his voice. "I didn't think you'd actually come looking for me. Besides, you won! You can just ask Esther for someone else to spar with."

Asher started to close the door, but Jasmine jammed her foot into the crack and forced it back open.

"That's not happening. I don't take pleasure in shattering your dreams, but I'm not here for you. I wasn't going to go looking for someone that abandoned his fellows without even letting them know."

*Okay, I was, but I'm not telling you that.*

"You weren't here to find me?" Asher blinked. "What in the world are you doing here, then? That's a pretty lame excuse, Jasmine. Even for you."

"What's that meant to mean?"

"Just… go," Asher said with a sigh. "I don't care about any of this anymore. I quit. None of it matters. You're the strongest warrior in Year 1 now. That's what you wanted."

Anger swelled in Jasmine's chest, but she bound it down before it could slip through. All the hours that they'd practiced. Every single humiliating defeat and hard-earned victory flashed through her head.

The constant training just to keep up with Asher – and eventually, to surpass him. Fighting was the one thing she was actually good at. The one thing she actually enjoyed.

*All this time, I thought you were the same. Insufferable asshole or not, I thought you got to the top of the class because you wanted to push yourself. Turns out that all you gave a shit about was the title.*

Jasmine's hand moved before her mind registered. Her fist caught Asher on the cheek and he staggered back with a curse, his eyes going wide in shock. Blood trickled down his lip and he wiped it away with the back of his hand.

For an instant, it looked like he was about to dive at her and start a fight. Jasmine tensed. Then Asher lowered his hands and just shook his head.

"Feel better?"

"No," Jasmine spat. "Not at all."

"Well, I'm sorry. Can you leave now?"

"Nope."

Asher ground his teeth. He wiped the blood from his lips with the back of a sleeve. "What is your problem? What do you want from me? I already told you. I don't care what you say. I'm not coming back. It's over, Jasmine."

"I'm not here for you."

Asher frowned. "What?"

"Not everything is about you, you arrogant prick. In case you didn't know, when you decided to abandon ship, I got selected to be a Keeper for some noble. Lucky me, right?"

Asher's face went white. "A Keeper? You're a Year One!"

"Tell that to Esther," Jasmine replied. "I assume you somehow overheard her telling me where to go. If you want to be an asshole, then go ahead. Just do it somewhere else. I'm not going to beg at your feet for you to come back. I'll find a different sparring partner – one that actually wants to get stronger. I guess I just misjudged you."

The two of them stared at each other for several seconds. Jasmine gestured irritably.

"What are you waiting for?"

"This is wrong," Asher muttered. "You aren't supposed to be here."

"Can you just get out of the way?" Jasmine demanded. "I need to see the noble. Did you bribe him to get into the room or something? This is a new low, even for you."

Asher pulled the door open fully, and Jasmine's eyes widened in spite of herself. The Starvein Hall rooms were considerably larger than the Keeper ones. A huge bed sat in the center, just below a large, curtained window.

Beautiful mahogany dressers lined one of the walls, opposite to a walk-in closet on the other. A large chest rested at the foot of the bed and there was a carved table made from the same wood as the dressers beneath a second window on the left side of the room with two chairs beside it.

But, even though the room was beautiful, it was surprisingly undecorated. It didn't look like anyone even lived in it. Everything was untouched and pristine.

"Where's the noble?" Jasmine asked, a frown crossing her features.

"You aren't lying about this?" Asher asked.

"I'll punch you again," Jasmine threatened, holding a fist up. "And you aren't going to get up from the second one."

Asher studied her for a moment before letting out a bark of bitter laughter.

"What's so funny?"

"Funny might not be the word I'd use," Asher said, shaking his head. "There's no other noble, Jasmine. It's just me. This is my room."

"Ha ha," Jasmine intoned. "Hilarious."

"I'm not joking," Asher said. His face was deadly serious – although his cheek was starting to swell up a little. He wiped the blood from his lip again, then grimaced. "Unfortunately."

Jasmine stared at him. "That's impossible. You were a Keeper."

Asher tilted his head to the side. "There's no rule against nobles being Keepers."

"Right," Jasmine said dryly. "You *chose* to be a Keeper instead of bending the universe to your will. Instead of the power to dominate nature itself, you elected to swing a pointy stick really hard."

"Being a Keeper is much more than fighting," Asher snapped. "And there's absolutely nothing wrong with being a little mundane."

"Don't get me wrong – I love my pointy stick. I'd just like to sling magic around even more," Jasmine said. She opened her mouth, but a set of hurried footsteps echoed down the hall before she could finish her sentence.

Even as she instinctively turned in their direction, a tall man strode out into the hall. He was middle aged, with thinning gray hair that did nothing to cover the arrogant expression on his hawkish face. Long, bluish-black robes rippled around his body with every step. They looked vaguely like a bedsheet, but Jasmine suspected that informing him of such would be a poor decision.

"Impressive," the man drawled, his voice nasally and somehow more irritating than Jasmine had expected it to be – and that was quite a feat. He looked straight past Jasmine, not even acknowledging her presence. "You've managed to cause a ruckus before even being here for a full day, Asher."

"Sorry for the disturbance, Starvein Qien. I let my emotions get the best of me. It's been a trying day," Asher said, inclining his head and letting his voice take on a respectful tone. "I didn't mean to cause any trouble."

"I'm sure you didn't," Qien said dryly. He took a step forward, passing Jasmine. "Please keep your future quarrels to an absolute minimum. I don't care who you associate with, but–"

Qien turned to nod in her direction, then froze as he looked her in the eyes. His hand shot out with shocking speed, grabbing Jasmine's chin and pulling her to meet his gaze before she could even react.

"Silver eyes," Qien breathed. "You are a Xolani. No horns, though. A mixed breed. I did not think such a thing was possible. What human could find one of those creatures attractive?"

Jasmine jerked her head out of the man's grip. He was fast, but not particularly strong. The urge to drive her fist into his stomach was strong, but striking a Starvein was a fast way to sign your own death – especially as a Keeper.

"My parents were both human," Jasmine said curtly. "The blood is from farther back in my line. I am not a Xolani. I have none of their magic. My eyes are just a different color. That's it."

"An unfortunate side effect of tainted blood, then. Shows to prove that even a single drop can ruin a pristine pool." Qien didn't sound completely convinced, but his eyes drifted to Asher. "I will take steps to ensure that such a drop never gets a chance to taint anything. You are already here against my will. Prove me wrong,

*Keeper.* Prove that you have a place as a Starvein – or you will be neither."

With that, Qien stormed down the hall. Jasmine watched him leave, rubbing her jaw, then shot a look at Asher.

"Who was that asshole?"

"One of my teachers, as of this morning," Asher replied, pressing his lips together in displeasure. A muscle in his sharp jawline twitched and he let out an exasperated sigh. "Were you serious about why you came here?"

"Trust me, this is the last thing I would lie about," Jasmine said, her shoulders slumping as the weight of her situation settled back in. Asher or not, she was still meant to somehow juggle being a Keeper and actually learning *how* to be a Keeper at the same time.

*And I started my job of being the ideal protector and assistant off by punching my charge in the cheek and then getting him into trouble with his teacher.*

*He deserved it, though. Prick.*

"Then I suppose you should come inside," Asher said wearily. He stepped back, leaving room for Jasmine to enter the room and holding the door open for her. "Is there any way we can convince Esther to change her mind? I didn't ask for this. I don't *want* this."

"Yeah? Guess what. Me neither. Trust me, I already did everything I could. The King himself ordered it, and the only idiot he was willing to waste on this was the unlucky highest ranked fighter in Year One. Lucky you."

"Tell me about it," Asher said, but there wasn't an ounce of humor in his voice. He shut the door behind them.

There was a small door on the right side of the room that nearly blended in with the cabinets. Jasmine had missed it when she'd first gotten a look into Asher's room, but there was no doubt in her mind that this was the entrance to her own room.

There was no handle on the door, but it swung open seamlessly when Jasmine pressed on it. The room beyond was… plain. It was made up of stone walls and a single, small bed. There were no windows or other ways to see out of it. If anything, it was more of a prison cell than an actual room.

A small bathroom was connected to her room – though it was more of a closet than anything else. It hadn't even been granted the liberty of a door and instead had a curtain that was pulled to the side to reveal a small sink and wash basin.

At the base of the bed was a small trunk bearing a scar at its top – a chest that Jasmine recognized. She'd put the scar there a few months ago by accident when she'd dropped her sword while polishing it.

"They sure move fast," Jasmine said, walking up to the chest and pulling it open. A large package wrapped in brown paper sat atop a pile of folded clothes. To its side was her whetstone and a small pouch of coin.

"It's… quaint," Asher said diplomatically from over her shoulder. "I checked the room when I moved in, by the way. There aren't any secret hallways or the like. It's safe."

*Quaint? This is the nicest room I've ever been in.*

"That's one way to put it," Jasmine said.

"Also, the door doesn't lock. It just swings."

"That's fine. I hate privacy."

"Look, I'm not the one that forced this to happen. I don't like it any more than you do. If you've got an issue, then take it up with Esther," Asher said, crossing his arms. "I've got things I need to do, though. I can't waste any more time."

He turned, letting the door swing shut behind him. Jasmine was pretty sure she was meant to follow after him, but after listening for a moment, it didn't sound like he'd left the room, so there was no need.

*Also, I don't want to follow him. Damn it all. I should be training right now. Why did it have to be me? Why did it have to be him?*

Jasmine pulled the package out of the chest and set it on the bed. A copper key had been tucked into a flap in the paper, likely the one that opened Asher's door. She tucked it into her pocket and pulled the wrapping away from the package. Jasmine immediately regretted it as she saw the glint of a pot. It was a set of cooking utensils.

"Fuck off," Jasmine muttered. She resisted the urge to shove the pots off her bed and instead stuffed them back into the chest and got about halfway through slamming it shut before she remembered that she wasn't supposed to be making any noise.

She shut the chest quietly, fuming to herself, and flopped onto her bed. It was the exact same one she had in her own room, but this bed felt a hundred times colder and less welcoming. The cold stone ceiling swam above her, drab and unforgiving.

Jasmine rolled over and buried her face in her arms. She didn't know if she wanted to laugh, scream into the bed, or just break down in tears. It didn't matter – she couldn't do any of it. There was no privacy. There was no leeway for her to feel anything.

There was only the duties of the Keeper.

# 5

Jasmine could only hide for so long. She was pretty sure that barricading her door would count as failing her duties. Only the Watcher knew how Esther was going to be judging Jasmine's performance, but she couldn't afford to fail.

Failure meant being removed from the Keeper order, and that meant return to the gutters. Icy spines pressed into Jasmine's back at the thought and she nearly retched. The mere idea felt like gargling sewage water, and that wasn't far from the truth.

She'd spent years surviving by begging, stealing, and running jobs for the gangs in the gutters. Dirty, rancid water and decaying rat were flavors that she doubted she'd ever forget – and they were flavors that she never planned to taste again.

Failure was impossible. It wasn't – it *couldn't* be an option. Shoving herself out of bed, Jasmine rose to her feet. Her eyes caught on her open chest, where the glint of metal pots still glistened.

The room was dark, but Jasmine didn't actually need all that much light. For that matter, she didn't need it at all. She hadn't been entirely truthful with Qien. Jasmine had never managed to manifest a single Xolani spell, but she *did* have their eyes.

To her, even the darkest night was clad in shades of gray rather than inscrutable black. And, to her displeasure, the pots weren't going anywhere. She let out a heavy sigh and grabbed a pan from the pile.

Jasmine padded over to her door and pushed it open, poking her head out into Asher's room. To her relief, he was sitting on his considerably larger bed, his legs crossed and eyes closed.

His features were relaxed and peaceful, as if he were asleep. Jasmine's eyes lingered on his face for a moment, tracing the sharp curve of his jaw and the almost-smile on his lips. The side of his face was still slightly swollen.

*Prick. If I could get away with sparring you now, you'd be stabbed a dozen times over.*

Jasmine crept over to the main door and slipped out, closing it behind her as gently as she could. She slid the copper key into the hole, locking it with a faint click. Still glaring daggers at the pot, Jasmine tucked the key back into her pocket and headed off down the hall.

After a few minutes of searching, Jasmine found what she was looking for – a kitchen. It had been down a few tight corridors and lacked all the décor that the rest of the Starvein Halls had, but that suited Jasmine just fine.

It was drawing near midday, and the duties of a Keeper included ensuring that her charge ate. The pot felt heavy in her hand as she stepped into the kitchen, glancing around. It was large and, to her relief, it was empty.

Several rows of metal boxes sat along the back wall beside a large set of cabinets. Across from them were a few burners with metal grates to slide wood into their bottoms and a single sink, with a large pot of water and a piece of soap at its side. A quick check of the cabinets revealed that they were full of flour, sugar, spices, and a multitude of other ingredients that she had absolutely no desire to get to know.

The boxes proved more promising. They were full of ice, with various foodstuffs preserved within. After a few minutes, Jasmine spotted a small crate of eggs in the corner of one. She pulled three eggs out, then closed the box and returned to the burners.

Placing her pot on top of the burner, Jasmine set the eggs on the countertop and knelt. Luckily, there was still wood inside, along with a small piece of flint to start a flame. She struck it, the sharp ring breaking through the silence.

A spark caught on the wood. Jasmine closed the door again and stared at the top of the burner. Out of the corner of her eye, she spotted one of the eggs as it started to roll off the counter. She lunged, grabbing it right as it fell.

Her victorious smirk vanished as the other two eggs rolled right past her hand, shattering against the ground.

Jasmine's eye twitched.

*I haven't even started yet.*

A minute of cleaning with a discarded rag that she found in a corner later, Jasmine retrieved two more eggs and stood before a heated burner with the pot upon it, three eggs watched under a careful eye before her.

*It's got to be hot enough by now, right?*

Jasmine cracked one of the eggs into the pot. It sizzled as soon as it hit the metal. She reached for a spatula – then cursed. She didn't have one with her. Her eyes shot around the kitchen and she spotted one on the other side of the counter.

By the time Jasmine retrieved it and got back to the pot, the overheated pot had already cooked the egg rather thoroughly. Jasmine pushed at it with the spatula, but about half the egg had gotten stuck to the bottom of the bot.

Still cursing under her breath, Jasmine cracked the other two eggs into the pot. A shard of one of the shells fell in alongside them, but she was a little more concerned with the loud, aggressive popping coming from the pot.

*Okay, maybe that was a bit too hot. I don't get it. The damn pot is hot. That means it should cook the eggs.*

*I mean, they're cooked, but –*

Jasmine flinched as the eggs popped again. She lifted the pot off the fire and fruitlessly tried to mix the eggs around with the spatula. The faint smell of burning food wafted off the pot and Jasmine stared down at her creation.

About half of it was completely stuck to the pot, and the other half was well on its way to getting up and throwing itself into the garbage in shame. That was quite the coincidence, as that was exactly how Jasmine felt.

*They're fucking eggs. I must have a defective pot. I'll just scrape this into the trash and give it another shot. They had like forty eggs, so I'm sure nobody will notice if twenty go missing.*

Jasmine turned, holding the pot out before her like a weapon – and found herself face to face with a very tired looking Asher. They locked eyes for several seconds. Jasmine yanked the pot back.

"What are you doing here?" Jasmine asked, desperately searching for something to pawn the pot off onto.

"Getting lunch," Asher replied. "I don't have a servant, you know. I have to make it."

He looked like he wanted to say something more, but paused. His eyes traveled down to the pot that Jasmine was unsuccessfully trying to maneuver behind herself.

"You made me lunch?"

"I most certainly did not. I was–"

"Definitely not cooking for yourself," Asher finished, a tiny smirk tugging at the corner of his lip before the weary expression returned again. "We both know you'd never do that. Haven't you been paying Lydia to cook for you ever since you got here?"

"Do you see Lydia around anywhere?"

"No, but I also know that I am a very hungry Starvein whose Keeper is bound to aid him in all things, and I currently find myself hungry."

"Your Keeper suggests you locate an alternate source of food."

"I'd much rather see what you made," Asher said, his grin returning. He made a grabbing motion with his hands. "Let's see it, Keeper. That's an order."

Jasmine's eye twitched. She drew in a deep breath and let it out slowly, holding the pot out before her. Asher looked down into it, then let out a snorting laugh. That would have been enough, but he doubled over, the laughter intensifying until tears streamed down his cheeks.

"Very funny," Jasmine said. "I'm glad at least one of us got some enjoyment out of this failure. Now, if you'll excuse me, I'm going to go scrape this out and try again."

"Please don't," Asher said as he caught his breath, wiping his face with the back of his sleeve. He straightened out and shook his head, letting out another quick chuckle before regaining control of himself. "I'd prefer not to waste food. I'll eat it."

Jasmine stared down at the homunculus she'd created in her pot. She was pretty sure it was wiggling of its own accord.

"I'm not sure that's a very good idea. This might not be suitable to be called food anymore." Jasmine could feel her ears turning red. She knew her talents well – cooking was far from one of them. Food didn't help her defeat an assassin or fight off a horde of enemies. It was a complete waste of time.

*On the other hand, if I was going to force anyone to eat this, it would be you.*

Asher walked over to one of the cabinets that Jasmine hadn't gotten around to checking yet. He pulled down a bowl and a spoon, then set them on the counter. He took the pot from Jasmine's reluctant hands and scraped as much of the egg monstrosity as he could into the bowl.

"Thanks for the food," Asher said, taking a spoonful and putting it into his mouth. Jasmine nearly looked away, but she forced herself to remain calm. There was always a chance that it wasn't as bad as it looked.

Asher swallowed, his face completely straight. He cleared his throat, opened his mouth, then thought better of it and put the spoon back into the eggs.

"If either of us want to survive this, maybe I should cook," Asher suggested. "I've been doing it all this time, so it's not really that big of a difference. We can pretend you did it if Esther asks."

"And then I get booted out of the program if it gets found out," Jasmine snapped. "It was one thing when I was in training, but I've now got to act like a real Keeper. I know you don't care about the order, but I do. I can't afford to fail."

Asher's eyes narrowed. Then he shrugged. "Fine."

Jasmine expected him to say more, but he didn't. To her surprise, he raised the spoon and shoveled another bit of burnt eggs into his mouth.

*I didn't mean you had to eat this crap. I would have found something less burn-able, but I can't really tell him that now.*

Asher polished the rest of the bowl off quicky – likely because he avoided chewing much to get the meal over with as quickly as possible. He set the spoon down and rose to his feet. Jasmine almost hoped he would tell her how horrible it was. At least that would have given her something to feel annoyed about.

Instead, Asher just gave her a curt nod and strode out of the kitchen, leaving Jasmine alone with the bowl, a spoon, and her pot – which still had eggs burnt into it. Her stomach rumbled, but now that Asher had left the kitchen, she didn't know where he was headed. If he wasn't in his room, he might not be safe.

*What if Esther sends a fake assassin after him or something?*

Jasmine swore. She poured some water into the pot, then washed Asher's bowl and spoon, returning them to the cabinet before jogging off after Asher. The pot could soak – she'd come back to it later that night. A twinge of pain in her stomach reminded her that she hadn't eaten yet, but the longer she left him alone, the more her mind screamed that Esther would try something while she was gone.

She jogged out of the kitchen to catch up with Asher, her hands clenched and she ignored her stomach as it rumbled. There would be time for her to eat once she had confirmed that Asher wasn't at eminent risk of death.

*I hate this. I hate this so much.*

# 6

By some miracle, Jasmine actually managed to catch up with Asher. She turned a corner and, in her pursuit, nearly ran him down on accident. He stood at the edge of the hall before a large tapestry, staring up at it with an inscrutable expression on his face. She skidded to a stop at the last second.

"What are you doing? Did you forget the whole conversation we had?" Jasmine demanded in an irritated whisper. "You can't just walk off!"

"As if someone's going to jump me in broad daylight in the middle of a hallway. I've been perfectly fine all the way up until today," Asher said curtly. "Besides, I have all the training you do."

"Two swords are better than one. And it doesn't matter what you think – what if Esther sends someone to test out if I'm doing my job? They smack you over the head and I get kicked out of the Sanctuary for failing my duties." Jasmine stepped closer to Asher, her eyes narrowing in anger. "I will not fail out. I *can't.* This is what I'm stuck with, and I'll be damned if I got this far just to get screwed by you being an asshole."

Asher blinked. For a moment, neither of them said anything

else. Then he pressed his lips together. "Fine. I won't interfere with your duties. Happy?"

"No."

Asher snorted. "Me neither. I guess that's how life works, though. What about my classes, *Keeper?* Do you plan to attend those as well? Or am I at risk of getting run through in lecture?"

It was tempting to say no. Jasmine almost did on the spot. A class was almost certainly safe – any of the teachers in Sanctuary were capable, especially the Starveins. The chances of something going wrong in one of their classes was next to nothing.

*This isn't just an assignment, though. I don't know if Esther will test me, or if there are actually real threats that might try something. The King himself asked for a Keeper to watch over Asher. If I screw this up, it's over. I'll be back in the slums and there won't be another chance to get out.*

*I'm not letting Asher out of my sight until Esther herself tells me I can.*

"I'll go with you," Jasmine said. "This time, at least. When I get a chance to talk with Esther, I'll figure out how much leeway I've got to let you breathe. I've still got class I have to go to myself, so I'm sure there's something we'll have in place."

Asher heaved a sigh. "Fine. It's not going to go well, though."

"It doesn't matter how it goes. They can take things up with Esther if they don't like anything."

"In that case, come on. I don't have that long before class, and I've already irritated Starvien Qien enough." Asher set off down the hall and Jasmine hurried to match his pace.

"The guy we saw a bit ago?"

"Yeah."

"The ass–"

"Yes." Asher glared at Jasmine out of the corner of his eyes. "And I'd appreciate if you don't make my reputation even worse than it already is. I don't need him to hear you insulting him."

They came to a stop at an open door that reached all the way up to the towering room's ceiling. By some mercy, the actual room beyond it was remarkably plain. At least, it was plain in comparison to the hall.

Two dozen chairs sat in a semicircle before an elevated stage. The chairs were all padded with soft silk, and about half of them were full. A chandelier hung from the ceiling, which was only a little taller than the one in the Keeper lecture room.

If anything, it was just a nicer version of the room the Keepers had. Its general shape was identical.

Qien already stood at the dais, tapping a finger against his thigh. He stood beside a large chalkboard and a pedestal, watching over everyone with a scowl. Several students were scattered throughout the chairs, and it became immediately clear that the class wasn't particularly tight knit.

The majority of the students sat in groups of two or three, with a few sitting entirely on their own. None of the groups sat anywhere near the others, so even though there weren't many of them, they were scattered throughout the room.

All the students wore fine clothes, many of which bearing family crests that Jasmine didn't recognize. Most importantly, everything looked remarkably ineffective at stopping a blade.

Asher headed into the classroom and sat down at a chair near the middle of the pack. Jasmine took the one beside him. The chairs here were *much* more comfortable than the stone wedges that she was used to.

Qien glanced at her out of the corner of his eye as they sat down, and Jasmine half expected the man to say something. But, to her surprise, he just turned his gaze away and continued tapping away impatiently.

Over the next few minutes, several more students entered the room. They either joined some of the existing groups or sat on their own. And, while some of the kids sitting next to each other spoke in hushed whispers, there was no communication between the invisible lines that separated everyone.

Jasmine shifted uncomfortably. Compared to the ribbing that usually heralded the start of Keeper classes, it was almost painful to sit through. The feeling couldn't have been any less tense.

More than a few times, Jasmine felt someone's gaze boring into her. She didn't even need to ask herself if it was just a feeling or not – the Starveins weren't particularly subtle, and it was easy to catch them in the act.

It looked like the interest was evenly split between her and Asher – though that might not have been a good thing.

Mercifully, Qien broke the silence by rapping a finger against the wooden pedestal before him to draw their attention.

"As many of you have noticed, we have a new addition," Qien said, interlacing his fingers and leaning on the pedestal. "Students, please meet Asher. He is a new Starvein that will be joining us today."

"I heard he was a Keeper," a girl with long, blonde hair said brusquely, not even pausing for a moment to even *try* to be polite. "What's a Keeper doing in here?"

Asher stiffened, but the motion was so imperceptible that Jasmine only picked it up because she sat directly beside him.

"Pina, at what point in my sentence did you mishear me?" Qien's glower was so intense that it could have melted through steel. "Asher is a Starvein, though he was a Keeper before. Whether he remains a Starvein is another question, but until he has proven to us that he is not who he claims, then a Starvein he remains."

Pina nodded and sank back into her chair. The look she sent over her shoulder at Asher and Jasmine said that she was anything but satisfied with Qien's answer, though.

"What about the girl with him?" A heavyset boy sitting in the chair beside Pina asked. "Is she also a Starvein?"

"No, Clarence. That would be his Keeper."

A small murmur ran through the room, though a single glare from Qien ended it in its tracks. He arched an eyebrow.

"Is something a matter?"

"Why does a Keeper need a Keeper?" Clarence asked.

Jasmine could have sworn the temperature in the room dropped as Qien's eyes bore into Clarence. She couldn't see his face, but the boy squirmed uncomfortably in his chair.

"Sorry. He's not a Keeper," Clarence said meekly.

"Ah. You must have misspoken," Qien said. "Do not do it again. And the answer is the same as the one that has always been. Tell me, Clarence. What is a Starvein?"

"A person blessed with the power to bend the universe to their will," Clarence said, unmistakable pride entering his voice. "We're the strongest warriors in the kingdom and the backbone on which everything is built. Without us, there is no Whitewater Kingdom."

*If you pat yourself on the back any harder, the friction will make your shirt catch fire.*

"Correct," Qien said with a curt nod. "And tell me, Clarence. We who are blessed to wield strength that can change the natural order of things – do you find that the magic comes easily to you? Does it spring from your blessed fingertips like an unstoppable fountain? Do you wake every morning with raw magic pouring from your eyes?"

Qien's voice intensified with every word, never quite getting to a yell but cutting through the room like a sharp knife. Clarence cringed into his chair.

"No, Professor. It is difficult."

"Yes. It. Is. Difficult." Qien punctuated every word by tapping his finger on the pedestal. "For some of us more than others. This is a good intro to today's lesson, so I must thank you."

Clarence did nothing but nod meekly.

"Pina, would you be willing to join me on stage?" Qien asked, but it was clearly not a question. She stood without word and walked up to stand beside the professor, whose gaze snapped over to Asher. "You as well please, Asher. Look lively, now."

Asher rose to his feet. Jasmine hesitated for a moment, then remained seated. Being in the room was enough. She didn't have to literally be nipping at his heels the entire time.

Before Asher had even taken a step toward the stage, Qien tilted his head to the side. "Why is your Keeper remaining behind? Call her to heel."

Jasmine's eye twitched in synchronization with Asher's. She stood and fell in behind Asher, joining him on the walk up to the stage. Qien indicated for them to stand to his right, then had Pina stand on his other side.

"To my left," Qien said, indicating Pina, "is a young woman who currently is toward the top of your class. She has remarkable control over the power that courses through her. Would you agree with this assessment, Pina?"

The blonde girl swallowed. "I would not argue with you, Professor."

*Good answer. That seemed like a trick question. At first, I thought Qien had it out for me or Asher, but I think he's just kind of a prick in general. Does he like anyone?*

"Wise. On my right is Asher – remind me of your training, Asher. How much power have you channeled before?"

"I have no training."

"You have no training." Qien nodded. He took a step back to open the space between Asher and Pina. "The two of you will duel. Partial power – there will be no fatalities. It goes until surrender, you move from your spot, or you are knocked unconscious. Begin."

Asher's hand shot for his sword. Pina brought her hands together, cupping them as if to hold water.

"Stop!" Qien barked.

They both froze.

"The mistake is mine," Qien said, his words dripping with false honey. "You are uneducated. When I say duel, then you are to use *magic*. Are you not a Starvein, Asher? A Starvein uses magic. They do not stab each other like savages – nor do they fling swords or other objects like some irate monkey. I am certain that you were only acting on muscle memory and did not actually plan to launch your blade at Pina."

*I can think of one person in this room who might benefit from a little stabbing. Might help him loosen up. Also, Asher was definitely just about to do that.*

"I am untrained in magic, Professor," Asher said, his voice surprisingly calm. Jasmine was pretty sure she wouldn't have been able to muster anywhere near the level of diplomatic calm that he possessed were she in the same situation.

"Is that so? Then I suggest you learn quickly. A Starvein wields magic, not blade. Resume the fight."

Asher pried his hands away from the hilt of his sword. At the same time, a faint chill ran along Jasmine's skin and called up goosebumps. Swirls of pale white energy were gathering in Pina's cupped hands.

Qien watched idly as Asher's back stiffened. Jasmine ground her teeth. It was pretty obvious what Qien was trying to get at. If he fought like a Keeper, then he'd be treated like one, so his only choice was to just sit there and either surrender like a coward or weather Pina's magic until he got knocked out.

*But... I'm not exactly a Starvein.*

Jasmine glanced at Qien, then walked right up to Pina. The girl barely even registered her – she was so focused on gathering her magic that she'd tuned out the outside world completely.

Reaching out, Jasmine gave Pina a light shove. The girl let out a yelp and staggered, tripping over her own feet and falling to her butt. All the magic she'd been gathering disappeared in a pop and a rush of cold wind.

"Ah. Pina loses," Qien said without a single note of interest in his voice. He turned toward Clarence. "Does that answer your question?"

Clarence was evidently bolder than Jasmine was, because he spoke up. "That wasn't a fair fight, though. She could have defeated the Keeper if she knew she was coming."

"No, she couldn't have. Keepers exist specifically because of our greatest weakness." Qien strode up to Pina, who still sat stunned on the ground. He reached down, grabbing the girl by her collar, and yanked her up to her feet. "We are powerful, but we are slow. Our magic can destroy battalions, but it cannot defend us from a sword wielded by a savage."

Jasmine tried not to bristle at that. She couldn't quite tell if Qien was insulting her or complimenting her.

"It takes us time to gather our defenses so that the very magic we draw on does not do what it did to the Xolani. A Starvein's most important power is not the strength of their magic but how well they can resist it. Fail to do so – try and call your magic too quickly or in too much volume – and your body will be warped and twisted as the magic consumes you from within."

Qien's eyes drifted down to Jasmine just for long enough for it to be clear what he thought of the Xolani. Jasmine kept her features expressionless, refusing to give the rude professor the satisfaction of a response.

She'd heard the stories of the Xolani Empire for long enough. When magic had been discovered hundreds of years ago, a select few of the Xolani been the first to learn to draw on its power – and the ones to sacrifice the most in learning to control it.

Too much magic warped humans, ripping them apart from within and turning them into magic-resistant monsters that only sought to consume more power. Unfortunately, that power generally came easiest when packaged in the form of the nearest mage.

By the time it was discovered that magic could be safely

controlled when used in small amounts or slowly enough to avoid overwhelming the user, the Xolani Empire had been destroyed from within.

*I don't see how it's their fault that they took the risks. You wouldn't know how to use magic if someone hadn't taken all the risks to find out the safe ways to use it.*

Jasmine's words remained unspoken, and Qien seemed satisfied with his demonstration. He flicked his fingers in clear dismissal. "Back to your chairs. Today, we discuss methods to reduce some of this weakness that was just demonstrated. The speed in which you can safely draw magic will determine if you live or die. Be prepared to replicate what I go over in this class. There will be a practical exam at the end of the week. I suggest taking notes because I will not be going over it again."

# 7

The rest of Qien's class passed in a crawling blur. He spent nearly two hours talking about casting methods, all the while drawing diagrams in the air with glittering black light. Jasmine understood exactly zero of what he spoke about, and it didn't look like Asher was in a much better spot.

When he finally clapped his class and dismissed everyone, the room emptied quickly. Nobody so much as stopped to give Jasmine or Asher a second glance – which she was thankful for.

They joined the line of students departing the room, not wanting to draw Qien's attention any more than they already had. The two of them wordlessly made their way back down the hall toward Asher's room, and neither spoke until all the other students had filed away.

"Well," Asher said as they arrived at his door. "That was horrible."

He reached into his pocket for a key. Jasmine beat him to it, pulling out the key that had been with her belongings and sliding it into the lock with a click.

"Was it?" Jasmine asked. "I originally thought Qien had it out for you, but it seems like he just acts like that with everyone."

Asher shook his head and pushed the door open. Jasmine followed him inside, closing and locking the door behind them.

"No, he definitely has it out for me. We didn't get singled out just because he wanted to remind everyone how useful a Keeper is," Asher said, running a hand through his hair and grimacing. "He did it to get their attention on us. Qien pointed out that I'm not a Starvein if I can't use magic, and then he proved that I can't use magic. Sure, you showed that Keepers are useful, but now they're wary of you as well."

"So...just learn magic?"

Asher threw his hands up. "Oh, of course. I should have thought of that. Just learn magic. Fantastic."

"Aren't you a Starvein?" Jasmine asked, blinking in confusion. "That's why you left the Keeper program, right? You've got magic."

"Yes, I have magic," Asher ground out. "But that doesn't mean I can *use* it. I don't know how."

"Isn't that the whole point of class?"

Asher glowered at Jasmine. "You're real great at the whole 'support' aspect of a Keeper. Half of our training was meant to be how you could be a confidant and assistant for your charge, wasn't it?"

"This is assistance. I'm giving you advice."

"Telling me to stop being bad at something is not advice."

"That kind of just sounds like an excuse to keep being bad."

"How is this meant to make me feel better?" Asher demanded.

"It's not. It's advice."

He opened his mouth, then closed it with a snap. He rolled his eyes. "By the Watcher's eyes, you're insufferable. I do appreciate your help in class, though. If you hadn't been there, I'm pretty sure Qian still would have singled me out and I would have gotten blasted with magic until I surrendered."

"Just my job, I guess. But… why not just surrender?"

"No. Don't suggest that again." Asher's features darkened and Jasmine almost flinched at the anger in his voice.

"I wasn't saying you should have, but there's no reason to take a fight you can't win," Jasmine said with a frown. "That's one of the things we learned. Always choose fights you can win. And if you can't win, change the fight. What, were you just planning to sit there and pray your magic worked until it did? Wait, is that how it works?"

"I'm not a Keeper anymore, and no, it isn't," Asher said curtly. "I think I'm going to get some rest and study. Did you want to bring a chair in or something if you're going to watch me?"

Jasmine's stomach answered with a rumble before she could respond. Her cheeks reddened and Asher looked up at her, a grin stretching across his lips.

"Never mind. Go eat."

"But I–"

"I'm hungry," Asher interrupted. "And I don't think I'll be able to study without food. This is an order, by the way."

Jasmine pursed her lips. "You realize I don't have to do what you say, right? A Keeper isn't a slave. My job is to protect you."

"Are you going to be doing that when you're starving?" Asher countered. "I won't leave the room, okay? You don't have to starve yourself because you're terrified Esther is going to fail you."

It was a tempting offer. Now that she wasn't doing anything, it was hard for Jasmine to deny that she was starving. It wasn't like she particularly looked forward to eating anything she could cook, but even burnt trash would be better than nothing.

"Fine," Jasmine said. "I'll make dinner. Don't leave the room. Promise."

"I'll stay right here," Asher said, patting the bed. "But only so long as you promise to speak with Esther and loosen my leash a bit. There's no way normal Keepers stalk their charges this closely."

"Speaking with Esther I can do," Jasmine said. "But I can't say what she'll say."

"Good enough for me," Asher said. A smirk flickered across his face. "What's for dinner? Not eggs, I hope."

"You'll find out when I decide myself," Jasmine grumbled. She unlocked the door and stepped outside, only pausing to lock it behind her before setting off in the direction of the kitchen.

The Watcher must have been smiling down upon her, because as Jasmine turned the corner of the hall, she found Lydia standing in the hall, a small bag clutched in her hands.

"Lydia!" Jasmine exclaimed, skidding to a halt. "What are you doing here?"

"Looking for you, idiot," Lydia said, her eyes lighting up as she laughed. The smile slipped from her face as she turned serious. "Are you doing okay?"

Jasmine glanced over her shoulder, but it looked like they were alone. "Relatively speaking? I guess. But–"

"Have you met any Starveins yet?" Lydia asked eagerly. "What are they like?"

"You already know. We've both met one."

"What? Who?"

"Asher."

Lydia's eyes widened and she took a step back. "You're screwing with me. Truly?"

"Completely serious." Jasmine placed a hand over her heart, then shook her head and heaved a sigh. "Guess who I got assigned to?"

"No way," Lydia said. "How? When did that happen?"

"Just now, apparently. I haven't really gotten a chance to ask him that much about it. My day has consisted of burning eggs, attending a class that made no sense and pushing a Starvein onto her ass, and then heading out to burn some more eggs."

Lydia sent Jasmine a pitying look, and a small spark of annoyance lit in Jasmine's chest. Even though she knew she was the one complaining, this was technically what they'd been training for. Lydia didn't have to act as if she was dying.

"Lucky for you I'm such a great friend," Lydia said, holding out the package. "I figured you probably hadn't learned how to cook over night."

The slight annoyance Jasmine had felt vanished in the blink of an instant. She took Lydia's offering with a grateful smile. "You're a blessing, Lydia."

"I know." Lydia flicked some hair over her shoulder, then gave Jasmine a smile and leaned closer as she lowered her voice. "But it's good to know he didn't jump ship and abandon you. And, of all the assignments you could have gotten, I guess this one isn't the worst."

"What do you mean?"

Lydia stepped back and crossed her arms. "Oh, come off it. You and Asher? Are you really telling me you'd have preferred some random prick? At least you know him."

"Yeah, that's true," Jasmine admitted. "It definitely could have been worse."

"Worse? Says the girl that *trained* with him every morning for the past few months? I'd be willing to bet you could point any part of him out in a lineup." Lydia waggled her eyebrows. "Know your enemy, right? Every part of them."

Jasmine's cheeks flushed red. "We were just training. We didn't do anything else."

"Your loss." Lydia smirked. "Guess you didn't have time with all that training. Good thing you've got so much more now."

Jasmine glared at Lydia, which only made the other girl snicker harder. For a moment, Jasmine almost felt like things were normal again. The feeling was welcome – and it lasted for far too little. Lydia's smile faded and she nudged Jasmine's foot with her own.

"Hey, I'll be here for you when I can. Esther's really cranking the work up on us, so I don't know if I'll be able to help you out with everything else as much as I used to, but…"

"You've already done more than enough. Thank you, Lydia. I was going to have to learn to do the rest of a Keeper's duties at some point anyway. You're right. Asher can be a cocky prick, but he's still Asher."

Lydia wiggled an eyebrow again and Jasmine groaned. "Stop it."

"Nope." Lydia flashed Jasmine a grin. "If you really wanted me to stop, you'd make me. By the way, Esther said she was sending someone to you to go over more of what your responsibilities are. It's how I got the excuse to come talk to you."

"That's a relief. I was wondering what I was meant to do about classes." Jasmine said, holding Lydia's package closer to her chest. "What is she having the rest of our class do?"

"Pretty much everything you'll be doing, just with practice charges and not for as long."

"You're really going to be busy, then." Jasmine grimaced. "Are you going to be fine without our practice sessions? You really need to pick a weapon and stick with it."

"Don't remind me." It was Lydia's turn to grimace. "Maybe you can find some time to tutor me when I get time to make you more food."

"So long as I actually have any free time left to myself. I guess we'll find out," Jasmine said.

"It's a deal. Take care of yourself, Jas. You should probably go back to babysitting Asher, though. Esther didn't say who she was sending, and I don't know when he's going to show up."

Jasmine nodded. "That's probably a good idea. Thanks for the food. You're a life saver."

"And don't forget it," Lydia said, raising a hand in farewell.

Jasmine felt another swirl of gratitude toward her friend grip her chest as she rushed off.

If it hadn't been for Lydia, she wasn't sure if she'd have made it this far in the Keeper program. Before reaching the Sanctuary, Jasmine hadn't had anyone she trusted, much less could have called a friend. But now, the idea of continuing on without having someone to vent and laugh with filled her with dread.

There was still a small smile on her face when she got back to Asher's room. By the weight of the package, Lydia had made more than enough food for both her and Asher to eat.

*I really do need to figure out how to cook better, though. I can't keep relying on Lydia for it. I'd rather not be eating ash for three meals a day.*

She unlocked the door and stepped inside. A small part of her expected to find the room empty and Asher gone, but she was relieved to find that he still sat in his bed, hunched over a book.

"Back already?" Asher pulled his gaze away from the book. "That was fast."

"We got lucky," Jasmine admitted. "Lydia made us food."

Asher's eyes lit up and he eagerly set the book to the side. "Really? That's incredible! Her cooking is amazing."

*You don't have to sound that excited about it.*

"Wait, you've had her cooking?"

"Yeah, she traded it for sparring lessons once. It was great. Unfortunately, I don't think she liked the lesson much."

Jasmine set the package on a small table in the corner of Asher's room and started to unwrap it. "You forgot to hold back, didn't you?"

"What's the point of sparring if you aren't trying? You're meant to get better, not just have fun."

"Not that I disagree, but now you know why you didn't get any more food from her." Jasmine pulled the last of the wrapping away to reveal several bamboo disks, each stuffed full of delicious-smelling marinated beef. Her mouth watered at the sight of it.

Asher pulled a chair out and sat down at the table. Jasmine quickly retrieved some utensils from her room for both for both of them and sat down beside Asher, interested in nothing more than sating her gnawing hunger.

And, for as long as she ate, she could pretend as if everything was normal.

# 8

The meal was delicious, and it was painfully short. Jasmine and Asher demolished every last scrap of food, leaving the bamboo scraped clean.

"I wish I learned to cook like that," Asher said with a satisfied sigh. "It's not really that fun, though."

"Weren't you literally making fun of me for the exact same thing?"

"Well, yes. I never said I was that much better. I mean, I remember to use oil before putting the eggs in a pan, but I don't think that's much to be proud of. Just because I don't know how to fly doesn't mean I can't point out when a bird is drunk."

Jasmine wrapped up the box so she could clean and return it to Lydia when she had a chance, then frowned. "What kind of analogy is that?"

"I made it up."

"I could tell," Jasmine said with a shake of her head. "It sucks."

"Very motivational of you."

"Just go do whatever it was that you were doing," Jasmine grumbled, standing up and tucking the box under her arm. "I'll probably get a visit from someone Esther sent pretty soon. They'll tell me how much of a life I'm allowed to have or if I need to walk an inch behind you for the rest of the year."

Asher pressed his lips together and looked away. "I'm sorry."

"About what? I'm the one that punched you."

Asher reached up to touch his cheek, then laughed. "Not that. I'm sorry you're caught up in this."

"Did you arrange it?"

"What? No."

"Then I don't want your pity. It's not your fault," Jasmine said with a sigh. "It's just what we're stuck dealing with – at least, for now. Maybe we'll find a way out of it. I'm not some wallflower that needs you to feel bad for me. This is what I was training for."

"What we were training for," Asher said, so soft that Jasmine barely even heard him. When she looked over, he just shook his head. "No matter. You're right. This is our lot now. I've got a lot of catchup, so you'll have to excuse me. Stay out of my way, and I'll stay out of yours. As much as that's possible, at least."

With that, Asher grabbed his book and returned to his bed. He was clearly done with the conversation, and that was just fine with Jasmine. She headed into her own, considerably smaller, room and set the box down in the corner.

Jasmine sat down on her bed and flopped back, staring up at the plain stone ceiling. Despite all the time she'd spent training with Asher, she'd barely actually spent any time with him outside of work.

She'd genuinely looked forward to their sparring matches. No matter how rude or annoying Asher was, he was still a fun opponent and occasionally said something amusing – not that she'd ever admit it to him. Now, she wasn't sure if they'd ever get the chance to spar again. Starveins didn't use swords, and a Keeper was meant to protect their charge, not smack them around.

*And of course I punched him in the face right off the bat.*

*Meh. He deserved it. Besides, with all the cheap shots he's given me in and out of sparring matches, I feel like I could sucker punch him ten more times and still be behind in count of low blows.*

Even still, it didn't feel like Asher liked the situation any more than Jasmine did. She still had no idea why he'd have chosen to be a Keeper over a Starvein, but he'd done it, nonetheless. Jasmine bolted upright as a thought struck her.

*Shit! I completely forgot what Esther said. The noble who I got assigned to had his entire family assassinated. He got pushed to be a Starvein because the rest of his family is dead, and a Keeper can't run a house.*

Jasmine buried her face in her hands and groaned.

*I was so shocked to see Asher that I completely forgot about the damn reason why he needed a Keeper in the first place. His family got killed, and the first thing I did was punch him in the face. Damn it.*

Jasmine stood to go back into Asher's room, then paused with her hand on the door, a heavy weight settling in on her shoulders.

*How am I even supposed to bring this up? Sorry for punching you, I forgot your parents are dead?*

Turning away, Jasmine let out another muted groan and ran her hands through her hair. Bringing the topic up now would just make things worse. He was probably in mourning, but he was apologizing to *her.*

*I'm an awful friend.*

Jasmine paced around her bed for a few minutes, trying to think on if there was anything she could do, but no ideas emerged. Chances were, Asher didn't even realize she'd been told about what had happened to him.

*Part of a Keeper's role was to give advice. Maybe I can just wait until he brings it up to me? It would just be part of my job, and then I'd be able to say the right thing then.*

*Except he's probably never going to bring it up because my advice sucks. Agh. I hate this. Why couldn't stabbing things just fix all my problems?*

Jasmine flopped back onto her bed. There were still a few hours left in the day, but she wasn't in the mood for any more work. She was barely even still in the mood to be thinking. After a few more minutes of lying face down on the rough, scratchy blanket, Jasmine rolled over and stripped out of her clothes.

She dragged herself to the bathroom. It wasn't all that much worse than what they'd had in the Keeper dormitories, and anything was better than going for months on end without clean water in the gutters.

Still, the lack of a door was... unsettling.

Jasmine finished preparing for bed a few minutes later and flopped down, letting out what must have been her tenth sigh that day. Light still trickled into her room from Asher's, and she watched her reflection in the polished blade of her sword leaning against the wall.

Slowly, reluctantly, sleep welcomed her into its embrace.

Jasmine's eyes snapped open. The air in the room felt stuffy and heavy. Her skin itched from the uncomfortable sheets, and her stomach was clenched in unease. She couldn't recall having any dreams or nightmares, but her back was streaked with sweat.

Sitting up, Jasmine pushed her covers back and grimaced as she blinked, trying to figure out what time it was. Whoever had built her room hadn't seen fit to grace her with a window, so there was no way to check easily.

The back of her neck prickled. Even though she'd only been trained to fight like a Keeper for a few months, she'd lived the other nineteen years of her life in the gutters, where instinct was generally the first thing that kept her guts separate from a dagger.

*Something feels wrong.*

Jasmine pulled her pants and shirt on, moving as silently as she could. There was always a chance she was wrong – it wasn't like the day hadn't gone poorly enough already. She didn't want to add waking Asher up in the middle of the night because she missed her old room to her list of mistakes.

Scooping the sword up from the ground, Jasmine crept up to the door that separated her from Asher. There didn't seem to be any noise coming from the room beyond.

*This is stupid. I should just go back to bed.*

Jasmine ignored herself. She pressed a hand against the door, suddenly grateful for its lack of a locking mechanism. Pushing it open just a crack, Jasmine peeked into Asher's room.

Silver moonlight poked through the cracks in his curtains, washing out over his bed and pushing the shadows back to the room's corners. He slept on his side facing away from her, his back rising and falling gently with every breath.

Jasmine slipped through the door, letting it close behind her. She held her sword in a loose grip at her side. The feeling in her gut hadn't abated in the slightest. A faint rustle outside caused her to spin, bringing her sword to bear only to find the culprit was nothing but the wind dancing through the trees outside.

*If Asher wakes up and sees me swinging a sword around his room in the middle of the night, he's going to think that I'm trying to kill him.*

She sent one last glance around, squinting into the shadows, but she found nothing within them. The room was perfectly silent. Pristine. Everything was in order – except for her. Jasmine lowered her sword, but still she hesitated.

*His family got killed. They definitely had guards as well. Probably at least one Keeper too, but they still died. The only advantage I have is that I know the assassins are coming. But it's not like anyone would try to make a move in the middle of the Sanctuary. It would be a suicide mission. I'm overreacting.*

But, no matter how Jasmine's mind tried to convince her body, her feet wouldn't budge. She grit her teeth and repressed the urge to sigh. Judging by the position of the moon, it was only a few hours until morning.

*If I'm wrong, so be it. You know what? Maybe Esther is going to send a fake assassin. That would be just like her – and if I'm not ready for it, she'll prove that I've failed my duties and I'll be scrubbing toilets for a week.*

Jasmine leaned against the wall and rested her sword at her side, watching the window out of the corner of the eye in hopes that it would make the sun come faster.

It didn't.

Minutes ticked by in an agonizingly slow march. Asher slept on, blissfully unaware of her presence watching over him. She resisted the urge to drum her fingers on the wall or start pacing around.

Despite Jasmine's best efforts, the mixture of boredom and weariness started to eat at her awareness. Her eyelids fluttered and more than once she was tempted to give up and just head back to her room to get what sleep she could still salvage, but she resisted the urge.

*I've wasted this much time. I might as well see it through.*

Something shifted in the darkness. The drowsiness vanished as a pump of adrenaline slammed into her like a runaway horse. A flash of silver shot across the room, illuminated only by a brief instant by the moonlight.

Jasmine lunged out of the way, and a loud thunk rang out as a dagger slammed into the wall where her head had been an instant before, burying itself up to the hilt. A dark form lurched from where the dagger had come from – moving not toward Jasmine, but for Asher.

They moved too fast for Jasmine to make it in time – or, at

least, for her to make it herself. Rearing back, Jasmine flung her sword with all the strength she could muster.

The dark figure bobbed to the side, avoiding the sword but wasting a precious second in the process.

"Asher!" Jasmine screamed, sprinting for the intruder. "Wake up! There's an assassin!"

She didn't wait to see if Asher had heard her. Jasmine dove forward, slamming her shoulder into the mysterious assailant. The figure let out a pained grunt and both hit the ground in a tangle of limbs.

Jasmine rolled to the side, grabbing her sword from where it had fallen. This wasn't a training exercise. A powerful blow slammed into her chest, picking Jasmine up off the ground and launching her into the air.

She hit the foot of Asher's bed and snarled in pain. The cloaked figure was already standing, and they'd managed to grab her sword.

"What in the Watcher's eyes–" Asher started, blinking as he spotted the man. Jasmine grabbed him by the hair and slammed his face into the bed as the figure flicked another dagger, this one at Asher. The blade carved across the back of Jasmine's hand instead of impaling him in the side of the head.

Jasmine grabbed the blade from the bed and held it out before her. The back of her hand pulsed and throbbed in a way that a normal cut shouldn't have. Her eyes flicked down to the wound and her stomach knotted.

*Watcher, it was poisoned. I need to end this.*

The figure chuckled.

Jasmine didn't see them move, but she certainly felt it. Her head slammed into the wall and stars flashed in her eyes. She heard someone cry out, and it might have been her. The world swam before her eyes and Jasmine felt herself slump to the ground.

She couldn't feel her legs from beneath her, and darkness

threatened to swallow her vision whole. A loud, roaring ring in her ears drowned out the sound of the night, but through sheer force of will, she managed to keep herself conscious.

Asher lunged for the figure. Their hand shot out, grabbing him by the neck and lifting him into the air like a child. He yelled something, but Jasmine couldn't make out what it was.

One of Asher's knees slammed into the figure's face – and a flash of pain shot across his features. The figure didn't even flinch. Jasmine's fingers scratched on the stone as she tried to push herself upright.

"-finally found you." The figure's raspy male voice scraped through the ringing in Jasmine's ears. "Thought you were clever."

"Who are you?" Asher choked out, clawing at the hand wound around his throat. He kicked the hooded man in the chest to little more effect than his first attempt.

The man didn't reply. He dropped Jasmine's sword and pulled a thin, black blade from his belt with his free hand, flipping it to place its point right in the center of Asher's chest.

"Don't move too much now, little noble," the man breathed, letting out a raspy laugh. "I wouldn't want to push this too deep. Your brother was a feisty one. If he'd held still, maybe he would have survived."

"Bastard!" Asher screamed, slamming his knee into the man's face again. He snarled in pain, but the man didn't even flinch. Jasmine's eyes locked on her sword. Her entire body rebelled against her, but she couldn't afford to indulge it.

Lurching forward like a drunkard, Jasmine grabbed the hilt of her sword. With a roar, she swung it with all the might she still had left. The blade bit into the man's neck with a wet thunk. At the same time, Asher cried out in pain.

The assassin had driven his dagger into Asher's chest, though it had only made it about an inch deep. Swirls of black energy coursed around the knife's blade. Dread filled Jasmine's chest.

She didn't know what the dagger did, but she knew for a fact that it wasn't anything good. Lunging, Jasmine grabbed the blade and yanked it free. Jagged blades of ice ripped into her palm and she cried out in pain, dropping the blade as storm of pain raced down her arm and into her chest.

The hooded man dropped Asher and spun, backhanding Jasmine. She was slammed into the wall for the second time. Her sword stuck out of the man's neck, buried nearly halfway into it – and yet, he still stood.

Blood trickled from her nose and two hooded forms danced before her as her eyes tried and failed to focus on him. A dim voice in the back of Jasmine's head told her that she likely had a severe concussion.

"You damned incompetent fool. Now I'll have to deal with you as well," the man snarled. He reached up to his neck and yanked the blade free, sending a spray of blood out. With a clean swing, he spun the weapon around and plunged it for Jasmine's chest.

She tried to move, but there was nothing left to spend. She could do nothing but watch as the blade descended to take her life.

A loud clang rang out. Jasmine's sword spun free, clattering to the ground. A spray of blood splattered across Jasmine's face as a sword erupted from the center of the hooded man's concealed features.

She watched in stunned disbelief as the assassin crumpled at her feet. Standing behind him was a bald man, scarred man wearing a plain, well-kept suit.

"Thank the Watcher," Jasmine muttered as the world started to spin. "I was right. You know that? I was right. It wasn't just a feeling."

The bald Keeper said something, but Jasmine's ears heard nothing. The world spun, consumed by an ever-growing darkness. Then there was nothing.

# 9

Something rough pressed against Jasmine's cheeks. A vile smell slammed into her and her eyes snapped open. She doubled over, dry heaving and coughing in between desperate gasps for fresh air.

She nearly choked as she spotted the corpse lying on the ground in front of her. Memory came flooding back in a wave, and a pang of pain reminded her of the poisoned wound on her hand – a hand that was, to her surprise, bandaged.

Jasmine pulled her gaze up. The bald man sat on Asher's bed, watching her with flat eyes. He was corking a small glass vial full of large, glistening crystals – and Jasmine could smell the horrid thing from where she knelt.

"Who are you?" Jasmine asked, pushing herself back into a seated position. If he was an enemy, he wouldn't have killed the assassin and bandaged her hand. "What happened to Asher?"

"He lives," the man replied. He stood in a smooth motion. "As do you."

"I half wish I didn't." Jasmine grimaced, then looked out the window. The moon still hung in the sky, though it was lower than it had been before. It couldn't have been more than an hour or two since the attack. "And you didn't say who you were."

"Riker. A Keeper. You are Jasmine."

"How'd you know? Did Asher tell you? Where is he? He got stabbed by a pretty evil looking weapon. It might have had some magic in it."

"Esther called on my services. I arrived... later than expected." Riker's expressionless features for the first time, turning down in a slight frown. "I was waylaid. It seems the group that sought Asher's head anticipated my arrival and arranged for an ambush."

"You were delayed avoiding it?"

Riker's frown deepened. "No. I was delayed interrogating them. There were eight, and I had to cross-check their information with each other. It took some time."

"You killed eight people like this on your own?" Jasmine shifted in surprise and immediately regretted it as a spike of pain ran through her body.

"Yes."

"How?"

"By being better." The frown on Riker's face vanished, making it impossible to tell if he was joking or not. "It is within the duties of a Keeper."

"Esther never told us we could do anything like that."

"That is because Esther believes it best to coddle you. She thinks that you will learn best by focusing on the ground principles of our order rather than the power we – and our enemies – wield."

Jasmine swallowed. Her throat felt like the desert itself. "You mean magic? You're a Starvein, then?"

"There is more than one way to harness magic. With sufficient training, anyone can learn how to use some degree of power. Why do you think it was so difficult to strike the assassin?" Riker nudged the dead man with the tip of his shoe.

"You're telling me I can do magic? And Esther didn't tell us?"

Riker snorted. "And now you see why. You would attempt to channel magic as you are – and like your ancestors, it would consume you. Ignorance was your shield."

Jasmine opened her mouth to refute Riker, then closed it with a snap. Her mind was so fuzzy that she couldn't think of a good response, especially since he was right. If she'd known there was a way to use magic without being a Starvein, she definitely would have tried it.

*Isn't that Xolani magic? Wait. Esther sent him. There's no way she's trying to test me right now, is there?*

Gritting her teeth, Jasmine pressed her back to the wall and used it as leverage to rise. Asher laid in the bed behind Riker, a bandage wrapped around his bare chest. The wound left by the dagger definitely hadn't been significant enough for such extensive treatment – which meant it was either poisoned or magic.

*Shit.*

"Is he going to be fine?" Jasmine asked.

"He will live. The dagger was Xolani magic that I am not versed in," Riker said. "But it does not seem to be getting worse."

*I knew it. It was Xolani magic after all.*

Jasmine let out a relieved breath. Asher hadn't gotten killed – and she wasn't about to lose her spot in Sanctuary. A moment later, she winced. That last thought had been more than a little selfish.

"Thank you. I was dead if you didn't show up. Asher too," Jasmine said. Her hands tightened at her sides. "I wasn't strong enough to fight the assassin off."

"You did your role. Expecting a Keeper that hasn't finished her first year to stand against a trained killer of this level of talent is unreasonable. If we had more resources, this never would have happened. Unfortunately, things are not going well for the Whitewater Kingdom. We are beset on all sides."

"Then… not that I'm mad about it, but why are you here?"

"I owed Esther a favor, and she asked for my presence. I was able to free up some time."

A weight lifted off Jasmine's shoulders. "You're going to take over protecting Asher?"

Riker tilted his head to the side. "No. I do not have time to watch a baby Starvein. There are many noble families with many enemies. He is not the only one. Esther has requested exactly two hours of my day for the next few months."

"Two hours?" Jasmine blinked. "Why?"

"You." Riker stepped up to Jasmine. If the wall hadn't been directly behind her, she would have stepped back. "She feels that your tutelage must be accelerated, and has called me in to aid."

"Oh." The weight settled right back down on Jasmine's shoulders.

"Esther also said your fighting skills were above average," the scarred man continued, entirely unperturbed by her attempt to kill him. "Even if you sorely lacked in almost every other department."

"I'm glad to know my incompetence is so monumental that she tells people that aren't even in Sanctuary."

"A sharp tongue is not an often-used tool in our trade, but it has its time. You should learn when it is," Riker said. "I will only be providing a short amount of my time to Esther. One hour a day of my time will be dedicated to watching over your sleeping charge so that you may catch up with your responsibilities."

A day ago, Jasmine probably would have complained about only being given a single hour of free time. But if there was one assassin, there was almost certainly going to be more – and that meant one hour that Jasmine didn't have to worry about Asher getting run through.

"Thank you. I don't know what I can get accomplished in an

hour, but any help is invaluable. What about me, though? I need to go to class somehow, but how will I protect him while–"

"You will still not be attending."

Jasmine blinked. "What? Then I'm screwed. I'll fail the exam at the end of the year and I'll be kicked out."

"I will take over your tutelage, should you be willing to accept it," Riker said. "You will not fail under my guidance."

"I can refuse?"

"Yes."

Jasmine studied Riker. Something about him set the hair on the back of her neck on end. It felt more like she was talking to a ghost than a man.

"When would that even be?"

"When I have time."

"What about Asher? Don't I need to stay around him?"

"He will be accounted for."

"What would you teach me? Fighting?"

"I would teach you what a Keeper is required to know."

It wasn't much of a debate. There was just too much she had to catch up on. Jasmine had no idea who Riker was or how he knew Esther, but if he wasn't lying, he definitely seemed capable. Capable of what, Jasmine wasn't sure. But he was capable.

"Is that really enough to catch up with missing my classes? I'm still going to fall impossibly behind."

For the first time, a faint grin tugged at the corner of Riker's lips. "It is not about the time you have but how you use it. I can assure you – it is not the test you will fail. Either I will break you, or you will become the most competent Keeper among your peers. I suspect the former, but Esther seems to have a high opinion of you."

*She does?*

Jasmine opened her mouth, then let it shut. "It's not like I'm going to refuse an offer like that. I should be dead right now. If you can teach me to do what you did – if you can teach me magic, then I'll take anything I can."

"We shall see. To start with – you will not inform anyone of this attack."

"What? Why not? We need to–"

"The semblance of control can often be just as powerful as control itself. If people believe that Sanctuary has been breached, there will be chaos. This is not the first time our enemies have broken through our walls, and it will not be the last."

Jasmine swallowed. "You say *our enemies.* Do you know who's trying to kill Asher?"

"No."

For some reason, Jasmine didn't believe Riker. Unfortunately, he was about as easy to read as a stone wall.

"Fine. I won't talk about it, but can I tell Keeper Esther?"

Riker inclined his head. "Testing to ensure I am who I say I am? A wise choice. Yes. Esther is already aware, but you may speak with her – but no other."

"And what of Asher? You keep avoiding the question about how he's actually doing. Saying he'll live isn't much of an answer."

"He will wake in the morning, I suspect. You will inform him of our discussion."

"Do… do you think there will be more assassins?"

Riker sighed. "Yes. Most likely. Until we determine why they sought out your Charge, they will probably continue to send more. You will look into this."

"Me? But–"

"Gathering knowledge is one of the core aspects of a Keeper."

Jasmine got the feeling she was going to hear that particular line a fair amount in the coming days. The look in Riker's eyes told her that refusing wasn't an option, and she couldn't muster the energy to ask how she was meant to find anything out. All she could do was nod.

"I have more to accomplish tonight," Riker said. "You will be safe. Rest."

That was one command that Jasmine didn't need to be told to follow twice. She slumped back against the wall, too exhausted to do anything more, and fell into the waiting arms of sleep.

# IO

Jasmine woke to the sun on her skin. Her eyes fluttered open. She was still leaning where she'd fallen asleep against the wall just a few hours earlier, and a crick in her back made sure she knew it.

She shifted and was somewhat surprised to find that her body didn't ache nearly as much as it should have. Even her hand only felt stiff because of the bandages wrapped around it.

"Finally. You woke up. What in the Watcher's Eyes happened last night?"

Jasmine glanced up. Asher sat in bed, his hair sticking out in every single direction. If she wasn't so tired, she would have laughed.

"Assassins," Jasmine replied, a wave of relief washing over her at his voice. Riker hadn't been wrong. Asher sounded fine. "Were you just sitting there waiting for me to wake up?"

"Yeah."

"Why didn't you say something when you woke?"

"You looked exhausted, and it didn't feel like there was a

problem anymore. Esther stopped by this morning to let me know that there was nothing to worry about, but she didn't have time to explain much. I've been hoping you might be able to fill me in."

Jasmine gathered herself and rose to her feet, moving slowly in case a wound suddenly flared up. Nothing did. Against her better judgement, she unwrapped the bandages covering her hand.

She drew in a breath. The skin was almost entirely healed. There should have been a fairly deep cut left over from the previous night, but all that remained was a faint, faded scar.

"I'm not so sure I understand myself," Jasmine said, flexing her hand. "I couldn't do anything against that assassin. We should be dead, but a Keeper saved us."

"You couldn't?" Asher let out a bitter scoff. "More like I couldn't. From what I saw, you held your own."

"You were asleep when he showed up."

"And what were you doing?" Asher arched an eyebrow. "Looks like you managed to notice him coming just fine."

Jasmine rolled her neck, trying to see if there were any significant injuries left over from the previous night. She'd definitely had a concussion from how hard she'd been thrown against the wall, but her thoughts felt clear.

*Did Riker heal me somehow? But... he's not a Starvein. How much magic can he use? Watcher, I have so many questions.*

"I was awake. Something felt off."

"Something felt off?" Asher repeated. He huffed. "What, did you smell them coming?"

"I don't know, okay? I just woke up and something felt off. And just because I stabbed the assassin doesn't mean I was doing anything. He was about to kill me when the Keeper showed up."

"Riker, right?"

"Yeah. Did you overhear us talking?"

Asher shook his head. "Esther mentioned he'd occasionally be keeping an eye on me while you were busy. She also said things didn't look too good for your potential free time."

That brought a grimace to Jasmine's face. "No. They don't. I get an hour a day."

Asher didn't respond – and Jasmine appreciated it. She was pretty sure the only things he might have offered up in their situation were either a snarky comment or an apology, and she wanted neither.

"Are… you okay?" Asher asked after a few seconds of uncomfortable silence. "You got hit pretty hard."

"Riker healed me. I'm more concerned about whatever that knife you got stuck with did. Is the wound healed?"

Asher looked down at his chest, pulling at the bandages covering it. There was a small, x-shaped scar just over his heart, but it didn't seem to be anything more than just that. "I guess so. It felt like he was pouring coals into me when I got stabbed, though. I've never felt a weapon like that."

"It almost seemed like he didn't *want* to kill you," Jasmine said slowly as she tried to recall the exact details of what had happened the previous night. "Do you have any idea what the assassin was talking about?"

Asher was shaking his head before she finished speaking. "I wish I did, but no. Do you?"

"Why would I?"

*Riker might, though.*

"I don't know. I don't understand why any of this is happening. It's not like my family has–" Asher cut himself off and pressed his lips together. "It's not like they had anything that valuable. My parents were both shoddy Starveins. We don't have a history of controlling strong magic."

"I'm sorry about your family." It was Jasmine's turn to feel uncomfortable. She paused for a moment, then continued on with a wince. "Keeper Esther… she told me about what happened to them before I was assigned to you. I just didn't know it was *you*. I kind of forgot about it. I shouldn't have punched you."

Asher let out a bark of laughter. "I don't want your pity any more than you want mine. You weren't the one that killed them, and you saved my life last night. I'd probably dining with them in the Watcher's halls if you hadn't been awake."

"Would you be mad if I said half the reason I was so concerned was because I thought Esther might have been testing my skills, and that half the reason I was awake is because I didn't want to get kicked out of the Sanctuary?"

"Would you care if I was?"

Their eyes locked and neither spoke for a moment. A slight grin tugged at the corners of Asher's lips and he leaned back in bed.

"I can't blame you. If I was in your shoes, I'd probably feel the exact same way. Watcher, at least I had a place to go back to. If the result of failing out meant I was going to the gutters, I'd be just as worried as you were."

Jasmine's back stiffened. "How do you know about that?"

"Lydia's lips are a little looser than they should be, especially when it comes to bragging about how far her friend has come," Asher said with a chuckle. "It does explain why your fighting skills outclass everything else by so much, though. You've had a lot of catchup that everyone else didn't need to deal with."

"If you knew that, why did you give me so much shit for it?" Jasmine asked irritably. "And I need to speak with Lydia about not sharing secrets."

"Should have told her it was a secret. And I didn't mention it because it's a lot more fun not to."

Jasmine rolled her eyes. "You're insufferable."

"Thanks. I do my best," Asher said. He looked away for a moment, then made eye contact again. "Truce?"

"Truce? For what?"

"You want to make it out of Sanctuary as a Keeper. I want to make it out in one piece. I'd have preferred to be a Keeper, but I'll settle for alive. And feel free to correct me if I'm wrong, but you aren't going to pass with the way things are."

*And whose fault is that?*

Jasmine cut the annoyed words off before they could leave her mouth. It wasn't Asher's fault that she'd gotten assigned to him. As easy as it was to blame him, it wouldn't have been right.

*Riker did say he'd train me, but I still feel like Asher is right. An hour of training a day isn't going to change anything. I'm well and truly screwed.*

"Yeah. You're right," Jasmine admitted. "What are you going to do? Ask Esther to unassign me?"

"Already did," Asher said with a shake of his head. "This morning when she dropped by. She refused. Said that it was clearly working since I was still alive."

Jasmine ran a hand through her hair and laughed. "Of course she did. That sounds just like her."

"Either way, you're screwed as things are."

"Yes, I'm aware. Thank you for reminding me of my impending doom."

"Let me get to the point, would you?" Asher asked with an irritable sigh. "Work together with me. I can't teach you everything, but I can more than cover for some of the knowledge you're missing."

"You mean *you'll* teach me?" Jasmine asked incredulously.

Asher nodded. "Yes. As much as I can, at least. If I'm with you when you're doing Keeper stuff, then you're still protecting me, right? So you wouldn't be stuck wasting time just sitting around and watching me."

*That... is actually a pretty good idea.*

"Yeah, but what do you get out of it? That's a lot of time and energy you're committing that you should be using to learn magic and do… whatever it is a Starvein asked."

"I haven't figured that bit out yet," Asher admitted, scratching the back of his head. "I feel like I'm already in debt to you, so this should even the score. I guess you can just agree to help me out when I need it?"

The idea of getting taught by Asher wasn't exactly one Jasmine loved. She could already picture his smug laugh as he watched over her burning their meal… but it was better than doing nothing. He wasn't even asking for much in return – if anything, his request was just what she'd have been expected to do as a Keeper.

"So you just want me to help you with your Starvein training occasionally?" Jasmine chewed her lower lip.

"Yeah. And with other small stuff when it pops up, I guess."

"So… you want me to do my job?"

Asher sighed. "I want you to *want* to do it. I'd really prefer to know that you aren't fighting to keep me alive purely because you're contractually bound to do it, but because you want me alive."

She studied him for a few moment. For the first time, Jasmine finally realized that Asher really was a Starvein. His features were regal and more attractive than she cared to admit. It wasn't like she'd let that sway her, but he was actually handsome when he wasn't being a smug asshole.

"Fine," Jasmine said. "Truce, but it's going to mean you'll have to try not to be insufferable for too much of the day."

"Please don't make unreasonable demands." Asher held his hand out.

Rolling her eyes, Jasmine walked up and took his hand. At almost the exact same moment, his stomach rumbled loudly. Asher cleared his throat.

"Perhaps now is a good time for us to get started? I'm starving, and if there aren't any more assassins waiting to stab me on my way to the kitchen, I'd like to get some food."

"You should stay–"

Asher arched an eyebrow, and the look alone was enough to cut Jasmine off. "I think the first thing I'll be doing is teaching you how to avoid burning eggs."

"Yeah, that might be a good idea," Jasmine admitted reluctantly. "You'd better put a shirt on before you start walking around, though. Riker told me that we can't let other people know about last night. He's worried it'll cause a panic."

"Esther mentioned the same thing, but I guessed as much. What do you want to bet that Qien would shit his pants if he found out his precious Starvein Halls weren't as safe as he thought?" Asher chuckled to himself as he scooted over to the edge of his bed and swung his legs out from under the sheets.

As he rose, he let out a startled curse and staggered. Jasmine jumped forward, wrapping her arm around him before he could fall. His bare chest pressed against her shoulder as his entire body tensed.

"Asher? What happened?"

Asher pulled away from her, leaning back against the bedframe with a groan. He pressed his hand to the wound at his heart, then looked down and examined it with a pained grimace. "It felt like I was getting stabbed again. It's gone now. Just phantom pain, I guess."

Jasmine wasn't convinced, but Asher gently pushed her back. He walked over to the closet and pulled a shirt. He pulled a pair of pants out as well, then glanced back at her.

"Are you going to watch this as well?"

Jasmine's cheeks reddened and she turned away until Asher had finished changing.

"Right. I'm good. If there's anything that can be done about it, Esther will tell me. There's no point wasting worry about it now,"

Asher said, but it sounded as if he might have been telling that to himself more than anyone else. His voice was laden with a note of false cheer. "Let's go learn how to cook, shall we?"

As she turned back to Asher and got a look at the smug expression on his face, Jasmine couldn't help but get the feeling that she might have just made a deal with a devil.

# 11

Jasmine stared down her great enemy, and she had half a mind that it was staring back at her. The six eggs she had – carefully – liberated from their crate sat on the counter beside the lit stove. Beside them were her pots and pans.

"Why did you make me bring everything again?" Jasmine asked. "All we need is a pot. They're eggs. A pan is just a flat pot."

"This is why," Asher said. "You need to use them for their proper purposes. They're tools, just like weapons. It's not like a sword and a dagger are the same thing just because they're both pointy."

Jasmine's nose scrunched and she huffed. "Fine. I'll use a pan. I don't see the difference, though."

"It's easier to access the food on a pan, and they have less area that needs to get hot. It's better for frying stuff," Asher said. "Seriously, did you ever pay attention to any of Esther's cooking lessons?"

"I mostly daydreamed about fighting in them. They were really boring."

Asher sighed and pointed at the pan. Jasmine took it and set it on the burner. She reached out for an egg, then paused as Asher stared her down.

"What?"

"Oil," Asher said. "You need oil. Or butter. Otherwise, the eggs will stick."

"I knew that," Jasmine said, scanning the kitchen. Her eyes landed on a beaker near the stove and she grabbed it, briefly examining its contents. They certainly looked like oil. She sent a glance back at Asher, then went to pour some of it into the pan.

"Hold on," Asher said.

"What? I thought you said I need oil?"

"You do, but the pan needs to get hot first. Give it a minute or two, then hold your hand over the pan to make sure it feels hot before adding the oil in."

Jasmine scrunched her nose and lowered the pitcher. A minute passed and she did as he'd suggested, holding her palm over the surface of the pan. Asher put a hand on her shoulder, nearly making Jasmine flinch and touch the hot metal on accident.

"Use the back of your hand." Asher ignored her reaction. "It picks it up easier."

To her mild annoyance, Asher was right. The pan certainly felt hot, though that wasn't all that much of a surprise considering it was sitting on the fire.

"Okay. Now can I add the oil?"

"Yes, go ahead."

Jasmine took the pitcher and held it over the pan. Before she could do anything, Asher grabbed her hand. Jasmine froze.

"What? What did I do wrong?"

"No. I'm just helping to make sure you don't pour too much."

"Don't we want enough to keep the eggs from sticking?"

"The amount you think we need and the amount we actually need are different," Asher said, a small grin tugging at his lips. He nodded to the pan, and Jasmine tried to pretend she wasn't vividly aware of the warmth of his hand against hers.

Asher moved a little closer, guiding her pour. And, as he had said, he pulled her hand back after just a small drizzle – about ten times less what Jasmine had been planning to add. She gave Asher a suspicious look.

"*Are* you reading my mind?"

"What? No. Did you really believe I could do that?"

"Not at the time, but you're a Starvein. I don't know what you can do."

Asher grunted. "Yeah, me neither."

"Then how did you know I was going to pour–"

"I did it myself. The first time my mom taught me how to cook eggs, I poured half a jar of oil into the pan while she wasn't looking because I didn't want the eggs to be dry."

Jasmine knew she wasn't in any place to judge, but she couldn't keep herself from snickering. "I bet they weren't dry."

"Not in the slightest. Very oily. She made me eat everything. We don't – didn't – waste food in our house."

Jasmine's smile fell away. "I'm sorry."

"What did we agree about the whole pity thing?" Asher asked, moving her hand toward the handle of the pan. "Come on. Grab it. We need to swirl the oil around so it covers the whole bottom."

Jasmine moved the pan in a few swirling motions. Asher's grip tightened on her hand, his fingers interlacing with hers as he grabbed the pan together with her and lifted it into the air.

"Like this," Asher said, swirling the pan more aggressively. "We need to get the whole thing coated. You know it's hot enough because the oil is flowing easily."

They set the pan back down on the burner and Asher released Jasmine before nodding to the eggs. "Okay. Here's what we're going to do. Crack the eggs into the pan, but try to move quickly.

Once they're cracked, take it off the burner immediately and start mixing everything around."

Jasmine nearly opened her mouth to ask what the point of that was, but she caught herself. Considering how quickly the eggs had cooked the last time she'd made them, it wasn't hard to guess.

*I guess the pan is hot enough to cook them without any more fire. This is more stressful than I thought it would be.*

"It's not that time sensitive," Asher said, misreading the look in Jasmine's face. "I'll crack half of them if you get the other half."

He took one of the eggs and Jasmine took the other.

"Firm hit, but don't smash the thing to death. You just want to crack it." Asher demonstrated by rapping the egg against the side of the counter with a sharp crack. Jasmine shifted the pan away from the flame and Asher gave her an appreciative nod before cracking the egg into it in a smooth motion. Not a single piece of shell fell in and the egg sizzled as it hit the pan.

Asher discarded the broken halves of the shell and took another egg while Jasmine attempted to replicate his egg-cracking technique. She was rewarded with a slightly louder crack and a much crunchier looking eggshell, but it wasn't completely crushed.

Jasmine poured the egg into the pan, managing to keep her own contribution shell-free as well. Asher grabbed a pan from her supplies and started to quickly mix everything. "Get the rest of the eggs in, please. I'll mix."

Jasmine hurried to comply. The other four eggs all went into the pan one after the other, along with one or two pieces of eggshell that Jasmine fruitlessly hoped that Asher hadn't seen. Asher continued mixing throughout the entire time.

"There. See?" Asher asked, tilting the pan so Jasmine could see it better. "Scrambled eggs. Not burnt. A little runny. Perfect."

"Why are there so many steps that go into making bloody eggs?" Jasmine asked in exasperation. "I thought they were supposed to be easy."

Asher chuckled. "I don't know if I'd say that. I think anything becomes easier with time, but I've had a lot of shitty eggs. They're not the hardest meal to cook, but making them taste really good is a skill in itself."

Jasmine snagged two plates from her belongings and set them out for Asher to split their meal between. As she hunted for utensils, he wandered over to the cupboards and took out two wooden boxes, setting them down beside the eggs.

"Spices. Specifically, ashpepper," Asher said, opening them with a flourish. "Everything tastes better when it's hot."

"You spice eggs?"

"I spice everything. Pepper is delicious." Asher sprinkled more than a healthy share of the red spice over his plate. Jasmine was pretty sure that he had more spice than eggs. Asher tilted his head to the side. "Want some?"

"I'll try a pinch, but not nearly as much as you put on."

"It's fine. We can't all have perfect taste buds." Asher sprinkled a tiny amount of the pepper over her eggs, then hit each of their dishes with a small pinch of salt. "There. Now we have eggs."

Jasmine gathered everything they'd used to cook and washed it in the basin – cooking experience or not, she was more than aware of how important it was to take care of her weapons. When she finished, she followed Asher back to their room so they could eat in peace.

*I'm glad nobody else was using the kitchen when we were. That would have been embarrassing.*

Asher was oblivious to her thoughts. He just set the plates down on his table and the two of them sat down to eat.

The eggs were great. They weren't quite as good as whatever Lydia did when she made them, but they were leagues better than the monstrosity she'd prepared the previous day. And, though Jasmine wasn't eager to admit it, Asher had been right about the pepper. It did taste good.

"So?" Asher asked. "What do you think? Did I do a good job of teaching you?"

Jasmine scrunched her nose. "Yeah. Don't make me say it again, though."

"I wouldn't dream of it." Asher chuckled, holding his hands up in surrender. His smile faltered, replaced by a pained grimace, but it only lasted for an instant before his normal expression returned.

"Are you okay? Is it the wound?" Jasmine pushed her chair back and moving to stand beside him. "We need to talk to Esther about it."

"I'm fine," Asher said, waving her away. "It just stings a bit every once and a while. If there was something that could have been done about it, she would have said something."

"Just because we don't know what to do about it doesn't mean you should ignore it."

Asher crossed his arms. "So what do you want me to do? I don't suppose you happen to know the way to cure this?"

"Of course I don't, but if it's poison, then the more you move around, the more it'll spread through your system. You should be sitting and staying as still as possible – at least until Esther or Riker come by and tell us more."

"Oh, come on. I'm not doing much. It's not like I'm sparring."

"Sit."

"You aren't my–"

Jasmine arched an eyebrow. "I'm your Keeper. We agreed to a truce, right? That means you've got to actually treat me like a Keeper – which includes following any order I give you that relates to your safety."

Asher opened his mouth, squinting for a moment. Then he let it snap shut with a defeated sigh. "Yes, ma'am. What am I to do, then? Just sit and do nothing?"

"You were studying Starvein stuff last night, weren't you? Do that."

Grumbling under his breath, Asher trudged over to his bed and grabbed his book from his nightstand. He scooted into bed and leaned back against his pillow, burying his nose in the book. Jasmine looked from him to the dirty dishes on the table.

*I'm not sure it's safe to go wash these. I still don't know how the assassin got in last night, so I probably shouldn't leave Asher alone until I speak with Esther or Riker again.*

Looking around Asher's room, Jasmine's eyes landed on a small pile of books at the base of his bed. She'd have preferred to practice sparring, but it just wasn't the time, so she settled for hoping Asher's reading materials weren't completely mind-numbing.

The book Jasmine took turned out to be on the history of Starveins. It was far from the most interesting thing she'd ever read, but it was still better than nothing.

Several hours ground by.

"What about my class, ma'am?" Asher asked, breaking their silence as he looked up from his book. "Am I banned from that as well?"

Jasmine knew he was being intentionally annoying, but she still rolled her eyes. "Call me that one more time and I'll make you keep using it forever."

"How does that relate to my safety?"

"Punching you would make you less safe, and thus following my orders will keep you safe."

Asher laughed. "That's some convoluted logic. Fine. What about my class, *Jas*?"

"You're stealing Lydia's nickname for me?"

"What else am I supposed to squeal in terror when assassins come for my head? Jasmine is too long."

"It literally has the same number of syllables as ma'am."

"So you *want* me to call you that?"

"Oh, shut it. Jas works," Jasmine said, shaking her head and refusing to give Asher the satisfaction of a laugh. "And I'll be honest, I was hoping–"

There was a knock on their door. Jasmine grinned.

"Ah. There we go. I was hoping Riker or Esther would show up before your class."

"Better make sure it's actually one of them and not another assassin." Asher only sounded like he was half joking.

He actually had a good point, so Jasmine kept a hand on the hilt of her sword as she approached the door.

"Who is it?" Jasmine called.

"Keeper Esther," came the response.

Jasmine let out a relieved sigh and pulled the door open, stepping back so Esther could enter the room.

"I was really hoping you'd show up. Do you have any idea–"

Esther held a hand up and Jasmine's mouth snapped closed instinctively. The old Keeper closed the door behind her, then walked over to stand by Asher's bedside.

"My time is limited, so let me speak first," Esther said. "You can fit in your questions after. We have found some limited information about the assassin that broke in last night, but I'm afraid it's not as much as we had hoped."

"What kind of information?" Asher asked, his voice tense.

Esther's eyebrows furrowed as she pressed her lips together in distaste. "The kind that gets people killed."

# 12

"Keeper Esther, I think I already knew that I'm wrapped in something that gets people killed. My family is currently rotting underground," Asher said curtly. "I think I'd rather know *why* people are getting killed, if it's all the same to you."

Jasmine's eyes widened at the tone Asher was using with the Keeper. She'd had a similar level of irritation with the teacher once before, and it had resulted in a sparring match that had felt much more like a beatdown. Jasmine hadn't been able to properly hold a sword for a week.

But, to her surprise, Esther just let out a sigh. "I wish I could say, Asher. I spent some time investigating the body of the man that broke into Sanctuary last night. He was part of an organization that goes by the name of Last Light."

"Did they get their naming sense from a thirteen-year-old?" Jasmine asked.

Esther shot Jasmine a look and Jasmine reddened. "Sorry."

"Evidently they did," Esther said, a rare flicker of a smile passing over her weathered features. "But, regardless of their name, they're a dangerous order."

"What *are* they?" Asher asked. "I'll admit I didn't get to see much of the fight, but I kneed the assassin twice and he didn't even flinch."

Something passed through Esther's eyes, but it passed so quickly that Jasmine could have almost convinced herself that she'd imagined it. Almost.

"He had magically enhanced defenses," Esther said. "Most of the Last Light do. They have access to some of their own Starveins, unfortunately. Regardless of their power, I believe we should be more concerned with their goal. Your family had something they wanted, Asher."

Asher shrugged his shoulders, then winced. Once his features returned to normal, he held his hands out, palm up. "I don't suppose you know what it was?"

"The dagger you were struck with had Xolani magic in it. I have yet to confirm, but I suspect we will find that your family all bear similar wounds to the one you bear now – though they were not treated."

"I'm not sure I'd call it treated," Jasmine said. "He's still getting pain from it."

Esther's gaze sharpened. "You are?"

"We were getting to it," Asher said. "I occasionally get what feels like muscle spasms that originate at the location I was stabbed in."

"Nothing else?" Esther watched Asher carefully, but he shook his head.

"No. Nothing that I'm aware of."

Esther nodded. "Good. It's likely inconsequential, then. Keep an eye on it and let me know if anything goes awry or changes. I believe the dagger didn't pierce you deep enough to release its magic thanks to Jasmine's timely intervention."

"Not nearly timely or effective enough." Jasmine clenched her teeth and looked down at her hands. "I barely even stalled the assassin for more than a few seconds."

"You saved both your life and Asher's," Esther corrected. "The assassin was weaker than a fully trained Keeper, but far, far more capable than any year one trainee should ever dream of defeating. You did nothing wrong."

Asher looked like he wanted to get out of bed, but shot a glance at Jasmine and thought better of it. "So… what now? What do we do?"

"You? Nothing. You are students. You will study."

"But what about–"

Esther silenced Asher with a sharp look. "The mere knowledge that the Last Light is involved is disastrous. I shared it with you to sate some of your curiosity, not fan its fire. The Last Light are known for bringing down small kingdoms, and news of their presence in Whitewater cannot spread."

"So, what? We're meant to pretend this never happened?" Asher demanded.

"No. You are to prepare for the next attack and continue to work to grow stronger. Riker and I suspect that whoever hired the Last Light will not be satisfied with their failure, so more assassins will come. You will draw them."

"We're bait, you mean," Jasmine said.

"That is one way to put it. This is beyond us at this point. The kingdom cannot overlook the presence of the Last Light within it. We must take action to determine their goals and who is filling their pockets with gold – and Asher is our only lead."

Esther's voice brooked absolutely no room for argument. Jasmine and Asher exchanged a glance, but neither of them spoke. They knew the Keeper well enough to know that, when her mind was made up, nothing was going to change it.

"Not that you have held them very well, but do you have any further questions before I continue my investigation?"

"If this threat is really this big, shouldn't you be assigning Asher a real Keeper?" Jasmine asked. "What if I'm not strong enough to hold the next one back?"

"Why do you think Riker remains at Sanctuary?" Esther gave Jasmine a wry grin. "His true purpose is to lie in wait for the Last Light to strike again and hopefully take one of their men alive. Yours will be to hold them off until he arrives."

*Or, more likely, get myself killed. Unless I get much stronger, the next assassin I see isn't going to be screwing around. They'll know one of them has already gotten killed and will off me as quickly as possible.*

"Understood, Keeper Esther." Jasmine inclined her head. It wasn't like anything she could say would change Esther's mind, so there wasn't any point arguing.

"And what of my classes? And Jasmine's, for that matter?" Asher pressed. "Can we attend those? Or should we hide in my room until the next attack, counting the hours of our life as they slip away?"

"You will continue as if all is normal. Riker will handle Jasmine's tutelage and attempt to keep her up to speed with the rest of the class."

Jasmine's stomach clenched. Even though Esther spoke casually, she caught the faintest note of pity in her voice. The kingdom was sacrificing her as bait to lure the Last Light out. That was why they weren't getting a better Keeper to properly guard Asher.

Sure, there weren't that many Keepers available, but there was definitely a way to spare a talented one for a situation like this. No, they were *choosing* to leave her, knowing the Last Light would be more likely to bite and send another assassin when Asher's guard was incompetent.

*She's having Riker tutor me just to tide me over. The real reason I'm not in classes is she doesn't expect I'm going to make it to the next year and wants to make sure Asher doesn't get offed so fast that Riker doesn't have a chance to catch the killer.*

Jasmine's fingernails bit into her palm hard enough to draw blood, but she drew on every ounce of self-control she had to keep her emotions from showing on her face. She gave Esther an admittedly stiff nod.

"I don't have any more questions, then. Thank you."

Esther glanced to Asher, who shook his head.

"Well then. Get in touch if anything changes, but otherwise, continue as you have been," Esther said. She gave them both a nod, then strode out of the room.

Jasmine remained frozen in place, staring down at a discolored stone on the ground. Her palms throbbed, but she welcomed the pain. The Sanctuary had been her way out of being a tool for the gutter bosses that threw their gang members' lives away like worthless scraps.

It had been a way to make something of herself. To pay the kingdom back for saving her from that hellhole.

*Turns out, the only difference is that I get to wear fancier clothes and feel self-righteous about getting sacrificed for the cause. Hey, at least I'll bleed out on fancy stone instead of face down in a puddle of sewage.*

A shadow passed over Jasmine and her eyes jerked up. Asher had gotten out of bed at some point, but she hadn't even noticed him moving until he was right upon her. He stood awkwardly, as if fishing for the right words to say.

Asher was more than clever enough to have come to the same conclusions that she had, but it wasn't like there was anything he could say to change it. Thankfully, he didn't try to speak. Giving up on words, Asher carefully reached out and pulled Jasmine into a hug.

She managed to hold herself together right up until his arms wrapped around her. She collapsed into him, clutching at his shirt as her back heaved with silent sobs.

# 13

Jasmine gathered control of herself about five minutes after ruining the front of Asher's shirt. She drew a deep breath, steadying herself and chaining her emotions back under control. Tears wouldn't change anything, but that didn't stop them from making things feel just a bit better.

Asher released her as she shifted, taking a step back to give her some space. Jasmine swallowed. "I'm sorry. I shouldn't have–"

"You have every right to," Asher snapped. "They want you to die for this. We need to go speak with–"

"No. Don't bother," Jasmine said sharply. "Esther made her decision, Asher. I wouldn't be surprised if she wasn't even the one that wanted to make it, but what's done is done. You heard what Esther said. The kingdom needs the Last Light stopped. What's the life of one trainee Keeper in exchange for something as important as that?"

Asher's jaw clenched. He raised a hand, pausing for a moment before letting it rest on the nape of Jasmine's neck. She nearly batted it away, but was surprised to find that it actually felt more comforting than she'd expected.

"Well, I – fuck, Jas. I don't know."

A snort slipped out of Jasmine before she could stop it. "You're really going to insist on calling me by my nickname? Now?"

"It worked, didn't it?"

Jasmine buried her face in her hands and let out a muffled laugh. It was equal parts mental exhaustion and actual amusement. Asher's fingers ran through her hair, sending tingles down the back of her spine. She froze, and he did too.

"Sorry," Asher said, lifting his hand. "My mom used to do that for me when I was feeling sick. It felt nice."

"It did," Jasmine agreed, raising her head back and drawing another slow breath. She pressed her lips together as she let it out. "Thank you. And… sorry about your shirt."

Asher glanced down at it, then shrugged. "It's fine. I have more. If it helped at all, it was a worthy sacrifice. Truce, right?"

A slight grin flickered across Jasmine's lips. "Yeah. Truce. For whatever good that's going to do against a deadly assassin."

"We'll figure something out. Hey, if it's not just you fighting them next time, maybe we'll be able to hold them off until Riker shows up."

"Esther said that there wouldn't be any more Keepers coming," Jasmine said with a shake of her head. "They need to bait the assassins in, remember?"

"Not another Keeper. Me."

"What, you're going to keep guard over yourself?"

"No. You were waiting when the assassin showed up, weren't you? That's how you managed to do something before they just stabbed me. So you knew they were there."

"I guess. I just had a feeling."

"See? You had a feeling. So… just wake me up the next time. You managed to sense the assassin the first time, so I bet you could do it again."

"You really want to rely on that?"

"It's better than nothing." Asher shrugged. "Besides, it's worked once. That means it's worked every time so far."

"You realize I might just start panicking and having the feeling every single night, right? You'd never sleep again."

"Better that than ending up dead. At least for now. Right?"

Jasmine nodded slowly. "If you're sure, yeah. It would definitely help if you're actually awake when the assassin pops up – but I don't know if I felt the assassin coming or felt it when he was already in the room."

"Either way, as long as you wake me up the moment you feel something, it should be better than nothing. Now that I'm expecting it, I can roll out of bed and try to be ready to fight as soon as possible."

"Well, just remember you asked for it when I prod you awake in the middle of the night. I'm not sure if two trainees is going to be all that much better than one."

"It certainly can't be worse, though." Asher looked down at his hands, clenching them as his eyebrows tightened. "And, if I could actually use Starvein magic, that would change things as well."

"Is it hard?" Jasmine asked. "I always thought it… kind of just happened."

"Yeah. So did I," Asher muttered. He threw a glance back at the book on his bed, then shook his head. "I'll figure it out. I have to. If we could actually fight as a Starvein and Keeper duo, then maybe we'd actually stand something of a chance."

It was almost certainly wishful thinking, but that tiny spark of hope still caught in Jasmine's chest. If – and it was a big if – they could actually fight together, there was the slightest chance they'd survive the next time an assassin showed up.

Of course, that was contingent on the Last Light giving them enough time to learn enough to defend themselves, but Jasmine doubted they'd send an assassin so quickly after the first one died.

*At least, I hope they don't.*

"So all we have to do is find a way to help you learn Starvein magic fast enough that you not only catch up to your classmates but also surpass them. Easy," Jasmine said, a small grin playing across her lips.

"And we've just got to pair that with you getting good enough to fight a trained assassin. Should be simple enough." Asher crossed his arms as if in deep thought, then scrunched his nose and looked back at his book. "I guess I've got to get back to that stupid thing, then."

"Do you not like it? If I had the chance to learn magic, I'd drop everything for it. Bending the world to your will sounds... incredible."

"Maybe it's a good thing you don't have it," Asher said, eyeing Jasmine before giving her a small smile to show he was joking. "But no – that part is great. This is the part that sucks."

He picked the book up and flipped open to a random page, spinning it so Jasmine could see. She held her hands up defensively.

"Hold on! Isn't that secret or something?"

"Oh, I don't carc. Just look."

Jasmine dropped her hands without so much as a second thought and leaned in eagerly. Her excitement melted away in an instant. Instead of scrawling lines of magical guidance or shimmering runes, what she found was a very, very complex looking graph – surrounded by equations and writing that made absolutely no sense.

"What is this?"

"Magic," Asher grumbled, turning the book back toward himself. "The theory of it, at least. I don't understand anything. I've never done anything like this. It's written in common, but it might as well be a different language."

"You've got to do all that in your head to cast magic?"

Asher waggled a hand in the air. "Not really. It helps, though.

It's a way to understand the magic, and the more you understand of it, the better you can use it. Most of this is talking about the amount of power you can channel based on your mental fortitude before you accidentally draw too much and..."

He trailed off, then made a gesture with his hands.

"Pull a Xolani?" Jasmine finished.

"Yeah."

"That's not good. Maybe avoid that."

"You think?" Asher huffed in annoyance. "I'm trying. It's not nearly as fun as sparring was. At least I could do that with someone – but the mere idea of asking any of the other Starvein students, much less Qien, to practice with me feels about as appetizing as a pile of cow dung."

"Is there any way I can help?"

"Eventually, yes. Once I figure out how to get my feet out under me and can use magic, then I'll need someone to practice against."

"You're going to try to blast me?"

"Nothing like that. From what I've read, keeping concentration and calling magic while stressed are the biggest difficulties a Starvein faces."

"Ah. You want me to throw things at you while you try to call magic."

Asher grimaced. "When you put it like that, no. But... yeah. I guess so."

"Well, I'd be happy to oblige." Jasmine adjusted her shirt, which was still wrinkled from the events of the previous night. She really needed to change out of it.

"Don't get too eager. I've got to figure out the basics first. And, speaking of which, I'm pretty sure it's almost time for class. We kind of slept pretty late into the day, though I'd say it was fairly justified."

"Just give me a second to swap out of this." Jasmine plucked at her shirt. "Don't leave without me."

"I won't," Asher promised. He sat back down, hiding a slight wince in the process. A small frown crossed over Jasmine's face, but there wasn't anything she could do about it. Esther had basically said he'd get over it, so that was that.

*Actually, can I even trust her? I'm easy enough to sacrifice, but is it really that much of a loss to the kingdom if Asher dies too? Taking out a nasty organization at the cost of a gutter rat and a single Starvein in training isn't really that much worse than just the gutter rat.*

Jasmine's mood soured again. She changed out of her clothes, tossing the old ones in a pile at the base of her bed, and pulled on a new, identical, set. There wasn't much variation in Keeper uniforms, which were made far more for practical use than comfort, but at least it saved her from worrying about what to wear.

*I'm far from a healer, though. If I can't ask Esther about the wound, who can I ask?*

Her question remained unanswered as she headed back into Asher's room. They wordlessly set off to Qien's class, both lost deep in their own thoughts.

# 14

The class was largely filled by the time they got there. Jasmine and Asher took the seats they'd had the previous class, settling in to wait until Qien started to teach. This time, some of the other students didn't even *try* to hide their interest.

*Great. Qien's demonstration definitely ended up getting more people to pay attention to us. Just what we needed.*

Fortunately, it didn't take long for Qien to start class. He launched into what Jasmine suspected to be complex magical theory that made absolutely no sense to her, and judging by the look on Asher's face, it wasn't clicking much better for him either.

While all the other students listened intently, Jasmine took some time to study the classroom – or, more accurately, the students in it. The seats they'd chosen weren't the best for looking at the majority of the others in the room, as they were right in the center next to the isle and a number of students were behind them.

She recognized the girl that she'd pushed the previous class – Pina, if she remembered her name correctly – and the boy beside her, Clarence. They were both completely focused on Qien, hanging on to every word he said.

*I suppose they don't have a choice, considering they're in the front row.*

Pina's quill scratched against her paper like a runaway horse as she furiously wrote down every single word that came out of Qien's mouth. It was actually somewhat impressive. If she moved much faster, Jasmine suspected her paper might catch fire.

Without names to match with the other Starveins, Jasmine ended up resorting to grouping them by trait. As far as she could tell, even with all the split off little groups, there were three main classifications that the Starvein students fell into.

The first type was named after Pina. They sat rod-straight and dutifully listened to everything Qien said, and many of them wore jewelry or had not-so-subtle additions to their already fancy Starvein robes that made them stick out like sore thumbs.

The next type were the Clarence lookalikes. They gravitated toward the Pinas, sitting beside them and paying attention through one ear. Their attention was split between studying the other students and occasionally prodding their Pina to mutter something. Some of them sat in larger groups, but they all gravitated at least one Pina.

The final group were the isolated students. The ones that that sat alone in their group of seats. There wasn't any real pattern in their behavior, but it was clear that they were ostracized to some degree by the rest of the class. Some of them were even reading their own books, tuning out Qien entirely.

For his part, Qien didn't seem to care if anyone was paying attention. He just kept talking away, only stopping to answer questions whenever someone called something out. As rude as he was, Jasmine started to appreciate the professor's efficiency.

He only cared about teaching the students that were listening. The other ones didn't get any time wasted on them. And, while he was snarky with every question he got, Jasmine was pretty sure he *was* answering them.

So long as she wasn't the one his ire directed at, it was actually rather interesting. The minutes ground on, and Jasmine's observations slowly started to become less interesting. There was only so long she could go people watching.

*I wish I could practice something useful. Maybe I should actually bring a book with me next time. At least that would –*

The back of Jasmine's neck prickled. She stiffened instantly, looking to the left. A girl sat four seats away from them, a small orb of white magic twirling between two of her fingers. Her clothes were above average in quality, though not as fancy as some of the other students. She wore a golden necklace around her neck, the top of it just barely poking out above her shirt. Jasmine locked eyes with her and the girl's eyes widened in shock.

There was a soft pop and the bolt of magic leapt from her fingertips, streaking through the air and leaving a trail of small crystals behind it. Qien's hand snapped up, almost of its own accord, and he clenched his fingers like he was grabbing onto a floating bedsheet.

The magical bolt sputtered and vanished. Streaks of energy swirled down from where it had been, gathering above Qien's palm before he crushed it within his grip. The professor's cold eyes flicked over to the girl.

"Esmarelda," Qien said, his voice deadly calm. "Did you lose something?"

"I – uh, I was just trying to practice some of what you were talking about," Esmarelda stammered. "I got distracted and–"

"I can excuse poor attempts at magic," Qien said, cutting her off. "I can excuse disruptions of my class for the sake of learning. What I *cannot* excuse is distraction. Do you know what happens to a Starvein that does not have control?"

"They die, Professor."

"They die," Qien mocked, striding down the aisle to stare the mollified girl down. "They do not just die. They turn into Xolani and murder everyone that they hold dear as the magic rips their mind apart from the inside – a fact I discussed *yesterday*!"

By the time he was done speaking, Qien's voice had raised to a roar. Esmarelda cringed back in her chair, her eyes darting around in search of help and finding nothing.

"I – I'm sorry."

"You are still dead," Qien said. His eyes flicked over to Jasmine. "You. Xolani. What would you Keepers do if someone failed utterly and miserably in their training?"

The eyes of everyone in the class turned to Jasmine.

"Probably run laps around the classroom for the rest of class," Jasmine said with a wince. She'd been the subject of that particular punishment more than a few times. It wasn't fun – especially because Esther would whack the runner with a wooden cane if they ever ran at anything less than full sprint.

"Is that all?" Qien's brow furrowed. "Less than I expected."

"It's pretty bad when you're completely out of breath and have to keep pushing. Sprinting when you can't even breathe anymore isn't a fun experience. It usually doesn't happen to anyone more than once or twice before they learn."

Asher glanced at Jasmine out of the corner of his eyes. She did her best to avoid meeting his gaze.

*I'm more than aware it happened to me about eight times. There's no way I'm going to admit it, though.*

"What do you think?" Qien asked, turning back to Esmarelda. "Is that sufficient punishment? Or would you prefer mine?"

Esmarelda practically leapt from her seat. She sprinted past Qien and started to run laps around the room. Qien watched her go, then nodded and strode back to his podium, where he started to teach as if nothing had changed.

*What in the Watcher's Eyes is his normal punishment if that's how she reacted to it?*

Jasmine didn't get to find out. The rest of the class passed quickly, though it started to get a little distracting when Esmarelda's desperate wheezing grew louder. She wasn't in anywhere near as good shape as the Keeper students, and it showed.

Still, the fact that her legs continued pumping and she refused to slow down told Jasmine that Qien's punishment was to be avoided at all costs.

Almost an hour later, Qien dismissed the class. Esmarelda collapsed on the spot, drawing in desperate, ragged breaths. Not even glancing in her direction, Qien strode out of the room. The rest of the students followed suit.

"What's his normal punishment?" Jasmine whispered to Asher.

"I've literally been here just as long as you have," Asher muttered back. "I have no idea, but let's make sure not to find out. What happened between you and Esmarelda? I saw her looking at us."

Jasmine rubbed the back of her neck and chewed her lower lip. "I got the feeling again. It came when she started casting that magic thing. She was looking in our direction when she was doing it, so she got surprised when I spun and lost control, I guess."

"You felt her casting magic?"

"I don't know what I felt. I thought someone was just watching us, but maybe it was the magic. Is that possible?"

"Again, no clue. When I say I barely know any more than you do, I mean it." Asher rose to his feet. "Should we check on Esmarelda? It looks like she's about to pass out."

Jasmine and Asher walked over to Esmarelda, and Jasmine knelt beside her. The necklace around Esmarelda's neck had hiked itself up, revealing the top of a spiraling pattern. She was still desperately trying to gather her breath, but she was conscious.

"Still alive?" Jasmine asked.

Esmarelda let out a groan, mustering the energy to roll over and lie on her back and squint up at them as she lifted a hand to wipe the sweat from her forehead. She glanced down at her chest and pulled her clothes back into place with a grimace. "It could have been worse."

"What would he have done normally?" Jasmine asked, not able to keep her curiosity in check.

A shudder passed through Esmeralda's body. "Made me use all the magic until I was completely drained."

*That... doesn't really sound that bad. Qien seems pretty strict on safety, so I doubt it would be dangerous. What's the punishment?*

"You don't get it," Esmarelda said, her tone strained. "It's because you don't have magic. Imagine feeling like you haven't eaten or drank anything in a week. It's like that, but worse. He did it to me once and it felt like my stomach was going to invert. I couldn't see straight for a day, and it took me two before I felt normal again. Starveins can't live without magic."

"Ah," Jasmine said lamely. "That sucks."

Esmarelda let out a weary laugh. She pushed herself into a seated position, then plucked at her shirt. It was completely soaked through with sweat. Letting it slap back against her skin, she grimaced.

"Sucks is an understatement."

"Why were you trying to cast magic in our direction in the first place?" Asher asked.

"I wasn't! I was just practicing when your Keeper turned around and stared me down like she was going to run me through," Esmarelda exclaimed. "I didn't think anyone had noticed, but she moved so damn fast that I lost my concentration."

"Maybe Qien had a point," Asher said. "That doesn't seem safe."

*I was thinking it too, but damn. You could have been diplomatic about it. What happened to all those etiquette lessons you were lording over me?*

"Yeah, I'm aware. I'm not normally this easily distracted. I just wasn't expecting you to glare at me the moment I started."

"Sorry," Jasmine said. "I thought you were looking at us."

"What, do you have eyes on the back of your head or something? How'd you even know that I was using magic? Did I make noise? I was trying really hard to be quiet."

Jasmine shook her head. She rose to her feet and held a hand out. Esmarelda studied it for a moment, then accepted the hand and let Jasmine pull her up. She wobbled for a moment, nearly falling over before Jasine steadied her. Esmarelda gave her a small nod of appreciation.

"I didn't hear anything," Jasmine said, taking a step back once Esmarelda was standing on her own. "I don't really know what set me off. Maybe I saw it out of the corner of my eye?"

"Some perception you've got if that's the case. Either way, I owe you one."

"You do?" Jasmine blinked.

*I thought she'd be pissy about getting forced to run laps.*

"Yeah. I told you – if you hadn't been here, Qien would have drained my magic. I'll run laps any day over that. At least all I have to worry about now is some sore legs and a bruised ego. Well, and a change of clothes. These are going to reek so bad that the Watcher smells them from his seat in the sky."

"Ah. Well, you're welcome, I guess."

*A Starvein that isn't a conceited asshole? I didn't think that was possible. Did she hit her head at some point while she was running? Or maybe you can just exercise the rudeness out. That's an interesting idea. Maybe all Starveins should be forced to run laps.*

"Well, I'm going to go waddle out now," Esmarelda muttered, looking up the stairwell leading out of the room. "I'd offer my help if you needed it, but I don't think there's all that much I can help you with."

"It's fine. We can just call it even." Jasmine shook her head, then paused. "Actually, wait."

Esmarelda raised an eyebrow. "If you're going to ask me to teach you magic, then the answer is no. Not because I don't want to, but because you can't learn it. It would just be a waste of time."

"Not me," Jasmine said. Asher shot her a panicked look, but she ignored it and nodded in his direction. "Him."

"Come on," Asher complained. "Seriously? I don't need–"

"This is a safety related matter," Jasmine said, cutting him off and crossing her arms.

Asher's mouth snapped closed and his lips pressed thin. "Fine."

Esmarelda looked from Asher to Jasmine, a grin flickering across her lips. "I thought the Starveins were meant to be in charge of the Keepers, not other way around."

"It's a partnership," Asher corrected, glaring at Jasmine. "And, unfortunately, she's a bit power hungry."

"You're telling me you actually need help with magic?" Esmarelda asked.

Jasmine gave Asher an encouraging gesture, and he returned it with a look that promised she'd pay for it later.

"I suppose I've been having a bit of trouble figuring out how to use magic, but it's not like I've had all that much time to figure anything out."

"Wait, really?" Esmarelda frowned. "I kind of figured you already knew what was going on."

"Why would I know what I'm doing? I literally just joined the Starveins. I was a Keeper up until a few days ago," Asher said, baffled.

"I kind of assumed that you were a prodigy. Nobody gets added to the program in the middle of the year," Esmarelda said, studying Asher as if seeing him for the first time. "You mean you're completely untrained? You've never used magic at all?"

"Never."

"You didn't have an awakening?"

"If I knew what that was, I could answer."

Esmarelda shook her head in disbelief. "It's when your magic comes out for the first time. It happened to me when I was eight, and it usually happens pretty early on. Starveins naturally channel magic, right? Our bodies have some degree of magic in them, it's just really low. That's what lets us control it. And, if you don't use magic for long enough, it starts to eat at you and build up in your body – until it reaches a certain threshold and all comes pouring out."

"I can say with certainty that that's never happened, because I've never used magic."

"And you're sure you're a Starvein?"

"Quite," Asher said dryly. "Do you really think I'd be here if I wasn't?"

"No," Esmarelda admitted. She chewed her lower lip. "This is really weird. I've never met a Starvein that hadn't awakened at our age. You aren't going to be able to use any magic until you manage to awaken. That's what establishes the connection."

"Do you happen to know how to trigger an activation?" Jasmine asked eagerly.

"Try to get in a stressful situation, I guess? It wasn't really a conscious decision for me. I got mad that my parents wouldn't let me have a second dinner." Esmarelda rubbed the back of her head. "I don't really know what else to say. You could try asking Qien."

Asher grimaced and shook his head. "He'd probably boot me out of the program on the spot if I admitted I couldn't use magic. Thanks for the help. At least we have something to work on before next class."

"No problem. Sorry I couldn't be of more help." Esmarelda shrugged, then started up the stairs and headed out of the class, leaning against the wall for support. Asher and Jasmine watched her leave.

"Well, shit," Asher said once she was gone. "What in the Watcher's eyes do I do now? I've never heard of that."

"Was an assassin not stressful enough? Maybe you should have been awake for more of it," Jasmine said with a smirk. "At least we have something to work toward, though. That's better than nothing."

"Yeah, I suppose so." Asher pursed his lips, then shook his head. "Well, no time like the present. Let's head back to my room and see if you can manage to stress me out enough to force my magic to awaken, shall we?"

# 15

"Close your eyes." Jasmine stood at the foot of Asher's bed, tapping her foot impatiently.

"I don't see how that's going to accomplish anything," Asher protested. He sat on his bed, facing away from her. "This isn't going to–"

Jasmine prodded Asher in the back. He let out a startled yelp, then doubled over with a grimace. "Watcher's tits! What's your problem?"

"Sorry," Jasmine said, pulling her hand back and wincing. "I thought surprising you might trigger the awakening."

*And it was kind of funny.*

It had been about an hour since they'd gotten back from class, and Jasmine had been trying to find ways to scare Asher's magic out of him the entire time. It was definitely a fun way to pass the time, but she got the slightest suspicion that she was enjoying it more than he was.

Asher rolled over and stared up at the ceiling, letting out a groan. "This is impossible. Maybe I'm adopted and I was never a Starvein at all."

"Do you think that's possible? It could explain why you haven't awakened."

Sitting up, Asher squinted at Jasmine. "Just so you know, that's generally the point where you try to assure me that I was definitely my mother's son, not agree with me."

"Why? It was a good theory."

"Well, I'm not adopted. I look really similar to my dad and brother, so unless they just happened to get lucky with their choice of adoption, that isn't what's going on here."

"Was your brother a Starvein?" Jasmine asked.

Asher nodded. "Yeah. Not a particularly good one, but he was. He left Sanctuary four years before I joined it."

"Well, damn. So the problem isn't your lineage."

"Yeah. It's me." Asher snagged his book on magic and flipped through it irritably. "This explains why I couldn't do anything in here at least. Hard to *feel* anything when there's nothing to feel."

"Do you think we should actually talk to Qien? He didn't seem like that bad of a teacher," Jasmine said. "Maybe he'd actually help."

"I might not have a choice if I can't figure anything out by tomorrow," Asher admitted reluctantly. "He said there would be a practical test at the end of the week, and its Seventhday today. I don't have that long to figure out the basics and not completely humiliate myself."

"You know, I could always just keep pushing your classmates over. It's not like they can protect themselves that well."

"Until you run into one that can cast a little faster than you expect. If you're able to fight, then you're able to get hurt." Asher shook his head. "And I'm a pure liability until I can use my magic. Besides, Qien only let you fight last time to prove a point. He might not let you do it in the future."

"Fine, fine." Jasmine held her hands up in surrender. "I won't make you do it. It was just a suggestion. I'm not really sure what else we could do."

"I didn't mean to snap at you," Asher said, letting out a heavy breath. "It's just frustrating. If I don't have magic, I don't see what the point of any of this is. I could have just stayed a Keeper. It's not like you can lead a noble house without it. They'd be better off handing what remains of my house to someone else to look after.

*I do wonder what happened to the people living on his land. Do they just remain unmanaged and unprotected until Asher graduates? It's going to be at least 5 or 6 years before he can leave Sanctuary.*

Jasmine resisted the urge to voice her thoughts. Asher had more than enough to deal with at the moment, and speculating about it wasn't going to help either of them. He was right – what they needed was a way to get his magic working. Unfortunately, knowing that wasn't quite enough to actually accomplish anything.

A shadow crawled across the room as the sun started to set.

"Maybe we should just get dinner," Jasmine suggested. "The solution could come to us while we aren't expecting it."

"What, do you think the answer is going to be written in the eggs?"

Jasmine opened her mouth to reply, but Asher slid off the bed and spoke again before she could.

"Never mind me. I'm irritable. Let's go see what we can throw together – though there are probably going to be other people using the kitchen right now. Are you fine with that?"

"I'll make do. We can't skip dinner because I'm too embarrassed to admit that I'm a horrible chef," Jasmine said, walking up to the door. "What do you think we should make?"

"I wouldn't mind some meat. Steak, maybe?" Asher suggested as he joined her. Jasmine pulled the door open – and the back of her neck erupted in icy tingles.

She threw herself into Asher, sending both of them crashing to the ground. They hit the ground and she rolled over, her hand flying to her sword and pulling it free of its sheath even as she rose, only to freeze in place.

Riker stood on the other side of the door, a bemused expression on his face.

"Interesting," Riker said.

"Shit," Jasmine muttered, sheathing the sword and holding a hand out. "Sorry, Asher."

"Better bruised than dead," Asher said, accepting Jasmine's hand and letting her pull him to his feet. "That was some fast reaction timing. Does he smell or something?"

Jasmine couldn't even bring herself to scold Asher for his attitude. Riker was working with Esther. If he wanted to insult either of them, she was more than happy to encourage him from the sidelines.

"She feels my magic," Riker said, stepping inside. He closed the door behind him with his heel.

"How? Jasmine is a Keeper," Asher said with a frown. He blinked, then reassessed her. "She is, right? Don't tell me you're also a noble."

"She is not a Starvein," Riker said before Jasmine even had a chance to respond.

"What are you implying, then?" Jasmine asked. "You mentioned this before as well. How could I be sensitive to magic if I don't have any?"

"Not being a Starvein and having magic are not mutually exclusive. The Xolani are not Starveins."

"I'm not a Xolani."

"But you have Xolani blood," Riker pointed out. "And, just like Starvein magic, it can become more influential as you age – and as you experience stress."

"You're saying that I can use Xolani magic?" Jasmine asked, not sure if she should be excited or terrified. There were a lot of stories about the Xolani, and not a single one of them had a happy ending.

"That is yet to be seen," Riker said with a shrug. "Using magic and having sensitivity to it that's left over from a diluted bloodline are separate things."

"But you said–"

"Almost anyone can use magic with sufficient training. It is not your Xolani blood that enables it. I am, unfortunately, nothing but a normal human."

"That's not true at all," Asher interceded. "The whole reason Sanctuary exists is to train Starveins and Keepers to aid them. If anyone could learn magic, then it would be much smarter to teach as many people as possible. It's not like the Whitewater Kingdom has bodies to spare. More mages means more combatants against the other Kingdoms."

"Refuting information because you do not understand it is the act of a fool," Riker said. "Starveins are *better* at accessing magic. This does not mean they are the only ones that can use it."

Riker held a hand out, his brow furrowing in concentration. The book on Asher's bed trembled, then lifted into the air. Jasmine and Asher watched in mute disbelief as it lazily floated over to Riker, who plucked it from the sky.

"That's impossible," Asher muttered. "Why didn't anyone tell us?"

"Because now you want to learn."

"Of course we do!" Jasmine exclaimed. "I mean… Asher *needs* to learn, and if I can use magic–"

"You can't."

Jasmine's eye twitched and she resisted the urge to throw her hands up into the air in frustration. "You literally just said–"

"I said you could learn it. As you are now, you cannot use it."

"Those are semantics."

"We are Keepers. Words should only be half-truths when we intend them to be," Riker said.

For a moment, Jasmine was nearly overwhelmed with the urge to point out that Esther had set her up for failure and she wasn't going to be anything when an assassin killed her or she failed the exam at the end of the year, but she repressed it, her hands clenching at her sides.

"Well, can you teach me?" Jasmine asked.

"No."

"Did you come here purely to annoy us?" Asher's eyes narrowed. "Because it's working. Stop screwing with Jasmine and give her a straight answer."

Riker's eyes crinkled ever so slightly in what have been amusement, but they returned to normal so quickly that Jasmine almost convinced herself that she'd imagined it entirely.

"Jasmine cannot cast magic as she is now. As you pointed out, Sanctuary exists for Starveins. Your kind have access to a flowing ocean just beneath the surface. She has a wellspring deep below the ground. It will take immense training to access it consciously."

"You could teach me, though," Jasmine pressed. "That's the whole reason you mentioned it."

"I mentioned it because knowledge is power. If you wish to learn magic from me, then you will need to be able to master the core tenets of a Keeper."

"What do those have to do with magic?" Jasmine's brow furrowed. "Keepers don't use magic."

"Magic is more than you believe it to be, but that is irrelevant to this discussion. A Keeper must be in perfect control of every part of themselves. Their mind – their muscles – their thoughts and words – everything. This level of discipline will be what permits you to safely access magic."

And, just like that, Jasmine's hope evaporated. If she had to completely master everything that a Keeper stood for in order to use magic, having magic or not was irrelevant. There was no way to do it before the end of the year, much less before an assassin ran her through.

"I'm going to be dead before I become a master Keeper," Jasmine said with a defeated sigh. "Why would you dangle something like that in front of me when there's absolutely no chance of achieving it?"

"You do not need to become a master Keeper," Riker corrected raising a finger into the air. "You must master the Keepers tenets. It is more mental than anything else. You could achieve it tomorrow should you have sufficient enlightenment."

Jasmine perked up. Riker was right – that was a lot more realistic. If all she had to do was change her attitude a bit to learn magic, that wasn't so hard at all.

"I just have to think about things differently? I can do that."

"And I will teach you," Riker finished with a nod. "That is why I am here. We will have to... accelerate certain aspects of your training."

"Accelerate?" Asher sent Riker a suspicious look. "What does that mean?"

"It is not your concern."

"What? She's–"

"She is a student," Riker said, his tone as flat as a board. He turned to match Asher's gaze, his face unreadable. "One with a purpose, but a student, nonetheless. Would you deny her training?"

"I didn't say that. I'm saying whenever someone says accelerate, they usually mean they're going to make it way worse. Are you actually going to help her? Or are you just going to feel better about yourself by putting her through the wringer and then leaving her for dead at the end of it, claiming you did your best and it couldn't be helped?" Asher's tone was perfectly even despite the anger in his eyes – exactly how a Keeper's should have been.

"My purpose is not your concern. All that matters is if Jasmine wants my training or not," Riker said. "Decide. I have better things to do with my time than argue with children."

It didn't take her long. No matter what the training was or how hard it would be, Jasmine couldn't pass up on the opportunity. Accelerated training seemed like the only way she'd be able to get strong fast enough to survive the next assassin attack.

"If I accept, what about Asher?" Jasmine asked. "What if the Assassin shows up while we're training?"

"He will be protected," Riker said, not expanding. Jasmine and Asher exchanged a glance.

"If you really want to do this, don't worry about me," Asher snapped. "I'm not a helpless child. I'll manage to survive on my own for an hour a day."

"Then I want to do it," Jasmine said.

"Good. Then come. We are already eating into our hour," Riker said. He pushed the door to the room open and stepped out, turning to look back at Jasmine expectantly.

After one last exchanged glance with Asher, Jasmine followed after him.

# 16

Riker led Jasmine through the Starvein Halls for several minutes before abruptly coming to a stop beside the wall. Before Jasmine could ask what he was doing, Riker pressed his hand against the adorned stone.

A crisp click rang out and a rectangle of stone slid inward, revealing a hidden doorway. Riker pushed it to the side and the stone grated against the ground, opening out into a small, largely unadorned room.

Without looking to see if Jasmine was following, Riker ducked inside. Jasmine hurried to keep up with him, then turned back and watched as the stone rumbled shut behind them. Several faint *whumps* broke the darkness as torches flickered to life along the room's walls.

There was a thick straw mat covering the center of the room. Beside Riker was a large wooden desk and several large shelves. Jasmine's eyes were immediately drawn to the other side of the room, where a wide assortment of weapons hung from the wall.

"Stop," Riker said.

"Stop what?"

"You are looking at the weapons," Riker said, stepping out onto the center of the mat and crossing his arms behind his back. "You are not ready for them."

Jasmine tried not to let the disappointment she felt show, but she could tell she did a poor job of it.

"I guess that's fair. You were just talking about the mind stuff. So… what are we doing, then? Just talking?"

"This is part of the problem. Esther told me about some of your past." Riker started to walk in a circle around Jasmine, forcing her to turn to keep watching him. "You value fighting because it was blade that granted you freedom. Your skill with a knife was enough to draw the King's eye when you tried to rob one of his guards and actually managed to deflect a blow, yes?"

Jasmine's cheeks reddened. "Yeah. One blow. It wasn't really that impressive."

"It is impressive. You have natural talent and the drive to make it into skill." Riker came to a stop and turned to stare into Jasmine's eyes. "However, you have made a grave mistake. You failed to hone all of your weapons."

"What do you mean? I've done everything I could to be the best warrior–"

"Have you?" Riker interrupted. "What is a warrior without his sword?"

She opened her mouth, then paused. It felt like Riker was asking a trick question. She thought through it for a few moments, chewing her lower lip. "I don't know. Does he have other weapons?"

"You tell me."

"I guess he's still a warrior," Jasmine said.

"With what weapon?"

"Maybe he has a dagger. Or his fists and feet. You never stop fighting until you're dead."

"Good." Riker gave her a curt nod. "And what if you are tied up and bound? Hung from the ceiling and unable to move? Are you defeated?"

Jasmine's brow furrowed. "I guess so?"

"Wrong," Riker snapped. "A warrior does not give up until they are dead. Your mind is a weapon. Your words are a weapon. And you – you are unarmed."

Jasmine winced. Riker's words were harsh, but he didn't give her time to dwell on them long. He strode over to the wall and took a wooden sword, tossing it to her. Jasmine snatched the blade from the air.

"I thought we weren't going to use this yet."

"I changed my mind," Riker said. "Normally, I would focus on the area that you lack training in, but we do not have time. Thus, we will do both at once."

"You're going to teach me how to act like a Keeper while we spar?"

"I am going to teach you how to *be* a Keeper while we spar," Riker corrected. He took a sword down for himself, and a shiver ran down Jasmine's spine a she turned back to face her.

Her years in the gutters had taught her when a mark was easy. There were a lot of telltale signs – the way they stood, the look in their eyes, how loose the drawstrings on their belts were. The guard that she'd tried to pickpocket had been half-asleep, and he'd had enough coin to feed her for a month.

He'd been an easy target. But Riker – up until a moment ago, he'd just felt like a sharp-tongued butler. She'd logically known that he was a Keeper, but he hadn't felt all that threatening.

Now, every one of Jasmine's senses was screaming at her to turn and flee. His eyes were hungry, like those of a starving wolf who had cornered its prey. Riker held the blade easily in his hands, as if it were an extension of himself.

Jasmine raised her sword, shifting back instinctively. It wasn't like there was anywhere she could have run, even if she wanted to.

"We will begin with the most important trait. Not for Keepers, but for you." Riker's sword whipped out. Jasmine raised her own blade to block it – and cried out in pain. It felt like she'd tried to block a falling boulder.

Her sword flew from her hands and slammed into the wall with a loud crash. Jasmine lowered her smarting hands – and her eyes went wide. Riker was swinging again. She dropped to the ground, just barely getting out of the way of a brutal swing as it whistled over her head.

Rolling to the side, Jasmine ran over to her sword and brought it to bear, spinning back to face Riker.

"Perseverance," Riker said, pointing his sword at Jasmine. "And tenacity. A Keeper must weather everything that life throws at them and come out standing."

Jasmine swallowed.

Riker meant what he said – and Jasmine was pretty sure he didn't know the meaning of the word *restraint.*

The past thirty minutes had involved Riker following Jasmine around the room, speaking on the reasons why Keepers were the way they were whilst beating her half to death with his sword.

Her breath came in desperate pants and pain pulsed along every single spot in her upper body. It felt like Riker was intentionally striking a new location every single time to make sure nothing came out unscathed.

"This is the attitude you must have," Riker said, his sword tearing through the air for her shoulder. Jasmine jumped back, avoiding the blow by an inch. "Pain can be overcome. Broken bones can be surpassed. Your mind must not break."

"My sword's going to break if you keep swinging like that," Jasmine said through desperate breaths.

"Perhaps," Riker allowed. "Do not dodge the next strike. Block it."

Jasmine grit her teeth and planted her feet. Riker was upon her in an instant, his sword crashing down. She lifted her own blade – and, as usual, it was smashed from her numbing fingertips. Jasmine stumbled, the vibration from the strike running all the way through her arms and into her chest.

She didn't let herself feel the pain for long. She lunged, grabbing her sword and bringing it back, even as Riker repeated the strike he'd just used. Jasmine whipped her blade up for a second time.

And, to her surprise, Riker's sword slammed to a halt. A ripple of force still drove into her, but she'd blocked the blow.

"Why did that work?" Riker asked remaining in place so Jasmine could take in the scene. "What did you change?"

"I – I'm not sure."

"It is the position of your sword," Riker said. "You blocked at the hilt, where you had more leverage."

"I – huh. I guess so," she said, using the moment to gather her breath. "What... what does that mean, though?"

"It means you persevered through one blow," Riker said, a faint smile flickering across his features. "Now do it against another."

The training lasted for another half an hour. Jasmine didn't block another blow, and not once did Riker relent or go easy on her. Her bruises had bruises, and some of those had bruises too.

Jasmine's throbbing fingers could barely still hold her sword, but she refused to leave it on the ground. She couldn't even muster the strength to bring the blade properly to bear, but she held onto it with everything she had.

Finally, Riker lowered his sword. "We're done."

"We are?" Jasmine wasn't sure if she was relieved, confused, or both. "But all we did was spar."

"Did we?" Riker returned his sword to its spot on the wall, then raised an eyebrow. "I would disagree. You simply learn better with blades than you do with words. I would say that you have understood the essence of a Keeper's perseverance."

"This is just how I always train," Jasmine said, still breathing heavily and trying to control her exhaustion. Riker took the sword from her, practically prying it from her fingers, and hung it up with a shrug. "Perhaps. And yet, for the last thirty minutes, you did not budge from your spot. You are not running anymore."

Jasmine looked down at the ground, her eyes widening. Her sweat had formed a small ring on the mat around her. Riker was right – she'd barely even been aware of it, but she hadn't moved at all.

"Is sitting and getting hit by everything really a good thing?" Jasmine asked.

"If it is a choice between you or your Charge? Yes." Riker shrugged, then gave her a small smile. "But, personally, I suggest you block."

Jasmine couldn't keep herself from letting out a laugh. "Thanks, I guess."

"Thanks are not needed. We are finished for today. You will rest and recover by tomorrow. We will continue where we left off."

*I'm not sure I'm going to be able to pick a sword up tomorrow, much less spar with you again.*

Jasmine didn't voice her thoughts. She took one look at Riker, then gave him a curt nod. "I'll be ready."

"Perseverance," Riker said approvingly. He pressed his hand to the wall that they'd entered the room through and it rumbled open. Jasmine stepped through and he followed after her, the wall grinding shut behind them.

"That's it for today, right?" Jasmine asked.

Riker's face was back to its normal, expressionless self. "Yes. Your body cannot handle any more. Return to your room."

She didn't need to be told twice. Training was great, but

Jasmine was exhausted. All she wanted to do was get dinner out of the way and then collapse in bed and sleep until the sun rose again.

"Thanks for the class, Riker. If I somehow end up not dying, I'll appreciate it," Jasmine said. She would have raised a hand if she still had the energy to, but instead settled for one last nod before heading down the halls in the direction of Asher's room.

# 17

"Watcher's eyes, what happened to you?" Asher lowered his book, getting out of his chair as Jasmine unlocked the door and walked into the room.

"Training," Jasmine replied, grimacing as she fought to muster the energy to lock the door behind her. Every movement of her arms felt like she was trying to push the world back. "It went well."

"You look like you're dead on your feet."

"I'll sleep soon enough," Jasmine said. A yawn threatened to force its way between her lips, but she forced it back and shook her head. "Right after I make dinner. I'm starving."

Jasmine turned toward her room, then paused. Asher's dining table had two plates on it, each covered with a large, silver bowl. Her brow furrowed. "What's that?"

"I got hungry," Asher said, clearing his throat. He set his book down on his bed and pulled a chair out. "And you were out for longer than I was expecting, so I made dinner myself."

"What? But it's my–"

"Oh, shut up and eat," Asher said, jiggling the chair impatiently.

"We're working together, remember? I'll be more than happy to let you cook when you've actually got the time for it, but you've got enough on your plate to accept letting me do it once."

Jasmine didn't even try to argue. After all, the food was already in front of her. It would have been a shame to waste it. She sat down in the chair and Asher pushed it in before sitting down across from her.

He pulled the bowls off their plates, revealing delicious-looking steaks. Jasmine's mouth started to water. She went to reach for her silverware, then paused.

"Wait. You said you were hungry."

Asher was already midway through cutting a piece of his steak off. He raised an eyebrow. "Yes?"

"Then why didn't you eat when you made food?"

"Oh, shut up and eat," Asher grumbled. "I thought I'd wait to keep you company. Is there a problem with that?"

Jasmine felt her cheeks color slightly, and she desperately hoped that it wasn't too apparent. "No. I was just wondering."

Jasmine picked her knife and fork up with trembling hands, inwardly cursing Riker. Her arms could barely raise above her waist. The mixture of exertion from blocking his strikes and pain from all the bruises was a lot worse than she felt like it should have been.

*I feel like I've got two limp noodles strapped to my body. It's not like this is the first time I've trained hard, even if this was probably one of the most brutal sessions I've ever had. What is wrong with me?*

"Are you okay?" Asher asked. He was somehow already halfway done with his meal, even though they'd only started eating a little while ago. "Is there something wrong with the steak?"

Jasmine's cheeks reddened even further. She drew on every last drop of strength she could muster. Moving the knife and fork to cut the steak felt like it was harder than blocking Riker's blows.

"Nothing is wrong. I'm just sore."

"Do you need help?"

"I'm more than capable of eating steak."

Asher arched an eyebrow, but he didn't say anything else. Jasmine sawed slowly at the steak, but she was pretty sure that gravity was exerting more pressure on her knife than she was. Her brow furrowed as her ears heated up.

*I am not losing a fight to an inanimate, cooked piece of meat.*

Her knife finally cut through, hitting the plate. She let out a smug huff, spearing the piece of steak with her fork and leaning down to pop it into her mouth, not wanting to have to move her other arm more than she needed to.

It was, without a doubt, the best bite of food she'd ever had in her life. A good portion of that was almost certainly due to how tired and hungry she was, but Asher's cooking definitely pulled its own weight.

"Well? What do you think?" Asher asked.

"It's really good," Jasmine said. "Better than Lydia's, but don't tell her I said that or I'll kill you."

She went to cut another piece, then caught sight of Asher's plate. It was empty. He'd already finished and was just sitting there, fingers interlaced.

"How long ago did you finish?"

"Just a bit."

"Have you just been watching me eat?"

"Hey, it's inspiring. I've never seen someone battle through pain so hard just to eat my cooking. It feels good."

Jasmine couldn't tell if Asher was joking or not, and she decided not to ask. She just let out a small huff and raised her knife once more, preparing to begin the arduous work once more. Asher reached out and pulled the knife from her hands, spearing the steak with his own fork and cutting a piece off.

He held it up to her. "Here."

"I told you I don't need help. I can–"

"Look. I'm going to sit here until you're done eating because that's the polite thing to do. So either you stay stubborn and put up with me staring a hole into your head for the next thirty minutes, or you let me help you. That's what a partnership is for, right?"

*Yeah, but you're trying to feed me with the fork you just used.*

Asher wiggled the steak around in the air. "Don't make me pretend this is a bird to get you to open your mouth. I'll do it."

Jasmine was pretty sure her ears had turned as red as molten coal, but she opened her mouth. Asher grinned and fed her the piece of steak.

"There. At least this way you'll get to eat the rest of it before it freezes solid from waiting outside for so long." He started to cut another piece.

Jasmine couldn't find any words to respond to that, so she settled for nothing. The less she had to think, the less embarrassed she'd have to feel. And, as long as she didn't think too hard about the situation, the meal was still delicious and not having to struggle for every bite wasn't exactly objectionable.

Before she knew it, the rest of the steak was gone. Jasmine barely stopped herself from opening her mouth when she realized that the plate was empty, but the slight grin that played across Asher's lips told her he might have noticed anyway.

"Next time, I won't train so hard that I can't move my arms," Jasmine promised. A small part of her that she refused to give voice felt slightly disappointed at that proclamation, which only made her embarrassment rise further.

"Are you sure? It was fun." Asher laughed at the expression on Jasmine's face and stood up, gathering their plates and stacking them up so they'd be easier to bring back to the kitchen. "I won't even dream of touching these until tomorrow. I wouldn't want to deprive you of your chance to do more Keeper duties."

"Thank you," Jasmine said dryly. "Let's just hope assassins don't show up tonight, or I might have to resort to limply slapping them."

"If I'm going to die, I'd rather do it seeing something funny. I can think of worse ways to go out."

"Don't tempt fate. Do you need anything else? Because, if not, I'm going to go wash off and collapse in bed."

"Please do. I won't hold you," Asher said, turning back to his book and flipping it open. "I'll just read a bit longer and then go to sleep myself. Don't forget. If you get that weird feeling again, come wake me up."

"I will," Jasmine promised.

She used her shoulder to push the door to her room open and made a beeline for the washbasin, only pausing to grab a change of clothes for the night.

Of all the benefits Sanctuary provided, clean, heated water was one that Jasmine would be eternally thankful for. Baths were more than just a commodity for anyone living in the gutters – they were the mark of wealth and power.

As for heated baths – unless the sun was so hot outside that it warmed the water, those were a thing of legend. On the other hand, Sanctuary had plumbing and firepits in abundance.

Jasmine slipped into her bath, a relieved sigh slipping from her lips as the tension seeped out of her body. Her arms ached just a little less – though she could still tell that scrubbing herself wasn't going to be particularly fun.

*I could always ask Asher to help.*

Jasmine's face went bright red as the thought sprung unbidden to her mind. She sank deeper into the water, grateful that there wasn't anyone that could see her.

*What's gotten into me?*

An answer to Jasmine's internal question didn't arise, so she let herself soak for a few more minutes until the water started to cool down. She pushed herself into motion, finishing up with her bath and taking care of the rest of her brief preparations for bed.

By the time she staggered out of her bathroom, she was already half asleep. Jasmine didn't even have the energy to pull her covers back. She just flopped down on them, then rolled over to stare up at the ceiling.

It was the same empty, depressing room that she'd fallen asleep in the previous night. The stone was just as cold and unfeeling, and the walls were just as tight. And yet, somehow, it didn't feel nearly as bad.

Sleep took her, and she welcomed it.

# 18

A pained groan ripped Jasmine from her sleep. Her eyes snapped open and she sat bolt upright, her heart slamming in her chest. She moved as quickly and quietly as she could, grabbing her sword from her bedside and pausing to listen.

*Another assassin? I'm not feeling anything off, though. Did I have a nightmare and somehow wake myself up?*

Jasmine crept toward the door. Even if it had been a nightmare, she wasn't about to risk it. As she raised a hand to push the door open, another groan broke the silence.

*Unless Asher already got stabbed, that definitely doesn't sound like an assassin.*

She pushed the door open and stepped into Asher's room. He laid on his bed, mercifully unstabbed. His face was twisted in a rictus of pain and he'd managed to throw his bed sheets off in his sleep, revealing the toned muscles of his bare chest.

Jasmine's breath caught in her throat. Thin black tendrils wound around Asher's chest just beneath the skin, originating at the point where he'd been stabbed the previous night. He groaned again, his hand clutching the sheets like he was trying to strangle them.

"Asher," Jasmine hissed, padding over to him. "Asher! Wake up!"

Asher didn't respond. His back arched and he let out a pained hiss. The lines covering him throbbed with dull, sickly energy.

*Watcher's eyes. How is this just fine? I don't know shit about magic. What am I supposed to do?*

Jasmine dropped her sword and reached out to shake Asher awake. As soon as her hand touched his shoulder, a jolt of ice slammed into her palm. It raced down her arm before she could pull back, driving into her heart like a spike.

She drew in a surprised breath, yanking her hand back and staring at it. The skin was unbroken. The grimace on Asher's face had faded slightly, but it returned an instant later as his wound pulsed.

Jasmine grabbed the blanket and threw it over Asher, using it to avoid touching him as she shook him as hard as she could. "Asher! Wake up!"

The only response was another pained groan – this one louder than the last. The pain was getting worse. Jasmine's eyes darted desperately around the room, but there wasn't anything to help.

Her hand brushed against his arm and Asher drew in a strangled breath. Another jolt of ice raced into her body. But, for a moment, the pain in his features flickered. It returned an instant later.

*Does it stop when I touch him?*

Jasmine didn't wait long to test her theory. She threw the blanket back and grabbed both of Asher's shoulders. Icy cold poured into her like a river, but this time, she didn't let go. The agony wracking Asher's body visibly left his features and the pulsing lines started to fade.

He drew in a gasp and his eyes snapped open. He sat up with a jolt, much as Jasmine had a few seconds ago, and unintentionally threw himself right into her arms. His heart slammed against his chest with such intensity that Jasmine could feel it.

"What – what happened? What was that?" Asher asked, his voice shaky. "I dreamed I was dying. Did I wake you up?"

"I don't think it was a dream," Jasmine said, moving back but not taking her hands off Asher's shoulders. The flow of ice had receded, but there was still a faint prickle against her palms. She nodded down to his chest, where the lines were still fading.

"Fuck me," Asher muttered as he followed Jasmine's gaze. "The Xolani magic?"

"I guess so. Are you… okay?"

"I think so," Asher said. They both watched the last of the lines fade into his chest. He touched the scar gingerly, then frowned. "It doesn't hurt anymore."

Jasmine carefully lifted one of her hands away, pausing to make sure Asher didn't react before she moved the other.

"How did you stop it?" Asher asked.

"I don't know. I just touched you on accident while I was trying to wake you up and it looked like it helped."

"Watcher," Asher breathed. "What did they do to me? I guess I owe you."

"Partners, right?"

Asher snorted. He propped his pillow up behind him, then did a double take. "Wait. Weren't your arms really sore?"

Jasmine looked down at her hands. A frown passed over her face as she flexed her fingers, then held her arms up above her head. "Yeah. That's weird. I feel fine. I feel pretty good, actually."

"Did you somehow eat my magic?" Asher asked, squinting at Jasmine. "Is that healthy?"

"If I knew, I'd answer. It helped though, right?"

"I'd say it did. You need to talk with Riker, though. I can't imagine whatever that wound was trying to do to me was good, and I don't want you dying with me if it's dangerous. No point to give them two kills for the price of one."

Jasmine rolled her eyes. "Considering I'm a dead woman walking, I'll probably take my chances. If you die, it's over for me. Doesn't matter how. I'll talk to Riker, though."

Asher nodded, then twisted to look over his shoulder and out the window. The moon was still high in the sky – it was early in the night.

"I guess I'll just go back to sleep?" Asher said after a few moments. "We can't afford to be awake all night."

"Probably for the best," Jasmine agreed. "Will you be fine?"

"I guess we'll find out." Asher gave Jasmine a grin, but it didn't quite reach his eyes. "Thanks for coming after me. Again."

Jasmine just nodded. She picked her sword back up, still marveling at the fact that her arms didn't hurt anymore. "Goodnight."

"It's a night," Asher agreed. "I just hope it's good."

Jasmine rolled her eyes at the lame attempt at a joke and headed back into her room, trying not to let her concern show on her face.

*I don't even think there's a point talking to Esther – not that I know where she is right now. Riker feels like he might be able to help, but he's equally unlocatable. I wish I'd asked how to get him when I needed his help.*

*I guess we'll just have to make it to tomorrow.*

Jasmine set her sword down against the wall and got back into bed. She held a hand up above her face. It wasn't just the soreness that had left – her bruises had faded as well.

*It's unfortunate I was half asleep when I rolled out of bed. I can't remember if I was sore before I touched Asher or not. There's no way I could have healed this quickly in any normal way, though.*

Unfortunately, try as she might, there were no answers to be found in the night. Jasmine let her hand drop and she let out a slow breath, trying to ease herself back into sleep. If she and Asher kept waking up in the middle of the night, the assassins weren't going to have to do anything else – they'd both die of exhaustion.

A muffled cry pierced Jasmine's rest. She burst into motion, rolling out of bed as the traces of sleep fell away. Cursing under breath, Jasmine darted for the door and into Asher's room.

The black lines coming from his wound had intensified to thick bands – bands that had somehow risen up above his body like tendrils that ended in jagged tips. Asher's eyes were closed in sleep, but his hands clawed at his chest, leaving bloody scratches in their wake.

*What in the Watcher's eyes is that?*

Jasmine didn't let herself think long enough to answer the question. She dashed toward the bed. The tendrils snapped toward her and she ducked, just barely clearing them as she threw herself onto Asher.

Spikes of ice dug into her palms and Jasmine hissed in pain, her grip involuntarily tightening on Asher's shoulders. The thought struck Jasmine that the magic from his wound might have gotten so out of control that touching him wouldn't stop her from getting stabbed by the tendrils, but it was too late.

She braced herself, squeezing her eyes shut and stiffening in preparation to get stabbed. Despite the freezing cold biting at her hands, they didn't give her the mercy of going numb and the pain remained constant.

A second passed. Two. The pain didn't abate, but now new pain came. Jasmine cracked an eye open. Whorls of reddish-black energy danced across her hands, swirling up and into her body.

The bands on Asher's chest had started to recede, the tendrils pulled back into him. His breath came in pained gasps, but his features weren't as twisted in pain as they had been a few seconds ago.

Jasmine didn't dare so much as budge. The cold sensation slowly started to recede as the energy faded, the last remnants draining away from Asher – and into her. He snapped awake a few seconds later, his eyes locking with Jasmine's.

"Well, shit," Asher said breathlessly, summing up Jasmine's thoughts in a perfect two words.

"Are you okay?" Jasmine asked.

"As before, better than I was." Asher grimaced, looking down at his chest. There was nothing left to see. The last traces of magic had faded away into Jasmine. "I feel normal for the most part, but this is a problem. I'm more worried about you. Are you really feeling fine?"

"As far as I can tell, yes," Jasmine muttered. Adrenaline still pumped in her veins and her heart thundered in her chest. "What in the Watcher's eyes did that dagger do to you?"

"Curse me to never sleep again, apparently."

Jasmine's heartbeat started to slow down to a more reasonable speed and she was struck with the realization that she was currently sitting on Asher's chest, pinning him to the bed. She reddened and carefully lifted a hand an inch, waiting to see his reaction.

"Not blowing up," Asher said. "I think it only happens when I sleep."

Jasmine shifted her weight off Asher, moving to sit beside him in bed while leaving one of her hands on his shoulder. Asher shifted into a seated position, then reached up to his shoulders. His hand came back slightly bloodied.

"Sorry," Jasmine said. "I think I scratched you on accident while I was trying to absorb whatever that magic was."

"If I have to choose between getting ripped apart from the

inside or a little scratch, I'll take the latter every single time," Asher said. He chewed his lower lip. "Fuck. You're sure you're fine?"

"As far as I can tell, yes." Jasmine cast her gaze out the window, where the moon had barely made any progress from where it had been when she'd last woken up. "I'm not going to stay fine if I can't get more than ten minutes of sleep at a time, though."

"I'm sorry. I could go try to find–"

"Esther?" Jasmine arched an eyebrow. "Did you really get the idea she'd care? I don't think either of us matter in the grand scheme of things, and if she actually knew what the magic did, she would have told us. I don't trust her."

"Can't say I blame you." Asher's brow darkened and he looked out the window. "You're right, though. At this rate, by the time another assassin shows up, we'll both be so exhausted that we won't even notice them until it's too late. What do you think the chances are that that this won't happen a third time tonight?"

Jasmine pierced Asher with a flat stare. "I'll give you one guess."

Asher sighed. "Yeah, I figured. I guess I'll just stay awake, then. You should go back to bed."

"That's not a solution. I need you to be able to fight as well, remember? That was the whole plan."

"Better one of us than neither. You can't keep waking up to save me."

"I'm well aware. The magic stops when I'm touching you, right? So all I have to do is stay in contact and you can sleep."

Asher nearly choked. He coughed into his hand, quickly turning away, but Jasmine caught a flash of red on his cheeks before he could hide it.

"I guess that would work," Asher said, clearing his throat again. "If you're comfortable with it. I mean, I don't want to–"

"The less you speak, the less awkward this is going to be," Jasmine said, relieved that Asher was too embarrassed to look at her. If he hadn't been, he would have seen that her own face was just as flushed as his.

Asher nodded and laid down slowly, letting Jasmine keep her hand on his shoulder as he moved. She doubted that the magic would return fast enough for it to matter, but at this point, neither one of them wanted to risk it.

She kept her hand between Asher and the bed, letting him lie down on it so she couldn't accidentally pull it away during the middle of the night. It ended up just below the nape of his neck, near his pillow.

"Are you comfortable?" Asher asked. "I can move if–"

"I'm fine," Jasmine said, determined not to think about how warm his skin felt against her hand. Asher's bed was considerably more comfortable than her own, and the pressure of his body against her palm felt oddly comforting.

Part of Jasmine expected she would be completely unable to fall asleep while lying just a foot away from Asher, but weariness overruled her embarrassment and she was fast asleep within minutes.

# 19

Gentle light bathed Jasmine's face. She woke slowly, her mind still in the comforting fuzz of dreams that she'd already forgotten. Her nose twitched and she went to scratch it, pausing as she realized that her arm wasn't responding properly.

She turned over, idly noting that her pillow seemed considerably more comfortable than she remembered – and found herself face to face with Asher. Jasmine nearly bolted straight upright as the memories of the previous night finally clicked back, but she managed to keep herself from moving at the last moment.

Either she or Asher had shifted during the night because they were only a few inches away from each other. He'd managed to completely pin her arm down rather than just her hand. Jasmine remained locked in place as she tried to think on how to extract herself without accidentally waking Asher up.

*He's still sleeping. If I stop touching him now, the magic might trigger and wake him up again. It's probably for the best that we both have enough rest. I guess I need to stay here.*

She wasn't as annoyed about that decision as she felt like she should have been, but Jasmine let her eyes drift back shut. There was nothing to be done about it.

Asher kept his breathing steady, vividly aware of Jasmine's arm beneath him. Her body was so close to his that he could feel the gentle warmth coming off it. At some point in the night, he'd managed to roll over to face her, but moving now would mean admitting he was awake.

He cracked an eye open to take a peek at Jasmine's face. Her head was stilted slightly toward him, her eyes closed in sleep. It was wrong, but he couldn't pull his gaze away. She was beautiful – but not as beautiful as she was when she was awake and smiling.

A memory of her sword knocking his from his hands and flicking up to his neck – the victorious smirk already playing across her lips – flashed through Asher's head.

*Damn it. I need to stop this. She's not here by choice. She's given so much for me already, and she can barely even tolerate me. But damn, she looks beautiful when she gets competitive. It's hard not to egg her on.*

*Actually, she just always looks beautiful.*

Asher forced himself to close his eyes again. The thoughts were just that – thoughts. A bitter smile flickered across his lips. As if he needed more reasons to hate the Last Light. A pang gripped his heart at the thought of his family.

He'd never been close with them, but they'd still been *his*. The assassins hadn't just taken them from him. They'd forced him back into the role that he'd hoped he'd avoided. The one that should have been meant for his brother, Jelan. The one that had actually been able to use his magic.

The one that hadn't been a disappointment.

*And to top it off, as if that wasn't enough shit, the girl I was going to ask to court is now my Keeper and I can't make a move on her without abusing the relationship a Starvein and a Keeper have.*

*Watcher. What did I do to deserve this?*

There was no response. Asher resisted the urge to sigh. Wallowing on his losses, especially his family, wasn't something he could afford to do. He didn't have the time for it yet. That would come when the Last Light were dealt with – or when he died. Whichever came first.

For now, all he could do was lie there and try not to feel too guilty about how much he was enjoying the feeling of Jasmine beside him. Close, but impossibly far.

A knock on the door broke the peaceful morning. Jasmine felt Asher rise off her arm, and she let herself open her eyes. Asher sat beside her, the sheets bunched around his waist. The sunlight had managed to land just so it illuminated his bare back, and Jasmine had to pull her eyes away from the muscles covering it before she got caught staring.

"Well, it worked," Asher said, touching the scar over his heart gingerly. "Thank you, Jasmine. I'm not sure what I'd do without you."

"Die, probably," Jasmine said, a small grin flickering across her face before the seriousness of the situation settled back over her. "You're okay, then?"

"Thanks to you, yeah. I am." Asher paused for a moment, searching for words. "I don't think I could have asked for a better Keeper."

Jasmine's cheeks flushed with a mixture of pride and embarrassment. She sat up and got out of bed, straightening out her clothes as best she could and failing miserably to remove the wrinkles from them. "I don't think that's true, but thanks. But… did I hear the door, or was that a dream?"

"No, I heard it too."

"It's probably Riker. He's got good timing. Hopefully he can at least take a guess at what magic was messing with you."

Jasmine walked over to the door and pulled it open, craning her neck back to look at Riker's face – but he wasn't there. Her gaze lowered and she blinked in surprise, her eyes not fully comprehending the face in front of her for a moment.

"Lydia?"

"Jas!" Lydia beamed at her. "I thought I'd come check up on you. You should… uh, probably fix your hair a bit. I've never seen you sleep in late, and it'll be bad if Asher–"

Lydia trailed off, her eyes moving past Jasmine and into the room, where Asher sat bare-chested in bed. Her eyes drifted back to Jasmine. "Ooooh."

"Wait. Stop," Jasmine said, raising her hands. "It's not–"

"You little liar!" Lydia exclaimed. She leaned in, lowering her voice to a conspiratorial whisper. "I *knew* you were full of it, for the record. There's no way you didn't take a bite out of that. You have to give me the details. Was–"

Jasmine clapped a hand over Lydia's mouth. Lydia licked her palm and Jasmine yanked her hand back with a curse, wiping it off on her shirt. "Seriously? What are you, ten?"

Lydia snickered and peered past Jasmine. "Hey, Asher. How's Jas treating you?"

"Better than I deserve," Asher said, sliding out of bed and turning to grab a shirt – only to reveal the scratches on the backs of his shoulders. Lydia opened her mouth, then closed it and sent a *very* pointed look at Jasmine.

"Stop," Jasmine begged. "Please."

"I bet that's not what you were saying last–"

Jasmine prodded Lydia in the stomach and the other girl

doubled over in a mixture of a laugh and a wheeze. By the time she straightened back up, Asher had gotten himself clothed. Jasmine sent her a pleading look and Lydia finally showed mercy, letting the topic drop.

"I take it things aren't as bad as they could be, then?" Lydia asked.

Jasmine glanced down the halls to make sure nobody was around, then pulled Lydia inside and closed the door behind her.

"Depends on what you mean by bad," Jasmine said.

"We're supposed to keep it secret," Asher pointed out.

"Don't worry. I won't spread rumors about you," Lydia promised, pressing a hand over her heart. "I swear on the Watcher's eyes. There's nothing I like more than forbidden–"

"Not that," Jasmine said quickly. She glanced at Asher, painfully aware of how hot her cheeks felt. Lydia was not helping the situation at all, but having another friendly face was a relief, no matter how shameless it was. "We can trust her, Asher."

"You're the Keeper," Asher said, inclining his head. "Despite what they said, I don't think just knowing is going to put her in danger – so long as she can actually keep a secret."

Lydia picked up on the serious tone of the conversation and her smile fell away. "What are you two talking about?"

"An assassin showed up two nights ago and tried to kill Asher," Jasmine said. "We barely managed to stop him in time."

"Watcher's eyes," Lydia breathed. "You beat an assassin?"

"More like I stalled him," Jasmine said. "Asher got stabbed by a Xolani weapon, and Esther seems to think that the assassins are going to come back. Did a guy called Riker show up and start teaching your class?"

"Yeah. He's really strict, but I think he's good. He definitely knows what he's doing. Why?"

"He was the one that saved us at the last second," Jasmine said. "If he hadn't popped up, then we'd both be dead."

"Well, thank the Watcher he did," Lydia said with a shake of your head. "You've got to be relieved, then. As long as that guy is around, you're safe, right?"

Jasmine snorted. "I wish. He's not actually watching over us all the time. He just happened to get there on time. Esther doesn't want it to be obvious that a real Keeper is protecting Asher or the assassins might give up.

Lydia's eyes widened in disbelief. "She's using you as bait to lure out an assassin?"

Jasmine's clenched tightened at her sides. "Yes."

"That rancid old dog," Lydia swore. "I always knew that she was an asshole under that polite exterior. Nobody makes people sprint until they throw up because they're a saint. She's just jealous because of how saggy her–"

Asher let out a snort of laughter and Lydia caught herself, clearing her throat. Jasmine was surprised to find how relieved she felt that Lydia had believed her without an instant of hesitation.

It wasn't like Esther had ever been excessively cruel to them before, so she'd half expected Lydia to scoff in disbelief at the idea that Esther was sacrificing Jasmine and Asher – but, now that she thought about it, it wasn't really all that out of character for the elderly Keeper.

*Everything she's ever done has been for the duty of being a Keeper and the kingdom. I guess she never cared about us as anything other than a job. I don't know what I would have done if Lydia didn't believe me, though.*

"Well, look on the bright side," Lydia said. "It looks like you're getting along better than you did before. That's good, right?"

"Yeah." Jasmine snorted. "We can hold hands and prance on our way down to the afterlife after an assassin kills both of us."

"It's not Lydia's fault," Asher said. "But Jasmine is right. We're relatively screwed, and you should be careful. You don't want to get wrapped up in this, or Esther might genuinely end up adding you to the sacrifice list."

Lydia's face paled, but she stood her ground. "She can't do anything if she doesn't know. I had no idea things were this bad, though. I – wait."

She grabbed Jasmine by the arm and pulled her close so she could whisper into her ear.

"Didn't you say the noble you got assigned to had his whole family killed?" Lydia whispered. "So Asher…"

Jasmine winced and nodded. "Yeah."

"Shit," Lydia said. "I'm sorry for your loss, Asher."

"It's fine," Asher said, pressing his lips together. "We weren't close. I'd rather not dwell on the past until we've dealt with the future."

"Is there anything I can do to help?" Lydia asked. She paused for a moment, then cleared her throat. "Uh… other than helping fight. I'm not really all that great at that, and I'd prefer myself unstabbed."

"Can't say I blame you," Asher said. "But I think it's probably best you avoid getting wrapped up any further. I don't think cither Jasmine or I want to see someone else get killed for this."

"Asher is right," Jasmine said. "Just knowing that you're looking out for me helps more than you realize, Lydia. Also, thanks for the meal yesterday. It was incredible."

"I'm great, I know." Lydia smirked, but the smile fell away quickly as a frown replaced it. She chewed her lower lip. "You're sure there isn't anything you need, though?"

"I'm not sure you could help us with it, even if there was," Jasmine said. "Do you really want to get on Esther's bad side? Asher wasn't joking. If she was willing to toss us to the side, she probably wouldn't mind adding you to the pile."

"I'm not going to try to fight Esther," Lydia said with a snort. "I'm not suicidal. But you've got to be trying to train really hard, right? Maybe I could get some of the other students together and we could help get food or the like to you. That would save a lot of time, right?"

The offer was tempting. It really was. Jasmine nearly said yes on the spot, but she caught herself. It would bring too many people into the fold. Even if Lydia came up with an excuse to justify it, it just wasn't safe.

With incredible reluctance, Jasmine shook her head. "Thank you, Lydia, but I can't accept. It's too dangerous. Asher is teaching me how to cook, and I'm sure it won't take as long once I stop ruining half the ingredients I touch. I definitely wouldn't say no to any of your food when you have time to make it, though."

"Fine. I'll think of something else, though. I'm not leaving you like this, even if Esther will. Maybe I could help make traps! You could rig the windows."

*That's... not the worst idea.*

"You know how to make traps?" Asher asked, blinking. "When'd we learn that?"

"Personal skill." Lydia grinned. "I'm great with ropes too. If Jasmine needs lessons, send her to me."

"Lydia!" Jasmine hissed.

Lydia snickered. "I should probably get out of here before someone notices I'm visiting. Can I get my plates back so I can bring something back tomorrow?"

Jasmine hurried to comply, mostly so she wouldn't leave Lydia and Asher alone in the same room for too long. She grabbed the wrapped box from where they laid in her room and scurried back into rejoin the others.

"Here," Jasmine said, handing the box to Lydia. "Thanks again. You have no idea how good your timing was."

"Don't worry about it. I've got your back," Lydia said. "But you can return the favor if you really want to."

"Really? How?"

"Send any cute Starvein boys my way. Girls too, while you're at it. I think I'd actually prefer the latter. Make sure they aren't assholes first, though," Lydia said. She went for the door, then paused. "On second thought, they can be a bit of an asshole. They've just got to be cute enough to justify it."

Jasmine rolled her eyes. Lydia wasn't very good at being serious, but something about her made it impossible to remain worried.

"Noted," Asher said, not even the slightest traces of amusement in his voice. "I'll keep an eye out."

"She was joking," Jasmine said.

Lydia just winked. "Don't get killed tonight, okay? I'm going to be really pissed if I make you food and there's nobody to eat it."

She pushed the door open and poked her head out, checking to make sure Esther wasn't there before zipping out into the hall.

"Well," Asher said after a moment. "She's… energetic."

"Tell me about it," Jasmine said. She glanced down at her rumpled clothes, then gingerly touched her hair. Lydia was right – it definitely looked like she'd just rolled out of bed. "I'm going to go get ready for the day."

"Sounds good," Asher said. "After that, I think I might need you to throw some things at me. I need to try and get my magic working. If I don't, forget the assassins. Qien is going to kill me first."

# 20

Asher sat cross legged on his bed, his book on magic open in his lap and his eyes closed. Jasmine stood across from him, armed with just about every balled-up sock that she and Asher had between them.

"This doesn't feel like it's going to work," Jasmine said.

"Just start throwing them. I need to trigger my activation event."

"By having a sock lobbed at your head?"

"It'll be stressful. Have you ever tried to focus on something while someone is distracting you by–"

A sock bounced off his head. Asher flinched and swore under his breath. "I wasn't ready."

"You told me to start," Jasmine said as she picked up another sock. "For the record, I still don't think this is going to work. Besides, what's the point of having the book open? Your eyes are closed. You can't read it."

"Maybe I'll absorb something by being next to it," Asher grumbled. He drew in a deep breath, letting it out slowly as his forehead creased in concentration. His tongue poked ever so slightly out of his lips as he tried to connect with his magic, and –

Another sock bounced off his head. Asher's eye twitched. A laugh nearly bubbled out of Jasmine's mouth, but she managed to strangle it at the last second. She wasn't so sure if it was the kind of stress Asher needed, but it was funny.

She threw another sock, then followed it up with a second one right after. They each struck the center of his forehead. Asher ignored them, fully focused on his meditation. Jasmine went to throw another sock, but paused.

*I guess they should be more of a surprise, right? If he gets used to getting smacked with socks, then they aren't going to be very surprising.*

Jasmine lowered her hand to wait for a more opportune time to throw. Now that it was silent, it was hard to keep ignoring her thoughts. And, especially with Asher's eyes closed, it was hard not to stare at least a little.

It wasn't like there was anything else to do. She'd never really had time to think about anything other than survival in the gutters. And, even after she'd gotten to Sanctuary, the only thought on her mind had been survival and getting stronger.

Jasmine's hand tingled as her thoughts drifted back to the previous night. The warmth of Asher lying beside her. The gentle curve of his lips and the cocky smirk that usually resided on them.

She shook her head in an attempt to clear it and grabbed a sock, throwing it at Asher's head. He let out a startled curse.

*I can't think about this. I'm a Keeper. We agreed that we'd both do our jobs so we wouldn't end up dead. It's my job to protect him, not ogle him.*

Asher's toned jaw clenched in irritation, and Jasmine caught herself staring at it. She grabbed another sock and threw it at him, but it flew right past his face and missed completely.

"Did you just miss?" Asher asked, a grin pulling at the corner of his lip.

The second sock hit him straight in the face, shutting him up.

*I don't think this is working.*

"I don't think this is working," Asher said. "I'm not stressed. I'm just annoyed."

"That's because there's no threat to you from a Watcher damned sock," Jasmine said. "If anything, you're just getting surprised."

"It was an idea, okay? Do you have a better one?"

Jasmine chewed her lower lip in thought. "What if we sparred? You could try to connect to your magic while I try to beat you up."

"That sounds horrible." Asher tossed his book onto the bed and stood up. "Perfect. Normal sparring is already stressful. Doing it with my concentration split is a great idea. You're a genius."

"I was joking," Jasmine said, following after Asher as he headed for the door. "Don't you think we should stay here in case Riker shows up? We need to talk to him about your wound."

"If he was going to show up, he would have. Whether it happens now or later doesn't really matter. It's not like he can uncurse me, or he'd have done it already." Asher shrugged as they walked. "I'd rather just keep doing what I can. I don't want to rely on other people."

"Fair enough," Jasmine admitted. "You do realize that if you want this to be stressful, I can't hold back?"

"Hey, I can take a little pain."

"We'll see."

They arrived at the Keeper training grounds some time later, claiming an unused room for themselves. Jasmine and Asher both selected a wooden sword and stood across from each other in the center of the ring.

"So how are we doing this?" Jasmine asked. "You aren't planning to sit down or anything, are you?"

Asher shook his head. "No. That would just be the sock thing all over again, just more painful. I need to feel like I'm in danger, so I guess we should just spar like normal. I'll try to connect to my magic while we do it. The book had some suggestions on ways to establish the connection."

"Don't you think you'd have already done it if it were that easy?" Jasmine frowned. "We've sparred before."

"Which is why I need you to come at me as if you were an assassin. I need to feel like I'm really in danger," Asher said. "Just... try not to kill me. And if I suddenly freeze up or start doing some Starvein stuff, don't keep smacking me."

Jasmine sent him a doubtful look, then shrugged. "If you're sure. You know more than I do."

"Not by much," Asher muttered. He raised his sword, settling into a fighting stance. "Okay. Don't stop until I tell you to, though. The only way to make it feel real is to replicate a real situation as much as possible. Its either this or we'll be waiting for the next assassin to pop up."

"Ready when you are."

"I'm ready."

Jasmine lurched forward, sending her sword whistling at Asher's side. He shifted his blade to block the strike and Jasmine redirected her sword before it could touch, aiming for Asher's fingers.

He yanked his sword down, managing to block the strike safely. The movement put him off balance, and Jasmine took the opportunity to jab for his stomach. Asher twisted out of the way, but Jasmine didn't let off the attack.

She pressed him relentlessly, refusing to give him an opportunity to strike back. Almost unconsciously, she started to copy the movements that Riker had been showing her the day before. The relentless, constant advance, only pausing for long enough to give Asher an instant to recover.

Asher faltered under her assault. He skipped to the side, catching a blow to the stomach in the process. Grunting in pain, he tried to retaliate with a swing at her legs, but Jasmine swept him off his feet before he could get close.

He hit the ground with a grunt and rolled to the side, narrowly avoiding Jasmine's sword as it plunged into the dirt.

"Watcher's eyes, are you actually trying to kill me?" Asher cursed as he scrambled back upright.

Jasmine didn't respond. She intensified her assault, hammering blows into Asher's sword. He gritted his teeth, but his defense was even worse than it normally was. It was clear that trying to split his attention between the fight and calling on his magic was too much to handle.

*I'm not stopping until he asks me to. This is what he wants.*

Her sword slammed into Asher's again, ripping it from his hands and sending it spinning across the room. He swore, earning himself a sharp rap across the shoulders as he turned to grab it.

Jasmine lunged, throwing her own sword to the side and sweeping Asher off his feet. He went down with a grunt and Jasmine jumped on top of him, locking her legs around his and grabbing his hands. She yanked them above his head, pinning him to the ground.

Adrenaline and energy pumped in her veins. She didn't know what it was, but she felt *strong.* Stronger than she ever had before. Asher's hips bucked beneath her as he tried to throw her off, but he couldn't get her to budge.

Jasmine grinned down at him, her hair hanging around her face as he writhed beneath her. "You're going to have to try harder than that. You're dead, Asher. Or worse, kidnapped."

He gritted his teeth – and a spike of ice drove into Jasmine's chest. She drew in a startled breath and pulled back, but the sensation didn't relent. Frost felt like it was blooming inside her, stretching out to fill every part of her body. A flash of black light lit Asher's eyes, flickering through them like a bolt of lightning.

"Jas! Are you okay?" Asher asked worriedly.

The sensation vanished. Jasmine's heart thundered in her chest.

"You did it. Didn't you feel the magic?"

"I did?" Asher blinked, and for a moment, the only sound in the room was their heavy breathing. "I didn't feel anything at all."

"Your eyes flashed black," Jasmine said. "They're gold again now, but for a moment, they changed color. That's definitely magic. I thought you were trying to freeze me solid. You're saying that wasn't you?"

"Seriously?" Asher's brow furrowed. "I didn't feel anything, and I never would have tried to use my magic *on* you. But if you felt something... it's not my curse, is it? It didn't hurt you?"

"I feel fine," Jasmine said. She leaned back, only half aware that she was still sitting on Asher's waist until she felt something shift. Her eyes darted down to his and their faces both reddened.

Jasmine hurriedly got to her feet, then held her hand out. Asher took it, letting Jasmine pull him to his feet. He adjusted his clothes, then cleared his throat.

"You're sure you're fine?"

"Yes. You did magic," Jasmine insisted. "Do it again."

Asher closed his eyes and pressed his lips together. Jasmine watched expectantly. A few seconds passed, and he opened them once again, shaking his head.

"It's not working."

"You probably need to replicate the feeling you had a moment ago," Jasmine said. "Whatever you're doing now is wrong. You just look constipated."

Asher let out a snort of laughter. "I didn't do anything that different."

"Just walk me through it. Sometimes things make more sense when you say them out loud. What were you thinking?"

"I was just thinking about the fight."

"Seriously? That's it?"

It took Asher a moment to respond. "Yeah."

Jasmine's eyes narrowed. "Think deeper. You hesitated for a moment. Come on, Asher. Wasn't the whole damn point of this to take it seriously? Why are you half-assing it?"

"I told you!" Asher snapped. "I was just thinking about the fight!"

Jasmine shoved him back a step and he stumbled, catching himself before he could fall. "What's your problem?"

"Replicate it, then," Jasmine said. "Come at me."

Asher didn't wait to oblige her. He shot forward, but Jasmine was faster. Either Asher was distracted or he was still thinking too much about magic, because she slipped right past his guard.

She slammed her shoulder into Asher's, twisting his body and slamming him to the ground. He let out a grunt, trying to roll free, but Jasmine wrapped herself around him. The strange energy was pumping in her body again, making every movement stronger. Making every movement faster.

Within an instant, Jasmine had Asher completely pinned. Her legs locked around his and her arms pressed his to the ground in an inescapable hold. Their faces were just inches away from each other.

"Think!" Jasmine snapped. "What were you–"

An icy spike that was starting to grow familiar slammed into Jasmine. She tensed and drew in a surprised hiss. Asher's eyes flashed black just before she released him.

"There! You did it again. Did you feel it?" Jasmine demanded, ignoring the chill as it faded. "What did you think about?"

"You!" Asher snapped. "Okay? I was thinking about you."

They stared at each other. This time, Jasmine didn't move to get off Asher.

"I'm sorry. I shouldn't have said anything. Ignore me," Asher said, pressing his lips together and turning his head to avert his gaze.

*What do you mean me? What were you thinking about me?*

Jasmine only barely managed to stop herself before she could ask. They were trying to make Asher's magic work. That was it. He was just distracted.

"Wait," Asher said, stiffening beneath Jasmine. "That's it. You."

"Me? What do you mean?"

"You were absorbing my magic at night," Asher said, starting to speak faster as excitement entered his words. "I think it goes the other way, too. What if the Xolani dagger messed with my magic? I think you're somehow storing it. I don't think I can use my magic unless I'm in contact with you."

# 21

"Do it again, then," Jasmine said, grabbing Asher's hand.

He hesitated for a moment, then nodded. Spines of ice prickled at Jasmine, but now that she was ready for it, it wasn't as much of a surprise as it had been before.

"Okay," Jasmine breathed. "Yeah. I believe you."

"Does it hurt?" Asher asked worriedly. "Are you–"

"Watcher's eyes, I'm not a baby. If it hurt, I'd tell you," Jasmine said, keeping her hold on Asher's hand and not letting him pull away. "Do something with it. Your magic can't just be making me feel cold, can it? I also felt… strong. Like, a lot stronger than normal."

"Wait, cold?" Asher frowned. "Hold on. That's what I'm supposed to feel like. One moment."

The tip of Asher's tongue poked out of his mouth as he focused. The frost within Jasmine shifted. It coursed down her arm and through her fingers. Asher drew in a surprised breath. His eyes flickered, crackles of black energy lighting them up.

"Can you let go of one hand?" Asher asked.

Jasmine obliged, and Asher lifted his right hand. He pressed two fingers together and pulled them apart slowly. Black electricity crackled between them, hissing and popping hungrily. It fizzed out an instant later and Asher let out a victorious laugh.

"Hah! I did magic!"

Jasmine let go of Asher's other hand, a grin crossing her own lips.

"More like you can steal mine."

"You stole it first," Asher said, smiling up at her. His eyes twinkled with delight. "I can't believe it. I thought I was the world's worst Starvein. Magic is supposed to come easy. The hard part is not taking too much, but I couldn't use it at all. This makes so much sense."

"Although it does make me wonder why you couldn't do it before," Jasmine pointed out. "It's not like Starveins are made. They're born."

Asher's grin faltered for a moment. "Yeah. That's a good question – but right now, I don't care. I'm too happy."

"Do you think it's possible you're somehow draining magic?" Jasmine asked. "Maybe you could do it by touching other people with magic in them?"

"That's possible. We'll have to test it." Asher chewed his lower lip. "And we need to figure out what's going on with you. If you're actually somehow housing my magic, I'm worried about what it might do to you. You aren't a Starvein."

"Somehow, I don't think this is a common occurrence. I doubt we're going to get help from anyone, but I'm not sure if telling Riker or Esther is a good idea. Are they really on our side?"

Asher made a good point. Jasmine scrunched her nose. "Damn. Why does this have to be so complicated? What about Qien?"

"We might not have a choice. He's an asshole to everyone," Asher muttered. "And that might include Esther and Riker. I don't want to put you at risk on accident."

He made to get up, then paused. "Are we still sparring or something?"

"No. Why?"

"You're still sitting on me. I can't get up."

"Oh. Right. Did you want me to get up?"

"I didn't realize not getting up was an option," Asher said slowly.

Jasmine's ears heated and she shot to her feet, brushing herself off.

*Did you want me to get up? What kind of lame line is that? Did I get hit on the head?*

Asher stood up and adjusted his clothes. He cleared his throat. He held a hand out and concentrated on it for a moment, then sighed. "Well, I can't use it again. It definitely only works when we're touching."

Jasmine held her hand out. Asher made to take it, then paused. "We should wait. At the very least, I'd like to talk to Qien and get his take on this."

"Probably a good idea," Jasmine said, letting her hand drop and ignoring the small pang of disappointment that ran through her. "I guess we should go find him, huh?"

"Yeah. Let's do that and then go get some food. I don't know about you, but I'm starved."

Jasmine nodded in agreement. They grabbed their swords from where they'd fallen on the ground and returned them to their proper places on the wall before setting out to find Qien.

Despite the potential threat of the situation, Jasmine couldn't help the small flutter of excitement in her chest. She didn't technically have magic of her own, but sharing it with Asher – that wasn't too bad either.

They found Qien about thirty minutes later. The Starvein Halls were huge, and it turned out that there was more than one teacher there. That surprised Jasmine, as the Keepers had only had Esther for as long as she'd been there, but that evidently didn't hold true for the nobles.

She and Asher located three other professors before they finally managed to get lucky and located one of Qien's classes just as it started to wrap up. The two of them waited outside in the hall as the students piled out of it, not going in until everyone had left.

Qien stood at the stand, sifting through some papers and organizing them into the front flap of a book. He glanced up as they approached, his lips pursed in disapproval.

*I swear Qien left first in Asher's class. Does he just like these guys more or something?*

"Mister Asher. Xolani," Qien said, greeting them in turn. "It is not yet time for our class."

"I know," Asher said. "There's something really important I'd like to speak with you about."

"You may save it for class," Qien said curtly. "I have better things to do with my time than answer why you can't use your magic."

*Did Asher talk to him about it before?*

"I'm not here about that," Asher said. "I'm here because I *can* use my magic, and it doesn't work the way it should."

"I can assure you that your magic works exactly as it does for everyone else," Qien said, his brow furrowing as the annoyance turned to mild anger. "Everyone interprets and uses magic differently, but the core aspect remains the same. Now, if you would, please get out of my way."

"No," Asher said. "I'm not making things up. I can't use my magic unless I'm touching Jasmine."

Hearing it like that sounded a lot more embarrassing than

Jasmine had expected it would, but she didn't let it show on her face. The last thing she needed to do was blush in front of Qien.

The professor paused. The papers in his hands wilted slightly as his grip slacked. "You what?"

"I can only use magic when I'm touching Jasmine," Asher repeated. "And I don't feel it – she does. I think she's somehow storing my magical energy, and she might even be using it."

"Wait, what?" Jasmine asked. "I didn't–"

"You were stronger and faster than normal, right? That doesn't just randomly happen. You were using magic," Asher said.

"You are claiming that the Xolani is housing your magic, and that you have none without her?" Qien asked, his eyes narrow.

"Yes."

That seemed to keep his attention. Qien set his papers down and stepped around the podium, crossing his arms in front of his chest and pressing his lips so thin that they turned white. His gaze bored into them like a drill. "Go on, then. Demonstrate."

Asher held his hands out and focused on them. Several seconds passed. Nothing happened. He licked his lips, then raised his eyes back to Qien. "I'm not sure how to show you that my magic *doesn't* work. It just won't."

"Then show me how it does work," Qien snapped. "I am not interested in hearing of your incompetence."

Asher held his hand out to Jasmine. She took it. Asher sent her a questioning glance, making sure she was ready. Jasmine inclined her head slightly, bracing herself. Spines of ice prickled within her, coursing down her arm and into her chest.

A crackle of black energy flitted through Asher's eyes. He pulled his fingers apart and lightning arced between their pads, hissing and popping hungrily.

"See?" Asher asked. "And I–"

"Hold still," Qien barked. He grabbed Jasmine's arm and yanked her hand out of Asher's grip.

"What was that for?" Jasmine asked, pulling her hand out of Qien's thin-fingered grasp. The man was surprisingly strong for his build. He looked like a small breeze could have blown him over, but her wrist throbbed faintly with the force of his fingers.

Qien ignored her. His eyes were locked on Asher's fingers, which still had lightning crackling between them. Asher followed his gaze. None of them spoke for a second.

"Hold it," Qien ordered. "Do not let the energy fade."

Asher's brow furrowed, but whatever he was doing didn't seem to do much. After just a few more seconds, the last traces of magic faded away and he shook his head helplessly. "I tried, but it feels like I'm trying to scoop water from an empty well."

"Which means you are either an anomaly or incompetent." Qien took Asher's wrist between two fingers, not even bothering to hide his annoyance. Even though he was clearly interested, the professor was making it abundantly clear how much he disliked them.

*What is this guy's problem? I'm not asking for him to treat us like little princes, but would it kill him to at least be slightly respectful?*

"What are you doing?" Asher asked.

"I am diagnosing. Use your magic and see if it works when I am the one in contact with you."

Asher turned his attention to his other hand, but it quickly became clear that nothing had changed. "Nothing. It feels like it isn't there at all."

"Close your eyes."

"Why–"

"I did not ask. I told," Qien said curtly. "As of the moment, I have a mind to believe that you are simply so starved for the touch of the Xolani that you have rendered yourself incompetent. If that is the case, I will hang you from the rafters by your feet until the blood drains from your loins and back into your head."

Asher's jaw clenched – but only for an instant. He closed his eyes, keeping his expression even. Quin snapped his fingers impatiently, gesturing to Jasmine.

"Touch his hand with a single finger," Qien said. "Asher, attempt to use your magic when contact is established."

Jasmine reached out, but Qien caught her hand before she could reach Asher. She looked at him in surprise. The professor held a finger to his lips, then rested one of his own fingers on the back of Asher's hand.

A second passed.

"I told you to use your magic," Qien said, irritation seeping into his voice. "What are you waiting for?"

"I'm trying!" Asher protested. "What did you do? Why isn't it working?"

"Continue trying. Jasmine, touch him with a second finger," Qien said. He dragged Jasmine like a ragdoll, pressing one of her fingers to Asher. The way he was handling her felt more like the way one would a random tool rather than another living being.

But, the moment Jasmine's finger touched Asher's skin, jagged spikes of ice dug into her innards. The feeling was far stronger than it ever had been before, and Jasmine let out a hiss of surprise and pain. A loud crackle ripped through the room as a swirl of black lightning roared to life between Asher's fingers.

Qien removed his finger, watching Asher's expression like a hawk. Nothing changed. He put his finger back, then tossed Jasmine's hand away. Several seconds later, the magic faded away and dissipated into tiny wisps.

"How odd," Qien murmured.

"What? Did you find something out?" Asher asked. "And can I open my eyes?"

"Yes," Qien said. "And yes. It appears I was incorrect. You are indeed an anomaly. If only you had chosen something useful to be unique in."

Asher rubbed the back of his hand. "So it's not just some kind of mental block?"

"It is not. You are drawing magic from the Xolani. Congratulations. You have found a new way to disappoint me." Qien grabbed Jasmine's chin and pulled her head up to study her face, once again moving with far more speed than his frame should have been possible with.

Before Jasmine could even process it, Asher slapped Qien's hand away from her. The professor's eyes widened.

"What are you–"

"Ask before you touch her," Asher snapped. "She's not your student. She's my Keeper."

It really hadn't been that big of a deal, and Jasmine had been more annoyed than anything else, but warmth welled in her chest at the protective anger in Asher's tone. She was pretty sure it wasn't going to end well, though. Disobeying Qien when they were asking for his help was a great way to get kicked out.

But, instead of getting angry, Qien let his hand drop. "My apologies. *May* I inspect you, Keeper?"

"Uh, yeah. That's fine," Jasmine said hesitantly, half expecting Qien to blow up in their faces. But, to her surprise, all he did was lean closer, peering into her eyes with a thoughtful frown.

"I am going to touch your arm." Qien's tone made it clear that he was not willing to word the request any kinder.

Jasmine nodded and Qien took her arm by the wrist. They stood in awkward silence for a few moments. A slight prickling sensation ran across Jasmine's skin. It was reminiscent of the energy that she felt when Asher had used magic from her, but it wasn't nearly as intense.

After nearly a minute, Qien let go. He wiped his hand off on his shirt, then let out a harrumph. "This is... odd. You have magic."

Jasmine's breath caught in her chest, and her best attempts to keep her expression under control failed.

*I'm a Starvein? I can use magic?*

"You are not a Starvein," Qien said, reading Jasmine like an open book and crushing her hopes before they could start to grow. "A Starvein's very existence is magic. Their bodies are infused with it, changed to be able to channel it without dying. You… your body is normal. But, for some reason, you have a store of magic within you."

"What does that mean?" Jasmine asked. "And what about Asher?"

"Asher appears to be the exact opposite of you," Qien said. "His body is changed, as a Starvein's should be. He is like a rough piece of quartz trapped in a craggy quarry – utterly worthless in his current form, but he has the potential that every Starvein does. And yet… there is no magic in him. He is empty, which should not be possible. A Starvein without magic is a dead Starvein."

"I'm pretty sure I'm not dead," Asher said.

"So I can see," Qien turned back to his podium and started to gather his papers back up. He piled them back into their folder and closed it, tucking it under his arm. "You are capable of channeling magic, but you do not have a store of it. The Xolani has somehow stolen your magical well."

"I didn't steal anything!" Jasmine exclaimed. "I–"

"At the moment, I am largely unconcerned with *how* you have come into possession of Asher's magical well," Qien said. He tapped his folder with a finger, then sighed. "Your situation is interesting and does warrant some degree of research, but it does not appear to be imminently dangerous. If we were in any other time, I would have been thrilled to spend extensive time looking into whatever it is you have done, but that is no longer the case."

"What do you mean? You can't help us fix it? I think I know what caused it. It was–"

"Stop," Qien ordered, cutting Asher off mid-sentence. "I am

aware of what you are about to mention. I believe you were informed not to go about spreading information. It is not safe."

Asher closed his mouth with a grimace. "So what are we supposed to do?"

"For the time being? Nothing. Your magic still functions. You simply need the Xolani by you. And, since she is your Keeper, that should not be much of a problem. If you want to speak to me on any other matters, I suggest you come by my rooms after lab."

Qien strode past them, pausing to glance back when he reached the top of the stairs. "Just do not forget that your magic is coming *from* the Xolani, so overdrawing will do to her what it did to her namesakes."

And, with that, he swept away and left them standing in the center of the classroom, unsure if they were better or worse off than they had been before.

# 22

The rest of the day passed quickly. Asher and Jasmine made lunch together in the kitchen about an hour after everyone else had already eaten – granting them free reign of its facilities without having to worry about someone seeing them.

Qien's class was about the same as it always seemed to be, and it passed by quickly. When it was done, Jasmine escorted Asher to Qien's office before setting back off to the kitchen – he wasn't going to be in danger while he was in the professor's office, and making something to eat early would save her a lot of time.

Riker was waiting for Jasmine at the door to their room. He didn't even say anything – he just set off down the hall. Jasmine cast one last glance at the door and her awaiting meal before following after him.

"Are you prepared for training?" Riker asked once they reached the training room and the wall had rumbled shut behind them.

"Can I ask a question first?" Jasmine asked.

"You may ask. I may not answer."

"Did you know about Asher's magic?" Jasmine watched Riker's

expression carefully, but he was about as easy to read as a dinner plate. There wasn't even a twinge of emotion in his expression.

"Asher is a Starvein."

"That's not what I meant," Jasmine said with a firm shake of her head. She was committed now. There was no point backing down. "You said I'd be recovered by today, but there's no way in the world a normal person would recover from the beating you gave me yesterday overnight. The only way that would be possible is if I had magic."

"Asher's magic?" To Jasmine's surprise, Riker's brow twitched in surprise. "That... explains much."

"Explains what? If you know anything about this, please tell me. We need every piece of leverage we can get."

Riker's features returned to their normal placid form. It was several long moments before he spoke. "It is possible to learn how to see magic. I can see it like strokes of a brush over the canvas of the world. You had more magic than you should have. I thought it was your Xolani blood, but it is possible that what I saw was actually Asher's magic."

"You can see – wait. One thing at a time. How can you see magic? Can I learn?"

"This is why I did not want to speak of it. It is a Xolani technique," Riker said. "And yes, you can. But no – you will not. Not today, at least. If there is magic in you that is not yours, then it is very likely related to the strange dagger that Asher was wounded with. You should be cautious."

"I know that," Jasmine said, clenching her fists at her sides. "I'm not stupid. We need everything we can get to survive this, though. If I don't take risks, then Asher and I are both going to die."

Riker didn't refute her. She was right, and they both knew it. He simply shrugged. "That is why I train you. Should you master the tenets of a Keeper, then I will teach you magic."

"Fine. Let's train, then. No point wasting time. What are we doing today? A new tenet?"

"No. You are not done with perseverance."

Jasmine frowned, her shoulders slumping slightly in disappointment. "I'm not? But yesterday you said that–"

"Your body has achieved it. Your fighting has achieved it," Riker agreed, cutting Jasmine off before she could finish. He walked over to the wall and took down two wooden swords, tossing one to her. "However, you have not proved that your mind is there. Not yet."

"My mind? What's that mean to mean? I don't give up. I never have."

"A good trait. If that is the case, today's lesson will be proof of your mental strength. We will speak and fight."

Riker's sword whistled through the air and Jasmine brought her own weapon up to block it. The force of the strike rippled through her body like a shockwave, but she weathered it.

"You grew up in the gutters of Rodridge," Riker said, striking at Jasmine again. She blocked the blow once more, nearly losing her footing in surprise.

"How–"

"I spoke with Esther," Riker said. "And you are not unique in your story. A child from the gutters, desperate to escape and willing to do anything to secure a life for themselves. Am I wrong?"

His sword slammed into Jasmine's again. It didn't even feel like he was trying to hit her – he was trying to knock the blade from her hands. Jasmine's grip tightened on the hilt and she bared her teeth.

"Yeah, it is. So what?"

"Who are you, Jasmine?" Riker's sword struck once more. Jasmine's fingers started to numb, but she held firm. "Why did you become a Keeper?"

"The King–"

"The King gave you a crumb." His blade slammed into hers again. Then again. She shifted her stance, trying to hold her ground. "Is that your only purpose? To accomplish the will of others?"

"I wanted to be a Keeper!" Jasmine yelled, driving Riker's sword to the side and thrusting her wooden blade at his chest. Riker moved impossibly fast and her strike was knocked to the side.

"Did you? Or did you desire safety? The Path of a Keeper granted you immunity from the horrors of life. But did you want to be a Keeper? Or are you a coward?" Riker was relentless. Every swing of his sword drove into Jasmine as if he was hammering in his words.

She refused to move. Even as her arms trembled and tingled, she didn't back up an inch. As long as her sword was in her hands, she wouldn't give in. "I'm not a coward. I chose this."

"You chose escape. Why have you done nothing since then? All you have learned to do is fight. You cannot cook. You cannot advise. You cannot comfort. You have learned the art of the sword, but you have not learned the art of war."

Jasmine's sword flew from her hands as a violent swing knocked it from her grip, sending it tumbling across the room. It bounced across the mat and came to a stop by the wall. Riker's eyes moved to follow the blade, then returned to Jasmine.

It was a challenge. She bared her teeth and lowered into a fighting stance. "I'm not moving."

"So you say," Riker said. His sword flicked out for Jasmine's shoulder. She shifted her body, slapping the palm of her hand against the flat of the sword. It was far from a perfect block, and the tip of the blade still connected. She hissed in pain at the loud smack that echoed through the room.

"So I say," Jasmine agreed through gritted teeth. "What's the point of this? I am a Keeper."

"You are *training* to be a Keeper. You are not one yet. A Keeper is their mind, not their body. But, if you claim to be a Keeper, this should be simple. Who *are* you?"

"I–"

"You are a gutterborn. You are a Keeper in training. You are a woman. You are a target. You are a sacrifice." Riker's sword slammed into Jasmine's arm and she bit back a cry of pain. "But what *are* you?"

"I don't know what that's even meant to mean," Jasmine said, her voice strained. Riker swung the sword and she ducked, avoiding the swing but still refusing to let her feet budge from the ground where she stood.

"I know you don't," Riker said. "Perhaps that question was too difficult. What do you stand for? What do you care about?"

"I don't know!" Jasmine snapped. "Survival, I guess!"

"Survival? A Keeper does not dream of survival." Riker's sword snaked around, somehow striking Jasmine on the back. It held force – just enough to knock her off balance. Her arms windmilled and she threw herself back, managing to keep her footing.

At this point, it was more than just a training exercise. Moving meant Riker won, and Jasmine refused to lose. Not here.

"A Keeper's goals are improvement. Their goals are to make a better life for themselves and for their charge," Riker snapped. Jasmine tried to block his sword swing, but she was just an instant too slow. He rapped her hard across the knuckles, a flair of pain racing down her nervous system.

"Then that's my goal. I want to get stronger."

"There is more to being a Keeper than strength. How can you guide another if you do not know yourself?" Riker demanded. "What do you love? What drives you? Is it the Kingdom? Do you love the king with all your heart? Would you give your life for him?"

Jasmine wouldn't. The King had given her a great opportunity – one that she'd never forget – but she didn't love him. The gutters existed in *his* kingdom. There were hundreds of other kids that had been just like her that died under his watch.

She'd only been chosen because she was bold and lucky. If it hadn't been for that, the gutters would have been all she ever knew.

"The King is sacrificing me. How could I?" Jasmine demanded. "Asher and I are just sacrifices for the Kingdom."

Riker swung his sword again and Jasmine blocked it, gritting her teeth at the flash of pain. Her body ached and begged her to give in and get her sword, but she refused it.

"If you do not love the King, then who do you love? What is your drive? I will answer these questions for you. You do not have an answer, because you do not know yourself. You cannot say if you are gutter trash or a Keeper because you do not know. A part of you remains in the gutters, waiting for you to realize who you have become."

The sword slammed into Jasmine's stomach. She doubled over, letting out a pained groan – but her feet didn't move. She grit her teeth and rose back upright, glaring in defiance.

"You cannot love the Kingdom because they have betrayed you, and yet you remain. A Keeper's mind must be focused. You must know what you are. You must know what you desire. Do you?"

Riker's sword struck Jasmine in the stomach again as she failed to block the blow in time. Bile built in her throat and she nearly crumpled on the spot as pain shot through her. The only thing that kept Jasmine from collapsing was sheer determination.

The pain from the injury started to recede, but Riker's words didn't. They rung in her mind like a bell that grew louder with every toll.

*He's right. I know how to fight. I could be a guard or a mercenary. What's the point of being a Keeper? The only reason I wanted to do it was because I wanted to get out of the gutters. I don't really care about the kingdom. I don't really care about the King, and giving either my loyalty is clearly a mistake considering Esther is throwing me aside like a used snot rag.*

*Why am I even here? I should just leave. Screw the assassins. Screw Esther, and the Whitewater Kingdom. Screw –*

Jasmine's thoughts ground to a halt. Leaving would mean abandoning Asher. It wasn't like she owed him anything, but he was in the same situation she was. His family was dead. His Kingdom was using him as bait, and there was nobody he could rely on.

The thought of dropping Asher to face his fate alone made her stomach clench. She knew without a shadow of a doubt that if their positions had been switched, Asher would have stood by her side.

*I can't leave him. It wouldn't be right.*

"I won't leave," Jasmine growled, meeting Riker's eyes and straightening back up. "I don't care if I can't answer any of your questions. A Keeper just has to take care of their charge, right? So that's what I'll do. Nothing else matters."

Riker grunted. Jasmine braced herself for another swing, but it didn't come. "Why? What is it that gives you strength? We must all draw it from somewhere."

"I don't know, okay?"

"Then you will fail." Riker lowered his sword and shook his head. "No more. We are done for today. You do not have the answer. You are not a Keeper."

"What? But the hour isn't up!"

"There is no purpose to continue. Before, we were training. Doing any more would simply be me beating you. Go back to your room. Think, and determine who you are. Because, if you do not, all you will ever be is the woman you were."

Jasmine's eyes prickled with shame. Riker strode past her, taking her sword from the ground and hanging their weapons up on the wall before leaving the room.

She stepped out after him, her fingernails biting into her palms as she struggled to keep herself from tearing up. Jasmine trudged back to her room, Riker's admonishments still echoing in her ears the entire way back.

No matter how bad she felt, she still had to make dinner if she wanted to eat anything that night.

# 23

Jasmine burned the eggs. She burned the steak too, but neither was completely inedible. Disappointment beat down on her shoulders like hammer blows as she returned to Asher's room, setting everything out on the table just a minute before he returned.

They ate quickly, both clearly exhausted in their own ways. It was far from the worst meal Jasmine had ever cooked, but it tasted like ash in her mouth.

"How did it go with Qien?" Jasmine asked, injecting false confidence into her voice as she gathered the plates and started to stack them up. "Did he decide to be helpful?"

"If you squint hard enough, maybe. I thought he'd want some form of payment, but it looks like he was just genuinely busy. He said he'd look into it, but not to expect anything special. Apparently, since my magic works normally when I'm touching you, it's not high on his priority list to deal with. Riker or Esther must have told him about the assassin, though. He knew about the Xolani dagger."

"Weren't they the ones that said to keep things secret?"

"Rules for thee, I guess," Asher shrugged. "Either way, we're on our own."

"Nothing new there."

"I suppose not. This spells a lot of trouble for us, no pun intended. If I need to be in contact with you to use my magic, then I don't know how useful it's going to be against an assassin. The whole point of a Keeper Starvein duo is to have one person up close and the other far back. At this point, if I need to be up close to do anything, I'd be better off focusing on my swordsmanship than my magic."

That wasn't a great solution, and they both knew it. Neither of them – no matter how much they practiced in the next few weeks – were going to be good enough to stand up against another one of the assassins for an extended period of time.

*The only way we've got a chance is with magic.*

"There has to be something you can use close up," Jasmine said. "Can't you find something faster, so you don't have to concentrate for a bunch of time when someone's trying to kill you?"

"It's not that simple. I could easily pull the magic quickly, even without any real training. You heard what Qicn said. The hard part is making sure the magic doesn't kill *you* in the process. Normally, you're supposed to regulate how fast you draw by the sensation of the magic coursing through you. I can't do that because you're the one the magic flows through first. I can't feel what you feel, so I need to be even more careful than anyone else."

"So all we have to do is practice and make sure that the amount of energy you draw isn't so much that I can't handle it, right?"

"I mean, sure," Asher allowed, reluctance in his tone. He chewed his lower lip, then let out a huff and pointed over to the corner of the room, just below his window. "There's also the problem of the actual magic. Let's say we're getting attacked, and the assassin is somewhere over there."

"Are we assuming we just jumped out of bed?" Jasmine asked.

Asher nodded. "You'd probably be between me and the assassin, somewhere about at the foot of the bed. I'd be just behind you, right?"

Jasmine walked over to where Asher had indicated, situating herself and turning to face the imaginary assassin. Asher moved behind her, standing at an arm's length.

"The last guy was throwing daggers, and you can't just stand and eat them," Asher continued, pushing Jasmine a few steps forward. "That means, after we realize we're under attack, there are only going to be a few moments before he starts attacking."

"I see the problem," Jasmine said, crossing her arms and frowning. "Either I stay next to you long enough for you to use your magic, risking us both getting hit by ranged attacks, or I run up to fight the assassin and you barely get any magic to work with."

"And if I run up with you, not only am I making one of your arms useless, I'm also just in the way. Using magic on the fly is next to impossible – it's too easy to mistakenly draw too much on accident. That's why Starveins need Keepers to protect them."

They both studied the position of the nonexistent assassin. Jasmine dug through her head for a way around it, but it wasn't looking good. Either Asher got time to use magic or Jasmine kept the assassin from getting to them – there didn't seem to be a good way to achieve both.

"What if I start throwing things back at the assassin?" Jasmine offered, her offer sounding weak to her own ears.

"Wouldn't stop him from targeting us, and I don't want you blocking anything with your body. I'd rather you survive the fight," Asher said with a shake of his head. "Besides, the last one used a poisoned dagger. Getting hit is as good as being dead."

"What about the weird speed and strength I was getting while we fought?" Jasmine asked, her eyes lighting up as a faint ray of hope broke through the exhaustion. "That was magic, right? And it's not like I can use your energy. I'm not a Starvein, after all. So that had to be you."

*Forget not being a real Keeper. If Asher can empower me with magic, I can still protect both of us.*

Asher's brow furrowed. "That… is a good point, actually. I don't think I was using it, though. I wasn't going to make you stronger while we were fighting. At least, I don't think I was."

He paced over to his bed and flipped through his book, searching for something. Jasmine looked over his shoulder, but the writing on the pages might as well have been written in a different language. She had no idea how Asher understood it.

"There are ways to use your magic to empower yourself," Asher said, stopping on one of the pages and tapping it. "And I've got no damn clue how to do it. This makes no sense to me. I mean – magic follows intent. I could do it, but I don't know how to do the part that keeps it from corrupting you."

"So what was happening during our fight? Because someone was using magic," Jasmine said. "Either it was you or me, and I know for a fact I wasn't doing any fancy stuff to keep myself from copying one of my ancestors and turning into a monster."

Asher shook his head helplessly. "If I knew the answer, I'd tell you. What I do know is we need to be even more careful than before. You need to warn me if you ever feel something off, okay? That's the only way I'll know if I'm using too much magic or casting it on accident."

"You can cast magic on accident?"

"Evidently," Asher said. "Unless it was you."

"I'm pretty sure it wasn't."

"Then it was on accident."

"Well, try to do it again. If you did it on accident, you should be able to do it on purpose."

"What if I–"

"Just do it," Jasmine said. "I'll tell you if something is going wrong, but I'm going to be just as dead if an assassin kills me as I will be if I turn into a monster. And, between the two, I'll take my chances with the magic."

Asher's hands clenched at his sides and he inclined his head, holding his hand out. Jasmine grasped it.

A second ticked by. There was a tiny prickle at the back of Jasmine's skull, but nothing else changed. She tried to stay patient, but after nearly a minute had passed, nothing felt different.

"What are you doing?" Jasmine asked.

"Trying to make the magic reinforce you. Really, really carefully."

"Well, stop being so damn careful. You aren't doing shit."

"I don't want to turn you into a Watcher damned monster!" Asher snapped, letting go of her hand and taking a step back. "What do you want from me, Jasmine?"

"I want you to try." Jasmine took a step a step forward to stand nose-to-nose with Asher and glare into his eyes, not letting him look away. "I'm not a fucking flower. I'll tell you if the magic feels off, but you've already done this before. How is this any different?"

*This is the only damn thing I can do. Let me do it!*

"I didn't know I was doing it before," Asher snarled, pushing Jasmine a step back. "I don't want to hurt you!"

"The assassin will definitely hurt me a lot worse than this will. If you can do it on accident, then you can do it on purpose."

"Just because it happened once or twice doesn't mean it'll happen again." Asher's jaw clenched. "I'll try later, once I've figured out how to use my magic better."

"Don't you understand? The assassins could show up tonight," Jasmine said. "There *isn't* a later. We could both be dead tomorrow. We could be dead tonight. Didn't we agree to work as partners?"

"We did, which is exactly why I'm not going to do something as stupid as flood you with magic just to see if it'll work," Asher replied. "Drop it, Jas. There are other ways we can deal with this."

"Tell me what they are, then. Give me one damn idea and I'll drop it." Jasmine crossed her arms and arched an eyebrow, waiting for an answer that she knew Asher couldn't give. He knew it too because he let out an exasperated sigh.

"You know I don't have one. It doesn't matter. This conversation is over."

# 24

Asher turned to storm over to his bed, but Jasmine grabbed his arm, yanking him to a halt. He stumbled and Jasmine shoved Asher back. He hit the wall with a surprised grunt, but the shock didn't last long.

It might have been because she was already tired from her training with Riker, but Asher overpowered her easily. He knocked Jasmine's hand away and grabbed her shoulders, spinning her around and effectively swapping places with her as he slammed her into the wall.

"What is your problem?" Asher snarled, his lips just inches away from hers. His breath smelled like vanilla. "Do you want to die?"

"I want you to stop being a coward," Jasmine hissed back. "This is my decision to make. If I could do this myself, then I would. We aren't in a position where we can turn down tools to survive. Why should it be different if you're the one that gets to control the magic?"

"Because it is. That's the end of the story. We can try to find something else out later, but I'm not risking it."

"You're going to say that about everything until we're both dead," Jasmine countered. "This isn't dangerous. We've already done it!"

"It could have been! We don't know."

"It's not like you can't stop if you need to. We're going in circles. Just do it."

"You know what?" Asher moved back, though he didn't take his hands off Jasmine's shoulders. His jaw clenched as he met her gaze. "Make me."

"I'm your K–"

"Don't pull that," Asher snapped. "It doesn't count and you know it. This isn't a matter of safety to me. Using magic is just as likely to kill both of us as it is to kill just you. If anyone has the power to make orders right now, it's me. And I'm saying no."

For a moment, the two of them didn't say a word. Anger and desperation swirled in Jasmine's stomach, forming into a pit that wouldn't disappear. Riker's words pounded in her mind.

*You don't know who you are. You don't know who you care about. How am I supposed to know any of that? I never had a damn chance to care! I didn't have the opportunity to sit around like some monk and think about life.*

"What's gotten into you?" Asher asked, his grip tightening on her shoulders. "You seem out of it. Is everything okay?"

*No, Watcher damn it. Everything isn't okay. This is the only path I can take.*

"I'm fine. You said that I had to *make you* do what I wanted." Jasmine slipped out from Asher's hands and took a step closer, pressing her body against his as she glared up at him. She could feel his heartbeat thump against her chest – and she could feel it quicken in response to her touch. "Were you serious about that challenge?"

"As if you speak in anything other than challenges," Asher

growled, not backing down in the slightest. "And you can't change my mind. Give up."

Jasmine's chest clenched as they stood there, a second of silence passing by. Two. The tension was so thick that she could have cut it. The logical move probably would have been to drop things as they were, but emotion had been bubbling up her entire life – and there was only so long she could keep the lid on the pot. There was only so long she *wanted* to keep it there.

Sure, Asher had a point. It was dangerous to push his magic. Esther had a point too. The Kingdom was obviously more important than her or Asher. Riker also had a point. She didn't really know why she was doing any of this.

Staying a Keeper meant nothing but trouble. It almost certainly spelled death, and she'd never cared for anything other than fighting. It had been all that had mattered.

But, as Jasmine stood there, staring into Asher's concerned eyes, equal parts angry and concerned, she realized that she couldn't stop being a Keeper.

The Jasmine of the past had a point once – she hadn't been able to rely on anything other than her own skills to survive. Showing weakness was a fast way to end up as another corpse in the gutters. Leaving room for others was a liberty that she couldn't afford.

It was a liberty that she hadn't been able to afford.

But it was one she wanted. Jasmine didn't care about the kingdom or being a Keeper or any of Riker's tenets. She just wanted to be able to live, and she wanted to be able to do it with the people she cared about.

Lydia was one, but Jasmine was surprised to find that the other was the cocky, annoying man standing before her, growing concern in his eyes.

He'd always been there when he could – and even when he couldn't, he'd tried to protect Jasmine by letting her think he'd left the Keeper program of his own volition so she wouldn't feel bad for him.

Riker's voice echoed through her head once more.

*Watcher help me, I think I've fallen for Asher.*

"What's going on?" Asher asked, releasing his grip on her. "Jasmine, you're acting really off. What happened? Are you okay?"

Jasmine barely even heard his words. All she could do was stare at him. She wasn't sure if she was *allowed* to fall for Asher. She was a Keeper, and he was a Starvein. There was no potential future there.

If anything, that thought only made Riker's voice ring louder. She shoved it away along with all the other thoughts.

*Forget if it's the right thing or if it's the safe thing. For once, I just want to do something because I want to do it.*

"Asher?"

He blinked at the change of tone in Jasmine's voice. "What?"

"Can I kiss you?"

Asher blinked in surprise, confusion rippling over his features – but it wasn't just confusion. There was a spark of desire in his eyes as well. The very same one that Jasmine knew her own eyes held. That was more than enough for her. Jasmine grabbed Asher by the collar of his shirt and yanked him down, pressing her lips to his.

Jasmine froze as Asher pulled back, breaking contact just enough to make room for them to whisper. For a moment, she feared she'd made a terrible mistake, but there was no mistaking the hunger in Asher's eyes. He wanted her just as much as she wanted him.

"Jas, I–," Asher said, his lips just inches away from hers.

"Shut up," Jasmine breathed. "Unless you want me to stop, I don't want to hear another complaint from your mouth and I'm giving you an order as your Keeper to keep going."

Asher's response was to shove her back against the wall.

Jasmine could feel every part of her body pressed against his as his lips met hers again. Tingles raced down Jasmine's spine and filled her stomach as she gave herself into the kiss. Some of the strength left her legs, but their embrace was so tight that she didn't need them. Jasmine's hands dug into the back of Asher's shirt and scratched his back, but neither of them cared. Asher's hands ran down Jasmine's body, pulling her waist even closer to his. For a single instant, his mouth broke contact with hers. "Jas, are you sure this–"

She kissed him again, then pushed him back from the wall and over to the bed. The back of his legs hit it and his lips broke from hers as he fell back with a grunt. She climbed on top of him, feeling his length stiffen beneath her.

Jasmine ground her hips against his and he groaned, reaching up and pulling her closer. She let him, but stopped just before her mouth met his again and pressed a finger to his lips, pushing him back down.

"Jas?" Asher asked, his voice husky and pleading. A thrill raced through her chest and she resisted the urge to pounce on him. The longing in Asher's voice was like music to her ears. She worked his hands under his shirt, pulling it off and throwing it to the side before throwing her own away.

"Do I win?" Jasmine asked, letting her lips brush against his nose. Asher's hands traveled up her body, feeling every inch of her. Thrills of pleasure raced through her and Jasmine bit her lip, grinding against him even harder.

Asher groaned in a mixture of desperation and defeat. "Yes. You win."

"You're mine," Jasmine whispered into Asher's ear. He was so warm beneath her. Jasmine could feel everything through his clothes – clothes that she desperately wanted to be rid of. She didn't think she could control herself for much longer, but she refused to give in. Not before Asher did. "Do you understand?"

Asher groaned and kissed the nape of her neck. Jasmine nearly gave in then and there, but she managed to pull back for just an instant longer.

"I want an answer." She ran her fingers along Asher's chest and he bucked beneath her. "Let me hear you say it. Say you're mine."

"I'm yours," Asher breathed, begged.

That was all Jasmine needed. She pressed her lips to his again, pulling him in as tightly as she could. Asher's hands tugged at her pants, pulling them off as she did the same to him.

For an instant, Asher paused, his heat pulsing against Jasmine. "Are you on–"

"Stop thinking so much," Jasmine growled, reaching down. Asher drew in a soft gasp at her touch, stiffening even further. "All Keepers are on herbs to avoid mistakes, idiot."

Jasmine leaned back and a moan slipped from her lips as they joined. Pleasure arced through her body and she ground against him, lowering as far as she could. She wrapped her arms around Asher and their lips pressed together again in desperate passion.

Jasmine rode Asher, her hands digging into his bare back as throes of pleasure raced through up through her body. She could feel Asher's warmth in her. The heat of his chest and his heavy breath against the nape of her neck nearly sent her over the edge instantly. It was more than just pleasure. It was safety. As long as she was in his arms, everything would be fine.

That might not have been true, but Jasmine didn't care. Asher's hands found her hips – and then went a little lower. He pulled her closer, and she melted into him. Their bodies were so intertwined that they couldn't have gotten closer if they'd wanted to.

Neither had anything more to say. Their bodies did all the speaking for them.

# 25

The bed sheets were in complete disarray, and Jasmine's limbs were entangled with Asher's, her legs locked around his and her head resting against the warmth of his bare chest. His hands wrapped around Jasmine's back, holding her close as if he feared she would run away. His fingers gently traced down her back, leaving a trail of warm tingles in their wake.

Asher's heart thumped with increased speed that Jasmine knew her own matched, and she could smell herself on his lips.

"In all other things you win," Asher muttered, his breath warm against Jasmine's ear. "I can't say no to you. Never could. But please – don't ask me to hurt you."

"I'm not asking you to," Jasmine said, giving Asher a tight squeeze and kissing his chest. "I'm asking you to trust me. We can do this. Together."

Asher let out a groan. "Fine. Just… don't take things too fast."

"Which things?" Jasmine asked, craning her head back to smirk up at him.

Asher's pushed her up with a leg and pressed another kiss to her lips, drinking her in for several seconds before finally breaking away again. "I think you know. I never realized you–"

"I didn't either," Jasmine murmured.

And, to some degree, she hadn't. Asher had always been there since she'd arrived at Sanctuary. He'd been a sparring partner and a friend. And, at some point, he'd become something more. The confident smile, his beautiful golden eyes and handsome features – his reliability and refusal to ever give up.

There had been a lot, but admitting that would have been opening herself up to weakness. Weakness that she couldn't have risked in the gutters.

*I'm not in the gutters anymore.*

"I've wanted to hold you like this ever since we met," Asher said, running a hand through Jasmine's hair. His grip tightened just enough to give it a soft pull and draw her eyes back up to his.

Jasmine could have stared into them for longer than she cared to admit, but she forced herself to speak anyway. "You're a Starvein. Is this okay? I'm not like you. I can't–"

"I don't care," Asher said, not letting Jasmine finish. "I never asked to be a Starvein. It doesn't matter what you are. Besides, who's going to object? It's not like anyone is left in my family to complain that I'm with my Keeper. The worst that could happen are some mildly annoying rumors."

"But what about the king? Your duty as a noble? What if we made a mistake? I don't want to put you in a position where–"

"Don't care, and don't care. You've got my magic," Asher growled, grabbing her chin before Jasmine could avert her eyes. "And you've got more than just that. I don't care what you are – all that matters is that you're mine."

There wasn't a speck of doubt on Asher's face. He meant every word coming from his lips. Even if it was the wrong decision, it was one they both wanted. Warmth spread through Jasmine's chest as she held his gaze.

The sense of comfort and safety she felt in his arms was insurmountable. Even if there were assassins breathing down their necks and the Kingdom couldn't have cared less, they weren't alone.

"You're *mine*," Jasmine corrected, a grin playing across her lips. "I'm your Keeper, remember?"

"I'd never even think about forgetting it."

Asher stroked Jasmine's hair again, pressing his lips to her forehead and inhaling deeply. He let out a soft sigh. "You smell incredible. Do you have any idea how torturous it was to sleep next to you and not be able to touch you?"

"I think I might have a bit of an idea," Jasmine said, leaning her head back against Asher's chest. Even though his muscles were nowhere near as soft as a pillow, they were somehow infinitely more comfortable. "Did you wake up before you said you did?"

Asher's cheeks went bright red. "Ah... something like that might have happened. I didn't think you noticed."

"I woke up earlier too," Jasmine admitted. "I didn't want to leave."

"Well, now you don't have to." Asher pulled her closer, almost suffocating Jasmine against his chest. She laughed, squirming in his grip to free herself.

"We have to get up eventually."

"Do we? It's already night," Asher said. "Stay in bed with me. We need to be in contact to keep the magic from eating me alive while I sleep, or did you forget?"

She had, actually. Jasmine blinked, flushing in embarrassment.

*So many things happened today that it completely slipped my mind. Riker kind of completely wiped my brain of everything that wasn't what we spoke about.*

Some of Jasmine's bruises throbbed at the thought of Riker, but she pushed him out of her head. There would be time to deal with that tomorrow. She wasn't sure she had answers to his questions yet, but she had more than she did a few hours ago.

"Jas?" Asher asked, drawing her attention with a gentle touch to her bare shoulder. "Are you okay? Not having second thoughts again, are you?"

"No. Nothing like that," Jasmine said with a small smile.

"Really? Not at all?"

"Okay, maybe a bit," Jasmine admitted. "I'm still worried that this is dangerous. We could be making a mistake."

"Even if we are, I don't care. It's a mistake I want. I'd rather make it and find out I shouldn't have than wait around and wonder what could have been. I should have talked to you about this months ago, back when I first started thinking about it."

"It's probably a good thing you didn't. I didn't think about anything like this until today."

"Today? Damn," Asher said with a chuckle. "You work fast. It took me months to even work up the courage to want to try to ask you if you wanted to court, and then everything went straight downhill right before I could."

"Are you complaining? I could have done the same."

"Not at all. I love a woman that knows what she wants."

"Good."

Asher looped an arm around Jasmine's waist and pulled her closer to him, spooning up behind her as he threw his arm over her shoulders and yawned. "You think this is enough to make sure the magic doesn't blow me up?"

"Someone's getting comfortable too fast," Jasmine said, suppressing a laugh. She pulled the sheets tighter around them.

*This is definitely a lot more comfortable than sleeping with my arm stretched out to my side. Warmer, too.*

The light coming through the window had already dimmed in the wake of the night, and Jasmine felt a wave of weariness settle in over her shoulders. The mixture of physical and mental exhaustion finally caught up to her, and Asher's arms were impossibly comfortable.

*I really hope assassins don't show up tonight, or I might end up sleeping through it.*

"Goodnight," she murmured. "We'll have to get up early tomorrow to make breakfast. I'm going to be hungry."

Asher's laugh tickled her ear. He gave her a light squeeze. "Goodnight, Jas."

# 26

The Watcher was merciful that night. Jasmine and Asher's sleep went uninterrupted, and they were spared the attention of any assassins. Unfortunately, His grace ended right as the morning dawned and a knock rang out on their door, rudely pulling Jasmine from her rest.

She blinked heavily, jolting in surprise at the intrusive noise. For a moment, she completely forgot what had happened the previous day and couldn't figure out why there was someone wrapped around her like an octopus.

The memories flooded back and Jasmine relaxed, granting herself one more second to enjoy the comfortable moment. All the pain from the bruises that had covered her the previous day was gone and – more importantly – Asher's magic hadn't flared up again.

Jasmine forced herself to sit up.

"You okay?" Asher asked, his voice drowsy and content. "I don't want to get up yet."

"There's someone at the door," Jasmine said, rolling her eyes. She untangled herself from Asher with more than a little difficulty, then hurriedly did her best to get her hair back into at least a somewhat respectable appearance. Giving up, she grabbed her shirt from the ground and pulled it on.

*If this is Esther, I'm going to be pissed.*

"Who is it?" Jasmine raised her voice just enough to be heard on the other side of the door.

"Who do you think it is?" Lydia's voice replied. "How many people do you have knocking at your door at this time in the morning? If you're that much more popular than I am, I'll be mad at you."

Jasmine pulled the door open. "Lydia! I didn't think you'd be back so soon."

Lydia had another package of food in her hands and a smile on her face as Jasmine stepped back to let her inside. She arched an eyebrow at Jasmine once the door was shut behind her.

"Nice look, Jas. You've got a little something on your neck there. Were you training or something?"

Jasmine glanced down at her collarbone, where there was a rather prominent hickey staring back at her, only partially covered by her shirt. Her cheeks went bright red and she quickly straightened her clothes to cover it.

Lydia looked from Jasmine to Asher. Her mouth made a small '*o*' shape and she slung an arm around Jasmine's shoulder, turning her away from the bed and leaning in to whisper.

"You little liar. Don't even *try* to deny it. That was a hickey, wasn't it?"

"We… might be dating now," Jasmine whispered sheepishly. Her cheeks hurt from how hard she was blushing, and she was pretty sure that her face had gone about as red as a tomato. "But we weren't the last time you asked."

Lydia snorted and flicked Jasmine in the forehead. "Right. Only telling me after you get caught."

"I'm not! We really weren't–" She trailed off as she saw the grin on Lydia's face, then glared. "Stop screwing with me."

"Never," Lydia said with a smirk, releasing Jasmine from her grip and letting her back up a step. "You did make me start wondering if my senses were totally off, though. Not cool. I was starting to get worried I'd lost my ability to read people. Glad to know it was just the two of you being pansies."

"Says the girl that isn't dating anyone," Asher said. He slipped out of bed and walked over to the closet in search of a shirt. Both Jasmine and Lydia's eyes followed him, and it was Jasmine's turn to prod Lydia.

"Eyes off. Mine," Jasmine said.

Lydia snickered and handed Jasmine the package of food before raising her hands in defeat. "Just looking, not shopping. And you don't get to talk, Asher. You didn't have shit yesterday."

"Yesterday was the past. The now is all that matters."

"When did you become a philosopher?"

"Last night."

Lydia rolled her eyes. "Well, if you want me to keep bringing you free food, I expect you to put those talents to good use. All the people left in the Keeper program are hunks. Nothing wrong with that, but I prefer my romantic interests to have a bit more between the ears."

"Maybe I should set you up with Qien," Asher said dryly. "He'd definitely love the snark, and he's only twice your age."

"Try it and I'll season your eggs with a handful of salt."

"Scratch that. I'll have the hottest, smartest Starvein tied up on the footstep of your door by tomorrow morning."

"Better," Lydia allowed. The smile slipped away from her face as her expression turned serious. "How are things looking, though? With... well, everything."

"They're not as bad as they were, but it's still not good," Jasmine said. She didn't even bother wondering if it was safe to talk to

Lydia about what they'd learned. If she couldn't trust her friend, then she couldn't trust anyone. "I… kind of stole Asher's magic."

"You *what?*"

"For some reason, all my magic is stored in Jas," Asher said, rubbing the back of his head before shrugging. "I can still use it, but I need to draw it out of her instead of the environment like I should be."

"How in the Watcher's name did that happen? And can you show me? I've never seen magic up close."

Jasmine and Asher exchanged a look. To Jasmine's surprise, it wasn't outright refusal that she found in Asher's eyes. It was a question, mixed with more than a little concern. She thought for a moment, then inclined her head.

"We're still trying to figure everything out, but I don't think it should hurt if we keep it to what you've already done," Jasmine said. "Maybe show her what you showed Qien?"

"I can do that," Asher said. He walked up to join the girls and placed his hand on the back of Jasmine's neck, holding two fingers on his other hand up. A moment passed, and a tiny river of ice ran along Jasmine's spine.

A small crackle of black electricity popped to life as he pulled his fingers apart. Lydia watched with rapt attention until Asher removed his hand from Jasmine and the magic faded away a few moments later.

"Whoa," Lydia breathed. "That's incredible. I wish I could do magic."

*You probably can, if what Riker said is true.*

Jasmine opened her mouth, then paused. Knowing that she had the potential to use magic and yet wouldn't be able to do it until she mastered every part of being a Keeper had admittedly caused her more trouble than anything else.

*I'll tell her about it once I figure out anything myself. Riker could be full of shit, and nothing sucks more than false hope.*

"It's amazing," Jasmine agreed with a laugh. "It's too bad I can't use Asher's magic, or I'd never give it back to him."

"And I wouldn't want it back. It would be all yours." Asher's eyes darkened. "It brings nothing but trouble and death."

Lydia's smile fell away. "Sorry. I wasn't–"

"It's fine," Asher said. He shook his head, then shrugged. "There's nothing to be done about it now. That's about all that we've actually figured out. I need to learn how to use magic through Jasmine without accidentally hurting her, or I'm going to be completely useless as a Starvein."

"We'll find a way," Jasmine said. "We've already done it unintentionally when we were sparring, so I'm sure it won't be that hard. How are things with the rest of the Keepers though, Lydia?"

"About the same, just busier. Riker is a taskmaster, but luckily he's too busy to teach us too much. He just goes around and smacks us with a wooden sword. I heard you weren't going to be coming to classes anymore. Do you need me to take notes or something?"

"It would probably be really helpful if you could, but don't work yourself to death for me," Jasmine said. "I'll figure something out."

Lydia snorted. "Yeah right. You'd be screwed without me and you know it."

"Yeah, I kind of would be," Jasmine admitted. "Thanks, Lydia."

"You know it." Lydia flashed them both a quick grin, then glanced out the window. "I should probably get going. I'm going to get in trouble if I'm late to class again. I'll see you again soon."

"Tomorrow?" Jasmine asked.

"Probably not. Esther is doing some form of training thing where we pretend we're real Keepers for a day, and it starts before dawn," Lydia said with a gag. "I'll try to meet up again as soon as possible though."

"One day, I'll find time to visit you," Jasmine promised. "And I'll bring food."

"Only if Asher helps you cook it," Lydia said with a laugh. She pulled the door open and slipped out, waving to them before disappearing down the hall. Jasmine set the food Lydia had brought down on the table while Asher closed the door.

"She's a good friend, isn't she?" Asher asked.

"Tell me about it. I owe her a lot."

"We'll do something to show our appreciation soon. Maybe after we find a way to keep ourselves from getting run through in the immediate future."

"Seems like a sound plan to me." Jasmine unwrapped the food and started to set the table, feeling more and more grateful for Lydia by the second. She and Asher devoured every last scrap of the meal, then moved the box out of the way as they went to get ready for the day.

Jasmine cleaned herself off and changed into a fresh set of clothes. She returned to Asher's room to wait for him to finish up when someone knocked on the door for the second time that morning.

For a moment, Jasmine hoped that Lydia had returned – but this knock was heavier and louder than hers had been. She walked over to the door with a frown.

"Who is it?" Jasmine asked.

"Riker. I have come for our daily training."

*Riker? It's kind of early for him.*

"Don't we normally train at night?"

"My availability is not always constant," Riker said. "It will be now or not today."

Jasmine pulled the door open. She wasn't sure how she felt about seeing the Keeper. Emotion twisted in her chest like a knife, but she met his eyes without flinching. "Then it'll be now."

Asher stepped out of his bathroom, pausing as he saw Riker in the doorway. "Training already?"

"Yeah. I'll be back in an hour," Jasmine said, keeping her eyes locked with Riker's.

"Sounds good." Asher picked up on the tone of Jasmine's voice and wisely avoided saying anything else. He just grabbed his book and sat down on his bed, to flip through it.

Without another word, Riker turned on his heel and set off down the hall. Jasmine followed after him, determined to make sure that the training didn't go anywhere near how it had the previous day.

# 27

"Do you have the answers?" Riker held his wooden sword easily at his side. He stood across the mat from Jasmine in their training room.

"No," Jasmine replied. "Not all of them. There's no way I could get answers to that much so quickly."

"Then you have some." Riker lowered into a fighting stance and raised his sword. Jasmine mirrored his position.

"I have some," Jasmine agreed. She kept her eyes on Riker's sword. Normally, it was the eyes that gave away how people fought – but Riker's face was so impossible to read in its normal form that it was pointless.

"Are they enough?" Riker asked. He bounded forward, bringing his sword down for Jasmine's shoulder. She struck it at the hilt with her own, redirecting the strike so it whistled past her harmlessly.

"Yes," Jasmine said, meeting Riker's eyes and clenching her jaw. "They're enough for me."

Riker's sword moved again and Jasmine tensed, but the strike never landed. Instead of striking her blade, he took a step back and inclined his head. Jasmine's brow furrowed in confusion.

"What? Why'd you stop?"

"Because you have an answer."

"You don't even know what it is! How do you know it's right?"

Riker let out a short burst of laughter. "If you think there is any right answer to the questions I gave you, then you are wrong. It was not about having the right answer. It was about having confidence in *your* answer. There are times when a Keeper will be faced with odds that seem insurmountable. You will be tempted to quit or surrender. By knowing what you fight for, you will persevere. It does not matter *what* you fight for."

Jasmine blinked. She let her own sword lower. "I – oh. That's it?"

"That's it," Riker said. "Normally, I would have spent weeks on this lesson. You do not have weeks, though. Some corners must be cut. Some lessons must be hastened and made more painful. I told you it would not be pleasant."

"Yeah. It wasn't."

"Good. Then it is working. What will we work on next?"

"Isn't that something you should decide? I thought you were the teacher."

"And you are the student," Riker pointed out, resting his sword on the ground between his feet. "One whose very life depends on her abilities. What aspect of the keeper should you learn? They are all important, after all."

*The implication that etiquette is anywhere near as important as fighting feels like an insult on multiple levels. At the same time, I don't think he wants me to just say fighting. I'm pretty sure fighting is part of everything Riker teaches.*

"Maybe... strategy, I guess?" Jasmine asked. "Advising and the like."

"Strategy is a sound choice," Riker said. He turned, making his way over to the corner of the room and rooting through one of the shelves. Locating a flat wooden box, Riker brought it back over to Jasmine and sat down cross-legged on the ground before her.

"Sit." Riker opened the box and dumped a myriad of black and white pieces out onto the ground. "We will use this."

"A game?" Jasmine asked.

"It is called Gambit," Riker said, setting the board down and arranging the pieces on it so that all the white ones were on one end of the board and the black ones were on the other. "It is a strategy game in which the focus is to capture the leader of the opponent's army. I assume you have not played."

"Do you think we had time to play games in the gutters?"

"I will take that as a no," Riker said. "The game is simple in concept, which is why it will serve two purposes. The first will be to teach you the basics of strategy and techniques to turn the battlefield in your favor."

"And the other?"

"You will learn when you figure out what it is," Riker said with a wry smile. "I will explain what each piece can do. Then we will play."

That sounded… considerably less interesting than Jasmine had been hoping for, but she shrugged. Riker didn't strike her as the type of person to just play a game for the sake of it. It clearly had something to do with strategy, but she wasn't sure how playing a board game was going to teach anything truly applicable outside of the game's rules.

"You are incompetent. Perhaps you should have stuck to the gutters," Riker said, leaning back as he took yet another one of Jasmine's pieces.

Jasmine's jaw clenched as she tried to hold in her anger. She'd expected to play a game, but the past thirty or so minutes had been a steady deluge of insults and mockery. It was like Riker had suddenly decided she was the most pathetic creature to ever live.

She moved another piece on the board – and Riker claimed it immediately with a unit that Jasmine had missed.

"Maybe you would be better suited to cleaning toilets," Riker suggested. "You have the intelligence of a steamed rat. The gutters grew smarter on the day you left."

Every ounce of Jasmine's self-control was in full effect. She wanted to do nothing more than jump across the board and punch Riker in his smug face, but –

*Actually, fuck it.*

Jasmine lunged for Riker – and his sword whipped down on her hand. Jasmine cursed in pain, rolling across the ground and clutching her knuckles. "Why are you such an asshole?"

"You lose," Riker said, moving one last piece across the board. Jasmine squinted through the pain at the board, disappointment and anger intermixing. She had absolutely no idea how, but she'd only managed to claim a single one of Riker's pieces through the entire game. He, on the other hand, had taken every single one of hers.

It hadn't even been necessary to take them all. Riker could have won about twenty rounds ago, but he'd intentionally dragged it on until Jasmine didn't have a single unit left on the board to play with.

"Tell me why you lost," Riker said, the malice in his voice gone like a leaf in a tornado.

"Because I don't know how to play the damn game."

"Wrong. You lost because you were so furious you did not think properly," Riker said with a shake of his head. "You picked up on the game quickly, Jasmine. The reason for this humiliating defeat is not that you could not play. It is because you let me play for you. And, for the record, I do not believe any of the things I said about you."

The anger simmering in Jasmine's chest sputtered. She looked back down the board, a frown creasing her lips. "You're still a dick."

"An effective one though, yes?"

"I suppose that remains to be seen."

"So it does," Riker agreed, collecting the pieces and putting them back into the box.

"Isn't that kind of cheap? I thought the point was learning the game."

Riker arched an eyebrow. "Do you think your opponents will play fair? You could have asked me more questions about the rules of the game instead of trying to brute force your way through it by only using the techniques you knew. You could have ignored my insults and realized that I was simply trying to distract you."

Annoyance made Jasmine's nose scrunch. She crossed her arms and sat back, letting out a small huff. "Can we play again?"

"We are out of time." Riker put the pieces of the game back and hand closed the box, handing it to her. "Take this."

"Who am I supposed to play with?" Jasmine asked, accepting the box with a surprised frown.

"Yourself," Riker replied. "Or Asher. Or anyone else that you may interact with. It does not matter. Bring it to our next lesson. Today's is over."

That was about as cut and dry as it could get. Jasmine tucked the box under her arm, not sure how she was meant to feel. It hadn't exactly been a *bad* lesson. Riker's were as clear as day, but it wasn't really the most satisfying conclusion.

The whole way back to her room, Jasmine's mind was stuck on Gambit. Riker had definitely been trying to show her something with the game, and it wasn't just that she needed to keep her cool.

*This was meant to be about more than just strategy. It's making sure*

*I'm playing on my own terms. I still suck at the game, though. Forget getting emotional, I'm not winning against Riker until I get better. Maybe Asher will know how to play.*

When she got back, Jasmine wasn't surprised to find Asher hunched at his desk and poring over the book on magic. He barely even noticed her as she walked inside, but he flinched in surprise at the gentle click of Jasmine setting the board on the table.

"Shit. I didn't even realize you got back," Asher said, slumping back down and laughing. "I thought an assassin showed up while you were gone."

"Riker said you'd be safe while I was gone, and do you really think an assassin would use the front door?"

"Probably not, but who knows. Do you actually trust Riker, though?"

Jasmine pressed her lips together. That was actually a pretty good question. She certainly didn't trust Esther, and she was the one that had called Riker over. But, even though there didn't seem like a very good reason to, Jasmine found that she actually did trust the Keeper.

"I think I do, actually. Not that I think he'll do anything he didn't say he would, but I think he sticks to his word. I don't really have a good way to back that up, though. I could be wrong."

"Considering how apt your instincts have been thus far, I'd say I'll go with them," Asher said. He stood up, stretching his arms over his head and yawning as he popped his back. Walking over to join Jasmine, he nodded at the table. "What's that you have there?"

"Gambit. Riker is trying to teach me–"

"I love Gambit!" Asher exclaimed, his eyes lighting up. "He taught you how to play?"

"Yeah, kind of. I didn't realize you knew."

"I used to play it all the time as a kid," Asher said, pulling a chair out and sitting down. "You want to play?"

“I kind of suck.” Jasmine sat despite her words, opening the board up and pouring the pieces out onto the table.

“Bah. Everyone starts somewhere. It’ll be hilarious if we can get you pretty good at the game by the time you have your next class with Riker.”

“Don’t you have to practice magic? Your demonstration for Qien is tomorrow, isn’t it?” Jasmine asked hesitantly, but Asher was already starting to set up the pieces.

“That’s tomorrow. We’ll figure something out by then. We’ve got time for a game or two,” Asher said. Jasmine leveled a pointed look at him and he let out a sigh, his shoulders slumping. “I’m not going to avoid using it to keep from hurting you, okay? I’m just… pushing it back a bit.”

“Fine,” Jasmine said. “But we’re practicing tonight, okay?”

Asher grinned and moved a piece on the board, starting the game. “Deal. Let’s see what Riker taught you.”

# 28

Asher didn't hold back in the slightest, and Jasmine didn't win a single one of the four games they played. She barely made it any farther against him than she had against Riker, though Asher didn't make a point of taking every single one of her pieces before winning. He just did it normally.

Despite suffering four losses in a row, Jasmine appreciated Asher even more for his refusal to baby her. It was the exact same way he'd treating sparring, and it was the same way he went about everything he was serious on.

*Everything other than magic.*

Jasmine ignored the thought and rocked back, shaking her head and laughing. "Well, you won. Again."

"I've been playing for a lot longer than you," Asher said. "You're better than you were when you started, and that's what counts."

"Can't say I disagree." Jasmine started to pack the game up. It was getting late in the day, and it wouldn't be long before Qien's class started. "Do you think we can play again tomorrow, assuming we get time before Riker shows up?"

"Of course. Why not tonight?"

She arched an eyebrow. Asher grimaced and cleared his throat. "Right. Magic. Yeah. Don't give me that look. We'll practice. I promise."

Jasmine nodded. "Good. Let's get going, then. What exactly is it that you need to be able to do by tomorrow's class, by the way?"

"I need to channel magic safely for thirty seconds while keeping it controlled," Asher replied, rising to his feet and joining Jasmine as they headed out to go to class. "Qien strongly implied that we would be getting distracted."

"Is that difficult?"

"I wouldn't know. According to the book? Yes. It's not like I've actually tried doing it yet."

"And whose fault is that?"

Asher suddenly found the gold-covered walls fascinating. Jasmine just shook her head, not sure if she was meant to feel more amused or exasperated.

They got to class earlier than normal and claimed their normal seats without much difficulty. The only other people in the room were Pina and Clarence, who had been sitting in the front row before they arrived.

As they settled in, Asher's hand found Jasmine's and he interlaced his fingers with hers. He shifted his leg, blocking the motion away from any potential prying eyes before giving Jasmine a quick grin.

"Need to make sure I can use magic if I need to," Asher whispered into her ear.

Jasmine scrunched her nose. "You better actually mean that."

"Depends. Do I have permission?"

"You already know you do."

"Better to ask," Asher said, leaning back into his seat. He sent one more glance at her, then turned his attention to his other hand. A tiny prickle ran down Jasmine's back, but it was so faint that she could barely feel it.

"You need more," Jasmine said.

The feeling faded and Asher looked back to her, his brow starting to furrow. "How precisely can you feel this? I thought you could just tell if I was doing it or not."

"Why would you think that? I could feel you not taking enough when I was trying to get you to give me magic."

"I actually gave you some?" Asher blinked in surprise. "I thought I didn't do anything and you could tell I wasn't drawing on it."

"No, you drew a little. Isn't that pretty normal? I can basically feel what you should be able to feel, right?"

Asher shook his head, then froze in place as an idea struck him so clearly that Jasmine could practically see the change happen in real time. "Watcher's Eyes."

"What?" Jasmine asked. "What is it?"

"You're not a Starvein," Asher muttered.

"No shit," Jasmine said. "You just figured that out?"

"You're missing it. The whole reason Starveins can safely use magic while the Xolani mages failed is because we're functionally shittier mages. We can't use as much energy. We can't sense as much energy. That's the whole point. It's harder for the magic to overwhelm us because we're worse at channeling it. But you – you aren't a Starvein."

Realization struck Jasmine just as hard as it had hit Asher. They exchanged a shocked look, then quickly turned to see if anyone had overheard their conversation. Mercifully, Pina was currently being distracted by Clarence and nobody else had arrived in class yet.

"I haven't had any problems from you using the magic before, though." Jasmine had to take extra effort making sure her voice didn't accidentally get too loud in her excitement. "Does that mean you just haven't used enough?"

"I don't know," Asher admitted. "It's not like I've used that much, but I'm pretty sure any amount of magic should be too much for someone who isn't resistant to it."

"I'm not sure if that's true." Jasmine leaned in, putting her lips just beside Asher's ear. She wasn't willing to speak any louder than the faintest of whispers. "Don't you remember what Riker did? He wasn't a Starvein."

Asher's brow creased as he thought back to Riker's demonstration. Confusion intermixed with it and he rocked back on his heels, shaking his head.

"Shit," Asher muttered. "What does this mean for us, then?"

"What it means," Jasmine said, squeezing his hand to get his attention and draw his eyes back to hers, "is that I can tell exactly how much magic you're using for something. So, if I know how much you're using, I should be able to figure out when you're using too much, right?"

"I'm not so sure that's true," Asher said with a hesitant frown. "You're assuming you know what the tipping point is. You might not be able to feel it until it's too late."

"But if you keep the energy you draw to levels below what you've done before, it should be safe, right?"

Asher opened his mouth, then paused. Jasmine had him trapped and they both knew it. He thought for a few more moments, then finally let out a huff and gave her a small nod. "Yeah. I suppose you're right. You tell me the literal instant it gets anywhere near the most I've ever pulled though, okay? Actually – tell me when it gets halfway there."

"Deal." It was Jasmine's turn to hesitate for a few seconds before speaking again. "Do you think this means we're technically more capable than a normal Starvein?"

"We'll have to look into it. Maybe Riker will know. I'm not sure if it's something we should address with Qien. Somehow, I'm not sure if he'd appreciate hearing that a *Xolani* can do anything better than him, and I don't trust him not to try to make you do something that isn't safe."

Jasmine hid a laugh. She could picture the irritated scowl on Qien's face at the insinuation that she had the potential to do any sort of magic better than him. Riker was probably a much better person to pry with questions. Even if he wasn't a Starvein, he seemed to know more than his fair share about magic.

A faint tingle ran down Jasmine's spine, barely more than the previous time he'd tried to use magic.. "Use more. About twice that amount."

The feeling intensified, creeping up until it felt like there was an icicle braced against her back. She gave Asher a small nod and he pulled his fingers apart. Energy snapped and fizzled between them, swirling into a tiny ball.

A few seconds later, the chill faded and the magic blipped out. Asher sent Jasmine an excited look. "Watcher. Why didn't we do this from the start?"

"Because you're stubborn," Jasmine said. "And, if we had, it might have stopped at that."

Asher paused as he thought back to the events of their discussion the previous day, likely recalling exactly what their argument had led to. He cleared his throat. "Never mind. I'm glad it took this long."

Jasmine rolled her eyes. "Just start thinking about how you're going to pass the exam tomorrow and how we can push this. We've got a lot of work ahead of us."

"I think that might be an understatement."

Jasmine blinked, turning to see that Pina had twisted in her chair and was looking straight at them. Evidently, she'd been speaking a bit louder than she thought she had. Her eyes narrowed.

*How much did she hear?*

# 29

"Care to elaborate?" Asher asked, his features darkening.

"You heard me," Pina said. "I still don't understand what a Keeper is doing in our class. You've yet to do even the slightest bit of real magic, and the only thing I've actually seen you cast is the training exercise that we learn as children."

"He's not a Keeper," Jasmine said. "Not anymore. Did you not hear Qien?"

"I didn't ask you, Xolani," Pina said.

Asher's hand tightened around Jasmine's as a streak of anger flashed through his eyes and stiffened his back. He shifted forward in his chair, but Jasmine beat him to it.

"You have a problem with me?" Jasmine asked.

"A problem? You aren't important enough to have a problem with," Pina said, her features twisting in distaste like she'd stepped in a pile of cow dung. "You're a half-baked Keeper from the gutters that couldn't even stay in her own program. I suppose it makes sense. What else would a Starvein that can't even use magic deserve?"

Jasmine could feel Asher was about an inch from rising out of his chair and punching Pina square in the nose. In the Keeper program, that wouldn't have been a problem in the slightest. Half their problems were ended with fights – but that wasn't how they worked here.

*If Qien walks in on Asher punching this stuck-up bitch, he'll be in a ton of trouble. That might be exactly what she's aiming for. I'm not sure why Asher is taking the bait so hard, but it's just a strategy to get him pissed off.*

*This is exactly what Riker was doing.*

"You're talking a lot of shit for a woman who'd bend like a reed in the lightest breeze," Jasmine said, squeezing Asher's hand sharply to stop him from doing anything stupid. "Don't forget how slow your magic is. The worst Keeper in the world could use your face as a floor scrub if they wanted to."

Pina's features narrowed in annoyance more than anger, but Jasmine had taken the wind out of her insults before they could get the wanted rise out of Asher. She opened her mouth, then paused and her eyes flicked up.

Jasmine turned, following Pina's gaze, as Qien strode into the room. He didn't even give them so much as a second glance as he approached the front of the class and walked up to his podium, setting down a bundle of papers and starting to prepare for whatever he would be teaching.

"Did you want to say something else?" Asher asked, his voice cool. "Or did you just like staring?"

Pina pressed her lips together in irritation and turned away from them without so much as a sound. Beside her, Clarence shifted uncomfortably. He rooted through his bag and buried his nose in a book he'd brought with him, doing everything he could to ignore the stares boring into Pina's back.

"What's her problem?" Asher muttered. "She was really going after you. I've got half a mind to–"

"Don't. She was trying to rile you up on purpose," Jasmine said in a low tone. "I don't think she actually gives a shit about me."

"Why? What in the world is she getting out of having a stick so far up her ass that it's threatening to poke out her mouth?"

"No idea," Jasmine admitted, hiding a laugh. She'd never seen Asher so irritated at someone, and she couldn't deny it felt more than a little nice to know how much he cared. "You don't need to get that angry on my behalf, though. Insults aren't going to kill me, but getting in trouble is the last thing we need right now."

Asher grimaced, then scrunched his nose and let out a huff. "As usual, you're right. I don't know how you just sit around when people basically spit in your face."

*Well, considering Riker did it to me a few hours ago and I tried to break his nose because he pissed me off so much, I'm not so sure I can say much without being a hypocrite.*

"Practice," Jasmine said, putting on a sage air. "Once you know what someone's trying to do, it's easier to counter it."

*Is this how Riker always feels? No wonder he's teaching me. It feels cool to pretend to know what I'm doing.*

Asher rolled his eyes and nudged her with his shoulder. "Give me your hand back. I need to be able to do magic if Qien calls on me."

His fingers found hers and they interlaced beneath the cover of their legs. It wasn't like they needed to be in such close contact. Simply touching the sides of their palms would have been enough, but Jasmine was not about to complain.

Students continued to filter into the class, taking their seats one by one. One of the last to arrive was Esmarelda, who made her way across the rows and squeezed past Asher – only to sit down next to Jasmine instead of returning to her spot from the previous day.

"Mind if I sit here?" Esmarelda asked, pulling a book out of her bag before Jasmine could even respond.

"Help yourself," Jasmine said. "It's not like I own the seat."

"Some people would disagree," Esmarelda said with a small grin. "Seat space is a coveted thing, you know. It's basically an alliance."

"This is a class. What are you allying over?" Jasmine's brow furrowed. "Like study partners?"

"That, but also the exams. A lot of them are taken in groups, and we usually get to choose who we work with," Esmarelda explained. She pulled a bottle of ink and a quill out of her bag's side pocket, then opened the book and placed them on the side of the small table sticking out of her chair. "Generally, the good noble families stick together. And, if you aren't one of the stronger families, you latch onto one and hope that you can make friends."

*I suppose that explains the seating arrangements. All the people with the fancy clothes are the good families – no brainer. That makes Pina one of the strong or rich ones. Spoiled brat.*

"Where do you stack up in that regard?" Asher asked. He winced as soon as the words came out of his mouth and held his free hand up in a placating motion. "Not that I care where you come from. I was more wondering why you weren't sitting with anyone before."

"I prefer to work alone." Esmarelda gave them a small shrug. "I wouldn't say I'm half-bad at magic, but I don't really like having to rely on people who are always waiting to get something back from me. It makes me feel dirty, like some form of magical concubine who gives out magic instead of her body. If I'm choosing who I help – that's a different story."

"Why us, then?" Jasmine asked. "Asher can't even cast magic properly yet, so I don't think either of us are going to be able to do much for you in class."

Asher glared at Jasmine. "Come on. You don't have to rub it in. I'm getting better."

"I'll compliment you when you deserve it," Jasmine replied

without missing a beat. She grinned at him. "And that means you have to practice first."

Esmarelda pointed her quill at Asher. "And that's the reason I wouldn't mind hanging around you two."

"What, because I suck? That's cold."

She raised a hand to cover a laugh. "No. Because you don't care how good I am, and because you helped me out without any real intention of getting anything back. Those are decent enough reasons, are they not?"

"It was Jasmine that helped you, not me."

"She's your Keeper. Your actions are one and the same."

Jasmine and Asher exchanged a glance, then shared a shrug.

"Well, I'm never opposed to more friends," Jasmine said. "Welcome aboard."

"I don't know if I'd go that far. Let's start with acquaintances. And, as acquaintances, I have to ask. How screwed are you for the exam tomorrow?"

Asher thought for a moment. "You know, I think I should actually be okay. Your advice was pretty useful. As long as Qien isn't looking to screw us over, I think I'll pass without too much difficulty. You?"

"About the same. I'm not about to let myself get distracted so easily again." Esmarelda glanced at Jasmine out of the corner of her eyes. "I wish I had a Keeper to cover me while I was using my magic. I'm jealous."

"Sorry. She's mine," Asher said. "I know another one in the market, though. She's pretty."

Esmarelda blinked, then arched an eyebrow. "Are you trying to set me up?"

"Let's just say I owe her a favor and she's on the market."

"As much as I appreciate the offer, I'm more of a man kind of gal," Esmarelda said. "That's sweet of you, though."

"Hey, I tried." Asher shrugged. "Jas, you're going to have to back me up the next time Lydia comes by. I bet she won't believe me when I tell her I gave it a shot."

"If you don't mind me asking, where in the noble families do you fall?" Jasmine asked. "Your clothes put you around the middle, but you've got that really nice necklace. I'm not sure if this is an offensive question or something like that, I was just curious."

Esmarelda touched the golden band that ran around her neck and beneath her shirt, then laughed. "This? It's just an heirloom. It's not really worth much. My family is actually on the lower end of things."

Before anyone could respond, Qien rapped his knuckles on the podium. Everyone turned their attention toward him as he stepped around the stand and crossed his arms behind his back.

"I hope everyone is prepared for tomorrow," he said. "As previously discussed, the exam will cover your ability to maintain concentration while casting magic. However, the exact details of the exam have… marginally changed."

A few low mutters ran through the classroom, but they were silenced by a single sharp glance from Qien. He didn't even have to say anything. Nobody was willing to risk his wrath by drawing extra attention.

"What are the changes?" Clarence asked from beside Pina, his tone wavering. "Will we be required to learn anything new before tomorrow?"

"New? No. I'll be explaining the exact details tomorrow to make sure none of you try to find ways to work around the exam. Life is full of surprises, and adapting to them will be an important skill. All you need to know is that you'll be expected to perform as you always have. I will not ask you to do anything out of your capabilities. Are there any further questions?"

Nobody spoke up, but it wasn't because they didn't have questions. The look in Qien's eyes said that anyone who made him pause for any longer was going to severely regret the experience.

*I guess that's one way to make sure you don't have to spend time explaining the exam. Nobody can be confused if everyone's too scared to speak up about it.*

"Good," Qien said with a curt nod. "Then we will begin today's lesson."

# 30

The class passed without anything of note, and before Jasmine knew it, Qien had gathered his books from the podium and departed the class. She blinked herself out of her mild reverie as Pina and Clarence strode past her seat near the aisle.

Pina very pointedly didn't look in their direction as she passed. Esmarelda tilted her head to the side, then jerked a thumb in Pina's direction.

"What's her problem?"

"Me, apparently," Asher said with a shrug. "She's not a fan of the fact that I was a Keeper."

"Seriously? Weird. She never gives a shit about other people," Esmarelda said as she threw one last glance at Pina's retreating back. "She's so self-absorbed with her magic practice that I figured she forgot there were other kids in the class. Did you antagonize her?"

"Not beyond when Qien had me push her onto her butt," Jasmine said. "But she didn't even seem that pissed about that. Her attention was on Asher, not me."

"Huh. Well, I'd stay out of her way if I were you."

"What, is she going to try to jump us in a dark alley?" Asher asked, only half joking.

"I highly doubt she'd ever do something to straight up break a rule. She's from the Ardfell family. They've got really high standards for her, and I've heard she's got a personal tutor that occasionally comes to Sanctuary. If they found out she was cavorting with people beneath her station, they'd probably punish her."

"Why should we be scared, then?" Jasmine frowned. "Seems like she should be the one avoiding us, not the other way around."

"Because if she doesn't like you, then the rest of the class is going to do what she wants to avoid getting on her bad side. The Ardfell family is pretty big, you know. One of the larger noble houses in the kingdom."

Asher yawned. He gathered his notes up and rose to his feet, stretching his arms in the air above his head before shaking his head and shrugging. "Whatever. I don't care what she thinks. Does this mean you want out of the alliance or whatever?"

Esmarelda snorted. "I was already sitting alone. I've got no interest in getting cozy with an Ardfell. They didn't get their strength and power by playing nice. Pina and her entire family are bad news."

"Good to know. You think tomorrow will be a group exam, then?" Asher asked.

"Probably. It seems like the kind of think Qien would like." Esmarelda scratched at the side of her cheek. "Well, I'm off. I've got some stuff to practice before tomorrow. See you both then."

She raised a hand in farewell, then gathered her belongings and headed out of the class. Jasmine and Asher weren't far behind her. They set a course back for their rooms. Exam or not, there was only one thing on their minds, and there wasn't any reason not to try it anymore.

*We need to find out how to use Asher's magic.*

As soon as Jasmine closed the door behind them, Asher set his notes and book down on his desk and turned back to her. "You're good to test the magic now?"

"I've been the one bugging you to do it this whole time. Yes, I'm good to do it."

"I didn't think it would be safe before," Asher said defensively. "I mean – if you had no idea how much magic was flowing, it would have been a huge problem. But now that we know that isn't the case… okay. When you feel the magic, it's like this cold, prickling sensation, right?"

Jasmine nodded. "Like ice running through my veins and along my back."

"Okay. I think that's pretty normal, although I haven't heard about the back part before. From what I read, Starveins are supposed to feel magic like a faint tickle through their entire body. As it grows stronger, we can feel it start working its way toward our head. That's when we have to stop. So, if that ice ever gets close to your neck, you make me stop immediately."

"Okay. What else do I need to know?"

"Well, there are a bunch of techniques that we can use to increase the flow of magic so it doesn't take forever to use it, but they usually come with the risk of filling you faster and resulting in… well, we get to repeat the mistake the Xolani did."

"Maybe we avoid those for now," Jasmine said with a grimace. She cracked her neck and flexed her fingers to get herself prepared. "It didn't feel like your magic was all that slow in the first place. Let's just start by slowly pushing up the magic you can draw until it begins getting close to our limit. If I don't know where to stop, it'll be hard to warn you."

Asher paused for a second, then inclined his head. "That seems reasonable. But please, be really careful. Don't forget I can't feel anything when I'm using the magic, so you'll have to be the one to stop me before I go too far. I don't want to kill you."

"You won't," Jasmine said. She held her hand out. "Go on."

Asher took it. He drew in a deep breath, then locked eyes with Jasmine. She gave him a slight nod, and a tiny prickle ran along her back. Dark energy flickered through Asher's eyes like sizzling bolts of lightning.

Moving at the speed of a snail, the feeling started to intensify. The tingles ran down Jasmine's back and spread throughout her veins. She shivered involuntarily and the sensation instantly abated.

"I'm fine," Jasmine said. "It's nowhere near my neck yet. I can feel it in my arms, though."

"That's it?"

"Yes. Keep going."

Asher reluctantly started to pull energy again. Jasmine drew in a sharp breath as the sensation sharpened. Tiny shards dug into her back, pushing over the border of mildly uncomfortable into nearly painful.

More of the ice crept throughout her, an invisible frost wrapping her in its grip. Jasmine's breath came out in puffs of white mist, but it had yet to travel anywhere higher than her chest. Asher sent her another concerned glance, but Jasmine just nodded for him to keep going.

Seconds ticked by. Something deep inside Jasmine pulsed hungrily, and tingles of anticipation made her ears ring. Blood rushed in her body, coursing with adrenaline. It seemed like ages had passed when the chill finally reached up, passing her collarbone.

"Stop," Jasmine said.

Asher released the magic instantly. A tremor ran through Jasmine's body as the cold drained away, spiraling into her chest. She let out a shaky sigh. "Watcher's eyes. That was *intense.*"

"Intense? Not agonizing?"

"Agonizing? Not at all. I mean, it wasn't comfortable by any means, but it wasn't exactly bad."

Asher squinted at Jasmine. "Are you a masochist?"

She choked. "What? No."

"I have no idea how much magic I was using, but you should have been screaming in pain at the amount I think we drew," Asher said, shaking his head in disbelief. "The book says drawing magic for more than ten seconds is already risking a lot. That was at least a minute. You didn't lie about where you felt the magic, did you?"

"Of course I didn't. I'm not trying to kill myself," Jasmine said, crossing her arms. "This means we can use a lot of magic?"

"A lot?" Asher let out a stunned laugh. "No. We can use a ridiculous amount. Starveins spend years trying to build their well of magic up as big as yours."

"You know, it's technically yours."

"Who cares whose it is," Asher said with a dismissive wave. "It's ours, if you prefer that. Whatever it is, this is unbelievable. We probably have more raw magic than Qien."

"What now? Test what it does?"

"We need to figure out how quickly you get the magic back. Starveins collect it passively, kind of like rain in a bucket. Everyone gets it back at different rates, but it's usually around an hour to a day to recover so long as you didn't completely run yourself dry."

"Huh. That's why Esmarelda was so scared of getting drained. If you completely run out, it takes longer to recover."

Asher nodded. "Seems that way. Ideally, we'd probably want to test that, but with the exam tomorrow..."

"Not a good time," Jasmine agreed. "So we shouldn't test my recovery abilities yet."

"Probably not. I guess that just leaves actually casting magic instead of feeling how much you can hold at once," Asher said, a note of reluctance in his voice. He shook his head and set his jaw. "Right. I'm ready to do it if you are."

"You know I am. What are you going to try to do? The exercise that Qien showed in class?"

"Yeah," Asher said. He gave Jasmine's hand a soft squeeze. "I know you can probably handle more, but I'm still going to go slow. I don't know if the draw is going to get more intense when I'm actually casting magic."

"Sounds like a good idea. Let's do it." Despite Jasmine's confident words, she couldn't shake at the snake of fear that ran down her back. The idea of getting transformed into a mindless, magic-devouring monster wasn't exactly a pleasant one.

*I can't mention anything about it. Asher will never go through with this if he thinks I'm worried.*

A tiny chill pressed against Jasmine's palm. She waited for a moment, but the feeling didn't get any stronger. Her brow furrowed.

"You'll need more than that, Asher. It took almost twice the amount just to make the crackly thing between your fingers."

"Oh. Really?" Asher's brow furrowed in concentration. The magical pull intensified, but Jasmine got the feeling it wasn't quite enough. "Is this better?"

"I think you probably need a bit more, but I don't really know what I'm talking about. It just doesn't *feel* like enough."

"Let me try with this first," Asher said. "I'm going to draw the magic out now."

Jasmine nodded, and the cold sensation raced out from her palm and into Asher. Energy swirled to life above his right palm, condensing into a hissing ball of black and faint red power. It spun for all of a second before collapsing in on itself and disappearing with a tiny pop.

The smell of ozone filled the air, and they both scrunched their noses.

"Okay. You were right," Asher admitted. "I didn't use enough. How in the world did you know? Did you read my book or something?"

"No. Your book makes no sense. It just… felt right, I guess."

"Good to know." Admiration lit in Asher's eyes and he shook his head with a chuckle. "You're incredible, you know that? I really should have expected this. You could detect the assassin's magic too. I guess you're just really sensitive to magic for some reason."

"Huh. I didn't even think about that being related to this, but it makes a lot of sense," Jasmine admitted.

"Try again?" Asher asked. Jasmine nearly laughed. The fear that he'd had was starting to evaporate, and she was surprised to find that her own apprehension was leaving with it. Asher wouldn't do anything that could hurt her.

"Yeah," Jasmine said. "Let's keep at it. We're going to smash tomorrow's exam, no matter what Qien throws at us."

# 31

They practiced through the rest of the day, and to more success than Jasmine could have dreamed of. By the time they finished, Asher was summoning magical energy to his hand even faster than Pina had been.

"I feel like I'm cheating," Asher muttered as he watched the power dissipate. "I barely even have to concentrate because you're the one taking all the pain for me. It's too easy."

"Well, don't forget the drawbacks. We've got to be in contact for it to work."

Asher flashed Jasmine a grin and tugged on her hand, catching her off balance. She stumbled forward and he stepped into her, wrapping his arounds her in a tight hug.

"I don't see it as a drawback," Asher whispered into her ear.

Tingles ran down Jasmine's back, and they weren't because of magic. She laughed into his collarbone and gave him a quick kiss before pushing him back a step. "Stop that. We can't get distracted right now. After the exam, okay?"

"After the exam," Asher allowed reluctantly. "You're sure the pain isn't bad, though?"

"I told you it doesn't hurt. It's just prickly."

"If you're sure," Asher said. His stomach rumbled and they both looked down at it. Asher cleared his throat. "I think it might be time for dinner."

Jasmine looked out the window past Asher's shoulder. It was well into the night and the moon had already lifted into the sky.

"The kitchen's probably empty. Now's as good a time as any. I'm pretty hungry myself."

Their path decided, they slipped out into the hall and made for the kitchen. Mercifully, Jasmine's prediction had been correct. It was completely abandoned when they arrived.

"Are you thinking anything in particular?" Asher asked, looking through the cupboard and squinting in the dim light that came from lanterns hanging along the walls.

"Food is good."

"Gee, thanks," Asher grumbled. "Aren't you supposed to be asking me this question?"

"You're the one teaching me," Jasmine said with a snicker. "I can make eggs, steak, and salad. That's about it. If you want something new, you'll have to show me how to make it."

He pulled a potato out of the cabinet and held it out. "Oh, I haven't had a baked potato in ages. This could work, and they're really easy."

"Let's see it, then. What do I do?"

"Just follow along. I'll show you what to do this time since it's so easy."

Jasmine did, and she had to admit that Asher hadn't been wrong. Making a baked potatoes was definitely simple. All they had to do was get the oven heated and wash the potatoes in the meantime. Then, once the oven was hot, they just drizzled oil and salt over the tubers before tossing them in to bake.

"Right," Asher said. "Forty minutes and they'll be done."

"Forty?" Jasmine's eye twitched. "I was hoping that would be like five or ten."

He rubbed the back of his head sheepishly. "Yeah. I kind of forgot how long it takes potatoes to bake. They taste good, though."

"I've had them before. Lydia made some," Jasmine said. She scrunched her nose, then sighed. "Well, whatever. We've already started, and now I want potatoes. So I guess we wait for an hour."

They stood in silence for a minute, leaning against the counter and watching the light from the fire beneath the oven. Jasmine snuck a glance at Asher, only to find that he was looking at her out of the corner of his eyes.

"What?" Asher asked. "I'm allowed to look, aren't I?"

Jasmine scrunched her nose.

*We're done with magic for the day. I think I'd prefer you'd do more than look, but I literally just told you a few hours ago that we would stay focused until the exam was done tomorrow. Damn it.*

"Yeah," Jasmine grumbled. "You can look."

Asher inched closer to her and slipped his hand around her waist, pulling her against his side. Jasmine met his gaze, and he lifted an eyebrow, letting a familiar smug look slip across his lips.

"What? It's practice for magic."

Jasmine opened her mouth, then turned to glance over her shoulder. The kitchen was empty. Nobody in their right mind was going to be using it this late at night. She looked back to Asher and pressed her chest against his. "You know, you have to be able to use magic while distracted."

"Yeah?" Asher leaned closer, brushing his lips against her forehead.

"Do you think you might need some practice ignoring distractions?" Jasmine asked.

"Only one way to find out," Asher murmured, pulling her up against himself and kissing her on the nape of her neck.

They nearly burned the potatoes.

Jasmine and Asher stared at the baked potatoes on the plate before them. Tiny wisps of steam and smoke rose off them – perhaps nearly had been a bit of exaggeration. The potatoes weren't *not* burnt either.

Jasmine adjusted her crumpled clothes in case someone happened to walk in, then cleared her throat softly. "I'm... less hungry than I was before."

"I'm not," Asher said, the look in his eyes making it very clear that he wasn't talking about the food. He pulled Jasmine in and gave her another quick kiss on the forehead. "But I'm not a savage, and you were right about the exam tomorrow."

"Tease," Jasmine grumbled, grabbing a potato and taking a bite out of it.

"Do you *want* me to fail? Because I'll happily stay up all night."

"I think I'd be failing in my duties as a Keeper if I encouraged that. Just eat your damn potato."

They finished their meals in peace, if not slight tension, and then headed back to their room to prepare for the night. The Starvein Halls seemed empty at night, devoid of the light that normally made their golden murals shimmer.

"Everything fine?" Asher asked. "You look concerned."

"I'm fine, sorry." Jasmine shook her head, pulling her mind back from its wandering thoughts. "The Starvein Halls are just kind of creepy at night."

"Tell me about it," Asher said.

They got back to his room and slipped inside. Jasmine checked the door to make sure it was locked, and then they both quickly set off to take care of their preparations for the night and following morning.

*I don't know why, but I kind of feel uneasy. This isn't the same sensation I had when the assassin showed up. Is it about the test tomorrow?*

When Jasmine returned to Asher's room, she did a quick check of the windows before leaning her sword up against his bed where she could reach it quickly if she needed to. Asher stepped out of the shower, his shirt held in one of his hands, and took a single look at Jasmine before figuring out that something was wrong.

"Are you okay?" Asher asked with a concerned frown. "What's going on? Did I–"

"Nothing you did." Jasmine shook her head. "I don't know why. I'm just nervous about the exam, I guess."

"About if I'll pass?"

"I don't know." She ground her teeth and clenched her jaw, glancing at the windows one last time before letting out a heavy sigh. "Whatever. There's nothing we can do about it. I don't even know why I'm concerned."

"Is it like... normal concern? Or magical?" Asher asked as he sat down on his bed and tossed the shirt into a small pile of dirty clothes at the base of his closet.

"I think it's just normal. I'm not getting the weird tingling that I did before."

"Then it'll be fine. You don't have to worry about me, Jas. I can handle myself. And, even if I fail, it wouldn't be your fault. Qien isn't going to expect me to be top of the class the first week I arrive."

"Logically, I get that." Jasmine flopped down on the bed and looked up at the ceiling, bunching the sheets up in her hands. "I don't even think you'll do bad. We were doing great today. I feel like we shouldn't have any trouble."

"If you aren't sure what you're worried about, then try not to give it attention," Asher suggested, sliding under the sheets. "If you stress about something you can't control, you only suffer twice."

"That's... actually rather sage. Your saying?"

"My dad's," Asher admitted. "One of the few good ones he had."

"It is good." Jasmine rolled over, pulling the sheets back and sliding beneath them.

Asher brushed a hand across her shoulders, then wrapped her in his embrace. She let out a soft sigh, and a smile flitted across her lips as his warm breath tickled her collar bone.

"If I hold you close enough, will you feel better?" Asher asked. "I don't want you stressed and sleeping poorly before the exam tomorrow."

"I guess there's only one way to find out," Jasmine murmured. "Goodnight, Asher."

Asher gave her a soft squeeze and a gentle kiss on the neck. "Goodnight, Jas."

# 32

Jasmine awoke to a shadow looming over her. She launched herself out of bed before she knew what she was doing, hitting the ground with a grunt and grabbing her sword as she rolled to her feet. Asher dove in the other direction, coming up with his own sword clutched in his hands.

Riker stood at the foot of their bed, a flat expression on his face. He didn't seem concerned with Jasmine's slamming heart or horrified expression.

"What are you doing?" Jasmine exclaimed, trying to get her adrenaline under control.

"Seriously, if you're going to watch, you need to at least ask first," Asher said, letting out a huff. "What in the Watcher's name, man?"

"You were not answering the door," Riker said. "I came inside. And, when I did, I wondered how sensitive you would be to my presence."

"So you… just stood and stared at us while we were sleeping?" Jasmine demanded.

"Yes."

"How'd you get through the door without making any noise?" Asher asked, not lowering his sword. "There's no way I was sleeping that deeply."

"I picked the lock, of course." Riker stared at Asher like he was an idiot. "How else would I have done it? I could have picked the lock on the windows as well."

"Picking locks isn't the behavior of a normal person. That's something an assassin would do."

"It is the behavior of a Keeper. We are capable," Riker said simply. "And Jasmine – for your information – it appears that your intuition did not detect me until I was about to stab you."

"You were about to *stab* me?"

"I was strongly considering it. I wanted to see if it picked up on magic or intent. It appears it is both." Riker shrugged. "You're welcome."

"I'm not saying thank you for that," Jasmine said, but some of the adrenaline had finally started to leave her limbs. She let her sword lower, but she didn't put it away completely. "You nearly scared me half to death."

"At least you were prepared. I came to tell you that we will not have class today. I have something I need to deal with."

"Like what?" Asher asked. "And couldn't you have left a note?"

"A note could have been intercepted. I wanted to ensure that the message was delivered. I trust you will continue the lessons we started yesterday, Jasmine?"

Jasmine nodded, then let out a slow breath and took control of the last fragments of surprise, shoving them away. "Yes. I think I've started to figure out what you were getting at."

"Good," Riker said. "Tread carefully. Do not slack on your training."

With that, he turned and strode out the door, closing it gently behind him. Jasmine and Asher stared at it in silence for a few seconds, then looked to each other.

"Watcher's eyes, he's *weird,*" Asher muttered, looking down at his bare chest. "I can't say I like being stared at when I sleep."

"Tell me about it." Jasmine grimaced. Sunlight had just started to filter in through the windows, so it was still fairly early morning. It was quite a while until it would be time for the exam. "Well, I guess we're up now. I don't think I can sleep after that."

"Me neither," Asher said. He let out a sigh and set his sword down. "Want to play Gambit? I don't really feel like practicing magic so close to the exam. I'm already feeling pretty confident after yesterday."

"You practiced for a few hours at most. That's enough?"

"It's not really difficult when you're the one doing all the work," Asher said with a shrug. He walked over to his closet and pulled on a shirt and pants, then looked back to Jasmine. "Unless you think you need more practice yourself? I just don't want you to run out of energy by surprise midway through."

"I suppose it's probably better to be safe than sorry if you're confident," Jasmine allowed. "Fine. Give me a second."

She headed into her room and pulled on a fresh set of clothes before finishing her preparations for the day and heading back to rejoin Asher. He'd already set the Gambit board out on the table and had laid the pieces on it.

Jasmine sat down across from him, still somewhat off guard from their rude awakening.

*Of all the days to do that, why today?*

"Should I try to find a way to get a better lock for our door?" Asher asked, reading Jasmine's thoughts with a single look at her expression.

"As if that would stop him. He'd just pick that one too," Jasmine said with a small laugh. She shook her head. "Don't worry about it. I'm still on edge. Let's just play so I can take my mind off this."

"Whatever you want," Asher said with a shrug. He took a piece and moved it across the board. "Your move."

Jasmine didn't win any games, but she got closer to it than she had the previous day. Asher lost more pieces and, even though he'd been trying as hard as he could from the start, Jasmine could see his posture change as their games progressed. He leaned in closer to the board and his eyes narrowed in concentration. Every move he made took just a bit longer, but he still managed to claim victory in every match in the end.

That didn't bother Jasmine in the slightest. At the rate she was improving, she was pretty sure she'd start claiming victories off Asher in just a few days. And, considering she'd never played Gambit before yesterday, that would be a pretty respectable achievement.

"Has anyone ever told you how damn good you are at Gambit?" Asher asked after they'd taken a break to eat lunch. "It's kind of scary."

"You still won all the games," Jasmine pointed out.

"For now. You're going to blow me out of the water soon enough. I guess you were a better Keeper than me all along, huh?"

Jasmine glanced at Asher in surprise. "That isn't true. I–"

"It's fine," Asher said with a laugh. "You don't have to feel bad about the truth. I was better than you at fighting for a while, but only because I had formal training. Everything else was just because I had experience and you didn't. You're going to be a terrifying Keeper when you graduate."

"If I graduate."

"When," Asher corrected, catching her eye. "I know you will, just like I know I'll be able to handle the Starvein program as long as you're by my side – both figuratively and literally. Qien's eyes are going to pop out of his head when he sees how much magic I can control."

*Well, I certainly can't complain about that attitude.*

"Let's see it, then. Shall we go to class?"

"Yeah, I'd say it's about time," Asher said with a grin. "Let's go."

# 33

Much of the class was already there when they arrived. Pina and Clarence stood near the front, and Jasmine spotted Esmarelda waiting for them near their normal seats. She gave them a nod as the two arrived and sat down beside her. Esmarelda looked like she'd run the entire way over. Her forehead was covered in sweat and her clothes were matted to her back.

"What happened to you?"

"Slept poorly," Esmarelda replied with a grimace. "And somehow took the wrong turn on the way here and didn't realize for nearly ten minutes. I sprinted the whole way over."

Jasmine suppressed a laugh and chose to look around the rest of the room, sparing Esmarelda any further embarrassment. Even Qien had already arrived and stood by the podium, drumming his fingers on the wood impatiently. He was poring over a piece of paper before him, his brow furrowed in either irritation or concentration. Possibly both.

"Why's everyone so early?" Jasmine asked.

"Test day," Esmarelda replied with a shrug. "And people are

nervous about the change of plans. Qien doesn't really do that often, so I'd imagine people are scared that it might be more difficult than they expected."

"You're also here early," Asher pointed out.

"I didn't exclude myself from people." Esmarelda flashed a grin at them and shrugged. "I'm sure it'll be fine, though. Qien isn't trying to fail us. I think."

That wasn't particularly reassuring, but Jasmine couldn't bring herself to respond. Even though she wasn't actually the one taking the exam, she felt anxiety build in her stomach and form a knot within it. She sat back in her chair, biting her inner lip and wishing the exam would just start already.

Asher's hand found hers and gave it a quick squeeze. He nudged her with his shoulder as she glanced at him.

"What?"

"It's fine," Asher said. "Even if something goes wrong, it's not the end of the world."

"I know, I know," Jasmine muttered. "I just don't want you to fail."

"In that case, I won't."

Jasmine bit back a snort. "Just like that?"

"You asked for it, so I'll deliver. Simple, right?"

She rolled her eyes, but somehow, Asher's words actually worked a little and some of the stress receded. Minutes passed, and the rest of the class filed into the room.

Qien finally looked up from his podium and scanned over all the students with his cold gaze. He pushed the papers he was studying into his folder and stepped around the podium.

"I see all of you have arrived. You are various stages of early. Good. Being prompt is vital for a Starvein. I'm sure you're all waiting to hear how the exam has changed, yes?"

Nobody said anything, but the intensity of the stares boring into Qien definitely told him all he needed to know. The corner of his mouth curled upward.

"Today's exam will take place outside of Sanctuary."

Jasmine's eyes widened and she exchanged a shocked look at Asher. The other nobles didn't look too surprised, though.

"Do the Starveins normally get to leave Sanctuary?" Jasmine whispered to Esmarelda.

"Yeah. Why? Do Keepers not?"

"No," Jasmine muttered, leaning back into her chair and shaking her head in disbelief. "They don't."

Qien continued on, unaware and uncaring of their conversation. "It will be different in a few ways. I wanted to find a way to more properly test all of you and ensure you were getting an appropriate level of real-world training. As it turned out, I got lucky. One of my colleagues is running an exam for her own students today, and we've decided to coordinate to achieve the best results for both of us."

"We're going to be competing with another class of Starveins?" Clarence asked. "Is that fair, Professor Qien? We're the only first year students, so there's no way we'll win."

"You would be correct if I was referring to the other Starvein classes," Qien said with a dry laugh. "It will not be them you go against. It will be the Keepers."

"We're going to be fighting Keepers?" a girl on the side of the classroom asked. "Didn't the demonstration a few days ago show that was basically impossible for us in our current state?"

"If it was a real fight, most likely." Qien nodded, then held a finger up. "But you will not be directly fighting them. Whoever struck first would always win, and we do not want casualties from you striking them with your magic. Instead, we will be playing something of a competition. You will be broken into groups of three, and you will go against Keepers in groups of the same size. The Keepers will not be allowed to seriously injure you, but they will be attempting to capture you. In turn, you will attempt to stun them with a weak bolt of magical energy. Any Keeper that is stunned will be treated as dead. The last group standing wins."

"Isn't that rigged for the Keepers?" Esmarelda sent a glance at Jasmine. "They're faster than we are. If they just rush us, we're very unlikely to win."

"They will not be allowed to seriously injure you, as I mentioned," Qien said. "In fact, this competition is skewed toward the Starveins, not the Keepers. Because they cannot remove you from the fight, so long as you can keep your concentration whilst under attack, you should be able to hit your opponent."

"What if we panic and use too much energy? I haven't been in a real fight before," Clarence said nervously.

Qien's cold gaze bored into Clarence's skull. "If you do anything more than stun anyone, I will drain your magic, strip you naked, and hang you from your heels in the Keeper quarters for a day. Starveins are nothing if not controlled. If you cannot control your power, you do not deserve to be called a Starvein. I would prefer to see you broken and bleeding than I would to hear that you are so incompetent that you could not restrain your powers. Do I make myself clear?"

Qien's words were a sharp knife that carved through the classroom. Clarence shrank before him, giving a hurried nod. The professor's eyes traced over the room, waiting to see if anyone else had questions.

Jasmine's stomach churned. Esther was somehow involved in the exam. It was odd, feeling so strongly against someone that had once been a mentor to her, but Jasmine couldn't bring herself to view Esther with anything but disgust.

*I never thought I'd actually be going directly against other Keepers either. But... this feels like a pretty good turnout for me, now that I think about it. Having someone to physically intercede with anyone attacking would put Asher at a huge advantage.*

"There is one final component to this exam," Qien said. "Esther and I have worked together to choose the most appropriate teams to account for weaknesses and strengths. They will be assigned shortly when we arrive."

*Shortly? It's going to take at least an hour to get out of Sanctuary.*

As if Qien could read Jasmine's mind, he held a hand out behind his back. His lips pressed thin and a crackle of blue energy arced through his eyes. A dull glow enveloped his fingers and swirled out at his palm.

Seconds ticked by. The class watched in rapt attention as the energy behind Qien started to intensify. Bolts of hissing energy arced free of a swirling blue disk that expanded behind him, growing until it was twice as wide and just as tall as he was.

Qien removed his hand and let out a slow breath. He shook his head, then nodded to the newly formed portal. "Get on with it. Even I do not have the energy to sustain a portal like this for a long period of time. And, needless to say, if you do not enter, you fail."

That got the class moving. Everyone shot to their feet and lined up, heading through the portal one by one. Jasmine tensed as she drew up to it, stepping into the popping energy and squeezing her eyes shut in preparation.

It felt like she'd plunged into a pool of freezing water. Jasmine drew in an involuntary gasp as a familiar freezing sensation rushed over her entire body. The experience lasted for less than a second, and her foot hit grass a second later.

She'd emerged into a grassy clearing inside a forest. The students that had gone through the portal before her were already standing around, looking around nervously.

Jasmine shook herself off as the last remnants of the sensation faded away and stepped to the side as Asher emerged from a twisting blue disk behind her. The rest of the class piled out behind them and Qien was the last to come thorough, holding a bag in one hand.

He flicked his fingers and the portal snapped shut, leaving them all in the clearing. Qien then opened the bag in his other hand.

"This has tokens for each of you. When you defeat someone, take their token. If you are defeated, you are to give up your token. The Keepers have their own, of course," Qien said. "And, before you ask, this exam is purely focused on control for you. There will be no trickery allowed with your tokens. Keep them on your person at all times. If you are defeated, give it up without complaint. Do not attempt to falsify or conceal tokens. I will find out, and you will regret it. Am I clear?"

Everyone nodded, and Qien passed the tokens out. To Jasmine's surprise, Qien actually gave her one as well. She studied the wooden disk. It was a small, coin-sized piece of wood with an S carved on both faces.

While everyone looked at their tokens, Qien started around, grabbing students by the shoulders and dragging them over to their assigned teams.

*So much for all the alliance stuff that Esmarelda was talking about. Maybe we'll still get lucky and –*

Qien put his hand on Esmarelda's shoulder and pushed her over to stand by Clarence, who had another boy on his team that Jasmine didn't know the name of. She grimaced and gave Esmarelda a small nod.

*So much for that.*

Most of the class had already been assigned to their teams by the time that Qien drew up to Jasmine and Asher.

"The two of you gave me some trouble," Qien said. "Obviously, I cannot separate you from your Keeper. However, I do not believe it would be fair to allow you such a significant advantage by having a four-person group. I will give you two options. First, the Xolani will not be allowed to participate at all. She will only be allowed to follow you. In this scenario, you will be given two more members. Alternatively, she may choose to aid you and will count as a member of your team, but I will not permit her the use of her sword."

"What? Why not?" Asher asked. "That's not fair."

"Because she would be too effective," Qien said dryly. "I am not a fool, and Esther is not either. She is capable with the sword, and it would trivialize the exam. If you wish for her to be able to directly assist you in the exam, then she will give me her sword for its duration."

Jasmine and Asher exchanged a glance.

"I want your help. Screw the sword," Asher said without a second of hesitation.

"You'll be at a disadvantage at that point," Jasmine warned him.

Asher shrugged. "Don't care. I trust you more than a random Starvein. I don't know two other people in the class, and Esmarelda is in another group already."

Jasmine reached down and removed her sheath from her side, handing it to Qien. He took it with surprising respect, inclining his head slightly to her. "I will take care of your weapon until I return it at the end of the exam."

"Thank you. We get a third person though, right?"

*We can do this. It's not ideal, but Qien isn't trying to separate us. Even without a sword, I know I can hold most of the other Keepers in my class back for at least a bit.*

"Of course. As you are now technically weaker than the other teams in the class due to your unique... limitations, I have assigned you the most competent Starvein to attempt to balance your group."

Jasmine's confidence evaporated like a puddle in the desert, her grin fading away.

*Oh, you've got to be kidding me.*

"Pina, please come over here," Qien said. "You'll be with Asher and his Xolani."

# 34

Qien didn't wait around to see their reactions. He moved on, herding the other Starvein students into their groups and dismissing them to the corners of the clearings. Jasmine and Asher stood several feet away from Pina, who hadn't so much as glanced in their direction once since they'd been put together.

"Is he trying to make us fail?" Jasmine muttered.

"He is trying to make me fail," Pina replied, glaring at Jasmine. "I do not have a single Starvein on my team."

"It's not like we can do anything about it now," Asher said with a sigh. "Unless you want to ask Qien to reconsider?"

"That would result in me failing the exam and nothing more." Pina crossed her arms. "Are you so stupid as to think that Qien would change his mind?"

"Look, you're the one complaining," Asher said. He stretched his arms over his head and rolled his neck, starting to get limber in preparation for the exam. "Jasmine and I can hold our own. Have you considered the part where we're technically at an advantage compared to the other teams?"

Pina snorted. "Only if you mean to club our opponents with your fists like a Keeper. And, if you do that, do not expect to pass the exam."

"Why are you so insistent that Asher isn't a Starvein?" Jasmine asked. "You don't know him. Just because he's new to the program doesn't mean he's completely incompetent, you know. It's pretty close minded to just assume he's helpless."

"If he was not completely pathetic, then he would have started in the Starvein program, not transferred into it. I have more respect for *you* than I have for him, and that's not saying much," Pina spat, glaring at Asher. The disgust in her features was so intense that Jasmine almost took a step back.

"What in the Watcher's name did he do to you?" Jasmine asked, glancing at Asher in befuddlement. He looked equally confused.

Before they could press the matter any further, Qien clapped his hands together in his signature method of getting their attention. Everyone turned toward where the professor stood at the center of the clearing.

"It's just about time for us to begin," Qien called. He paused for a moment to ensure that everyone was listening before starting back up again. "I'm certain you can all figure out how the semantics of this will work. You will travel out into the forest with your team. The Keeper teams are in another clearing in this forest. Do what you will in order to come into contact with them, but the only way you pass is if you use your magic to defeat them. Once you have fought a team and either lost or won, you are to return to this clearing immediately, your hands over your head to indicate you are no longer part of the exam. Needless to say, if you raise your hands into the air and have *not* finished the exam – you fail."

Excitement and anxiety intertwined in Jasimine's chest. She snuck a glance at Asher, but his features were just as confident as they always were. Jasmine let a breath out and shifted her stance. It was just an exam. They'd prepared for it. Even without Pina's help, they'd make it through.

"Last rule. No interacting with the other Starvein teams. I don't care what the reason is. You will not so much as look at each other. Good?" Qien waited for no more than a second before clapping once more. "In that case, begin! This exam will last for a maximum of one hour. I look forward to hearing of your success."

"Let's go," Pina barked, striding into the forest. Asher and Jasmine exchanged a glance, then hurried to catch up with her. Pina certainly didn't make it easy, though. She set a brisk pace, moving through the trees without any attempts at stealth.

"I thought we weren't going to be working together," Jasmine said as they caught up to her. "What's this now?"

"We're stuck with each other," Pina said curtly. "I do not plan to fail, so you will both just act as bodies for me. Stand in front of the Keepers and let me deal with them."

"Yeah, that's not happening," Asher said. "I'm passing this exam of my own volition."

Pina snorted in response. "Delusional. If anything, you would have cheated. It disgusts me that you're in this program at all. Just stay out of my way and remain silent."

Jasmine grabbed Pina by the shoulder, spinning her around. Pina's eyes widened in shock and anger. She made to throw Jasmine's hand away, but she wasn't anywhere near strong enough to move her.

"Seriously, what is your problem?" Jasmine demanded. "Out with it. Now. You're causing so much damn noise that the Keepers will hear us coming from the other end of the forest. What's your issue with Asher?"

"Keep your nose out of–"

Jasmine shook Pina with just enough force to cut her sentence off. "I am not in a good mood, Pina. Answer the damn question. If Asher actually did something that you deserve to be mad at, he's going to apologize, and then we're going to work as a Watcher damned team."

"I am?" Asher asked, blinking.

Jasmine ignored him and continued. "And, if he didn't, you're going to shut your mouth and work with us. I'm not giving you an option. Qien has made it pretty clear he doesn't give a shit about me, and that means he won't stop me if I knock you in the head and leave you right here."

"You wouldn't dare. I'm from –"

Jasmine arched an eyebrow and Pina's voice trailed off. "I'm a gutter rat, Pina. I clawed my way through life until I got into Sanctuary, and all I've done since is train. You probably think I've got bricks for brains, but guess what? That means I'm not going to think through the consequences of my actions. I don't care what family you're from. I don't care who you are. Just answer my damn question."

"Fine," Pina spat. "I don't want to work with some pathetic fool who couldn't manage to stay in the Keeper program so he begged his family to pull him into the Starveins so he could keep living in ease. I hate people that just get given handouts, and Asher is the worst of them. Choosing to be a Keeper is fine. You lot have your purpose – but failing and then falling back on being a Starvein just because you have noble blood? Pathetic."

Asher and Jasmine both stared at Pina in befuddlement.

"What?" Pina demanded. "Why are you looking at me like that? Are you so stupid that–"

"What are you on about?" Jasmine asked. "Asher's family got fucking killed. They're all dead. He didn't *choose* to be a Starvein. He was forced to do it because, if he didn't, there would be nobody left to lead his family."

Pina blinked, confusion entering her features. "What are you talking about? That's not what–"

"It's been like a week!" Jasmine pressed on, not giving Pina a chance to say anything else until she was finished. She couldn't talk about the actual assassins, but she wasn't going to stand around and let Pina spit filth about Asher. "And the whole week, he's been doing everything he can to learn magic. You've been practicing your whole damn life, but he only just figured it out. How is it fair to hold that against him?"

"You're lying," Pina said, her voice flat. "Just what I'd expect from–"

"Not one more word." Asher's voice was as sharp as a knife. He grabbed Jasmine's wrist, pulling a faint thread of magic from her. It swirled into a ball above his palm, dark energy crackling in wait. Pina's eyes went wide.

"I thought–"

"I'm fed up with how you talk about Jasmine," Asher snapped. "There's nothing wrong with being a Keeper. I think it's laughable that you claim to hate people that are given handouts when you're in the most spoiled group of brats to ever live. Jasmine has worked for every damn thing in her life tirelessly. I don't give a shit if you don't like me, but if you can't even stick to the ideals that you claim to stand for, you're the one that's worthless."

Asher held Pina's gaze, his jaw clenched in anger. The magic crackled in his palm, equal parts a threat and a testament to his claims. But, oddly enough, Pina didn't look scared. She just looked increasingly baffled.

"This makes no sense. You can't cast magic," Pina muttered, squinting at Asher as if someone had replaced him when she wasn't watching. "And I didn't hear anything about your family. What in the Watcher's name are you talking about? I thought you just failed out of the program."

"Failed out? I got ripped out," Asher snapped. "How does this matter?"

"She said that you–"

A stick cracked to their side. Asher and Jasmine both burst into motion, but Pina lacked their Keeper training and didn't respond with nearly as much speed. Jasmine shoved Pina to the ground and a bundled rock sailed over her head, hitting the tree behind them with a loud thump.

Jasmine grabbed Pina and yanked the other girl to her feet. "No more talking. All our arguing brought another group to us. Get your magic ready."

Asher had managed to keep his hold on Jasmine's wrist and raised his other hand, summoning a swirl of magic back to his palm. Pina's eyes darted around the treeline and she held her hands out, cupping them to try to summon her own magic.

The argument must have unsettled her far more than Jasmine had thought it would, because she wasn't summoning the power nearly as quickly as she had during the demonstration a few days ago in class.

There wasn't any more time to worry about Pina, though. Jasmine squinted into the trees, where two Keepers stepped out to meet them. Jasmine didn't recognize who they were – they'd wrapped themselves in dark green robes to camouflage their appearance, and all three held wooden swords in their hands.

*The other one is still hiding somewhere in the forest. They're probably waiting to find an opening while we fight and knock us out at range. We need to deal with these two as quickly as possible. I need to make sure their focus is on me.*

"Hello," Jasmine said, lowering into a fighting stance and swaying in place. It wasn't easy to move around while holding Asher's hand, but she didn't plan to move. All she had to do was make sure the Keepers couldn't get past her. "I don't suppose you want to re-introduce yourselves? I can't recognize you with the wrappings."

The Keepers raised their swords and charged as one.

*Ah, well. I guess I should have seen that coming.*

*Whatever. Sorry, guys. You're not getting past me.*

# 35

In all the training Jasmine had done, she'd yet to actually practice fighting against two people at once, much less doing it while trying to protect two Starveins. However, she was still the top ranked fighter of the first year Keepers, and Riker's training hadn't been for nothing.

The first Keeper swung the butt of his sword at Jasmine's head, aiming to knock her out. She twisted out of the way and drove her knee up between his legs. He let out a pained grunt and staggered back, going bowlegged. Jasmine didn't have time to capitalize on her advantage. The other Keeper lunged forward, thrusting his sword for her stomach.

His goal was likely to force her to move out of the way and expose Pina or Asher, but Jasmine had absolutely no plans of budging from her spot. Jasmine's hand snapped out and she struck the flat of the wooden blade with her palm, knocking it to the side.

She whipped her foot out in a violent kick, driving it straight into the first Keeper's chest as he started to raise his sword again. He staggered backward with a grunt – and a tingle ran down Jasmine's neck.

"Drop!" Jasmine yelled.

Asher ducked down beside her as a rock whistled past his shoulders. He shot back upright, nearly pulling his hand from Jasmine's in his haste, and thrust his hand toward the first Keeper.

The orb of dark light leapt forth, streaking through the air and slamming into the boy's stomach. There was a deep thrum and a ripple of air buffeted Jasmine's hair back. With a startled cry, the Keeper was launched off his feet.

He flew through the air and slammed into a tree with a loud crack before dropping to the ground, his head slumping forward. Jasmine nearly cheered, and her moment of distraction almost landed her a sword strike to the knee.

She blocked the blade just in time before giving the Keeper a firm shove. He was stronger than Jasmine had expected and only staggered a foot back, but that bought just enough time for Pina to finally gather her magic.

A streak of grey light carved through the air and drove into the second Keeper's chest, winding around his body and yanking his limbs to his sides. He pitched back with a curse, struggling futilely against the bonds.

Jasmine spun toward the direction that the rocks had come from and squinted into the forest, trying to pick up where they'd come from.

"Don't let your guard down," Jasmine warned. "The last Keeper is still out there. We can get the tokens after he goes down."

"I could start shooting magic," Asher offered, turning his back to Jasmine's and scanning the forest through squinted eyes. "Could get lucky."

"Don't waste your energy. He'll have to show himself eventually," Jasmine replied. "Just get more magic ready."

A faint chill bit at her palm as he did what Jasmine suggested. If this had been a real fight, Jasmine suspected the other Keeper would have ran for it. There was no point fighting three prepared opponents when the first two of his allies were already downed.

It wasn't a real fight, though. It was an exam – and it wasn't one that Jasmine suspected retreat was a viable option in. The last Keeper would be forced to attack soon.

Seconds ticked by. Pina summoned another orb of magic to her palms, then sent it into the cursing Keeper. He stiffened and slumped, unconscious. Pina shifted uncomfortably, and Jasmine didn't blame her. The last Keeper was definitely taking their time. It was the right move, too.

Jasmine exchanged a quick glance with Asher. Her eyes dropped to the magic in his free hand for a moment, then lifted over to the forest. They didn't say a word, but they'd spent more than enough time together for Asher to nod his understanding.

*The longer this goes on, the more distracted we get and the more likely he hits a lucky shot. He doesn't know that I've got some weird Xolani danger sense, though. I just need to wait for him to attack again and point Asher in his direction. Magic moves faster than rocks do, but I can't pretend like the rock wouldn't knock one of us out on the spot if we got hit in the head. I can't let my guard down.*

The seconds turned to a minute, and the minute to two. Jasmine's concentration started to fray. She was tempted to run into the forest in search of the last Keeper herself, but that would have been monumentally stupid.

"Where's the last one?" Pina hissed, her voice taut. "What in the Watcher's eyes is he waiting for?"

"I don't know," Jasmine muttered. "But I wish he'd just do something already. I'm about to lose my shit."

"Isn't this kind of against the spirit of the exam?" Asher asked. He sounded strained from the effort of keeping the magic permanently ready to bear. Asher nudged the bound Keeper's shoulder with his foot. "This is meant to be a challenge in concentration, not stamina and mental resilience. Where's your friend, man?"

"I don't think he's going to answer," Jasmine grumbled. "Pina knocked him out."

"It was part of the exam. What do you want?" Pina demanded.

The back of Jasmine's neck tingled like ice water had been poured onto it. She drew in a strangled gasp and moved purely on instinct, kicking the hardened wood sword from the ground and yanking Asher to the side.

He let out a curse and stumbled as Jasmine shoved past him, raising her weapon. A flash of silver carved through the air and thudded into the flat of her blade. The point of a dagger sprouted from Jasmine's sword, stopped only by its hilt. It quivered just a few inches away from her face, the force from the strike nearly having been enough to drive the dagger into her eye even with the sword blocking it.

A man wrapped in dark green clothes identical to the ones the Keepers wore stepped out of the forest, a slender blade in one hand and another dagger in the other. Jasmine's blood ran cold.

*That's not a Keeper.*

"Run!" Jasmine yelled, grabbing Pina and shoving her into motion, even as the assassin reared back and flung a second dagger at them. "Get Qien!"

Jasmine whipped her sword out, knocking the dagger from the air with no small amount of luck. The sheer force of the throw still sent a tremor running down her arm, but it was nothing compared to what Riker had done to her.

Pina turned and sprinted in the other direction, moving as fast as her feet could carry her. Jasmine had no idea if she was running for her life or to comply with her orders, but she didn't have time to find out. The assassin didn't even glance in Pina's direction. He sprinted toward Jasmine.

Asher thrust his hand toward the assassin and a streak of black light carved through the forest. In an impossible display of flexibility, the man vaulted straight over the bolt of magic, procuring a second dagger from within his sleeve by the time he landed.

*That's the same kind of dagger the last assassin stabbed Asher with.*

There was no time to think about anything other than survival. Jasmine's blood pounded in her ears and adrenaline wrapped her heart in a vice grip. The assassin charged, swinging his blade at her neck.

She couldn't duck – that would put Asher right into the assassin's path. Instead, Jasmine caught the strike on the edge of her sword, shoving it out of the way. The sword carved clean through her weapon, severing a large chunk of wood and sending it tumbling to the forest floor.

Jasmine drove her foot into the assassin's stomach, trying to shove him back with all the might she could muster. It worked no better than the first time she'd tried kicking one of the Last Light assassins, and her best efforts didn't even budge the man.

His sword flashed, moving with incredible speed. Every bone in Jasmine's body screamed at her to duck and avoid the attack. The only thing that kept her in place was Riker's training, and even that was only holding on by a strand.

Jasmine slammed her sword up, just barely managing to redirect the strike and losing another chunk of her weapon in the process. Jasmine felt ice running through her veins as Asher drew magic in.

He hurled an orb of reddish-black energy at the assassin, but the man twisted out of the way and avoided the attack. Jasmine couldn't help but notice that he was actually trying to dodge Asher's blows. That meant they actually had a chance to do damage.

"We need to hold him down," Jasmine hissed to Asher, barely managing to block another attack and turning her sword into a dagger as another piece of it was carved away. "He's scared of your magic. You can't miss the next one. We don't have time."

"I can't hit him! He's too damn fast!"

"Then I'll hold him down."

The assassin's next attack slammed into Jasmine's sword, but she let it fly from her grasp instead of trying to hold onto it. Cold pricked Jasmine's spine. The sword flicked for her head, but she shoved Asher back and leaned out of the way, letting it flash past her harmlessly.

The move should have been impossible. Her reaction felt like it had happened in a split second, and it gave the assassin an instant of pause as well.

"You," he hissed. "You are no Starvein. You used the siphon?"

Jasmine's response was to drive her open palm into the man's face with all the force she could muster. She doubted it would do much damage, but the nose was one of the easiest spots to attack on the body, so there was a chance –

There was a loud crunch. The man screamed in pain, stumbling backward as blood matted his face wrappings. Jasmine stared at her hand in disbelief, and understanding dawned on her.

*Asher is making me stronger with magic, just like he did on accident during our sparring match. It's the only kind of magic we can do when we aren't touching.*

The assassin lowered his stance – and then he blurred. Jasmine's eyes widened as she completely lost track of the man. Her neck practically froze and she shoved Asher away from herself with all the force she could muster.

Asher tumbled across the ground, rolling back to his feet across from Jasmine. The assassin's dagger flashed, narrowly missing where Asher had been standing. He spun toward Jasmine, his blade moving faster than she could react.

A line of white-hot pain erupted on Jasmine's chest as it carved across her. Jasmine didn't know how bad the wound was, and she didn't have time to figure it out. She lunged, grabbing the assassin's arm and desperately trying to rip the sword from his hands.

It was impossible. He was too strong. Even with Asher empowering Jasmine, it was like trying to wrench a brick from a wall, and now she'd wasted the few instants of advantage that she'd had.

The world felt like it ground to a halt. Jasmine saw the blade driving forward, prepared to punch into her heart, but there was no way for her to move fast enough to avoid it. Behind the assassin, she saw Asher desperately trying to call on his magic again, but he was already focused on Jasmine – there was nothing else he could do.

*Ah, shit. I'm dead.*

And, just like that, the world snapped back into motion. A streak of gray light flicked through the air and slammed into the assassin's palm. He let out a scream of pain as the blade flew from his hand, spinning through the air and falling to the ground several feet away.

Pina stepped out from behind a tree, her face pale but determined. Another orb of magic started to form in her palms. "I couldn't find Qien."

*I could kiss you right now.*

Instead, Jasmine tried swinging at the assassin again. Her fist passed through the air harmlessly as he blurred into motion. Jasmine lunged – she could barely track his movements, but she still knew where he was headed. Her fist slammed into the back of the assassin's head as he reached for his sword, sending him stumbling. Unfortunately, he still managed to grab his blade and bring it to bear.

"Round two?" Jasmine asked, baring her teeth in a desperate attempt to keep the assassin's attention on her. The moment he went for Asher or Pina, it was over. "I've gotten cut harder in training. Don't you feel a bit pathetic struggling against a girl half your size? I've felt more threat from fish bones than I do from you."

The assassin flicked the blood from his sword and let out a dry laugh. His words came out nasally because of his broken nose. "Mouthy little deadling. No need to try so hard to keep my attention. You used the Siphon. You've already got it. I'll have to take my time with you."

*That's the second time he's mentioned a siphon. Does he mean the dagger the other assassin stabbed Asher with?*

"What's that? I can't hear it over you choking down your own blood."

The assassin dashed, flicking his sword at her neck. She just barely managed to duck out of the way in time. Her plan had been successful – the assassin was definitely focused on her. Now all she had to do was survive for long enough for Qien to show up.

*I just hope I don't get run through or bleed out before he gets here or we're all dead.*

# 36

Blows rained down on Jasmine, moving so quickly that she could barely keep up with them, even with the magical energy coursing through her courtesy of Asher. Not even being freed of her need to stand in one spot and stand between Asher and the assassin was enough.

She bled from several cuts all over her body, some far more serious than others. The worst of them was the deep wound running diagonally across her chest, weeping so much blood that it had completely stained her clothes.

Adrenaline and magic were powerful, but they weren't enough to stave off the growing exhaustion. The world was getting heavier, and Jasmine was getting slower. Despite Asher and Pina's best attempts, neither of them had managed to land so much as a blow on the bandaged man.

Time was running out. Qien was still nowhere to be seen. The inside of Jasmine's mouth felt impossibly dry. She ducked out of the way of a swing, hissing in pain as the sword caught her shoulder and opened yet another stinging cut.

She was putting up a respectable fight, but it wasn't enough. She knew it, and the assassin did too. Her one hope had been that he would overstep and make another mistake, but it never happened.

Instead of rushing for the kill, he was content to whittle away at Jasmine. He didn't expect them to get reinforcements, and he was clever enough to recognize that she had the chance to hurt him.

*Damn it. Why couldn't I have gotten a stupid assassin? If something doesn't change, I'm dead.*

Jasmine twisted out of the way of another stab and lunged, trying to catch the man off guard. He skipped back, avoiding the blow and flicking a dagger at Asher. Jasmine swore, drawing on her aching muscles and blurring into motion.

Ice raced through her veins as she crossed the ground, bringing the stump of her sword down and knocking the dagger from the air. She stumbled, coughing up blood and nearly tripping over her own feet.

Even as Jasmine raised her cut up blade to defend herself, she knew the assassin was coming – and she knew she wasn't fast enough to block the next blow. She gritted her teeth, mentally screaming at her muscles to comply.

More ice spread through her body, its greedy fingers digging deep into her. It crept toward her neck, threads of frost reaching to consume her. Power surged within her limbs and she leaned back with incredible speed, avoiding the strike.

Jasmine spun, lashing out with a powerful kick. It slammed into the assassin's chest and he tumbled back, rolling to absorb the shock of the blow. A streak of gray light shot from Pina's hands, but the assassin vaulted off his hands and avoided the magic. The assassin laughed as he landed and flung a dagger at Jasmine.

*How many damn daggers does this guy carry?*

She stumbled, just barely managing to avoid the flying blade. The icy magic continued its creeping advance within her. Blood trickled from Jasmine's nose, tasting like iron against her lips. Shapes and colors spun around her, but she refused to give in.

*I can't give in. I need more.*

The assassin sprinted toward Jasmine, bringing his sword up for a finishing blow. She gritted her teeth, desperately reaching for more power – but nothing came. It felt like she was clawing at a brick wall.

Shock widened her eyes, but it was too late. She didn't have the time – or the reaction speed – to react. She wanted to open her mouth, to yell to Asher to run. That she wasn't enough to handle an assassin, even with him and Pina backing her up.

Instead, all she could do was watch as the sword streaked for her neck. Something slapped into her hand, yanking her back. The tip of the assassin's sword streaked past Jasmine's nose, just barely nicking it. Jasmine just barely caught a glimpse of Asher's determined face before he shoved her behind himself.

Asher thrust his hand forward, but it wasn't light that spilled forth. Burgundy red tendrils erupted from his arm, snapping out like a bed of snakes. It was the same sickly magic that she'd absorbed from his body at night.

Letting out a surprised curse, the assassin stumbled back – but he'd somehow been caught off guard. One of the bands managed to latch onto his hand. A loud sizzling noise rang out and the assassin roared in pain. He brought his sword down, severing the strand of magic even as smoke rose up from his palm.

"Asher," Jasmine coughed. "What are you doing? You need to–"

"The other way wasn't working," Asher said, gritting his teeth. The tendrils of magic whipped at his side, hungrily seeking a new meal. "We're doing this together. For real, this time. You aren't fighting alone."

"This is not possible," the assassin hissed. He took a step back, holding his sword defensively before him. "You used the Siphon! How does he–"

A streak of gray light screamed past the man, streaking just past his shoulder as he twisted out of the way. The light twisted as it passed him, curving to whip back at his back. The assassin caught notice of it at the last moment and tried to dodge, but it was too late to completely avoid the attack.

The magic caught him in the shoulder and, with a loud crack like a falling tree, he was sent spinning. Asher thrust his hand forward and the tendrils erupted, reaching out to grasp for the assassin.

They wrapped around the man's right leg, binding it tightly. He let out a scream of pain, desperately swinging his blade to sever them. Asher's hand felt limp in Jasmine's palm. He was covered his clammy sweat, and agony twisted his features.

"Thanks, Asher," Jasmine said, grabbing Asher's hand. Ice prickled her neck as she drank the magic from him. The pain faded from his features and he looked to her in shock, but Jasmine didn't stick around to watch his expression.

She ran forward, diving as the assassin started to rise. She drove her shoulder into his already-broken nose. He grunted, and the moment of surprise was just enough to wrench the sword from his grip.

With a cry, Jasmine spun the blade around and plunged it down into his eye. Even though Asher was no longer empowering her with magic, the blade hit home. It slammed the assassin's head into the ground, pinning it there as Jasmine threw the entirety of her weight behind it and drove the sword down through the man's head and the earth alike.

Her grip slackened. Jasmine slipped, falling to her back beside the man as a hysterical laugh slipped from her lips. The world swam above her and her consciousness fluctuated like a candle before an open window.

Asher grabbed Jasmine, pulling her into his lap and desperately patting at her cheeks. "Jasmine! Are you okay?"

"What do you think, idiot?" Jasmine asked with a pained laugh. "I feel like I got stabbed. A lot."

Asher yanked his shirt off, tearing strips off it hurriedly as he worked to bind her wounds. Darkness threatened to encroach on Jasmine's vision, but she fought it off. "Did you make sure he's dead?"

"Nobody survives that," Asher snapped. "Stop talking and rest. You did it."

"We did. I would have died on my own," Jasmine muttered. Asher swam before her, and for a moment, it looked like there were two of him. A tiny grin flitted across her face.

*Huh. Two Ashers. That would be kind of fun. I wonder –*

"Jasmine!" Asher gave her a gentle shake and she blinked, shaking her head.

"What? What is it?"

"Your eyes were about to close," Asher said, pulling another binding tight. Jasmine winced. She didn't know when, but he'd managed to wrap most of her wounds in the blink of an eye.

*Or did I just lose track of time? Everything seems so fuzzy.*

She blinked, pushing her weary brain to work. "We won?"

"Yes, we won," Asher brushed the hair out of her eyes and wiped some of the blood from her face with a scrap of his sleeve. "Just relax. Pina, find someone. Where in the Watcher's eyes is Qien?"

"Wait. What about the exam?" Jasmine mumbled. The world was spinning again, her head like a bag of bricks. "You still need to pass."

"Forget the exam," Asher said. "You need to rest. Just focus on staying awake."

Jasmine's mouth worked, but no more words came out. She stared up at Asher's face as it grew hazier by the second. A tiny breath slipped out of her lips as the last of the energy her body had to give was spent.

She could hear Asher yelling, but his voice sounded distant. So, so distant. Darkness rose up like a rushing ocean, swallowing her in its entirety, and Jasmine knew no more.

# 37

Jasmine woke to soft blankets enveloping her. Her body felt like it had been run over by a pack of horses. She tried to sit up, but the thought was instantly abandoned as the wound on her chest flared in pain.

"Jasmine!" Asher's voice said from above her, each word laden with relief. "Don't move. You need to recover."

"Why can't I see?" Jasmine mumbled, her voice feeling gummy.

"Just a warm compress on your head. Hold on." Asher's fingers ran along Jasmine's head and light suddenly returned as he lifted a warm, wet towel off her head. Jasmine blinked heavily.

"What happened? Where am I?"

"Back in our room," Asher said. "It's okay. We're safe. Do you remember what happened?"

Jasmine's brow scrunched, and she nodded. "Yeah. We killed the assassin, and I think I passed out a few seconds later. You – wait. You used your magic. On purpose – and without touching me!"

"That's the first thing you ask about?" Asher let out a laugh and ran his hand through her hair, massaging the top of her head in gentle motions. "But yes, I did. I was so scared that you were going to die that I... well, I don't actually know what in the Watcher's eyes I did, but I did something."

"I hope you can do more magic than just that," Jasmine said with a small grin. It felt painful to smile, but that didn't stop her. The pain meant that she was still alive. "What happened after I passed out?"

"Qien showed up about ten minutes later." Asher's brow tightened in anger. "He was getting distracted by some stupid argument two other teams were having on the other side of the forest. Pina managed to find him and he ended the exam, bringing you back to Sanctuary. Since then, we just had some healers take a look at you and I've been sitting by your side until you woke up."

"How long has it been?"

"Three or four hours. They thought it would be longer, but I guess not even unconsciousness can keep you down." A smile flitted across Asher's face and he leaned down, giving her a soft kiss on the forehead. "Don't push yourself any harder, please. You need rest."

"Forget that," Jasmine said, grimacing as a flicker of pain ran through her. "Did Qien say anything about the assassin? What about the third Keeper in the group we were fighting? Is he–"

"He's alive, somehow," Asher said, raising a hand to stop Jasmine's questions. "They found him unconscious with what would have been a fatal stab wound out in the forest. The healers took care of him, just like they did for you. And, for the record, your wounds were somehow more serious. You nearly bled out."

Jasmine breathed out a sigh of relief. "What matters is that we aren't dead, not how close to it we got. So... did you pass the exam?"

Asher stared at Jasmine in disbelief.

"What? We did this shit for a reason, didn't we?"

"Who gives a damn if I passed?" Asher demanded. "You nearly died!"

"Yeah, but did you pass?"

Asher's anger evaporated as he let out a burst of laughter. The tension left his shoulders and he slumped, shaking his head in mirth. "Yes, Jas. I passed. Qien judged that the three of us defeating an assassin was slightly more difficult than fighting another Keeper."

Jasmine snorted and immediately regretted the decision as it sent another wave of pain through her body. Concern passed over Asher's features.

"Be careful, Jas. Don't hurt yourself."

"I'm fine. I could just picture Qien saying something like that," Jasmine said. The smile faded from her face as the severity of their situation set back in. "Do we know what happened out there? How did the assassin know we'd be out in the forest?"

"I wish I knew. Qien seemed completely shaken up about it, and Esther wasn't even at the exam. She apparently had something to take care of and assumed that one professor would be enough."

Jasmine's expression tightened. "That seems…"

"Suspicious," Asher finished. "Yeah. It was her idea to do this exam as well. I think she might have been trying to use us to lure the assassins out."

"That bitch," Jasmine started to sit up, then hissed in pain. Asher gently pushed her back down.

"Don't!" Asher snapped. "You need to heal, Jas."

"I know, I know. I'm just so damn mad." Jasmine's fists tightened into balls at her sides. "If the point was to lure the assassin out, what in the Watcher's eyes was she doing? Why didn't anyone show up to help us?"

"I don't know. I'd ask, but I won't be leaving your side until you're better and something tells me she doesn't plan to give you a bedside visit."

"She better not. I'll knock her teeth out."

"Not like I wouldn't love to see that, but I don't think it would be a good idea. She's still a fully-fledged Keeper."

Jasmine let out a sigh and scrunched her nose. "Yeah, I know that. It's nice to imagine, though. And look at you, sticking by me. I thought I was the Keeper here."

"I've got all the training you do and then some, and we're partners. That's what we do for each other, right?"

Jasmine smiled. "Yeah. Thanks, Asher. I'm definitely not going to say no to getting pampered for a little. I just wish we weren't dangling on the end of a fishing hook."

"Yeah. Me too," Asher said. "As soon as you're walking around again, we're going to get some answers. If not from Esther, then from Riker."

"Who was also conveniently busy today," Jasmine said, her brow furrowing. "Something is going on."

"Yeah. So I've gathered," Asher said. He pressed his lips together, then shrugged. "We'll deal with it or we'll die, eh?"

Jasmine snickered, trying to keep herself from moving too much. "Don't make me laugh right now."

"Sorry," Asher said. "Is there anything else I could do right now?"

She thought for a moment, then sent a small smile up at him. "You know, my pillow isn't very comfortable. I think a lap might be better."

"I can arrange for that." He shifted beside Jasmine, gently shifting her head into his lap while making sure not to move her too much. Jasmine was pretty sure she wasn't so injured that she couldn't have moved herself, but it really did feel nice to be taken care of, so she let him do all the work without an ounce of guilt.

"That's much better," Jasmine said. A small shiver of pleasure ran down her spine as Asher gently ran his fingertips down her arms and up her shoulders. "And you can keep doing that too."

Asher laughed. "Any other requests?"

"Not yet, but I'll let you know if I think of any. Maybe I should get myself cut up more often. I could get used to this."

"Please don't. Just ask and you can get it whenever you want, but I'd much prefer you not to get nearly killed in the process."

"I think that's an acceptable tradeoff," Jasmine said, pausing for a moment in mock thought.

She didn't say anything else for the next few minutes, content to lie there and enjoy the feeling of Asher's hands against her body. She wouldn't have said that it was worth the pain, but now that the worst of the pain was over, it definitely wasn't anything to complain about.

"So you haven't figured out how to do the tendril stuff on command?" Jasmine asked, breaking the silence.

"Can't you stop working for five minutes?" Asher asked. "Just relax, would you?"

"I did. It's been five minutes exactly."

Asher rolled his eyes, then shook his head. "Unfortunately, I've got nothing. Granted, I haven't tried to do it since you collapsed, but I just can't remember what it was that I did. We can try to practice once you're back in shape, but I'm not doing anything before that. I don't know what absorbing magic will do to you in your current state."

"Fair enough," Jasmine allowed. "Then you may go back to your earlier actions. They were aiding in my recovery."

Asher laughed and obliged her. At least, he obliged her for about two more minutes before someone knocked on the door. They exchanged a glance. Asher raised Jasmine's head, swapping his lap out for a pillow as he stood.

He grabbed his sword as he approached the door. "Who is it?"

"It's me," a female voice came from the other side. Jasmine's brow furrowed as she tried to place it, but her memory felt a little fuzzier than usual and she couldn't quite remember who the voice belonged to. It certainly wasn't Lydia.

Asher pulled the door open, and Jasmine blinked as she realized who the voice's owner was. Pina stood on the other side of the door, her gaze averted as she chewed her lower lip.

"Pina? What do you want?" Asher asked.

"I'm here to check up on Jasmine," Pina admitted after a second of delay. "I… I want to apologize. I don't think I've treated you properly."

Jasmine blinked. She certainly hadn't been expecting that. It wasn't like she knew Pina much at all, but the other woman had struck her as haughty and stuck-up, not the kind of person to apologize when she was in the wrong.

"Oh. Well, apology accepted, I guess," Jasmine said. "Just don't be such an ass in the future and we're good. Oh – and stop being rude to Asher as well."

"I'll apologize to him in a moment," Pina said. She pulled her gaze up to meet Jasmine's and her features hardened. "First, I think we need to talk."

# 38

"Talk? Why?" Jasmine asked.

Pina glanced over her shoulder. "Can I come in?"

Asher looked at Jasmine, who nearly shrugged before she stopped herself. "Yeah. That's fine, I guess."

"Thank you." Pina stepped inside and Asher closed the door behind her. They both walked over to the bed, and Asher sat down beside Jasmine. Pina stood at the foot of the bed awkwardly, then grimaced. "I don't know the right way to say this, but I think someone tried to set me against you."

"What do you mean?" Asher asked, leaning forward. "Did someone tell you that there would be an assassin at the exam or something?"

"No, nothing like that." Pina looked like she wanted to shrink in on herself and disappear. She bit her lower lip and clenched her fists. "I was an idiot. Someone told me that Asher dropped out of the Keeper program because he couldn't handle the workload, and that you were just some random gutter rat that was clinging onto him to avoid your responsibilities as a Keeper."

"What?" Jasmine demanded. "Who? And why?"

"I don't know." Pina's cheeks reddened even further in shame. "I overheard someone talking about both of you while walking to class, and I'm ashamed to admit that I believed them without spending any effort to verify their words. They... made sense, I suppose. I'd never heard of someone transferring into the Starvein program in the middle of their Keeper training. Nobody chooses to be a Keeper, so it just doesn't make sense. Everyone would just start as a Starvein."

Pina realized what she'd said and winced again. "Shit. I'm sorry. I didn't mean–"

"It's fine. I don't care," Jasmine said, her mind spinning. Pina's accidental insult barely even registered. The rumors Pina was talking about didn't make any sense. Nobody had any reason to think anything of them before they'd joined the Starvein program. It didn't make sense for rumors to go around before they'd had a chance to meet anyone. "Do you remember anything about the person you overheard?"

"No," Pina said, shrinking in on herself even more. "I only saw their back, and it didn't really register at the time. I thought they were just a student in an older year. I was particularly sensitive to the rumors about Asher because everyone thinks I've just been handed everything I've worked for, but my family hasn't given me a scrap. I've clawed my way to the top of the Starvein program on my own work, not because my dad is a powerful noble. I hate people that don't work for what they have."

"It almost sounds like the rumor was specifically targeted to piss you off," Asher muttered, a deep frown on his face. "It doesn't even make sense. Rumors are usually based off some kernel of the truth, but I've never done anything to make it seem like I didn't enjoy being a Keeper. I only joined the Starvein program because my whole family was murdered."

Pina winced and looked away. "I'm sorry. I–"

"You weren't the one that killed them," Asher said, his voice terse. "Just drop it. All we can do is try to figure out what's going on. Do you really remember absolutely nothing about them?"

"Nothing. I believe it was a girl around our age or close to it, but I wouldn't swear by it. I know I should have tried to verify the rumors, but I know they're obviously not true now."

"Were you intentionally trying to get Asher to start a fight with you yesterday, then?" Jasmine asked.

"I – yeah. I was. I had pretty good reason to suspect that Qien would put us on the same team, so I was hoping I'd avoid that if he couldn't take the exam," Pina said. "I'm deeply sorry. My failure to act according to my position has caused both of you a lot of trouble, and you saved my life today when you could have easily let me die, even after how I treated you."

"Of course I did," Jasmine said, giving Pina an aghast look. "You were an asshole, but that doesn't mean I wanted you dead!"

"That's how I know you aren't a Starvein," Pina said with a pained laugh. "In true, the nobility are worse than the gangs that dwell in the gutters. We just stab each other in the back instead of in the chest."

"We did that too," Jasmine said.

A snort slipped out of Pina's mouth and she raised a hand to cover it.

"If you happen to hear anything else, would you try to find out more or tell us?" Asher asked. He glanced at Jasmine, and his eyes narrowed. "Someone's trying to kill us, and the professors aren't helping."

*That's an understatement. The professors might be the ones trying to do the killing, even if they aren't holding the knife themselves.*

"So I gathered," Pina said. She paused for a moment, then swallowed. "I know I don't have the right to ask, but Qien told me that I was not allowed to tell anyone about what happened. They're covering the whole thing up. Could you tell me what's going on?"

Asher and Jasmine exchanged a glance. Pina had already seen

the assassin, and she'd come back to fight with them even after having an opportunity to run. It wasn't like their situation was going to get any worse by disobeying Esther at this point.

"What do you think?" Asher asked Jasmine.

"Sit down," Jasmine said, giving a small nod to the chair by Asher's desk. "It's a bit of a story."

# 39

"I can't believe it," Pina muttered. "This is unacceptable. The King–"

"Doesn't care about us," Jasmine finished. "He got me into the program, but because I was a passing fancy, not because he truly cared about me. And, if you think about it from his perspective, why wouldn't he be willing to sacrifice one noble and a gutter rat? It's a cheap cost to root out a group of assassins this strong."

"It goes against everything we are meant to stand for as Starveins!" Pina snapped, pounding a fist against the table. She realized what she'd done a moment later and yanked her hand back, her cheeks flushing. "I am sorry. I let my temper get the better of me. I'm… more emotional than I should be today. I suppose a brush with death has a way of doing that."

"Are you kidding? This is much better than how you act in class," Asher said with a chuckle. "At least you seem like a real human now."

"Forget about that. This can't be allowed to continue," Pina insisted. "We need to tell others."

"And then what?" Jasmine asked, already shaking her head. "The fact of the matter is that nobody will do anything. The Last Light are a threat to the King and the nobility. They're not going to pass up the chance to get rid of them."

Pina's lips pressed together in anger. "But..."

"It's life," Asher said with a shrug. "You can't unkill my parents and brother, and you can't make the kingdom suddenly give a shit about Jas and I. Watcher, I bet nobody would even believe us. All we have as proof is our own words."

"Then I will help," Pina said.

"How?" Asher asked. "With all due respect, my room isn't big enough for three people, and I'm not looking to have someone new move in."

"Not like that," Pina said, glaring at Asher. "That would be too obvious. But I can still help. You're new to magic, right? I can help teach you. I've been practicing magic since I awakened as a child. You've got some of the fastest magic I've ever seen, but it's really clear that you aren't using it properly."

Asher opened his mouth, then paused. "That... might actually be really useful now that you mention it. It's better than asking Qien for lessons."

"I feel like it isn't enough, but it would let my own conscience rest easier. I do not think I could leave things as they are."

"Then we'll happily accept your help," Jasmine said, and she meant it. It didn't matter how Pina had acted before – as far as she could tell, the girl genuinely seemed deeply apologetic for her actions. She and Asher didn't exactly have many allies to rely on, so they couldn't afford to refuse one.

"I'll try to see if I can figure out who was spreading the rumors as well," Pina said. "Clarence is good at projection. I'll ask him to look into it for me."

"Is he your boyfriend or something?" Asher asked. "He always sits next to you in class."

"Nothing like that. He is betrothed to a woman from a different family, but we have something of an agreement. He pretends to be one of my clinger-ons so I don't have to deal with other worthless Starveins trying to get into my good graces, and I let him pretend that he is on good terms with me to his parents."

"It sounds like he is on good terms with you if you're doing something like that," Jasmine pointed out.

Pina scowled, then let out a sigh. "I suppose we are friends. He will help and not ask questions. I assume you do not want me to tell him the circumstances."

"It's best you don't." Asher shook his head. "It's not even safe. Who knows what could happen if people find out. It's just not worth the risk. Not yet."

Pina inclined her head. She pushed her chair back and rose to her feet. "Then I will respect your wishes. We can practice your magic tomorrow, Asher. I will need time to remember all the lessons I started with as a child."

"I'll look forward to it, but make sure they're things I can do here," Asher said, nodding to Jasmine. "I'm not leaving her side."

"I will," Pina promised. She hesitated for a moment, then turned toward the door. She only managed a grand total of two steps toward it before a knock rang out and they all froze.

Asher snagged his sword again.

"Do you frequently have visitors?" Pina asked. "This seems a bit much."

"Funny. I was just thinking the same thing. I'm starting to feel like I'm stuck in a loop," Asher muttered. He strode up to the door. "Who is it?"

"Me, dumbass!" Lydia snapped from the other side. She rattled the door handle. "Let me in before I kick your damn door down. I want to see Jasmine."

Pina narrowed her eyes and cupped her hands, clearly thinking that Lydia was a threat. She paused when Asher lowered his weapon and pulled the door open. Lydia shoved past him without a second of hesitation, her eyes locked straight on the bed.

She let out a relieved sigh as soon as she saw Jasmine awake. "Oh, thank the Watcher. You're alive. It was the Last Light again, wasn't it? What in the Watcher's eyes are those instructors doing, bringing you out of Sanctuary when they know there are fucking assassins trying to kill you? This is it. I'm going to hide a rat in Esther's bathroom and nail her door shut the moment she goes inside."

Lydia let up on her tirade for just long enough to draw in a breath – and froze as she saw Pina standing in the corner of the room, staring at her with a shocked expression. Lydia closed her mouth, then cleared her throat.

"Uh... oops. I didn't see you had someone else here."

"I thought you were avoiding telling people about this," Pina said suspiciously.

"Lydia, meet Pina," Jasmine said, suppressing a laugh for the sake of her aching body. "And Pina, this is Lydia. She's the only other person we've told about this."

Lydia flicked her hair back and extended a hand. "Pleasure. I'm Jasmine's best friend and the better chef between us. Are you a Starvein, then? What are you doing here? And why is Jas telling you anything? Are you a friend she's been hiding from me?"

Pina, clearly taken aback by Lydia's energy, paused for a moment before she slowly reached out to take her hand.

"I – yes. I'm a Starvein," Pina said. "I just happened to be present when an assassin went after Jasmine and Asher."

"She saved our lives," Asher put in. "I suppose Jas saved hers in return, so we're even. Still worth mentioning, though."

"Ah. You should have led with that. Pleasure to meet you, Pina." Lydia gave Pina's hand a firm shake, then spun back to Jasmine. "You. Are you okay? How bad are the wounds?"

"I'm fine," Jasmine said with a smile. Lydia's energy was infectious, even when she was just concerned. "A bit hungry, I suppose, but I'm alive and I think I'll recover. At least, I assume Asher would have told me if I wouldn't."

She sent him a pointed look and Asher raised his hands defensively. "The healers said you'd make a full recovery, just as long as you give yourself time to heal."

"Good. See?" Jasmine asked. "I'll be fine."

"Just making sure. I need to run, then. I told Esther I was going to the bathroom. I'm supposed to be in class right now."

Lydia darted over to the door, then paused and glanced over her shoulder. She gave Pina a once-over, then nodded to herself and darted down the hall. Pina stared at where she'd been standing, then turned to the others.

"Who was that, again?"

"Lydia. She's trustworthy," Jasmine said. "Just a bit... much. Couldn't ask for a better friend, though."

"I can imagine," Pina murmured. She shook her head and cleared her throat. "I need to leave as well. I shouldn't trouble you any longer. If there's anything else you need before tomorrow and you think I can help, find my room."

"We appreciate it," Asher said. He extended his hand to Pina. "New beginnings?"

Pina clasped his hand and they shook. She then turned to Jasmine. "I'd shake your hand as well, but..."

"The thought is what counts. Just be careful. You're wrapped up in this too," Jasmine warned.

"I will," Pina promised. She gave them one last look, then stepped out of the room and closed the door behind her with a click. Asher locked it, then walked back over to rejoin Jasmine on the bed.

"Well," Asher said. "That was... something."

"I don't think it could have gone better," Jasmine said with a small smile. "I love Lydia."

"I can see why," Asher said. "I feel like I got a burst of energy just from standing next to her. She's a force of nature. I still like you more, though."

Jasmine laughed, and she was surprised to find it wasn't quite as painful as she'd been expecting. "It's not a competition."

Asher just arched an eyebrow in response. "Of course it isn't. Nobody else can compete."

"Stop," Jasmine pleaded. "You're going to make me laugh again."

"Sorry, sorry." Asher held his hands out in defeat. He paused for a second, then shifted closer to her. "So, does that pillow still need replacing, or have you decided it's better?"

Jasmine smiled up at Asher. Even though they'd just narrowly survived their second assassination attempt, she was surprised to find that she wasn't nearly as terrified as she should have been. They'd done better than they had the first time. Sure, it hadn't been a perfect success, but they were all alive. And, if Jasmine got lucky, her wounds would heal as she slept, just like the bruises that Riker had given her.

*We can do this.*

"I think we'll need to test which is more comfortable," Jasmine said. "We can start with you."

# 40

The next week passed with a surprising lack of incident. Jasmine found her wounds improving at an incredible rate, though they improved particularly fast over the nights. It clearly had something to do with how she was absorbing Asher's magic, but neither of them knew how and there wasn't anyone to ask.

Riker hadn't made an appearance since the day of the exam, and Esther had been equally absent. The only professor either of them had interaction with was Qien, and that was only because Jasmine insisted that Asher attend the classes without her. He would have stayed by her side if she'd let him, but there was no point holding him back.

It wasn't like she was going to be able to fight an assassin off in her current state, and Pina was already keeping an eye out for him in class. Pina came by their room several times that week to give Asher some basic tutelage on magic, and Jasmine had to admit that Pina definitely knew what she was doing.

In just the few days that passed, Asher's grasp of magic expanded by leaps and bounds. He still couldn't replicate making the tendrils, but he was already catching up to Pina in just about everything.

It did feel a bit awkward to just lie in bed while Asher and Pina worked beside her, but there was nothing else to be done. And, as fast as Jasmine's injuries were fading away, it was only by the end of the week that she found herself fully in control of her body again.

Jasmine could barely even find a word to describe the relief she felt when she woke up on the eleventh day after the fight and found that her wounds had finally stopped aching. There was still a thin scar along her chest, but everything else had almost completely faded away.

The bed beside her was colder than she expected, and she rolled over to find that Asher wasn't lying in it. Even as a frown crossed her lips, the door opened. Asher stepped into the room with a plate of pancakes and eggs balanced on one hand, pausing as he saw that Jasmine was no longer asleep.

"Jas! How are you feeling?" Asher set the plate down on the table. "I made breakfast. You know, I'm really starting to feel like the Keeper here. Maybe I should try to enroll in both programs at once."

Rolling her eyes, Jasmine yawned, arching her back and stretching her arms over her head to make sure that the wounds were actually as healed as she hoped they were. Nothing hurt, and her grin grew wider.

"I can move around again normally. I'm healed."

"Seriously?" Asher strode over to her. "Xolani magic is incredible. No wonder they all used so much of it. I can't believe you're completely recovered from several nearly mortal wounds in just a week. Actually, I don't believe you. I need to check."

Jasmine laughed as Asher gently pushed her back into the bed, pulling her shirt up as he ran his hands along her body in search of wounds. His fingers traced up the scar on her chest, sending tingles through her body.

"Seems healed."

"I'm not sure," Jasmine murmured. "You might need to double check."

It was Asher's turn to let out a laugh. He leaned down, pressing his lips to the scar and kissing his way up it. His hold on her was far more gentle than normal – likely worried that he'd mistakenly aggravate a wound that he couldn't see.

Asher worked his way up to Jasmine's neck, slipping under the covers beside her in the process. He let his lips brush across her collar bone, his warm breath sending shivers down her entire body.

"How are you feeling?" Asher asked. "I don't want to–"

"I'm feeling like you should be doing just about anything other than talking right now," Jasmine said into Asher's ear. "Get back to work."

"With pleasure." Asher slipped out of his shirt, pressing his bare chest to hers. Jasmine only had time to draw in a shaky breath before his lips met hers with a hungry, passionate fervor.

His hand drifted lower, gently working Jasmine out of her pants as she worked her hips against his. She moaned into his mouth and he pushed her head into the pillow, still handling her as if she might break.

Jasmine reached down and yanked Asher's pants off in a sharp motion. His length stiffened against her hand and she arched her chest, pressing against him.

"Rougher. I don't need protection," Jasmine ordered, her voice a throaty growl.

Asher obliged. He pushed her down into the bed, then started kissing his way down her body. She moaned, practically writhing in pleasure.

Asher kissed every single part of her, not even stopping for so much as air before working his way back up to her lips. He wasn't asking permission anymore, and she didn't want him to.

Jasmine locked her legs around his and he entered her, sending another wave of pleasure through her so intense that she nearly turned into a puddle. Asher's hands gripped Jasmine's hair, pulling her head back with just enough pressure to pull her lips to his.

She wrapped her hands around Asher's back and pulled him in, not wanting to ever let go. They drank each other in like water in a desert, hands roaming and clutching at anything they could grasp.

Asher had taken her orders to heart. He pulled away and pushed her down, pinning her shoulders to the bed. His hips moved in a steady, rhythmic motion as he thrust into her. She bucked against him, her legs going weak.

Jasmine reached up and pulled Asher back down to kiss him again. In that moment, nothing mattered other than them, and that was just how she wanted it.

Asher's heartbeat thumped against Jasmine's ear. She looked up into his eyes, her arms wrapped around his chest and a leg over his waist. The smile on his features made his eyes shimmer like pools of liquid gold and sent another warm shiver through her body. He massaged her head gently with one hand while of his hands while the other cupped her backside.

"I love you," Asher murmured. "I don't know if it's too early to say that, but I've never met anyone even remotely like you. Everything about you is incredible."

As Jasmine looked into Asher's eyes, the feeling she found within them was warmth and comfort. There hadn't been room for love in the gutters – but she wasn't in the gutters anymore, and she never would be again.

"I love you too. And you're pretty special yourself."

Asher pulled her in for another gentle kiss. As they pulled apart, he glanced over at the table where their breakfast sat. "I… think our food may have gotten a bit cold. Sorry."

"I'd say it was worth the tradeoff," Jasmine said, squeezing him with her legs. But, before she could say anything else, her stomach rumbled. Her cheeks flushed a bright red as Asher burst into laughter, giving her a tight hug.

"I think your stomach might disagree. Hold on to me."

He scooped Jasmine up, holding her close to his chest with one hand. She kept her legs wrapped around his waist to avoid falling off as he made his way over to the table and grabbed the plate of food with his free hand.

Asher then made his way back to the bed, lowering into it and keeping Jasmine leaning against his chest. "There. Now we can eat here."

"We'll get the sheets dirty, though."

"I think that ship has long since sailed," Asher said dryly. He tore a piece of pancake away and brought it up to her lips. "Open up."

Jasmine rolled her eyes, but she did as he asked, letting him feed her. The pancakes were definitely a little cold, but they still tasted good.

"Well?" Asher asked. "Too cold?"

"I'm not sure," Jasmine said with a coy smile. "I need another bite to make sure, but my hands are preoccupied."

Asher laughed and pulled another piece of pancake away to feed her. Even though the food itself wasn't warm, his chest and embrace were. It was the best breakfast that Jasmine could ever remember having.

# 41

After breakfast was finished, Jasmine and Asher spent some time cleaning up the bed – and themselves. Once they'd finished getting ready for the day again, the two met back in his room.

"We've got some time until class, but I'd make sure you're ready for it," Asher said. "Qien is probably going to want to speak with you. He's been pretty hard to read in these last classes, and he hasn't talked to me at all. I don't know what he's going to say."

"As if there's anything he can say that'll affect me." Jasmine shook her head and shrugged. "It's fine. I think I'm much more interested in figuring out what you can do after all that training with Pina. By some stroke of luck, there haven't been any more attacks while I was injured. We can't count on that forever, though. I doubt the Last Light is going to give up after two of their people got killed."

"Yeah," Asher said, his brow darkening as he clenched his hands. "And we barely won that last fight. You nearly died. I need to be able to do more."

"You saved me," Jasmine pointed out.

"I only had to save you because I was just standing on the sidelines being completely useless while you fought for our lives. Sure, you were getting empowered by my magic, but I need to be able to do more."

"Well, only one way to do that. We try to practice."

"Yeah," Asher said with a firm nod. "I won't be holding back. Not anymore. Back to the training rooms, then?"

"Sounds good to me," Jasmine said with a grin.

They set off without any more hesitation, making for the training rooms as fast as they could without drawing undue attention. Nobody bothered them on the trip over, and it didn't take long until they arrived in the Keeper section of Sanctuary and hunted down an empty room.

*I suppose we could have used the room that Riker trains me in, but I still have no idea how he gets in and out of it. Maybe I should ask him the next time he shows up – or if he shows up. It's been quite a while since I last saw him.*

"Everything okay?" Asher asked, peering at Jasmine with a concerned frown. "Your wounds aren't still acting up, are they?"

"Nothing like that. I'm totally fine. I was just trying to figure out if Riker was ever going to show back up," Jasmine said with a shake of her head. "It hardly matters now. Let's just focus on magic."

"Okay. Just wanted to make sure," Asher said. He reached out for Jasmine's hand, then caught himself and pulled back. "I guess I should try to call the creepy tendrils first, shouldn't I?"

"Probably for the best," Jasmine said with a nod. She walked to stand just beside Asher, ready to touch him at a moment's notice. "Just do it in the opposite direction from me. I heard what happened to the assassin, and it didn't sound fun."

"I will," Asher promised. "Assuming I can actually call them up, that is."

Jasmine gave him an encouraging smile. Asher's brow furrowed and his lips pressed thin as he looked down into his palms, concentrating with a terse frown. Several seconds passed, but nothing happened.

"I wasn't looking at your face during the fight, but you seem really focused right now," Jasmine observed. "Is it possible that you're trying too hard? Maybe it needs to come more naturally. Normal magic is pretty easy when we're in contact, right?"

"I – yeah. I suppose so," Asher admitted as he scrunched his nose. His face relaxed, but not fully. "It's kind of hard to make yourself not try on something you're trying to do, though. It's like the exact opposite of my goal."

"Well, focus on something else. Just try to reach the magic subconsciously… or something like that. Didn't Pina's lessons talk about any of this?"

"Most of her stuff has been about actually controlling the magic and having it do more of what I want. Right now, we're just using it as raw energy. Doesn't do much other than knock things around or make them fall unconscious through magical shock. That clearly wasn't what I was doing with the tendrils."

Jasmine crossed her arms and chewed her lower lip in thought. "You were doing it entirely on accident at night. Do you remember why?"

"No, not really. It was just… sleep. Sleep, and then pain and fear. That was just about it. It's not like it's happened recently because you've been sleeping by me. Do you think it would be a good idea to try to sleep alone and see if we can figure out what causes it?"

Jasmine could tell by the tone of Asher's voice that he couldn't have liked the idea he was suggesting any less if he physically wanted to, and she wasn't a fan of it either.

"I don't know if that's the best idea for a variety of reasons." Jasmine said as she shook her head. "The chances of something going wrong are way too high, for one. You've done it outside of sleep, so you should be able to replicate it. Maybe just think back to the emotions you felt when the assassin was attacking."

Asher pursed his lips, then started to walk in a slow circle as he thought. "I can't pin exactly what emotions I was feeling, though. There was definitely fear. Surprise. More than a little anger and concern. Panic as well. Basically every bad emotion, now that I think about it."

"Great. Can you replicate it?"

"If I could, I'd have done that already," Asher grumbled. "Emotions are emotions. People can barely even control them normally. Completely faking them is a whole new field."

"Maybe you could just try to focus on one?" Jasmine suggested, tilting her head to the side. "We could just try to make you angry or the like."

"Do you not remember the socks? That didn't work."

"Oh. Right. Hm."

The two of them stood in silence for a few seconds, contemplating their options. The assassin hadn't managed to land a blow on Asher, so the strange magic he'd used was definitely under his control to some degree.

It hadn't been due to Jasmine either, as she hadn't felt any magic running through her when he'd used it. If anything, it was the opposite. She had to draw the power out of Asher to keep his magic from eating him alive.

"Maybe we should start with normal magic first," Jasmine suggested. "It might be easier to figure out what's going on after we see the basic stuff you can do."

Asher shrugged and held his hand out. Jasmine took it, and he turned his free palm up toward the ceiling. Ice pricked Jasmine's spine. Energy gathered within Asher's palm, taking just seconds before a ball of black and red power swam in wait.

"Whoa. That really was fast," Jasmine said, her eyebrows raising. "If I'm not wrong, even Pina wasn't this quick."

"It helps a lot when you aren't dealing with pain and distractions. You make it easy."

Asher flicked his hand and the ball shot off in a streak of light, splattering against the wall and vanishing with a sizzle and a puff of smoke. He drew another one to his hand, then tossed it as well.

"I'm able to form about one of these every three seconds. Pina is at four and a half, so I'm a fair bit faster than her. And, since you're the one that has to deal with the hard part of magic, I don't have to concentrate as much on it either. You make this completely unfair."

Jasmine nodded absently, her mind drifting back to their fight against the assassin. There had to be something that had happened that would be useful for their training. Her brow furrowed as one of the lines he'd said resurfaced.

"The assassin said something about a siphon," Jasmine said. "I'm pretty sure he was talking about the dagger, and he definitely thought it was important."

"Yeah," Asher said with a nod, letting the magic in his hand fade as he dropped it. "And he also said that you somehow stole it... or something like that? The siphon definitely feels like the dagger, but you didn't still have the dagger."

"It's pretty clear that the dagger was the reason I somehow stole your magic," Jasmine said. "So I guess that means they were trying to steal your magic with the dagger?"

"Sound logic, but it doesn't even make sense." Asher shook his head in befuddlement. "It's not like my family put out any good mages. I was completely worthless at it, and my brother was middling at best. The Last Light was clearly hunting us. I just can't see why."

Jasmine shook her head. "Let's focus on what we do know. The dagger was a way to steal magic, and they targeted your family specifically. Anything else?"

"It makes some form of link between the person wielding it and the victim," Asher said after a moment. "And at least as far as I can tell, it's one way. You can't use anything without me giving it to you. You just happen to have your own magic that's muddling what comes from where a bit."

"I'd agree. There's also one of the last things the assassin mentioned. Didn't he look completely shocked that you were using the tendril magic?"

"Yeah, though I can't say I love calling it tendril magic. It makes me sound… gross."

Jasmine rolled her eyes. "Get over it or come up with a better name. Stay on topic."

"Fine, fine. Yeah, he looked pretty shocked. Almost as if he thought you were supposed to be the one tossing the magic around, and he just thought you were an amateur."

"Meaning the dagger was probably meant to steal the magic completely," Jasmine concluded. She chewed the inside of her cheek. "That makes sense. You make the link then kill the guy you're stealing from, so all his magic goes into you."

"That still doesn't tell us why they'd choose me or what it actually does, though. My family is – was – pretty damn plain. We weren't that great at magic. We weren't all that talented. We were just mages. That's it."

"Maybe that's the exact reason they targeted you," Jasmine said. Goosebumps ran down her back as she raised her eyes to meet Asher. "That's it, isn't it?"

"What is?"

"They went after you *because* you suck at channeling magic," Jasmine muttered, her theory gaining traction with every word she spoke aloud. "Remember the whole thing you told me about Starveins being able to use magic because they couldn't channel it as well as other people, while the Xolani were really good at it so they couldn't control how much they drew?"

Asher's eyes widened in realization and he swore under his

breath. "Watcher's eyes. We've been some of the least effective Starveins, which means if there's some kind of powerful magic someone is trying to use, the people most likely able to actually survive it would be my family. But... my family doesn't have anything like that. I can't see why we'd be important enough to send a group of powerful assassins after. It's not like there aren't other crappy Starveins in the kingdom."

Jasmine shook her head. "I don't know why either, but it's a start. Better than what we had before, at least. You're sure the tendril stuff isn't from your family?"

"Definitely not. We would have heard about it before, I'm pretty sure – and we're already pretty sure that the dagger's purpose was to steal magic, not give it. Right?"

"I mean, I suppose it's always a possibility that it did more, but we don't have any way to know. Can you start using magic again?"

"Sure," Asher said, forming a ball of swirling red in his palm. Jasmine peered at it, taking care to keep her distance.

"Do you know why it's the same color as the tendrils were?"

"Pina said everyone has their own color of magic. It's an expression of self, or something like that. Magic starts out pretty universal for all Starveins, but the stronger you get, the more unique your power becomes. The color is just the first element of that."

"Makes sense. So we don't know if the red is due to your magic or the dagger. Was your brother's magic red?"

"Unfortunately not to both questions. It was pink."

"Well, shit." Jasmine scrunched her nose. "And you can't form your magic into the tendril things?"

"Afraid not."

"Then there's only one thing I can think of."

"And that is?"

"We need to get our hands on the dagger again," Jasmine said, setting her jaw. "I'm not asking Esther for shit, so that means we need to speak with Qien."

Asher shook his head and shrugged. "I think I agree, though. It's the only thing I can think of. I'm certain Qien took the dagger from the assassin to study, so we'll confront him after class and see if we can make him give it to us."

# 42

Their plan in place, Jasmine and Asher spent most of the time leading up to class just practicing with normal magic. Asher mostly focused on his own abilities, though he spent some time empowering Jasmine so she could work on getting more used to her improved abilities.

The magic felt surprisingly natural and almost as if it were an extension of her body's normal capabilities, even though that couldn't have been farther from the truth. They also discovered that Jasmine had a pretty significant pool of energy to draw on, though the progression of the chill grew the fastest when Asher was empowering Jasmine.

They didn't get an exact number of how long she could use the power at once, but it seemed to be somewhere around two to three minutes before the ice reached her neck.

After they gave the magic another five or so minutes, it receded to the point where they could draw on it again – but it would come back slower than it had the first time. It continued to move slower with every time they used it up, so the two of them stopped around an hour before class to make sure Jasmine still had enough power to work with if the situation called for it.

With the extra time before class, Jasmine and Asher hit the kitchen to make lunch. They waited around for a few minutes for some other Starveins to vacate it before going in themselves. It wasn't like they couldn't use the kitchen when anyone else was in it, but cooking had become something that Jasmine didn't really want to share with anyone other than Asher.

They made a quick but tasty meal of steak and fried vegetables, finishing everything up and setting off to class just in time to get there just before the majority of the other students arrived.

Jasmine was mildly surprised to find that, when Pina showed up, she sat down a chair away from Jasmine's seat instead of returning to her normal spot at the front. Clarence, who was trailing after her, took the seat beside it.

*I suppose it makes a bit of sense since we're friendlier now, but I didn't expect Pina to actually change where she sat.*

Esmarelda was one of the last students to show up. She took the open seat that Pina had left, giving Jasmine a quick smile as she sat down and started pulling her belongings out. "Good to see you back. I was worried you weren't going to show again."

"Qien can't get rid of me that easily."

Esmarelda's lips curled down in a frown. "He actually tried to do something to you, then?"

"What? No. Well, I don't think so." Jasmine's brow furrowed. "What's the story as to what happened to me?"

"It doesn't sound very convincing when you're asking what the story is meant to be. Doesn't that mean you're covering something?"

"That depends on the answer you give me."

"Just that something went wrong during the exam and that Qien didn't account for it. Nobody's saying anything else. Are you going to enlighten me? I heard that someone took the identity of a Keeper and was trying to dig for information. Did you–"

"She won't be answering that," Pina said, giving Esmarelda a flat stare. "She is not. Qien expressly stated that anyone spreading unfounded rumor would be drained."

"Kind of a harsh punishment just for talking," Asher observed with a frown. "Why's he being so strict about it?"

"To avoid rumors," Pina said, giving them a pointed glance to remind them of exactly how much rumor had affected her. "And to maintain control of the class, I'd assume. It would not be a good outlook for him if nobody respected his orders anymore."

*That feels like a bit much, but no point pissing Qien off even further. I'll be doing more than enough of that when we talk after class and I try to get him to give me his dagger.*

"Bah. Since when did you care? You've been sitting around Asher ever since Jasmine got injured. What's up with that?" Esmarelda asked, cocking an eyebrow and staring Pina down. "Got any reason for it?"

"I am tutoring him."

"Sure. *Tutoring.*" Esmarelda scoffed and rolled her eyes. "As if anyone believes that. You should tell her to get lost, Jasmine. She's butting her nose in where it doesn't belong."

*Do these two have history or something?*

"I think Asher can make decisions for himself," Jasmine said. "And Pina isn't trying to do anything inappropriate. If she did, Asher would handle it. I wouldn't need to do anything. Besides, my job is to protect him from threats, not doe-eyes."

A smirk flickered across Pina's face for an instant before she took it back under control. Esmarelda let out a huff and leaned back in her chair, burying her nose in a book. Before Jasmine could say anything else, the class fell silent.

Qien swept down the stairs and over to his dais. He set his books down and glanced up, his gaze pausing as he spotted

Jasmine sitting beside Asher. It only took him an instant to recover, but it was still long enough for Jasmine to pick up on.

*Oh, yeah. He's definitely not happy that I'm here. But is he mad because he's uncomfortable he screwed up, or is he with Esther and ashamed that his attempt to use us as bait failed?*

There was no way to know the answer to that until class ended, and so all Jasmine could do was wait.

Class felt like it dragged on forever. When Qien finally dismissed everyone, Jasmine nearly leapt out of her desk in her haste to get down to Qien before he could leave the classroom. Instead, she forced herself to remain seated while the other students left.

Qien still had to gather his notes, and he wasn't moving as if he was in a hurry. That meant she wouldn't have to cause a scene running him down, which would obviously be preferrable.

"I take it you mean to speak with Professor Qien," Pina said as she stood.

"Yeah. I'm just waiting until everyone else leaves," Jasmine said. "I don't want to start something."

"That is likely a sage choice," Pina said with an approving nod. "In that case, I will leave. Are we still meeting to practice later today, Asher?"

"Yeah," Asher said absently. He glanced at Jasmine. "Do you think two hours should be okay?"

"We should be back by then, so sure."

Pina nodded, then set off out of the classroom with Clarence tailing behind her. He'd yet to say a single word to them. Esmarelda looked like she wanted to say something, but she just shook her head and headed out of the room.

Jasmine and Asher made their way down to the center of the room as the last of the students trickled out the doors behind them. Qien sighed as they approached, gathering all his papers into his folder and pressing it down against the podium.

"You have recovered faster than the healers expected."

"I guess I'm just hard to keep down. I hope you aren't disappointed," Jasmine said, unable to keep all of the anger from her tone. Qien clearly picked up on it, but all he did was collect his folder and tuck it under an arm.

"That remains to be seen." Qien made to step around Jasmine, but she moved to block him.

"We need to speak, Professor."

"Are you giving me an order, Xolani?"

"Jasmine," Asher corrected. "Or Keeper. The most Xolani presence we've seen is the daggers that the assassins keep trying to stab us with. The assassins that you nearly led straight to us while you were playing around with other students."

"Your exam nearly got me killed," Jasmine said. Her hand tightened on the hilt of the sword at her side. "I think you owe us a few answers as to how you screwed everything up so badly. Unless it was intentional?"

Qien's eyes narrowed and his lips pressed together. Neither of them spoke for a second. Finally, he let out a sound between a grunt and a sigh. "Then come with me to my office. I will not do this where others can watch."

He set a brisk pace out of the classroom, forcing Jasmine and Asher to break into a light jog to keep up with his long stride. The professor led them out the doors and down the glittering Starvein halls, not slowing for an instant.

Jasmine was pretty sure that Qien would loved nothing more than to leave them behind, but neither she nor Asher were willing to let him leave – and, unfortunately for Qien, they were in considerably better shape than he was.

A few minutes later, the three of them stood before a small, adorned door. Qien reached for the handle, hesitating for an instant before he pushed the door open to reveal an office. It was surprisingly plain in comparison to the rest of the halls.

There was a large wooden desk in the center with a single padded chair behind it. Shelves chock-full of books lined the walls and several more books were scattered across the table, some open. An open ink pot sat beside one of the books, a quill knocked askew and dripping ink onto the table beside it.

Qien walked around the table and pushed the chair back, though he made no move to sit down. He gestured impatiently to the door.

"Enter, and close the door behind you. There are no bugs in my office, and I would like to keep it that way."

Asher shut the door behind them as they entered. Jasmine let her gaze roam over the room, hoping she'd find the dagger just lying somewhere, but there was no such luck.

"Make this quick. I do not have time to listen to complaints for the next hour." Qien tapped a finger on the desk impatiently. "What do you want?"

"What do we want?" Jasmine demanded, nearly losing her cool on the spot. She wrestled her anger down, Riker's teaching ringing through her head, and let out a slow breath. "I want to know what happened, Professor. Why was there an assassin in the forest? It feels like they knew we were going to be there."

Qien's tapping echoed through the room, the only sound other than their breathing. The professor finally let out a sigh.

"I don't know."

Jasmine waited to see if he would add anything else, but he didn't. She crossed her arms. "Professor, I'm not trying to be antagonistic here, but that isn't enough. We nearly died. I *should* have died."

"I know!" Qien snapped, raising a hand and balling it into a fist. He nearly pounded it against the desk, but caught himself before he could and instead crossed his arms behind his back, his jaw clenched so tightly that the veins in his neck bulged like writhing worms. "There is a leak. Someone is feeding information to Last Light."

*Yeah. It's you. Or Esther, I suppose. Either way, no shit.*

"With all due respect, that's… not really a surprise to us," Asher said. "Keeper Esther hasn't made much effort to hide that we're being used as bait to lure the Last Light out. But just because she's willing to spend our lives doesn't mean we are."

"Ludicrous," Qien said with a dismissive wave. "Keeper Esther is an apt instructor if a bit brusque, but she is not attempting to kill you."

"Right," Jasmine said dryly. "That's why she's assigned a Keeper that hasn't finished her first year to the noble who is actively getting targeted by assassins. That's why she won't actually have the real Keeper that visited Sanctuary near us. Don't you think it's awful coincidental that Riker went off to do something right before we were attacked?"

Qien didn't respond immediately, which was a surprising point in his favor. He was actually thinking about Asher's question rather than just dismissing it on the spot.

"That was indeed suspicious," Qien allowed after a few seconds. "But there is nothing to be done. I regret what happened, but I cannot change the past. You lived. The assassin is dead. If you want my word that I will not force you to leave Sanctuary again until this issue has been dealt with, then you have it. Is that sufficient?"

*That's definitely something, but…*

"No," Asher said, answering for Jasmine. "It helps, but the assassins have gotten into Sanctuary before. If we're going to be playing games with our lives, then I think we should have all the tools to play with. Give us a fighting chance."

"And how am I meant to do that?" Qien arched an eyebrow. "Do you want me to personally train you? To ignore every other student in favor of a single one?"

"No," Jasmine said. "We just want you to give us the dagger you took from the assassin. That's it. We want to research it, and you've already made it clear that you're too busy to help us. So, in that case, it shouldn't be that much of a problem, right?"

Qien tilted his head to the side. "You want the Xolani artifact?"

"Yes. What's wrong with that?" Jasmine challenged. "It's what caused this whole mess in the first place, so it might be the key to finding out – well, anything. I'd say it's better than just sitting around and waiting to get killed."

"I suppose it would be."

Jasmine blinked in surprise as Qien walked around the desk and over to a bookshelf. He ran a finger along the book spines, stopping on a plain, gray manuscript and pulling it free.

*He's actually going to give it to us?*

"We can have it?" Asher asked, voicing Jasmine's thoughts.

"Yes," Qien said. "Despite what you seem to believe, I do not seek your death. I will not endanger or hamper the progress of the other Starveins – the kingdom cannot afford to make such a blunder – but if you wish to take your lives into your own hands, I will not stop you from inspecting the artifact. It very well may kill you, though."

"We're aware of the risks," Jasmine said. "Anything is better than nothing."

"Then you may have it, so long as you return it." Qien pulled the book open, revealing that a hole had been cut into its center in the shape of a dagger. And, within the hole was absolutely nothing.

The book was empty.

# 43

Qien's eyes widened in shock that was far too real for it to be an act. He spun, turning back to the bookshelf and flicking through the other books in it, pulling them out and tossing them onto his desk without a word.

Jasmine's heart sank into her stomach as Qien went through the entire shelf, then patted down the shelves. He pulled the shelf back to look behind it, but it became increasingly clear that the dagger wasn't where he thought it was. Finally, he turned back to them, his face a shade paler than it had been.

"The dagger. It's not here," Qien said, his words laden with disbelief.

"And I take it you didn't misplace it somehow?" Jasmine asked, knowing her question to be pointless. The hole in the book that Qien had first pulled out had pretty clearly been shaped perfectly so it wouldn't rattle or thump around. Someone had pulled the dagger out of the book.

"Of course not," Qien grabbed the book where the dagger had been meant to be and closed it, opening it once more as if that would magically make the blade appear. "Someone has infiltrated my office and stolen the artifact."

"Who even knew about it?" Asher asked. "Nobody just steals things randomly, and not like that. It was targeted."

"Nobody other than the two of you and Pina, who was present at the fight. The two Keepers were both unconscious, and the third never saw the assassin cut him down," Qien said. His knuckles turned white as he gripped the book in his hands. "My room was protected against intrusion. There is an assassin – or someone with the skill of one – currently within Sanctuary."

Jasmine was pretty sure that statement should have sent chills down her spine, but at this point, she couldn't even bring herself to be surprised. She exchanged a glance with Asher, who just sighed.

"Figures," Asher said. "I don't suppose it's you, and you'll try to stab us now? It would make things easier. We could get it out of the way."

Qien sent a glare at Asher. "I will not tolerate your sarcasm right now."

"There's not much else we can do," Jasmine pointed out. "I guess we could go ask Esther, but I get the feeling I know how that would go."

"No," Qien snapped. They both looked at him in surprise.

"Why not?" Asher asked. "Nothing changed for us, professor. Assassins got into Sanctuary before. It isn't really a surprise that they're back again. All we can do is keep trying to prepare to fight them."

"Not that. I meant Esther." Qien drew in a breath and let it out through clenched teeth. "I may have to retract my earlier statement."

"Which one?" Jasmine asked.

"Esther would have been aware of the dagger. Nobody else would have had the knowledge or ability to break into my office," Qien said. "They would have needed either the appropriate tools or an intimate knowledge of Sanctuary – and the assassin would not have broken into my room purely to steal an artifact. I would be dead already. That means it was someone who was hoping I would not notice its disappearance."

"Wait. You're saying you think Esther stole the dagger?" Asher asked, his eyes going wide. "That's going well past her just trying to use us as bait."

"I cannot think who else would have had access to or knowledge of the dagger," Qien said. He started putting books back onto the shelf, shoving them into place with loud thuds that accentuated the anger in his posture.

*If Esther did that... it means she's not just using us as bait, but actively trying to get us killed. That's a terrifying thought – but why would she want that? It doesn't make sense.*

"Why would Esther do something like that? Don't get me wrong – I hate her," Jasmine said. "But why would she steal from you?"

"If I knew, I would not be sitting here in befuddlement," Qien replied. He returned the last of the books to his shelf and clenched his fists, staring into their spines as if the answers he sought resided within them. "Never in my years of teaching has something like this happened within Sanctuary."

*Sounds like you really need to upgrade your safety measures. They're kind of pathetic.*

"That sucks, but it also doesn't help us. Jasmine and I need that dagger if we want to get stronger fast. It's our only lead."

"It isn't the only dagger that has been recovered." Qien turned to look back at them, his expression hard.

"You just said not to talk to Esther," Asher pointed out. "Did you change your mind?"

"No," Qien replied. He squatted, pulling open a drawer in his desk and rifling through it before pulling out an iron key. He set it down on the desk before them. "I said not to *speak* with Esther."

Jasmine nearly burst out laughing at the absurdity of the situation. "Are you telling us to rob Esther?"

"I am telling you to do nothing. Robbing a Keeper is a crime against the kingdom," Qien said sharply. His eyes narrowed. "But so is robbing a Starvein – and no law is worth more than your life. If you believe the dagger is key to your issues, then take steps to acquire it. Evidently, someone has decided the same thing. I believe getting one of the daggers may be in your best interest."

Jasmine and Asher exchanged a glance. It didn't take Jasmine long to decide, though. She pocketed the key.

*At least it's something. More than I thought he'd give, if I'm being honest. I was already planning on stealing it from him if he didn't give it to us, so I guess this is the best-case result given the scenario we got.*

"Thank you."

"Don't thank me," Qien muttered irritably. He pulled his chair out and sat in it, running his hands through his hair. "This is a damned fool thing to do, but the situation has deteriorated to the point where a fool's choice may be the only one that works. If someone has stolen the dagger from me, they are likely to be watching my movements to some degree as well. And, if Esther is indeed the culprit, then she will have others waiting to confront me if I attempt to search her rooms."

"What makes you think she has the dagger in her room at all?" Asher asked. "Even if she stole it, it could be anywhere."

"It could be," Qien agreed. "I do not know. I have no way of knowing. Perhaps the key will help, or perhaps it will not. That will fall to you – or you will choose to take the wiser path and forgo searching for the dagger. Regardless, when you leave my room, ensure you look angered. If we are being watched, you must look as if I did not help you."

*That's sound advice. Maybe Qien isn't so much of an asshole after all.*

"Why do you have a key to Esther's room in the first place?" Jasmine asked, unable to help herself.

Qien's lips quirked up in the faintest smirk. "I was nosy once as well, and I am older than I look. I have been at Sanctuary for longer than Esther has, and she is not the only one to have lived in the Head Keeper quarters. That will be all the answer you get. Leave. If you spend more time here and we are being watched, our enemy may get suspicious."

Asher and Jasmine nodded. As they made for the door, Jasmine turned to ask Qien one last question. "Are you going to try to bring in help or something? If there's one assassin, there could be more. We can't just keep fighting them forever, and everyone is in danger, not just us."

"We shall see," Qien said, his gaze drifting away from them. He shook his head and waved a hand dismissively. "Leave. And do not forget your expressions."

That, at least, wasn't too difficult. Jasmine was already suitably pissed, so the scowl on her face as she and Asher stormed out of Qien's office wasn't even fake. They headed straight back to their room, not wanting to lurk around in the large hallways waiting for a dagger to kiss their backs.

Shadows were already crawling across the tall golden arches of the Starvein Halls as the evening started to give way to night. The only thing that gave Jasmine any peace was that her neck had yet to start tingling.

They made it back to their room and, without even exchanging a word, thoroughly checked every nook and cranny of it before they allowed themselves to relax.

"Well," Asher said, sitting down on his bed, "shit."

"That's an understatement." Jasmine sat down beside Asher and he wrapped his arm around her shoulders, pulling her into his chest.

"Can't say the idea of robbing Esther isn't even slightly enticing, I have to admit," Asher said. "Somehow it feels like it would be really satisfying."

"Unless she's standing there and staring at us when we open the door," Jasmine said. A shudder ran down her spine. "Imagine we pull the door open and the room is pitch black. We step inside and Esther is there with the dagger in her hand and the assassins are flanking her."

Asher grimaced. "I really don't like the idea of pretending that Esther is one of the Last Light. It wouldn't make any sense, though. She's had ample time to kill us."

"Yeah," Jasmine muttered. She shifted her position so she was lying down with her head in his lap. "You're right. That doesn't make me worry about it any less, though."

Asher stroked his hand through Jasmine's hair. "We're not robbing her, then?"

"No, I think we should. We just... shouldn't do it at night. That's terrifying – and she's way more likely to be home at night. If we go some time midday tomorrow, our chances of the room being empty are way higher."

"Good point," Asher said. He paused for a moment. "And it also helps that we don't have to walk around Sanctuary at night."

"Yeah," Jasmine said, her cheeks reddening slightly. "That too."

"You're the one with the danger sense, so you better believe I'm doing what you suggest."

"Not because I'm your Keeper?"

Asher tussled Jasmine's hair, much to her annoyance. "That too. Either way, it might be better not to do anything today."

"Why not?"

"Because Pina is–"

There was a knock on the door. Jasmine bolted upright, but Asher caught her before she could jump and pulled her back into his lap.

"We're fine, Jas," Asher said with a laugh. "It's Pina. She was coming to help with my magic, remember?"

The smile faded away from his face and he stiffened. "Unless you felt like something was wrong and it's an assassin?"

"No, it's fine," Jasmine said with a shake of her head. "I didn't feel anything weird. I'm just jumpy. I have been since the exam."

"And we nearly got killed at the exam," Asher pointed out. He slipped out of bed and grabbed his sword. "I'm going with your brain here, not mine."

Jasmine drew her own weapon and approached the door, moving Asher a step back and letting her hand stay in contact with his in case he needed to use magic.

"Who is it?" Jasmine asked.

"It's me. Is now a bad time?" Pina asked from the other side of the door.

Jasmine breathed a sigh of relief. She pulled the door open and let Pina inside, closing it behind her. Pina glanced at the swords in their hands.

"Is something going on?"

They exchanged a look.

"Yeah," Asher said. He nodded to his chair. "You might want to sit down. It's not good news."

# 44

"That is not good news." Pina said once Asher finished bringing her up to speed on what had happened that day.

"Yeah, that's what I said." Asher pinched the bridge of his nose between his fingers and let out a pained sigh. "We're in shit. Either we do nothing and get stabbed, or we try to steal from Esther and probably get stabbed anyway."

"You are accusing Esther of treason. This is not something that will go over easily. She works directly for Sanctuary, so she represents the will of the king. Even without the standing of a Starvein, Esther is a very dangerous person to confront. Are you certain this dagger will make that much of a difference?"

Jasmine and Asher exchanged a glance. It wasn't an easy question to answer. There was no guarantee that the dagger would do anything. After all, its purpose may very well have already been finished – or it could just make things worse.

*We don't have anything else to go off, though. If I can't get my hands on the dagger, then Asher's only way to get stronger is to keep practicing. The assassin made it sound like the magic should be able to do more than what we were doing, and he recognized the tendrils of magic. There has to be a way to control them, and the dagger is probably tied to it.*

"It's hard to say, but I think it's our best shot," Jasmine said. She stood up and started to pace back and forth in the room. "We can't even consider how difficult it will be to actually use or test anything with the dagger. The first step is just getting the stupid thing."

"Then you have no choice. Esther is your best bet," Pina said grimly. "Although you could wait for another assassin to strike and take their dagger when they fall."

"Assuming we don't get killed in the process. Two assassins already got killed trying to get me," Asher pointed out with a shake of his head. "They've got to have figured out something is going on. The next one will be stronger, and I doubt we'll keep getting lucky."

"I'm not asking you to aid us in treason," Jasmine said quickly. "You don't have to–"

"It is my duty as a Starvein to take action if I have reason to believe that something is remiss and threatens the kingdom," Pina said, cutting Jasmine off and crossing her arms in front of her chest. "Even if we are wrong, aiding you is the only decision that I am willing to consider. I believe your story, especially after how incompetently the situation in the exam was handled."

Jasmine was surprised to find that Pina's words actually took a sizable amount of weight off her shoulders. Even though she'd gotten to know the other girl a little over the past week during her tutoring sessions for Asher, she wasn't certain she'd have called Pina a friend.

*Nobody can say that Pina isn't honorable when push comes to shove. I could have someone worse at my back, and I know for a fact that she's on our side. If she wasn't, she never would have saved us from the last assassin.*

"Does that mean you're going to break into Esther's room with us tomorrow?" Asher asked. Jasmine shot him a look and he shrugged. "The more help we get the better."

"I will help." Pina nodded. "Not that I have extensive experience breaking into places, but an extra body can't hurt."

They weren't in a position where Jasmine could reject Pina's offer. All she could do was give the other girl a grateful nod. "Thank you. I've broken into my share of places, but not in a long time. Having someone that can help act as a lookout will be really useful. We need to start working on a plan, then."

"Do you have one?"

"Not yet," Jasmine said, pressing her lips together and clenching her jaw. "But we will."

For the next hour, the three of them talked about the best time to try and break into Esther's room and various other activities that would almost certainly get them all booted out of Sanctuary if anyone had happened to be listening in.

As it turned out, no matter how dangerous confronting Esther was, there weren't really many different ways to go about it. Their best bet was to just wait until she was teaching a class, then break into the room while everyone was busy. As long as they were out before class ended, chances were that they'd get away with it.

Of course, that didn't stop them from poring over every single detail of their plan, trying to figure out where things could go wrong before they happened. No plan was foolproof, but the more moving pieces were accounted for, the less likely they would be to get surprised.

Their preparations were interrupted by a knock on the door. All three of them froze like blocks of ice, and Jasmine nearly tripped over her own feet mid-pace.

"Another one?" Asher muttered as he went for his sword.

Pina cupped her hands and drew magic into them as Jasmine approached their door. Her neck wasn't tingling, so she doubted they were in danger, but she was also starting to get tired of jumping at every single shadow.

"Who is it?" Jasmine asked, raising her voice just enough for it to be heard on the other side of the door.

"You're way too popular if you're getting visitors at this time of night," Lydia's voice came from the other side. "You and Asher aren't getting up to anything nasty, are you? And, if you are, do you have room for–"

Jasmine pulled the door open, suppressing a laugh as she dragged Lydia inside, closing the door behind her the instant she was through.

"You have both the best and worst timing ever," Jasmine informed Lydia.

Lydia glanced around the room, her gaze lingering on Pina for a moment longer than the others. "Oh, wow. You're getting adventurous, aren't you? Well, I've never been one to turn down a unique experience. I'll take this as an invitation and accept. I've never been with three people at–"

Asher laughed as the tension in the air cracked. He shook his head and waved Lydia over. "That's not what we're doing. Sorry to crush your hopes."

"Oh. Damn. This is just a normal boring gathering that I happened to stumble into, then? Also, hi Pina. Good to see you again."

"Hello. What exactly did you think we were doing?" Pina asked.

"Never mind that," Jasmine said hurriedly. "And I'd say this is anything but boring, Lydia. We're robbing Esther."

Lydia blinked. "Seriously? Damn, count me in. How can I help?"

"Just like that?" Pina asked, her eyebrows creeping up her forehead. "You don't even want to know what we're stealing or why we're doing it?"

"I mean, sure. But I'm in either way." Lydia flashed them a wide grin. "I've wanted to do something like that forever. Not to romanticize your life in the gutters, Jas. Sorry. It just sounds kind of cool to rob some powerful asshole."

"You realize most of what we did in the gutters was pickpocketing, not stealing from wealthy merchants and nobles?"

"Let a girl dream."

Jasmine rolled her eyes. "Well, we're robbing Esther of a dagger. The same one that Asher was stabbed with. We need it to try and figure out how to control his magic, but Qien's got stolen and we think Esther took it. Also, there's an assassin somewhere in Sanctuary. Did I miss anything?"

For a total of two seconds, Lydia stared at Jasmine in disbelief. Then she shrugged and nodded. "Understood. Esther is a traitor – no surprise there. She was already basically trying to get you killed. You missed one thing. How do I help?"

"Is she always like this?" Pina asked. "You barely even said anything and Lydia is already completely onboard. Is she insane? We are committing treason."

"Meh, I've done worse." Lydia rubbed the side of her neck, then frowned. "Actually, I don't think I have. But I'm sure I will at some point. Might as well get it out of my system before I become a Keeper for some stuffy Starvein that doesn't know the meaning of fun."

"This is fun to you?" Pina squinted at Lydia. "If you like this, then what are you scared of?"

"Probably the usual," Lydia said, rubbing her chin with a thoughtful frown. "You know. Dying alone and forgotten, without having accomplished anything meaningful. Failing to live up to my expectations and finding out I'm a terrible Keeper. Marrying someone boring. Eating Jasmine's cooking. That kind of thing."

Pina turned away, but Jasmine caught a glimpse of a small grin flickering across her features before she could hide it.

"Those are definitely not the usual fears," Asher said. "And I'll have you know that Jasmine's cooking is great. She just needed a little practice."

"Oh? I'll have to be the judge of that." Lydia crossed her arms and arched an eyebrow. A moment later, she scrunched her nose. "Well, assuming we survive this whole thing."

"That is certainly the goal," Pina said. "Our plan right now is not very much of a plan. Jasmine and Asher said that the Keeper classes start an hour before sunrise. We will go to Esther's room just after that time. While they break in, I will stand watch. Whether we find the dagger or not, we will leave within thirty minutes."

"Seems simple enough," Lydia said.

"Except for the part where there's an assassin roaming around Sanctuary somewhere. Maybe more than one," Asher said. He sat down on his bed and leaned onto his forearms, a frown playing across his features. "And something tells me that our luck is going to make sure we run into him in Esther's room. After all, if she's working with the assassins, that's where they'd be staying."

"Unless she *is* the assassin," Lydia pointed out.

"Possible, but we can't count on it," Pina said. "We need to assume that there may be another enemy. Maybe more. I think the most useful thing you could do would be to help me keep watch. If we hear Jasmine and Asher get into a fight or call out, then we'll both join them and forget about the watch."

"Works for me. And Qien won't help us at all? We're sure he isn't working with the Last Light himself?"

"Pretty sure." Jasmine pulled the key out of her pocket. "He was going to give us the dagger when we asked for it, but when it was stolen, he gave us the key to her room instead."

Lydia tilted her head to the side, a small grin forming on her face. "Why's he got a key to Esther's room?"

"Don't even insinuate that," Jasmine said with a shudder.

"Esther is ancient, and Qien seemed pretty pissed about the theft. He said that the key was from when he knew someone else that lived in there before Esther. They aren't doing anything."

"That's what you want to think. I bet Qien was mad because his lover betrayed him. That would be romantic. And depressing."

"I think your head may be attached slightly askew," Pina said with a shake of her head. "Nobody could ever find Esther attractive in that way. I have seen her before, and I suspect a prune has smoother features than she does."

"Hey, it's not about the outside. It's the inside that counts." Lydia paused for a moment, then frowned. "Wait, that's a good point. She's an asshole that pretends to be nice. Nobody would like that part of her either. Never mind, then."

"I think we might have lost our topic a bit," Asher said with a small laugh. "Is there anything else we can do to prepare? Because, if not, I think we should get some rest. I don't want to be tired while we try to do this tomorrow."

Everyone waited for a moment, but none of them spoke up again. Jasmine nodded.

"Sounds like the plan is sleep, then."

"I'm not so sure I want to head back through the halls right now," Lydia said, clearing her throat uncomfortably. "There's an assassin out there, and I'm suddenly considerably less excited about walking back to my bed. Jas, you're using Asher's bed now, right? Does that mean I can use yours?"

"It's fine with me," Jasmine said, sending a glance at Asher who shrugged in response. "I mean, we could walk you back to your room as well."

"Nah, I'll take your bed. I get the feeling it hasn't seen much use in recent days anyway." Lydia waggled her eyebrows. "Where is it?"

Jasmine pointed to the wall where her door was and Lydia pushed on it. She peered into the smaller room, then turned back.

"A bit small. I can see why you use Asher's bed. It'll work, though. Thanks."

"I'll head back to my room, then," Pina said. "Tomorrow, I'll meet you back–"

"Did you miss the whole bit about an assassin?" Lydia, shaking her head in admonishment. "Are you *trying* to get stabbed?"

"I don't live very far."

"And it doesn't take an assassin that long to stick a dagger in your back. I can walk you back to your room if you want me to."

*Didn't you literally just say no to us doing that for you a second ago?*

"That's fine. I really don't need–"

"Or we could split Jasmine's old bed," Lydia offered. "It's safer."

Jasmine nearly choked at the eyebrow raise Lydia gave Pina. It was hard to miss the offer in her voice. Nobody could say Lydia wasn't completely forthright about her thoughts, but there was no way that–

"That might actually be wise," Pina said. "Are you okay with that, Jasmine?"

"I – uh, yeah. Sure," Jasmine stammered, barely managing to get the words out of her mouth without tripping over them in surprise.

"Thank you," Pina said. She walked past Lydia and into the room.

"See you tomorrow," Lydia said. She winked at Jasmine, then let the door swing shut behind her. Jasmine and Asher exchanged a look.

"Lydia is terrifying," Asher said. "What she lacks for in literally anything she makes up for in boldness."

"Tell me about it," Jasmine said with a quiet, disbelieving laugh. "She's something else. We should make like her and get some rest, though. I don't want to be tired tomorrow."

Asher raised his eyes to the window, looking out into the night sky. He nodded and got into bed, laying his sword where he could reach it if he needed to. "Yeah. Sleep well, Jas. Tomorrow, we get some answers."

"Tomorrow," Jasmine agreed, getting in beside him. Asher pulled his shirt off and she wrapped her arms around his chest, pulling him closer as they settled in for the night. It wasn't long before an empty, dreamless sleep welcomed her into its grasp.

# 45

The next morning came in the wake of gray storm clouds. Jasmine was pretty sure she wouldn't have even woken up if Asher hadn't rolled out of bed and given her a quick kiss before starting to get dressed.

She squinted out the windows, the faintest traces of light muted. In the Keeper's room to the side, Jasmine could hear Lydia and Pina getting ready. Shaking her head to clear the sleep away, Jasmine grabbed her sword and strapped it to her waist.

Jasmine stretched her arms and shifted from foot to foot, getting some blood flowing. The anticipation for their upcoming task started to build in her chest. She drew in a deep breath and let it out slowly, flexing her hands to maintain control over her emotions.

"Feeling okay?" Asher asked in a low whisper.

"Yeah. I want to get this over with. The worst part is waiting."

"I'd say the worst part would probably be getting stabbed," Asher said with a dry smile. "Keeping the worst part as the waiting would be a blessing."

Jasmine rolled her eyes. She glanced over to the Keeper's door as Lydia pushed it open and stuck her head out. After verifying that they were awake, she stepped into the main room, followed by Pina.

"Sleep well?" Asher asked.

"Better than you could imagine. That bed really is small, but I can't say that I can complain." Lydia flashed a grin at Pina, whose face turned the brightest shade of red that Jasmine had ever seen.

*At least I know what I look like when Asher or Lydia tease me. I never thought Pina was Lydia's type, but then again, I didn't think Asher was my type until... well, until I did.*

"What're you thinking about?" Asher asked.

"You," Jasmine replied absently.

It was Asher's turn to be flustered. He got over it in a respectable second, leaning in to give Jasmine a kiss on the forehead. Lydia gagged.

"Stop that. I'm going to get jealous and embarrass someone."

"Please don't," Pina said. "We should stay focused. We don't have room for distraction right now."

"It's not distraction. It's a reason for us to win," Lydia corrected. "If you don't have something in life worth fighting for, then you have nothing worth winning for."

Pina opened her mouth, then closed it as she processed Lydia's words. A thoughtful frown crossed her face. "That's... very romantic of you."

"What can I say? I'm a pretty fantastic person." Lydia flicked her hair over her shoulder, then gestured grandiosely to the door. "Let's go. We have an old bat to rob."

"I said romantic, not fantastic," Pina muttered under her breath.

Jasmine grinned. "Lydia is right. Let's do this. Class should be just about to start, and the Keeper area of Sanctuary is a bit of a walk."

They all set off. Their steps echoed through the large, empty Starvein Halls. It was odd to be walking around them this early, before all the Starveins had started to move around. Despite their earlier banter, none of them spoke during the trip over.

Jasmine kept her hand on the hilt of her sword, running her fingers along the pommel in attempt to distract her mind. The closer they got to Esther's office, the tighter the knot in her stomach wound.

An assassin seemed to lurk in every shadow in the hall, but nothing was ever there when she double checked. Against all odds, their trip went entirely uncontested and they soon found themselves in the Keeper dormitories.

Jasmine had passed Esther's room several times since arriving at Sanctuary, though it felt like it had been years since she'd last been there. She led the small group down the considerably tighter hallways until they stood before the relatively plain door.

"Here?" Pina asked in a hushed tone.

"Yeah," Jasmine replied, fingering the key in her pocket.

"Okay. Lydia, head down the hall to give us warning if anyone comes from that direction," Pina said, nodding to their left. "I'll cover the right. Stay in range of being able to see the door, though."

"Good luck, Jas. You too, Asher. But most of it goes to Jas. No offense." Lydia gave Pina a mock salute and strode off. Pina nodded to them, then walked in the other direction.

Jasmine's hand felt clammy as she raised a hand and knocked on the door. If someone happened to be in the room, she didn't want to be caught trying to open the door with a key she wasn't meant to have.

There was no answer. Her heart thumped in her chest as she pulled the key out and slid it into the lock. With a gentle twist, the door clicked and swung open. Asher and Jasmine peered into the room.

It was… normal. Jasmine wasn't sure what she'd been expecting. A bed sat against the back corner beneath a window, neither large nor small. Beside it was a desk and two bookshelves. A trunk had been tucked beneath the bed, and several swords hung from the walls. An open door led into a plain bathroom, nothing of note immediately apparent.

*At least nobody is here.*

Jasmine stepped inside alongside Asher. Her gaze was immediately drawn to the trunk at the base of the bed.

"You check the shelves," Jasmine whispered. "I'll get the trunk."

Asher nodded and they split off. While he started ruffling through the books, flipping all of them open to check if Esther had utilized the same hiding method that Qien had, Jasmine dragged the chest out from beneath the bed.

A quick check revealed that it was locked, and another very cursory scan around the room failed to turn up any other keys. The lock was much too small to use the door key on, which meant that Esther probably had the key on her person somewhere.

Jasmine jiggled the lock, then rooted through her pockets in search of a metal hairpin. It had been a while since she'd last needed to use one, but some habits from the gutters died hard. And, despite what she'd told Lydia, there had been more than a few times when knowing how to crack a lock had saved her life and put food in her hands.

While Jasmine was slightly out of practice, the lock wasn't exactly the best one she'd ever had to crack. After about a minute of poking around and jiggling it, the mechanism popped open.

"Anything?" Asher asked, nearly making Jasmine jump. She glared at him and he held his hands up. "Sorry. I didn't mean to startle you, but there wasn't anything on the shelves. Just books and a normal dagger."

Jasmine let out a huff and turned back to the crate. She pushed the top back, letting it thump against the bedding. The inside of the chest had several packages wrapped in oilcloths, stacked up on each other.

Jasmine opened the first, but all it contained was a beautiful dress. A sudden feeling of snooping where she didn't belong set in on her shoulders. She rolled it back up and returned the package to the chest, picking up another one.

What she found in the next were travel clothes and a bag of trail mix. Jasmine's brow furrowed as she continued looking through each roll. Nothing really felt out of place. There were a variety of clothes, keepsakes, and other items that probably would have been valuable to Esther, but no dagger.

Jasmine piled the worthless packages up at her side until the chest had been completely emptied. There was nothing in it.

"Well, shit," Asher said. "Now what?"

Jasmine shook her head and sat back, her mind racing. They didn't have that much time to work, and they had to put everything back the way it had been before they left. But there was no sign of the daggers.

*We had to have missed something.*

She looked back over the crate, then paused and leaned back again. The floor of the crate felt like it should have been a bit lower than it actually was.

"What is it?" Asher asked.

"Hold on," Jasmine said, running her hands along the inside of the crate. When she found nothing, she tried the sides, pressing in on the ridges and pulling at anything that felt like it might have stuck out more than it should have.

Her efforts were rewarded by a faint click. The bottom of the crate slid slightly askew. A victorious grin crossed Jasmine's lips and she pulled the panel back, revealing one last package in a hidden spot at the base of the chest.

It was small, but the shape was right. Jasmine unwrapped it carefully, her fingers trembling slightly as she pulled the last flap out of the way. Within the leather was a thin, pointed dagger.

The very dagger that the assassins had wielded – but only one of them.

"Where's the other dagger?" Asher whispered.

Jasmine started to wrap the dagger again. "I don't know. This was only one. She should have two. The one from the first assassin in our room, and the one from the one at the exam."

"Do you think Riker took the first one?"

"No idea," Jasmine replied, stuffing the package into the back of her pants and pulling her shirt over it. "We'll figure that out later. Help me put everything back."

They hurriedly returned all the re-wrapped pieces of leather back to Esther's chest, then closed the lid and re-locked it. After pushing it back under her bed, the two straightened out the rest of Esther's room as fast as they could.

Jasmine did one last look to see if they'd somehow missed another hiding spot, but her stomach was nearly throbbing with pain. If anyone came back now, it would all be over.

"Forget it," Jasmine said, jerking her chin toward the door. "Let's get out of here before something goes wrong. We have what we needed."

Asher nodded and they slipped out, closing the door behind them. Jasmine stuck the key back in and twisted it, locking the door behind them. She could hear her heart thumping in her ears as she shoved the key back into her pocket.

Lydia and Pina both saw them emerge and walked to rejoin them.

"Did you find it?" Pina whispered.

"Kind of," Jasmine replied, resisting the urge to glance around like a thief. Even if that was what she was, she'd long since learned that people generally didn't get bothered unless they *looked* suspicious. "Let's get out of here. I don't think I'm going to be able to breath until we're back in Asher's room."

# 46

Every hall they walked past set Jasmine's hair on end, but nobody ever pulled them aside or even so much as noticed them. They soon left the Keeper section of Sanctuary and made it back to the Starvein Halls.

None of them even dared to speak. The whole operation had taken less than an hour including the walk there and back, so the Starvein Halls were still largely silent. Jasmine counted every door they passed up until they stood before Asher's room.

She couldn't believe that they'd made it back without even a single person so much as noticing that they were missing. Her heart was still pounding furiously inside her chest, demanding that she find a chair and collapse in it until she could convince herself that they'd actually gotten away with their heist.

Jasmine unlocked the door and stepped inside. The others followed after her, and Asher closed the door behind all of them. As soon as the lock clicked, Jasmine let out an explosive, relieved breath.

"Watcher's eyes," Jasmine said, pulling the leather-wrapped

dagger out and setting it on the bed. She sat down beside it, the adrenaline flooding from her veins in a rush. "I can't believe it."

"Things in life are often simple, but we build them up to be more than they are," Pina said. "What did you mean by not exactly finding what you were looking for, though? Is that not the dagger?"

"No, it's the dagger." Asher answered for Jasmine. "But we only found one. There should have been two. It's possible we missed it, but I don't know where else Esther could have hidden it. We have no way of knowing which assassin this dagger came from."

"Meaning you think Esther might not have stolen the dagger from Qien?" Lydia asked.

"Yeah," Jasmine muttered, unwrapping the dagger. She left it on the bed, not willing to touch the handle yet. There was no way of knowing exactly what the blade would do when she touched it, and she didn't want to do that until she was ready to actually deal with it. "But I don't have any way to know for sure. Watcher, Qien could have been a really convincing liar and might actually have the other dagger himself."

"No point doubting ourselves now," Asher said, putting a hand on Jasmine's shoulder. "What's done is done, and what matters is that we have a dagger."

"Although it does mean we technically committed treason," Pina said, clearing her throat. "If Esther didn't steal from Qien, then we're objectively in the wrong."

"Lydia?"

"Yes?"

"Could you distract Pina, please? I've come to appreciate her logic, but this isn't really the time for it."

"With pleasure. Call for us if you need something," Lydia said, grabbing Pina by the collar and pulling her in for a kiss. Pina let out a strangled noise of surprise, but her protests died off pretty quickly as Lydia pulled her back toward the Keeper room.

"You know," Jasmine said, watching the door swing shut behind them, "I'm not sure who's more shameless between you and Lydia."

"Definitely Lydia," Asher said. "Did you see how she kissed her? Gives me some ideas."

Jasmine let out a small laugh. "I'll take you up on that, but after we figure this out. I don't think I'm going to be able to sit still until we find *some* form of answer."

"Yeah, tell me about it," Asher muttered. "I'm here for you no matter what, though. Answers or not."

"Thanks, Asher." Jasmine squeezed his hand, then turned her eyes back to the dagger. It looked so inconspicuous, lying there on the oilcloth. If she hadn't known better, Jasmine would have assumed that it was just a random, thin dagger.

She rolled it over, squinting at the pommel to see if there was anything remotely useful inscribed on it. Unfortunately, it was plain. The only form of design on it at all was on the bottom of the pommel. A swirling pattern had been carved into the rounded metal, much like the center of a whirlpool.

"A whirlpool, huh?" Jasmine murmured. "That could definitely be related to being a siphon. Both involve water draining away. If there were any doubts that this was what the assassin was referring to, they're certainly gone now."

"It sounded like it didn't work, though," Asher said, his face just inches from Jasmine's as he tried to study the dagger together with her. "I think we can assume that this dagger was used on the rest of my family – and none of them survived the experience."

"Yeah. I'm sorry, Asher. I haven't forgotten, but you haven't been given time to grieve properly. I–"

"It's fine, Jas." Asher paused, then shook his head. "No, it's not fine. But there's nothing we can do about it, and it wasn't your fault. I mentioned them because I think it's possible that the reason the whole ritual with the siphon wasn't completed was because I didn't die. Maybe it was supposed to completely drain me of my magic but only managed to get part of it."

"That's possible, but the first assassin made it sound like there was more to it than that." Jasmine's brow furrowed as she tried to think back to the man's words. The whole night had been something of a blur, but there were still fragments floating around in her memory. "I think he implied that you might be able to survive if it worked, didn't he? That means death wasn't the goal. Something else was."

"That's a good point," Asher said. His jaw flexed and he let out an exasperated breath. "That was my one idea. Shit."

"If we can figure out what the original assassin was going for, I think we can figure out what this was for," Jasmine said, rocking back and chewing her lower lip. "Maybe the question shouldn't be what the dagger did, but how the assassin would have benefited from using it."

"That would be the question indeed."

Jasmine and Asher spun as a smooth, syrupy voice breached the sanctum of their room. Stepping out from the perfectly silent Keeper's door was a tall man clad in black clothes. A thick scar ran across his handsome face, and a mat of white hair sat on top of his head, and his eyes were silver. He had Xolani blood.

The man looked to be about ten years older than them, but Jasmine's eyes quickly caught on the two daggers at his hips – each identical to the one that sat on the bed before her.

Jasmine's neck hadn't given her the slightest warning of the man. She didn't have time to wonder why, though. She scrambled to her feet, drawing her sword and holding it before her. Asher drew his own sword.

"Who are you?" Jasmine demanded, her voice coming out a pitch higher than she'd hoped because of the surprise coursing through her system.

"Someone who has been waiting to meet the two of you for a long time. My name is Saleer," the man said, inclining his head and giving them a toothy smile. "You killed two of my subordinates, so I thought it was about time to come pay you a visit myself."

# 47

"What did you do with Lydia and Pina?" Jasmine growled, her knuckles clenched so tightly around the hilt of her sword that they turned white.

"The two girls that came into the room a moment ago? They live. I knocked them unconscious and gave each a dose of a Weeping Lilly. They'll be asleep for the next day. I'm sure you think some horrible things about my group, but we do prefer to avoid killing pointlessly."

"Say that to my family," Asher snapped.

"I said pointlessly. Death is a part of life, and for some, it comes sooner than others. Your family possessed something that we needed, Rockheart."

*Rockheart? Is that Asher's family name? I never even asked it. Nobody ever used them in the gutters, but that was because none of them actually had families to claim.*

"The first assassin you sent tried to kill me," Jasmine said tersely. She didn't know why the man hadn't attacked yet, but her neck wasn't giving her any warnings yet. For whatever reason, he wasn't triggering her senses. "Do I not count either?"

"You were in our way. That makes your death have a point," Saleer said, shaking his head with a sigh. "But, fortunately for you, you have proven that your life has worth."

*Saleer is talkative. I don't know why, but I don't care. If I can keep him talking, maybe he'll spill information about the dagger. And, worst case, the longer we can stall, the more chances someone finds out that this guy is here.*

"And how was that?" Jasmine asked, adjusting her grip on her sword hilt as her hands grew clammy. She shifted her stance, trying to keep the fear from showing in her posture.

"Killing two of my men caught my attention, but imagine my surprise when I heard that you managed to find a flaw with the siphon," Saleer said, running a fingertip over the handle of a dagger at his side. "Your magic interfered with it. And that, Jasmine, is fascinating."

Jasmine resisted the urge to take a step back. The hair all over her body stood on end. Saleer knew her name – and he knew how their magic worked.

"Someone was leaking information to you," Asher said. "Who?"

Saleer chuckled. "Why would I say that? I'm not an amateur. Sources are only good so long as nobody knows who they are. Although, I must admit that I enjoy a good game of cat and mouse as much as the next person. Perhaps more. There's a reason I've kept my hands clean for this long, but I couldn't risk your potential being wasted."

"Wasted?" Jasmine asked suspiciously. "How so? I'd say sending your men to kill us would be a pretty good way to waste our potential."

"And I would agree," Saleer said. "Which is why I came myself. Not to kill you, but to give you an offer."

"What kind of offer?" Asher asked. His voice was surprisingly measured. Jasmine knew for a fact that Asher had absolutely no plans of accepting anything that Saleer pitched to them, but it was a good way to keep him talking.

"The standard one. Truth, power, all of the sort," Saleer said with a laugh. "Surely you've heard stories of making deals with that which you fear. It's dangerous. It can destroy you. Whatever fairytale you wish to reference, all of them warn against taking any steps to ever break out of your place. Good citizens obey the king. Good Keepers don't question orders. Good Starveins maintain the order. Isn't that right?"

Saleer's voice darkened, a warbly, lilting note growing stronger with every word. His hands clenched around the hilts of his daggers. Fervor sparked in his silver eyes, and Jasmine realized that the man before them, no matter how charismatic his appearance may have been, was not fully present with them.

*Watcher's eyes. He's going insane from magic use, isn't he?*

"You have magic poisoning," Asher muttered. "You've lost it, haven't you?"

A cackle slipped out of Saleer's mouth. "Magic poisoning. Another lie from those who fear strength. I am in complete control of myself. The Xolani had greater potential than any other kingdom, but fear broke them."

Saleer released his dagger and raised a hand into he air. Strands of blackish red magic twisted out of his palm, curling around his fingertips and winding down his arms. It was the exact kind of magic that Asher possessed. The energy hissed and popped – and Jasmine finally realized what the tendrils had been.

They were roots.

A pulsating tree of energy formed in Saleer's hand. His fist closed around it, crushing the magic into motes of light that flooded back into his body.

"Magic is a tool," Saleer growled, a droplet of saliva dripping from his mouth and falling to the floor. He didn't even seem to notice. "A natural law, yes. But one that can be broken. One that can be bent to our will, and anyone with sufficient will and power can control it. Of course, not all magic is made equal. Not all *men* are made equal."

"You mean how resistant we are to magic?" Jasmine asked, watching Saleer's hands carefully in case he suddenly attacked. "That isn't something we can change."

"You are correct. It cannot be changed. Not normally." Saleer's lips split into a charming smile as his entire countenance shifted, the insanity vanishing in the blink of an eye. "But that resistance is not a permanent part of our bodies. It is part of the soul. And, when a portion of a soul is merged with another, it becomes harder for the magic to enter both. We can become greater than we were, but the transferring process is a brutal one. It is a process that cannot be done on a soul that allows magic to flow through it easily, nor can it be done with one that resists it completely."

"That's why you came after my family?" Asher asked. "We figured it out, then. You were coming for us because we were resistant to magic. Our souls could handle getting siphoned out, or something?"

"Precisely," Saleer said. "Very good. Your family was more resistant to magical corruption than almost any other Starvein. To be frank, you are barely a step above a normal human. But this very flaw is what allows the magic stored within the siphon to take root. The siphon is a key to the power that even the Xolani could not control – but with your soul, we can."

"So that dagger is just a pathway to opening up forbidden magic that we can't handle, and my shitty bloodline is so bad that it forms a buffer between you and the magic," Asher concluded, clenching his fists and glaring at Saleer. "You killed everyone because of that?"

"Yes. You are more intelligent than your father, and his soul worked perfectly. Unfortunately, he and the rest of your family failed to have bodies that were as resilient as their souls. They did not survive the process. But you – you will be different. I am certain of it."

"I don't think anyone survives getting their soul ripped out," Asher spat. "I'd be dead just the same."

"Wrong!" A fanatical light lit in Saleer's eyes, and he thrust a finger toward Jasmine. "You have begun to give a portion of your soul to Jasmine, but she has not returned hers to you. The ritual hangs incomplete, a quarter of the way done. Jasmine was not the one to pierce you with the blade, so the connection never finished. Complete it. A piece of your soul is already severed. It hangs suspended between the two of you. Give it to her, and take a piece of hers back. In doing so, you will become everything that I have sought to create. You will be perfect."

Spittle flew from Saleer's lips as his voice grew louder and more excited. He took a step toward them. The whites of his eyes had completely vanished, consumed by a silver as pale as the moon.

*Something tells me Saleer isn't telling us everything. There's no way this madman would care that much about us both achieving his goal. He's definitely planning to take it somehow, but it seems like he needs us alive to get what he wants. That can work to our advantage.*

"So you're not here to kill us?" Jasmine asked. She almost scoffed at her own words. "You only want us to – what, use the dagger?"

"Precisely," Saleer said. Fanaticism flared in his eyes and he drew the blades at his sides, pointing their tips at Asher and Jasmine. "You understand. Do it. Sprout the seed that has been planted within you and flourish into what we have forged."

*We, plural. He's not the one in charge of Last Light, then. There are others. Fantastic.*

Jasmine caught Asher's eye. She could tell that he was thinking the same thing that she was. Even though the whole reason they'd gotten the dagger was to try and use it, the absolute last thing they were going to do was what Saleer wanted. As soon as they did as he requested, there was nothing left to protect them.

"How can we trust you?" Jasmine asked. "One of the other assassins said that he'd just kill me and take the energy. Doesn't that mean you could just do the same to us?"

The smile on Saleer's face flickered and vanished. "Use the daggers."

*I knew it. He's going to kill both of us and take our magic the moment we do what he wants. I think the time for discussion is over.*

Ice prickled at Jasmine's back as Asher clearly came to the same conclusion. Jasmine kept her expression neutral as she felt energy start to flow into her, empowering her body. She knew more than well enough that she had no chance of actually keeping up with the assassins, but it did give her one shot at a surprise attack.

*I just have to make it count.*

"I should have known. I was mistaken. You are just like the rest of your family." Saleer's features tightened in rage. Strands of red and black roots wormed out from his shoulder and right arm, writhing like hungry worms. "And you will die like them as well."

# 48

Jasmine charged, drawing on every ounce of speed she could muster. The twisting roots coming from Saleer's body shot out to meet her, their tips opening up like the maws of starving beasts to clamp down on her flesh.

She twisted out of the way at the last second, letting out a battle cry as she brought her sword down toward the tall man's shoulder. A loud clang rang out as her sword met the blade of a dagger and slammed to a halt, sending a powerful vibration down her arm.

Jasmine threw herself back as a wave of magical roots crashed into the spot where she'd been standing, shattering the floor and worming beneath it. Tiles cracked and bulged as Saleer pulled the roots free, baring his teeth in a furious snarl.

She couldn't even see his arm anymore. The entire right half of his body was completely consumed by the vile magic. It bubbled and hissed, roiling like a thick broth over a flame. Red blurred for Jasmine's head, and she barely managed to tackle Asher to the ground in time.

It whipped past their heads and crashed into the wall, smashing through stone as if it were plaster. Dust rained down on Jasmine as she scrambled to her feet. She pulled Asher up with her. For a second, the power coursing through her body faded.

A bolt of red light leapt from Asher's hands, streaking through the air and slamming into Saleer's arm. It bored a hole through the roots, but they twisted and wound back over the wound, sealing it over in seconds.

Energy slammed back into Jasmine just in time for Saleer's next attack. She bounded into the air, almost failing to clear the grasping strands. By some mercy, Saleer seemed slower than the other assassins they'd fought.

But, as Jasmine brought her sword down on the magic and carved through the reddish-black trunks, severing them from Saleer's arm, she realized that while he was slower, he was by no means weaker.

There wasn't even a wound. Saleer's magic just kept growing, expanding and spreading its reach further along the room. Saliva dripped from his mouth, sizzling as it hit the ground. No trace of sanity was left in his eyes. All that remained was hunger.

"He's turning into a monster!" Jasmine yelled. "We need to get out of here!"

"I think it's too late for that," Asher yelled back. A root shot for him and Jasmine cut it from the air, stumbling as another one that she hadn't noticed rose up and wound around her leg. It sizzled as it caught her pant leg. Asher's sword carved the grasping tendril at the base and the part that had been touching her burned away into motes of ash. "We can't leave the others!"

Almost a quarter of the room was covered, and it had only been seconds. It wouldn't be long before the fight went from difficult to completely impossible. Jasmine's eyes flicked to the dagger on the bed. It was still there, lying in wait.

*Even if it's exactly what he wants, I don't think we've got a choice.*

"We need to be stronger!" Jasmine grabbed Asher and lifted him over her shoulder, jumping to safety a second before a wave of roots crashed down where they'd been standing. They melted through the floor and washed into the walls, ripping stone apart freely.

"Do it!" Asher yelled. "I trust you!"

Jasmine didn't have time to consider if that was the right call. She lunged, snagging the dagger from the bed. She narrowly dodged a grasping root as it went for her neck and spun the blade around, turning the point to face themselves.

*Fuck, this is such a damned stupid idea. Watcher protect me.*

"Stab me already!" Asher hissed, grabbing Jasmine's hand. "I'd say be careful, but I'd rather die at your hand than his."

*Aw, that's kind of sweet.*

Asher guided Jasmine's hand into his chest. An involuntary shudder ran through her body as she felt the dagger meet resistance and push through it. Asher's body arched in agony and he let out a scream of pain.

Power erupted within Jasmine. Hot magma pumped through the veins in her hand, ravaging her arm and twisting in to her chest. They wound around her heart and reached out toward her extremities. Bands of pain wrapped around her skull and consumed her thought, and she realized that she was screaming as well.

The roots that had been rushing toward them slammed to a halt and pulled back, poised like snakes ready to strike. Jasmine could barely bring herself to care. The pain was so all-consuming that nothing else mattered.

And then, in the flood of agony, there was ice. Relief clawed its way back into her, inch by inch. Jasmine forced her eyes back open. Asher's hand had found hers and he was squeezing it tightly, sending a river of ice in to combat the unrelenting heat.

The flow of power snapped shut. Jasmine ripped the blade out of Asher's chest and he crumpled, his hand slipping from hers.

Jasmine caught him as he fell, slapping the blade back into his hand and wrapping his fist around it.

"Wait," Asher wheezed. "I don't think–"

Jasmine plunged the dagger into her heart. This time, there wasn't even time to feel pain. It hit her with such force that Jasmine's mind couldn't even register it. The world exploded in a loud, buzzing screech, and then there was sheer nothingness.

Once again, the cold grasp of ice was what pulled her from the brink. Jasmine drew in a ragged breath, her eyes snapping back open as stars swam before her. Asher had ripped the dagger out of her chest and thrown it to the ground, blood still dripping from its blade.

Saleer watched them, his lips pulling back in a huge smile. They'd done exactly what he wanted them to.

"Yes," Saleer breathed. "Do you feel it? The power? Is it yours?"

Jasmine wasn't sure what she was meant to feel other than pain. The room swam around her. The only thing that wasn't moving was Asher, and she held onto him with everything that she had.

And then, like someone had ripped the scales from her eyes, there was clarity. The breath froze in Jasmine's throat. She could feel every single part of her body. Every single hair brushing against her clothes. The warmth of Asher's hand. The pumping blood in his veins.

Not just that. She could *feel* him. Even if Jasmine's eyes had been closed, she could have pointed Asher out with complete certainty. She could have said exactly how far away he was, and she could have described the expression on his face.

And, most of all, she could feel the storming magic burning within both of them. Heat radiated from Jasmine's chest, originating in the point that Asher had stabbed her.

"You did it," Saleer cackled. He moved in jerky motions, raising his remaining hand up and making a desperate, grasping motion in their direction. "Give it to me. Give me my power!"

The world snapped back into motion. The roots blurred toward them, and it immediately became clear that Jasmine's initial assessment of Saleer had been completely wrong. He wasn't slower than the other assassins at all.

He was faster. Much faster. Saleer had just been waiting for them to be forced to act. The path to the bed had been left open on purpose, all to make sure they completed the ritual. But there was one more factor.

Saleer wasn't the only one that was faster.

Jasmine erupted into motion and jumped forward, her sword a silver-gray blur as it cut the grasping tendrils apart before they could touch her. As her feet hit the ground, power forced itself out of its own volition.

Magic peeled away from her skin like the petals of burning flowers, fluttering in a miniature tornado around her. They gathered at her sword, melting into the blade. Wherever the petals touched Saleer's magic, his roots were burned away.

For the first time, a flicker of unease passed over Saleer's face. He opened his mouth, but Jasmine didn't get to find out what he was going to say. A pillar of intertwined roots identical to Saleer's ripped out of Asher's arm, tearing through the air. They slammed into Saleer's chest, shattering the roots that rose up to protect him, and drove the man into the wall.

Blood splattered from Saleer's mouth. It would only take another strike to finish him off – but a wave of weakness gripped Jasmine in its claws. She nearly dropped on the spot as she felt the magic surrounding her suddenly evaporate.

Stumbling, Jasmine pushed her body to move toward Asher. He dashed for her, grabbing Jasmine before she could fall. Power flooded back into her, though not nearly as much as there had been before. The world spun and danced before her eyes.

"We share the same pool of magic," Asher said, drawing in deep, desperate gasps as he struggled to catch his breath. He clutched

Jasmine's arms for dear life, both supporting and leaning against her. "We can't use too much at once."

"Just do whatever you did again!" Jasmine blinked heavily, trying to keep her consciousness from drifting away.

"Too late," Saleer hissed, bringing his hand down on Asher's magic and shattering the glowing wood to pieces. He dropped to the ground, the wound on his chest already starting to fill with magic and seal itself off.

He threw his head back and let out a roar. The ground trembled beneath Jasmine and Asher, nearly throwing them off their feet. Jasmine tried to draw on her newfound magic again, but it felt like she was trudging through waist deep mud.

Asher grit his teeth, raising a hand. Magic started to gather, but it wasn't going to be enough.

Saleer brought his hand down. And, out of the corner of Jasmine's eye, she saw the door to the Keeper room swing open, as soundless as ever. Saleer's roots surged forward as Lydia stepped into the open, rearing back and flinging a pan as hard as she could.

The pan sailed through the air and struck Saleer clean in the skull with a resounding clang. It knocked his head back and he let out a surprised cry of pain. The distraction lasted for no more than an instant, but that instant was the last one Asher needed.

A black root shot out of his arm, piercing through the air and driving clean into Saleer's eye. His body jerked back, stiffening. Jasmine felt energy flowing into her from Asher, and she drew on it without reserve.

Power surged back through her body and her foot hit the ground, flaming petals blowing up around her foot as the magic manifested itself. She exploded forward with a defiant scream, crossing the room and leaping into the air.

Jasmine drove her sword, cracked and superheated by her magic, into his heart. The blade shattered and she dropped to the ground, narrowly avoiding falling onto the bed of roots covering most of Asher's room.

Above her, Saleer's body stopped twitching. For a horrifying instant, Jasmine feared that he had somehow survived. Then tiny motes of ash started to rise up from him, blowing away in an invisible wind.

The sunlight broke through the cracks that Saleer's magic had made in the walls, illuminating him in golden light as his body disintegrated. His daggers dropped to the ground with a clatter.

"Watcher's eyes," Jasmine breathed, bracing her hands against her knees. She looked back at Lydia, then over to Asher. "We did it."

Then she passed out.

# 49

Jasmine woke nestled in sheets and pillows. It took her mind a moment to spin up to speed, but the sleep was ripped away as visions of the fight against Saleer flashed through her head. Her eyes snapped open and she bolted upright, surprised to find that her body didn't hurt.

She wasn't in Asher's room anymore. In fact, Jasmine didn't recognize where she was at all. The only thing that stopped the panic from building up in her chest was that Asher sat at a desk across from the bed, the assassin's dagger sitting on a roll of leather before him. He turned toward Jasmine as she woke, a huge grin crossing his features.

"Jas!" Asher exclaimed, pushing the chair back and quickly making his way over to the side of the bed. "Are you doing okay?"

"You know, I'm starting to feel like we've had this conversation before," Jasmine said with a laugh. "Passing out after fights is starting to turn into a habit. At least I don't feel like I fell down a cliff this time."

"So you're fine, then?"

Jasmine nodded. She flexed her fingers, then stretched her

arms out slowly. There was no pain. In fact, she felt better than she had in a long time. It was like she'd just woken up from the best sleep she'd ever had. Her body felt limber and relaxed, but not groggy at all.

"I feel great, actually. What happened? Where are we? Are Lydia and Pina okay?"

"It's fine, Jas. Everyone is okay. Well, almost everyone. Saleer is dead," Asher said, walking over to sit beside Jasmine and putting his hand over hers. "We killed him."

Jasmine leaned back against the headstand, her shoulders slumping in relief. "And the others?"

"Resting. Class was canceled. They couldn't cover Saleer's attack up like they could with the other incidents. Everyone basically got told that enemies of the kingdom tried to attack Sanctuary, but were defeated."

"The way you say defeated–"

"Esther and Riker took credit for it." Asher's lips pressed thin. "I was pretty pissed at first, but I actually think it might be for the best. The only people that knew about us using the daggers was Saleer, but the rest of the assassins in Last Light might figure it out if they knew we beat him. On the other hand, if the story is Riker and Esther handled it..."

"Nobody has any way to know," Jasmine concluded. She wasn't sure how she felt about that. It wasn't like getting credit for killing Saleer would have earned her and Asher anything, but it still rubbed her wrong. In the end, being safe was more important than bragging rights. "I guess that's probably the right move. Did you say Riker was back? I kind of thought he might have gotten killed."

"He was on some mission. I haven't spoken to him much yet," Asher said. "I think he and Esther are waiting for you to wake up. They want to talk to us."

"I'd imagine," Jasmine said, her eyes flicking to the dagger that still sat on Asher's desk. "Does she..."

"Know about the dagger? Yeah. They showed up shortly after Saleer died. It was hard to tell what Esther was thinking, but she didn't take it from us. Maybe she didn't realize who it belonged to, but I doubt it."

"How long was I out, then?"

"A day. You haven't really missed much." Asher glanced over his shoulder, then leaned in closer and lowered his voice. "Can you still feel our magic, Jas?"

She could. The wellspring of heat in her chest swirled like the currents of a powerful river, just waiting for release. It pushed against her from within, and the temptation to answer it was strong.

"Yeah. It's..."

"Incredible," Asher finished with a small laugh. His expression quickly turned serious. "Saleer was insane, but he was right. It doesn't hurt, does it? I've been worried it might affect you badly because you aren't a Starvein."

"It doesn't seem that bad. Just... warm."

"Yeah. The complete opposite of how it's meant to be," Asher muttered. He gave her hand a small squeeze. "But it's comforting. It reminds me of you."

Jasmine squeezed his hand back. "And I can't say I haven't always wanted magic. I guess I've just got half of yours now."

"Or I have half of yours," Asher joked. "I still have no idea how the siphon worked or what its real purpose was. Saleer had the same kind of magic that I did, but yours was different. There's something else going on that we haven't figured out, but now isn't the time to dig into it. Esther and Riker are hovering around outside, and I'm pretty sure they'll want to talk with you soon."

Jasmine wasn't sure how pleased she was to hear that. The idea of confronting Esther was simultaneously tantalizing and terrifying. Asher read the look on her face and pursed his lips.

"I know how you feel. We might actually owe her an apology,

which has been driving me up a wall. It doesn't look like she was actually trying to kill us. She was just a bitch that didn't care about us. Not exactly the same thing."

Jasmine's hands clenched, but Asher was right. All she could do was let out a heavy sigh. "Yeah. At least it sounds like she isn't going to accuse us of treason for robbing her."

"She better not. She had it coming."

Jasmine snorted. She shifted her blankets back and carefully rose to her feet. Asher held her hand, providing support. Jasmine didn't need it – her legs felt perfectly fine – but she accepted it anyway.

"There's a spare set of clothes in the bathroom," Asher said, nodding to a door at the side of the room. "You feeling good enough to get into them? I can help if you need."

"Are you asking that just because you want to see me naked?"

"I'm hurt. I was just offering to be a gentleman," Asher said, flashing her a sly grin that told her not a single word that had just come out of his mouth was true. "The offer still stands, though."

"I can handle it this time, if only because I don't want Esther to walk in when we inevitably get distracted."

Asher grimaced. "Okay, good point. That would scar me for life."

He let her hand go and Jasmine walked into the bathroom, where a fresh set of Keeper clothes sat on the basin. She changed into them and headed back out. Asher nodded to the door as Jasmine emerged.

"They're waiting. I could send them away if you wanted, though. Do you need more time to get ready?"

"Might as well get it over with," Jasmine said, shaking her head. She desperately wished she still had her sword, but her fight with Saleer had shattered it and turned it to slag. It wasn't like she could stab Esther anyway, but it would have been nice to be able to feel its comforting weight at her side.

Asher waited a second to make sure Jasmine was fully prepared before pulling the door open. Jasmine locked eyes with Esther. The elderly Keeper's face looked tired. There were dark bags under her eyes and her lips were a shade lighter than what she remembered. Riker stood behind her, his face as expressionless as ever.

"Jasmine," Esther greeted, stepping into the room. Riker followed her in and shut the door behind him.

"Keeper Esther," Jasmine said, successfully keeping the distaste from her voice. "You look tired."

"And you, for some reason, look perfectly well rested," Esther said. Her eyes drifted to the dagger on the table and she let out a dry laugh. "Despite how busy you've been."

*The absolute gall it takes to stand there and laugh at our desperate attempts to stay alive is infuriating. Watcher, I almost wish you really were one of the assassins so I could punch you in your wrinkled old face. I can't believe I ever looked up to you.*

None of the anger burning in Jasmine's chest made it to her face. Riker hadn't gotten time to teach her many lessons, but the ones he'd taught had stuck. She wasn't going to give Esther any advantages in their game.

"I did nothing but my duty as Keeper," Jasmine said. "I took every action I could to ensure the survival of my charge."

A smile pulled across Esther's lips, so small that it was almost unnoticeable. "So you did. And, against all odds, you killed a member of Last Light."

"Two members," Riker corrected. "Though the last man was different. Asher already told me of your fight. His name was Saleer, yes?"

Jasmine nodded. "Yeah. Do you know anything about him?"

"Yes. I was the one that put the scar on his face," Riker said. His features darkened and he shook his head. "That was some time ago, when he was far more than what he became. Asher told me he was consumed by his magic."

"It certainly seemed that way," Jasmine said. "He was insane, but he was terrifyingly strong."

"You were lucky to survive." Riker crossed his arms in front of his chest. "Both of you did well to defeat him, even without his sanity."

"And that is what we are here to talk about," Esther said, taking back control of the conversation. "Has Asher told you that we plan to take credit for his death?"

Jasmine nodded.

"And you have no objection?"

"I do what is necessary for the kingdom."

Esther tilted her head to the side, and a flash of approval flashed through Riker's eyes. He gave Jasmine the faintest nod.

"You have come a long way," Esther said. She glanced back at the dagger, walking over to the table and wrapping it back up in the leather. "Perhaps too far."

Jasmine didn't respond to that. There was nothing she could say about the theft that would help her situation. If Esther wanted to push on it, then all she could do was stand there and listen. But, instead, Esther set the dagger back on the table.

"I suppose there is nobody better to leave this with than you." Esther handed the dagger to Jasmine. The hilt of the blade poked out from the folds of the leather, as if surprised that Esther had given it away.

*What?*

"We can keep it?" Asher asked.

"Considering how closely it is tied to your magic? Yes. The Whitewater Kingdom is not doing well, Asher. We need every advantage we can get, and you have proven that you are more than just an incompetent Starvein."

*Ah. So now that we're worth something, you care. At least nobody can say you aren't consistent. Results are all that matter, and the people you lose in the process are irrelevant.*

"Do you think the Last Light will give up on trying to kill me, then?" Asher asked.

"Unlikely," Riker said. "The death of Saleer will only prove to them that there is more reason to claim your life. I would expect them to try even harder – but they will be more careful. I suspect the next attack will not come for some time. They have been making moves all across the kingdom, not just here. No matter how badly they want you, they will not overcommit. Their leadership is clever."

*Screw the rest of the kingdom. As long as we can get a breather, I'm happy. I don't even care if that's selfish. We've already done way more than we should have.*

"But the topic right now is of you, not everyone else," Esther said. She interlaced her fingers, then inclined her head to Jasmine. "I pushed you into a position that you did not want to be in. While the King ordered for someone to defend Asher out of duty to his family, you were ripped from your life. I owe you an apology."

Jasmine's mouth nearly dropped open, but she managed to keep hold of herself. There had been so many things she'd wanted to tell Esther. She'd wanted to laugh in her face, or gloat that she'd only apologized because Jasmine had proven her worth.

Instead, all Jasmine could manage was a nod. "That's life, I suppose."

"Asher has proven that he is important enough to garner further attention from the King," Esther said, raising her head and locking eyes with Jasmine.

Jasmine's blood ran cold. "What do you mean?"

"You have done far more than what should have been requested from you," Esther said. "If you would like, I can fix this. I can relieve you of your duties and return you to the Keeper program, where you can resume training as normal."

# 50

For a second, nobody spoke. Jasmine glanced at Asher. His face was straight, but she could see the nervousness beneath it that he was desperately trying to hide so that it wouldn't influence her.

A small smile passed across Jasmine's lips and she turned back to Esther, shaking her head. "No thank you. I like to finish what I start. I never left the Keeper program. I can guarantee that I'll pass any exam that you put in front of me. If anything, I'd just like to request that Riker continue teaching me. With that, I believe I can continue my current duties and graduate as a Keeper when the time comes."

Esther raised an eyebrow. Behind her, Riker smiled.

"Are you sure?" Esther asked. "Do not feel–"

"I've made up my mind. I'm not going to change it."

"Very well," Esther said. "Just remember that you chose this yourself. And yes, Riker will remain. He would have been Asher's temporary Keeper should you have accepted my offer, but I believe he is not opposed to giving you further tutelage."

"I am not," Riker confirmed. "It is rare that I find someone worth my attention. I will, however, apologize for failing to uphold my duties. When Saleer attacked, I should have been there to aid you. The two of you should not have had to fight him alone."

"Weren't you on a mission or something?" Asher asked.

"I was." Riker's features darkened. "A false one. The reports of the Last Light led me on a wild goose chase. By the time I realized that I was chasing nothing but shadows and returned to Sanctuary, Saleer had already attacked. There is someone leaking information."

"I… kind of thought it was Esther," Jasmine admitted.

Esther let out a bark of laughter. "I don't blame you. I would have, were I in your shoes. Blame is often drawn to the one who has done you the most wrong."

"So you don't have the dagger that someone stole from Qien?" Asher asked. "The whole reason we went to your room is because someone took it from him."

Esther shook her head. "I do not. We have already talked to Qien. You may speak with him personally if you'd like."

"I searched Esther's room," Riker provided. "As a precautionary measure. Esther did not have the dagger, but that changes nothing. There is a spy in our midst."

"Thank you, Riker," Esther said dryly. "But the chances of us finding the spy are likely zero. We must simply adapt. If we cannot find them, then we can feed false information or attempt to outmaneuver them."

"It would have to be someone who knew you," Riker said, pressing on and ignoring Esther. "Someone who has interacted with you enough to give the Last Light information about your comings and goings. Can you think of anyone who might have been privy to that?"

Jasmine's gut reaction was to scoff. Lydia would never have betrayed them – and she saved their lives in the fight against Saleer. And, while not as strongly, she felt the same about Pina.

The Starvein girl had proven to be a true ally and Jasmine refused to even entertain the thought of her turning against them. She'd also saved their lives against the second Last Light assassin, so it made no sense for her to be working with them.

"I can't think of anyone," Jasmine said. Her gaze fell down to the dagger in her hands. The spiral on its hilt managed to catch her eye once more, and a small frown crossed her lips. She turned it toward Esther. "Is this thing the symbol of the Last Light?"

"Yes," Riker said. "The assassins use it to identify themselves to each other. The symbol is not well known and can be easily disguised, so it can be a safe way to prove their identities."

She squinted at the pattern. It had caught her eye every time she'd seen it, but for some reason, she couldn't quite place why. The pattern wasn't really that unique. It was just a swirl. It wasn't like –

Jasmine's breath caught in her chest. Prickles ran down her arms and the back of her neck as a memory resurfaced. A golden chain, the top half of a swirl pattern poking out from beneath a shirt.

Esmarelda. More memories surfaced. The way she'd talked about power was strikingly similar to Saleer. She'd been covered in sweat right before the exam, as if she'd been doing something else beforehand. She'd tried to get into their team before Qien had randomized everything. Not just that – she'd pressed about what had happened during the exam. All the small events hadn't seemed particularly suspicious at the time, but together, pieces started to click together.

One final piece clicked into place. It was a stretch, but the moment the idea hit, Jasmine couldn't shake it. Esmarelda had seemed particularly interested in pressing for rumors – and rumor had been the very thing that originally made Pina dislike them.

*Esmarelda knew where the exams were. She got close to us and was constantly pressing for information. And, even though there wasn't a specific reason, Pina didn't like her. She could have subconsciously recognized her as the person that had spread the rumors.*

"Watcher's eyes," Jasmine breathed. "I think the spy was Esmarelda. She's a Starvein in our class that happened to get friendly with us. She tried to get information about what happened to us during the exam, and was going to be on our team for it before Qien made everything random. She wears a gold necklace with what I think might be the same spiral pattern on it. I only saw the top of it, but it looked kind of similar."

"Shit," Asher said, his eyes going wide. "I didn't see her necklace, but everything else lines up. She's the only other person we've spoken with."

"I will seek her out," Riker said. "You have done your role, Jasmine. Rest, and take the time you have bought yourself to recover. We have won the battle, but the war wages on. After I finish investigating Esmarelda, I will return to train you again. We have much to catch up on."

With that, Riker strode out of the room. Esther watched him leave, then returned her gaze to Jasmine.

"I will leave as well. I have much to account for and damage to patch over. Remember our story. It will keep further attention off your backs – and if you wish to survive the next year, secrecy will be vital. I do have one question, though. How was it that you defeated Saleer?"

"He was distracted," Asher said before Jasmine could even think of a response. "And I managed to get some of my magic off. It took him by surprise just enough for Jasmine to dip her sword into the fire coming off his own magic and run him through the heart with it."

"Then he has truly fallen. From the tales Riker told of him, I expected him to be a far greater opponent. He was right. You are lucky to live," Esther said. She shook her head and sighed. "Continue your training. And, if you ever do figure out how that dagger works, let me know. The kingdom could use an edge over its enemies."

Esther turned and followed after Riker, closing the door behind her. Jasmine and Asher exchanged a glance. For several seconds, neither of them spoke. Asher's last line to Esther had been a lie, but it was one that Jasmine would have made as well.

Even if she hadn't been trying to kill them, that didn't mean she was to be trusted. That particular secret was one that would be staying close to heart.

"Well," Asher said, breaking the silence. "We lived."

Jasmine burst into laughter. "For now, I guess. We need to get ready, though. The Last Light isn't defeated. They'll be back."

"Probably. I can't control the future and the past is already done. The now is all that matters." Asher pulled Jasmine's hands into his. "And, right now, I can't think of anywhere I'd rather be than with you."

Jasmine looked into Asher's eyes, squeezing his hands back. Asher was right. She had no idea what the future would hold for them, but it didn't matter. There would be time for training and preparation later. The Last Light would come, but they'd be ready for them.

Right now, Jasmine was exactly where she wanted to be.

# EPILOGUE

Esther strode down the dusty hall, her eyes cold as ice. Cobwebs long since abandoned lined the corners. Sanctuary was ancient, and the interlocking tunnels that connected it were older still.

She moved with purpose, her pathway lit only by the small candle in her hand. Esther arrived at an old metal door that hung slightly askew, torchlight spilling out from the room behind it.

The room was plain, bearing only a small storage chest, two chairs, and a table. A girl sat in the chair, hunched over the table with her face buried in her hands. A siphon rested on the table before her. She looked up as Esther arrived, the stress evident in her face.

"Esther. I–"

"Failed," Esther finished, closing the door behind her. "Idiot. How were you so obvious? Your only job was to gain information, not get so close that they could figure out who you were."

"It's not my fault! And I didn't fail – I stole the dagger from Qien, just like you told me to. I reported on what they were doing and where they were," Esmarelda said, pushing up to her feet. "And this isn't what I agreed to do. I said I would share information with you, not try to get people killed!"

"You were not granted entry into Sanctuary because we needed a few rumors placed and a few words spoken," Esther snapped. "You had a role to fulfill, and you do not get to choose what it is. We got you into Sanctuary, Esmarelda. We changed the documents to make a *bastard* daughter seem legitimate, so long as nobody pressed too hard. Do you think we did that for free?"

"I did everything you asked!"

"And yet, you were revealed. Even now, a Keeper comes for you," Esther said. "And, if he catches you, all your secrets will spill like fresh blood from a lamb. For all the Keepers claim to be, they are no kinder than we."

The blood rushed out of Esmarelda's face. "I need to leave, then. Reassign me. I can be useful in other ways, I swear."

"Do you really think we would leave you in Sanctuary to be tortured to death?" Esther snorted and shook her head. "At least you were wise enough to come to our safe room after you heard that Saleer died. If you had not, Riker would have found you before me. I trust you were wise enough to cover your tracks?"

Esmarelda let out a relieved sigh. "Thank the Watcher. Yes, I covered my tracks. He won't find the entrance, but I'm not cut out for this. I just wanted to learn magic and make a difference."

"We know," Esther said. "That's all any of us have wanted. Do not fear Riker. He is strong, but easily mislead."

"What will we do now, then?" Esmarelda asked. "Where will I be reassigned?"

"For now, nothing. Riker is waiting for us to act, so we will wait until his guard is down. He cannot guard our target forever, and there are far more targets than just this one." Esther pursed her lips. "And you are not being reassigned."

"What?" Esmarelda blinked. "I thought–"

A black root tinged with red whorls burst from Esther's palm, piercing across the room and driving into Esmarelda's heart. The girl's eyes widened in shock and disbelief. She let out a shocked, wheezing gasp as Esther ripped the root free.

Esmarelda crumpled to the ground, blood pooling around her. Esther heaved a sigh. Cleaning up the mess would be a massive waste of time, but it wasn't like she had anything better to do.

The Last Light were no strangers to biding their time. A flicker of silver glistened in Esther's eyes as she picked the dagger up off the table, examining the blade. Saleer had been a strong member, but he had already lost much of himself if he had been defeated by an untrained Keeper and a half-baked Starvein.

Today, they had lost. But, just as it always did, the sun would set and the moon would rise in its place. The Last Light would come for what was theirs.

They always did.

www.ingramcontent.com/pod-product-compliance
Lightning Source LLC
Chambersburg PA
CBHW020249030826
48979CB00030B/2680/J